A
TIME A

A SERIES OF CURSES NOVEL

CHRISTINE NORRIS

PAPER
PHOENIX

PRESS

Pennsville, NJ

PUBLISHED BY
Paper Phoenix Press
A division of eSpec Books
PO Box 242
Pennsville, NJ 08070
www.especbooks.com

ISBN : 978-1-956463-57-6
ISBN (eBook): 978-1-956463-56-9

Cover Image:
Rusty steampunk background with clock
and different kinds of gears © Ellerslie, www.shutterstock.com

Cover Design: Mike and Danielle McPhail, McP Digital Graphics

Interior Design: Danielle McPhail, McP Digital Graphics

DEDICATION

For Dad.

CHAPTER I

August 1868

L ATER, WHEN HENRY REMEMBERED THAT DAY, HE MOSTLY RECALLED that his shirt collar itched. The shouting, the weeping, the strange men at the back door, the pistol shot, and the terrific crash that Frau Weber's prized grandfather clock made as it smashed to the floor, weren't as important as uncomfortable clothing to a boy of nearly four.

He stood in a corner of the Weber's dining room with his back against the wall. His mother had instructed him to keep out of the way. She and Frau Weber rushed in and out of the kitchen, the bustles of their skirts bopping up and down. The reason for the party had been explained to Henry a hundred times, but he still didn't understand what all the fuss was about. It wasn't Weihnacten, or his birthday. Babies were born all the time. No reason for him to have to wear his church clothes *all day*. He had already had to dress for Sunday when it wasn't Sunday, then sit through the boring christening service in the swelter-ing church. Wasn't that enough?

He pulled at his collar, made with the lace his grandmother had crocheted for his christening gown. Mama reminded him about that every time she made him put it on. Pulling the collar didn't help with the heat or the itching, so he tugged on the cuffs, trying to cool his sticky, soaked-with-sweat arms. At least he wore short pants. If he had to wear the linen trousers that gentlemen wore all the time, he would surely melt into a puddle.

Frau Weber set a shiny wooden box on the table. Henry leaned forward to see, hoping it was full of candy. She lifted the lid. Sadly, it was only silverware. Frau placed a fork beside a plate, and moved it one way, then another, before taking out a knife and doing it all again. When she finished, she gazed over the table, her face all frowns and downward lines. Whenever his mother wore that face, it usually meant he was in trouble. But he had been standing here the whole time, not doing anything, so she couldn't be cross with him.

She twisted her hands around each other and pressed her lips together until they turned white. After a few moments, she smoothed her skirt.

"Oh, Marta, stop fussing. Everything looks wonderful." Henry's mother emerged from the kitchen carrying a tray full of gleaming drinking glasses. She set the tray on the sideboard and took Frau Weber's hand.

"Thank you, Sabina." Frau Weber patted Mama's hand. "I don't know why I am so nervous. I've hosted dozens of parties."

"This is an important party." Sabina put her arm around Frau Weber's shoulders. "A baby girl is a gift from God, and her christening is one of the most important days in her whole life, and yours."

Frau Weber wiped her forehead with the back of her hand. "A gift we thought would never arrive." She shook her head. "I don't know what's wrong with me. I just want everything to be perfect."

"And it will be, because you will be surrounded by friends and family and love. Oh, stop playing with it, Heinz. You'll make the lace filthy." The scolding was tossed at Henry over her shoulder as she disappeared into the kitchen again.

Henry, unaware his fingers had once again crept to his collar, pulled them back.

"It's so hot. And it itches. And I don't like being called Heinz." The last bit he mumbled.

Mama's ears must have turned to wood because she did not reply. Frau Weber finished setting the table. Using one finger, she pointed at each plate, counting to herself in German as she went around. She did it again, and again, and Henry wondered if she had forgotten how to count. He would help her. Being three and three-quarter years old, he knew how to count to ten in both English and German. He opened his mouth, the word *eins* on his tongue, but she held up her finger as if telling him to wait. She sucked in her breath and then let it out in a rush.

"Twelve. There are twelve. Good."

Henry didn't know if she was speaking to him or not, but decided it was probably better if he didn't say anything.

"Marta, something the matter?" Henry's mother returned from the kitchen, this time carrying a stack of linen napkins.

Frau Weber smiled. *She is a pretty lady,* Henry thought. "Nothing. Only double checking. Twelve guests at the table and twelve only. Thirteen is unlucky."

Mama laughed. It bubbled, like the Wissahickon Creek, where Henry went with Papa to fish.

"So superstitious! As if luck has not been your bosom friend of late!" Mama set the linens on the table and folded them, turning each into a fan before setting it above a plate. "The textile mill is doing so well you and Edmund were able to buy this beautiful home, the most elegant home in all of Germantown, perhaps in all of Philadelphia. And now you have been blessed with that angel sleeping in the next room. Misfortune would not dare to cross your path today." She placed the last napkin. "I hope I don't sound envious, Marta. You and Edmund have both worked so hard and been so patient. You deserve every bit of happiness. Just relax and enjoy this day."

With a sigh, Henry slipped from the dining room and crossed the foyer to the parlor. His good shoes clacked on the polished floor, but fell silent when he stepped onto the thick, flowered rug. All of the big windows were open, so the room was slightly less stuffy than the dining room. It was like their parlor at home, filled with fancy furniture that he was ordered *never* to touch. He supposed the same rule applied here, and so he put his hands behind his back, to keep them out of trouble.

Near the front window stood a bassinet. Covered in white cloth and trimmed in eyelet lace, it reminded Henry of an enormous wedding cake, except a sudden, terrible screeching erupted from it. Henry tiptoed across the room and peered over the edge.

A baby girl lay inside, her tiny arms waving madly, as if she were trying to swim through the air. Henry wrinkled his nose. His mother had called the baby an angel from heaven, but she didn't look like an angel, with her eyes clamped shut and her nose scrunched up and her mouth open wide.

"What's the matter?" Henry asked the tiny shrieking creature. His gaze traveled over the baby's small length, but saw nothing wrong with her. *Though, if they'd dressed me up like that, I might scream, too.* The long white gown with a matching bonnet was covered in so much lace she looked as if she had been covered in spun sugar, a decoration on the bassinet-cake. Henry couldn't imagine how much it must itch. Maybe that was why she screamed with all her breath. He glanced toward the dining room, but no one else seemed to be concerned.

"You shouldn't be crying. They're throwing you a party." The baby wailed louder, her face turning a brilliant a shade of red. Henry reached into the bassinet and placed a hand on her belly, rocking her gently, but she only cried louder.

Henry panicked—if someone came in now and heard her wailing, they might think he had done something. He pulled his arm out of the bassinet, his three- and three-quarter-year old mind scrambling. He could run and hide, but based on previous experience, it would only get him in more trouble. He tried humming a lullaby, the one his mother sung to him every night before tucking him into his bed. It did not help.

He stepped back and jammed his hands into his pockets. His fingers touched something hard and cold, the jagged edges digging into his fingers.

Surprised, he pulled out a small brass gear. He knew where it had come from, of course, but had forgotten it was in his pocket. Henry rolled it between his fingers, and the sun caught the polished surface, casting shards of golden light. He was so focused on the bit of metal it took a moment to realize the baby had stopped crying.

When her face wasn't all wrinkled up like a prune, she was kind of pretty. At least she no longer looked like a ripe tomato. Her blue eyes followed the shimmering light and made a soft gurgling sound.

"Do you like that?" Henry held up the gear so she could see it better, and her eyes followed the movement. "It's from Papa's shop." The baby did not reply, so Henry leaned a little closer and whispered. "He's very clever."

The baby, unimpressed by Henry's words, cooed as she watched the little gear dance in the sunlight. Henry smiled.

"Heinz Rittenhouse, what are you doing in here?"

Henry's mother filled the parlor doorway. She planted her hands on her hips, a scowl on her face that spoke of a thousand punishments.

"N-n-othing, Mama," Henry stammered. He backed away from the bassinet and stuffed the gear in his pocket. "She was crying, and I just wanted to..."

His mother waved away his excuses with one hand, the other still firmly attached to her hip. Her eyes closed in prayerful patience. "Never mind. Come with me." She took three steps and grasped his hand. "The guests will be arriving at any moment."

Henry groaned. "Why do I have to eat supper in the kitchen? I want to sit with you." It came out as a long whine, which he knew did nothing to help his cause but was unable to prevent.

"You know perfectly well why. This is not a party for children."

That made no sense to Henry at all—wasn't the entire point of the party to celebrate the *baby?* The child in question resumed her wailing almost the second Henry and his mother left the parlor.

The kitchen door was still swinging in their wake when the doorbell rang. Henry's mother rattled off instructions in German to the kitchen staff for his care. As she spoke, she plunked him into a chair at the kitchen table, planted a kiss on his head, and disappeared through the door.

Henry slumped. He knew he was going to be the only child at the party, which meant he had to sit in here and eat alone. There had been the smallest hope, now crushed, that his mother would let him sit with the adults. He rested his chin on the kitchen table and sighed. The kitchen was the hottest room in the house. He pulled at his cuffs again, his deepest desire to rip the shirt from his body, run down the road, and jump into the cool water of the creek. The front bell rang again and again, and soon the murmured sounds of adult conversation seeped through the kitchen door.

Henry finished his pork and dumplings. They were delicious, but not as good as his mother's. When dessert had been served, the activity in the kitchen turned to cleaning up. Henry remained at the table, rolling his watch gear along the surface with one finger, watching the teeth bite into the wood.

Maybe my gear is magic, he thought. *Maybe I can make time go faster, so I can go home and play.*

The front bell rang again, but Henry did not look up. The maid muttered something about the rudeness of being late, wiped her hands on her apron, and left the kitchen. Henry barely noticed she was gone, and he barely noticed when the cook disappeared a moment later, leaving Henry alone. He was busy imagining the gear to be a great metal machine, destroying everything in its path. Henry rolled the gear up the side of a flour canister. He was the commander of an army of kitchen utensils left to dry on the table.

It was the rising of voices in the dining room that made him stop playing. He paused, his finger on the edge of the gear, which hung precipitously over the lip of the open flour canister. He tipped his head toward the dining room, trying to hear what they were saying.

"I've given you my answer already. I will not change my mind. Now go, before I summon the police."

Normally, shouting would make Henry run in the opposite direction. But since he was not the one being shouted at, and he had never heard adults speak to each other that way, he slid from his seat and crept to the door. If the police were coming, he wanted to see.

He pushed the door open, just an inch, and peered into the dining room. Everyone was on their feet. Frau Weber stood closest to him, her hand to her chest, her face white as milk. Beside her stood Mr. Adler. He lived two doors down from the Webers and owned the general store, the largest shop on Germantown Avenue and the home of many delicious sweets. They were the only two people he could see. Both looked at someone on the other side of the table. Henry moved his head around, trying to get a better look. But he couldn't see anything else without opening the door further. Something told him that he should not, so he stayed right where he was and listened.

"You do not understand what you are doing, Edmund. Please, I implore you to reconsider." It wasn't a voice Henry recognized, but whoever it was sounded watery, as if he were about to cry.

Herr Weber's voice sounded stern but frightened. "This is how you ask me to reconsider, Alexei? By intruding in my home, interrupting my daughter's christening party, and threatening me and my guests with a pistol?"

A pistol? Henry had never seen a pistol up close. Only behind the glass of his father's case, which he was strictly forbidden to touch. He dared push the door open another tiny bit but couldn't see much more.

"You've left me no other recourse." The stranger's voice turned from watery to cold as brass in the winter. "I must be able to finish my work."

"Your work is unnatural." Herr Weber practically hissed the words. Henry turned his head and pressed his ear to the door opening.

"My work will save lives!" The stranger's sudden shout made Henry jump. "It could change the world. You must let me continue."

Herr Weber was not to be swayed. "You are playing God." There was a loud thump and the *clink* of glasses shivering against each other. "And I will not be a part of it."

"Then her death is on your head. And it is a debt that *will* be repaid." There was a loud *click*. Everyone in the room gasped. Henry put his eye back up to the gap. Herr Adler had moved to stand in front of Frau Weber, whose face was bright red and streaked with tears. The room turned silent, and even Henry held his breath.

The stranger's voice cut through the air like broken glass. "Shooting you would only be a moment's pain. Edmund Weber, you will feel the same agony that I feel. When you least expect it you will know the never-ending torment that comes when a piece of your heart is taken from you."

Frau Weber gasped, afraid. "You stay away from Sophie."

Henry nodded. *I knew she was trouble. All that fussing.*

The stranger continued, his tone low and dangerous. "You will never be able to hide or run. You will not have one moment's peace. That is my curse on your house."

Henry listened for Herr Weber's reply. He had finally worked up the courage to push the door open enough to get a peek at the man with the pistol, when the sound of tapping on glass made him turn around.

Two men stood outside the kitchen door. One was dark-skinned, wearing a rounded hat. Henry didn't recognize him. He didn't know the other man either, but he had the look of being someone he *should* know. He resembled Henry's father, but younger, and his eyes and chin were the wrong shape, more like his mother's. It was a very trustworthy face.

The argument in the dining room forgotten, Henry crossed to the door, ready to let them in. The two men seemed to argue. The dark-skinned man held the other by one shoulder, pulling him away. The man who reminded Henry of his father pushed the man's hand off and gestured wildly, his mouth forming words Henry could not hear through the kitchen door's thick, wavy glass.

Both men turned and looked right at him. The dark-skinned man looked at the other, anger puckering his mouth like a grape in the sun. The other stared through the glass at Henry, his mouth forming an O of surprise.

Henry met the man's eyes and his stomach rolled. It was the same queasy feeling he got when he came down the stairs at home and caught his reflection in the mirror at the bottom. He jumped back, startled and feeling dizzy. The man put his hand to the window glass, staring at Henry while the boy gazed warily at him, still feeling off-balance.

A terrific crash in the dining room, mixed with a loud *pop*, broke the spell. A great deal of screaming came from the front of the house, followed by the slamming of a door. Henry jumped and looked over his shoulder.

When he turned back to the kitchen door, the men were gone. Henry pressed his nose to the glass and looked about but saw nothing. He opened the door and stepped outside, the summer heat like a wall, causing sweat to run down his face and onto his lace collar.

The Weber's garden was empty.

CHAPTER II

December 1884

ENRY TRUDGED THROUGH THE SNOW, HIS HEART BEATING FASTER with every step he took down Germantown Avenue. He pulled his thick, warm muffler tighter against the biting wind, silently cursing his choice of fashionable but completely useless calfskin gloves, as he trudged through the snow wishing he had chosen one of the dozen woolen pairs his mother had knit for him.

It was only another half block to the Weber's house, but might as well have been a hundred miles. With each step he took along Germantown Avenue his heart beat a little faster. He rehearsed for the hundredth time what he planned to say to Sophie's father, and though he knew the words by heart he was terrified they would stick in his throat when the time came to speak them. Which was ridiculous—he had known Herr Weber since he was a child. Yet just the thought of this conversation made his hands go from frozen to sweaty. He patted his jacket pocket, checking for the precious bundle inside. With the other hand he reached into his other pocket and rubbed the case of his pocket watch with his thumb. The watch was a gift from his father, made by him and given when Henry had been accepted to the university. He had even used the small gear Henry had stolen as a child and played with for years in the works of the timepiece.

The Weber's house appeared before him, covered in garlands and red bows. The gingerbread trim, the snow in the yard, and the enormous wreath on the door turned the house into a Currier and Ives lithograph. Frau Weber loved the holidays. As one of the premier ladies of Germantown, she took her duties as hostess very seriously. Henry had planned this visit carefully, allowing himself plenty of time to complete his mission before the first guests were scheduled to arrive for the Weber's annual Christmas Eve gala.

He pushed open the beribboned wrought iron gate. The Christmas tree glittered and winked at him through the bowed parlor window. He could practically smell the mixture of pine and freshly baked cookies that he was sure would hit his nose the second he stepped inside. It had been this way every holiday season for as long as he could recall.

The familiarity of it eased his nerves a little, until an unexpected movement caught his eye.

Somewhere near the top of the turret on the corner of the house. The movement resolved itself into a person, bundled in heavy clothing. They clung to the copper drainpipe that ran down the side of the house. The topmost window of the turret stood open. A burglar?

The intruder was climbing *down*. The robbery had already occurred then, and Henry had caught the thief trying to escape. Henry marched right across the yard, his footprints marring the pristine snow, reaching the bottom of the turret just as the burglar's feet touched the ground.

"Hold on, you." Henry grabbed the shoulder of the thief's coat and shook him roughly.

"Henry Rittenhouse, take your hands off of me this instant!"

Henry was shocked into compliance. The thief had called him by name, but more shocking, the voice that came from beneath the flat wool cap was decidedly *not* male. A hint of blonde hair poked from beneath the burglar's hat, and when she turned around Henry was met with a pair of large blue eyes that blazed with anger.

Henry jumped back. "Sophie! I mean, Miss Weber. Please forgive me, I didn't know it was you." He paused, unsure how to proceed, his face suddenly hot enough to melt the snow. "Is there a reason you're climbing down the drainpipe?"

Sophie's lips curved into the smile that made Henry's heart jump. Had she possibly grown more beautiful since he had last seen her? Her transformation from annoying little girl into charming young woman seemed to have occurred overnight. The effect she had on him now was both maddening and extremely pleasant.

She planted her hands on her hips, one gesture that had survived from childhood.

"Because, silly, I want to go riding," Sophie replied as if she were explaining that the sun rose in the east.

"Shouldn't you be getting ready for the party?" He glanced at her scandalous attire—a pair of brown wool trousers and a peacoat, in addition to the hat—and turned his gaze elsewhere. "Pardon me if I'm being forward, why are you dressed so?"

Sophie heaved a sigh. "Because Mother and Father are being impossible. You know how obsessed they are with keeping me inside.

They sent me away to that prison they called a school, surrounded by its brick walls and iron gate and absolutely no privacy whatsoever. When I was younger it made a kind of sense, but I'm *sixteen*. I'm old enough to make my debut at the Assembly Ball."

Henry opened his mouth to reply, but she rambled on without stopping.

"Now their excuse is that it's not proper for a girl of my age to go unchaperoned, but they won't even let me out into the garden alone anymore. As if they are holding their breath, waiting for something terrible to happen. It's just possible I might die of over-protection. And tonight? With the entire neighborhood stuffed into the house and Mama hovering over me? If I don't get some fresh air, I will go mad."

Henry held back his smile, though he could not stop it from creeping into his eyes. Sophie's flair for the dramatic and willful spirit, both of which he used to find childish and irritating, had turned into the things he found most endearing about her.

"Sophie, I'm sure you're overreacting. They're your parents, it's their job to protect you. And as you said, it's Christmas Eve, when everyone in town will be arriving on your doorstep. I'm sure this is the one time when you will be missed. Come back inside and maybe we can convince them to let us go riding together for a little while." He held his breath hoping that she did not realize the implication of such an offer. Another half a year or so, she would be seventeen. It was absolutely inappropriate for him to ride alone with her, as they had done when they were younger. "With a chaperone, of course."

Sophie made a sour face at the word *chaperone*. She tilted her head in a most alluring way. "Let's not tell them and both go riding anyway..." Then she moved in close and spoke low, making the hairs on the back of Henry's neck stand up. "Come on, Mr. Rittenhouse, live a little. Have an adventure with me."

Henry took another step back, his collar and muffler suddenly feeling tight and his skin terribly hot. "I can't. What would people say? I won't bring a scandal on you or your parents." He wanted to go with her, ached to say yes to her demands. But he was so close to doing things the proper way that he could not spoil it now.

"Who would recognize me in this outfit? You worry far too much about what people will say, Henry." Sophie said the words gently. "You are brilliant. The world is waiting for you, all you have to do is spread your wings and fly. But you insist on remaining on the ground."

"It's smart to stay on the ground, and to think of the future." Henry put his hand into his pocket and squeezed the package inside. "And to take advantage of the opportunities that come your way." Which he would do if Sophie didn't muck up his carefully laid plans. "Come back inside, please? I was on my way to your house anyway. I... I have a gift for you."

Sophie's eyes lit up like stars. "Really? What is it?"

Henry knew if he played it right, he could still salvage the evening. "I can't give it to you unless you come back inside."

He pulled her gift from his pocket. A little box meticulously wrapped in silver paper and tied with a green velvet bow. He held it up to show her.

Sophie was not so easily tempted. She looked up at him, wide-eyed, through her delicate lashes. "Oh please, Henry. What harm would it do to give it to me now?"

Henry's conviction wavered, but he had been ready for her reply. "Because I want to give it to you properly, not skulking beside your house while you are dressed in boy's clothing." Words he never thought he would utter in his entire life.

Sophie retaliated with heavy artillery. She pushed out her lower lip in her very best pout. "It would be much better for you to give it to me now, while we're alone. Then you can keep my overjoyed reaction all for yourself."

Henry cleared his throat and pulled at his muffler to let the cold air run down his sweltering neck. "Miss Weber, you are treading the line of propriety." Though he meant it, it was not spoken to scold.

"I'm standing in the snow, dressed as a boy, speaking alone to a man who is not my father. I think the line has been well and truly crossed." Sophie reached for the box. "In for a penny, in for a pound! While I'm already on this side, might as well make it worth my while."

Henry, a champion fencer, had exceptional reflexes. Young and strong, and with steady hands. And yet, in the face of a sixteen-year-old girl, he was somehow too slow to prevent her from snatching the box from his hand and running away with it, all the while giggling with glee.

He heaved an exasperated sigh and chased after her, hoping to catch up before she ripped the paper off completely and he missed seeing her face when she opened it.

Sophie was fast, unencumbered by skirts. By the time Henry reached the walk, she was already around the corner of the house. He followed her footsteps in the snow. They led him between the Weber's house and the neighbor's, emerging into the alley that ran behind all of the houses on the street.

Trees lined the alley, their branches heavy with snow that hid Sophie from view. Henry followed her crystalline laugh further down the lane. Ahead, a door slammed shut, cracking like a gunshot in the snowy quiet. The only place she could go was the carriage house. By the time Henry reached the door his heart pumped rapidly, and not only from exertion. He paused, leaning against the wood to catch his breath.

Sophie vexed him in a dozen ways that both terrified and exhilarated him. He, as she had rightly accused him, was grounded. The world had rules, and he liked it that way. His staid nature had got him to the top of his class at University, and on track to be one of the most sought-after civil engineers in the city when he graduated. But when he was around Sophie, he felt off-balance, and just a little bit out of control. When she was near, the world shifted beneath his feet, leaving him breathless. And he didn't mind at all. She made him chase after dreams.

He put his hand on the door handle with the full realization that he had done exactly what she wanted.

"I hope you haven't opened that package yet, Sophie."

After the brightness of sunlight on snow, he was nearly blinded by the sudden plunge into darkness as he stepped into the stable. His eyes adjusted slowly to the lamp-lit space, the earthy scent of hay and horses heavy in the air.

"Sophie?" he called softly, and then listened. She was terrible at hide-and-seek. She always giggled and gave herself away. There was no sound except the neighing of horses and the cooing of birds taking shelter from the cold. He walked through the carriage house, peering into each stall, but only received strange looks from horses in return. He passed into the space where the carriages were kept, feeling uncomfortable as he looked inside the private broughams and phaetons of Germantown Avenue's finest families. But he spied no Sophie.

Had she gone straight through, sneaking out the front door then home again? She had wanted to ride, but still it was in the realm of possibility that she had left simply for a laugh. He opened the door and peered out, but saw no footprints in the snow.

"Sophie?" Henry called out again, hoping he had just missed her hiding place, trusting that the note of urgency in his voice would be enough to make her appear and allay his fears. Only his call met silence. And he spied something shiny on the ground, a bit of silver picked up by the lanterns.

A bitter knot of fear twisted Henry's gut as he leaned over and picked up a torn bit of wrapping from his gift.

"Sophie, please come out."

Even as he uttered the words, he expected no reply.

Sophie shivered with cold as she woke, and her head throbbed with a terrible headache.

What happened?

She concentrated, trying to bring the memory back, but there were only bits. The carriage house. A voice behind her, startling her. Darkness.

Darkness remained, but she was definitely not in the carriage house. The scent of horses and leather had been replaced by a stale, musty smell and the slight hint of lavender. She lay on her back, with something soft and silky beneath her. She continued to shiver—though she could not see, she was sure her breath fogged in front of her mouth.

When she tried to move, the pounding in her head made her stomach churn. *Why did I go into the carriage house?* Henry. The package. She had taken it and led him a snowy chase, then ran inside. Her plan had been to hide by her family's brougham and leap out to startle him, then reward him with a kiss. Sophie's cheeks flushed with warmth, which at least help abate the shivering.

Sophie closed her eyes and, between the beats of her throbbing head, tried to remember what happened. Someone had been in the carriage house, inside one of the stalls. He knew her name. The voice echoed like a long-ago memory, but the shadows hid his face. She had gone closer but found no one there. Sophie gasped when she remembered—a hand had clamped over her mouth, pressing a sweet-smelling cloth to her lips. Everything had turned to thick fog.

"Henry?" Sophie called softly. Her voice bounced back to her strangely, as if she was inside a small closet. She didn't expect a reply.

Wherever she was, Henry wouldn't have left her unconscious, in the dark. She teased him about being a stuffed shirt, but that same feet-firmly-on-the-ground attitude made him loyal to a fault. She had only called to break the silence, which pressed on her like a heavy woolen blanket.

A reply did come, however.

"It's all right, Sophia. You are completely safe."

The words sounded muffled. If she spoke inside a closet, the speaker addressed her from outside. The timbre and inflection bobbed like a bit of driftwood on the sea of her memory. Not Henry. The man from the carriage house. The man who sounded familiar but that she couldn't place.

The man who had *kidnapped* her.

Sophie tried to sit up, and her forehead collided with something solid and cool. She fell back, the dull throb in her head rang as if she had stuck her head inside a church bell. She raised her hands and found the barrier easily. She rapped on it with her knuckles. It sounded dull, as if it was made of thick glass. She ran her shaking fingertips along it, looking for an edge. The glass curved above her head and around to the sides before it met with cold, hard metal on either side of her body. It extended as far below where her hands could reach, and up above her head. She lifted a foot and met with resistance after only a few inches. Fear clamped her with an iron grip. She was encased in a glass-and-metal cabinet.

Click. Lights appeared above her. They were dim at first, but quickly brightened. Not gas, but brand-new incandescent bulbs. Her father had brought one home from the factory to show her. He was installing them for the laborers, so they could work later in the winter months without the danger of fire. The light revealed more of her prison. Glass above, metal below. She twisted her head to the side and caught a glimpse of white satin beneath her body.

The truth of her prison whisked the breath from her lungs.

Not a cabinet.

A coffin.

Sophie sucked in a huge gulp of air and expelled it in a lung-searing scream. Inside the enclosed space, the sound shattered her ears. She balled her hands into fists and beat them on the glass overhead, kicking with all her might. Her blows didn't make a crack.

"I would ask that you not struggle." The man stood out of view, keeping her from looking her captor in the face. "The machine is delicate, and precisely calibrated. Also, you might injure yourself. No matter what you might think, I don't want that."

Think? How could she think amidst the crushing eddy of pain, confusion, and panic? Her whirling thoughts, however, had caught on one word: *Machine.*

A face appeared above hers. Her heart galloped even faster. Here he was, a ghost of the past she could not name. He looked weary, his eyes deeply lined, his temples and well-trimmed moustache streaked with gray.

What is his name? It was on the tip of her tongue but slipped away.

"Where am I?" The room around her held no clues. Tools hung on the wall nearby, as if she were in a workshop of some kind. No one would find her. Another, more terrifying thought crept into her mind like a thief.

She involuntarily pulled her legs together and curled her hands into claws, ready to scratch his eyes out if he attempted to touch her. That was when she realized she no longer wore the trousers and man's shirt she had left home in. Instead, she wore a silk gown of pure white. A wave of nausea rolled over her, but she did not dare ask aloud the question burning in her mind.

"What are you going to do to me?"

The man focused on something along the side of the cabinet. "Miss Weber, I want you to understand something very clearly." He spoke quietly, but with a dangerous edge to his voice that made Sophie nervous. "It's extremely important that you understand that none of this is your fault."

His fingers danced along the metal, and Sophie tilted her head to try and see what he was doing. What appeared to be a series of knobs, dials, and gauges stuck out from the side of the machine.

She scanned the seam between the metal and glass, searching for some kind of catch or release. But there was nothing. The man—*why can't I remember his name!*—fiddled with the instruments some more, then straightened. He gazed at her for another moment.

"I'm so very sorry." His eyes gave truth to his words.

He stepped away, out of Sophie's sight. The pity in his voice brought tears to her eyes. They streamed down the sides of her face to pool on the satin.

"Why are you doing this, if you are sorry?" The words came out watery and broken as Sophie's breath hitched in her chest. "Please, let me go home to my family."

"Your family?" The words bit with a hard-edge, spit from his mouth as if they were poison. "Why should I let you go home to your family when your family has taken mine away?"

Sophie didn't understand what he was talking about, but his tone terrified her.

"No, my dear. I am sorry for you, but not for your family. This is their retribution. Now your father will see that I was right, and he will understand the cost of his actions." The man came back into view and knelt in front of the machine.

"You can stop, though." Sophie wiped at her tears, desperate. "You can release me. I won't tell a soul what happened, I promise."

The man hesitated, but did not look up.

"She would have been just like you, I think." He shook his head and hunched his shoulders. " Things are in motion, much bigger than you and I or even your father. It's too late. But do not worry. As I said, I have no desire to hurt you."

He stepped back from the machine, and Sophie saw his face once more. From his sorrowful expression, Sophie almost believed him.

Something beneath her clicked. A clock started ticking loudly, as if nearby. The air around her turned even colder, and frost formed on the machine's glass lid. Suddenly the edges of the world turned fuzzy. Her eyelids felt so heavy. She struggled to keep them open to no avail, and her arms and legs went numb from the cold.

As the darkness closed around her the man spoke.

"When you wake, the world will be a different place. Sleep well, Sophia."

"Tell us again what happened? Where is Sophie?"

"Exactly where was the last place you saw her?"

"What was she wearing, Mr. Rittenhouse? Please describe it again."

Henry sat in the Weber's parlor. He heard the questions being thrown at him, by the police, by Herr and Frau Weber, by his own parents. Nothing they said made sense, and they all sounded as if they were underwater.

He had returned to the house, hoping that Sophie had snuck home, changed her clothing, and waited for him as if nothing had happened. She loved to play just that kind of joke. But when he arrived at the Weber's front door, all his hopes were shattered. A black carriage bearing the Philadelphia Police Department's emblem on the door waited at the end of the walk. The horse that drew it snorted and stamped his feet in the cold. The Weber's door stood wide open, the festive decorations suddenly feeling ominous. Henry dragged himself up the front steps and across the porch. The moment he entered, a frantic Frau Weber asked him if he had seen Sophie, said she had gone missing. There were footprints in the snow that suggested a struggle.

Henry had considered, for half a heartbeat, about lying. He could have pretended that he had only just arrived at the house, and that the conversation in the snow, the chase, and what he found in the carriage house had never happened. But he was first of all a terrible liar. Secondly, he could not bear the look in the Weber's panic-stricken eyes. Guilt tore at his heart and mind and compelled him to tell the entire story, beginning from when he first saw Sophie climb down the rain gutter. He was getting Sophie in more trouble with her parents than even she imagined possible, but that hardly mattered. They might refuse him as suitor for their daughter, if they wanted, and blame him for her sudden disappearance. He could lose her forever.

He could live with all of it, if Sophie was found safe.

The whole affair played over and over in his mind, while the innumerable questions pelted at him remained muffled background noise. Had he seen anything out of place? No matter how many times he tried to eke more details from his panic-addled brain, he had to say no. He had heard nothing, finding only the bit of silver paper on the floor of the carriage house, mocking him.

Henry blinked. "What? I'm sorry, could you repeat that?" The sudden tone of the detective's voice had caught his attention. The detective, a thin man in his late thirties with graying hair, pinned Henry with a hard glare. "I asked, Mr. Rittenhouse, how you would classify your relationship with Miss Weber."

Henry narrowed his eyes and tilted his head, still trying to understand what it was the detective wanted to know. Then it hit him, and the detective's implication became as clear as the crystal of the chandelier above his head.

"Excuse me? I don't see how any of that is your business, sir." It wasn't that Henry did not want to answer, only that he wasn't exactly certain *how* to answer. He had known Sophie since she was born, their parents were best friends. She and he hadn't always been on the best of terms, especially when they were younger. But now...

He was sure that the Webers knew his intentions, but since he had not made the formal request, it wasn't a matter for public knowledge yet. Declaring his love for her out loud to a stranger were not how the words should first cross his lips.

The detective pursed his lips and studied Henry. "It is my business, Mr. Rittenhouse, to find Sophia. I need to know the nature of your relationship with her, because, quite frankly, you were the last person to see her. And we have only your word on the veracity of the events that preceded Ms. Weber's disappearance. My men have searched the carriage house and the surrounding area, and have found nothing that suggests a third party was present."

Henry jumped from his seat. "Detective... Thornton, is it? Are you implying that I had anything to do with Soph — Miss Weber's disappearance?" His face turned hot as anger flooded through him. "I implored her to come inside, but she ran off. I told you before, when I entered the carriage house, she was not there." He fumbled in his pocket, pulled out the piece of silver wrapping and thrust it under the detective's nose. "This was all that I found. It is part of the wrapping for the Christmas present I brought for her."

Frau Weber, perched on the edge of one of the upholstered parlor chairs, looked from Henry to the detective, her eyes wide. "You think Henry is responsible? He could no more harm my daughter than he could himself. You are mistaken."

The detective turned toward her, bobbing his head respectfully. "Of course, Mrs. Weber. I am only considering every possibility. It is my duty." He turned back to Henry. The look in his eyes said Frau Weber's speech on Henry's behalf had done nothing to dissuade the detective from considering him a suspect.

Herr Weber returned from the kitchen, a glass of water in his hand. He handed the glass to the detective. "You are wasting your time, detective. Mr. Rittenhouse had nothing more to do with my daughter's disappearance than I did."

The detective's mouth fell open, then closed again quickly, as if he were biting back words he knew would get him into trouble.

"Thank you for the water, Mr. Weber." His expression betrayed his thoughts — he considered *everyone* a suspect.

Herr Weber continued. "If my daughter does not return to this house of her own volition, there is only one person responsible."

Frau Weber, her face pale as the snow outside, rose from her chair. "Edmund, you can't possibly think... but we've been so careful."

His mouth a grim line, Herr Weber shook his head. "Marta, he was here. Four years ago. Remember?"

Frau Weber gasped, her hand flying to her mouth.

"That was why I insisted she be sent away to school, where she could be safe." He bowed his head, studying the pattern on the carpet. "It seems it was all for nothing."

The confused detective looked from Edmund to Marta and back again. "Mr. Weber, if you have any information, I suggest you give it to me immediately."

Edmund closed his eyes and sighed. "Detective, this is a family matter, which goes back to the days leading up to my daughter's birth. But it does not appear we cannot keep it to ourselves any longer. There is a man you should investigate."

A knocking at the door interrupted him. Frau and Herr Weber ran to the entrance hall, Marta calling out Sophie's name. Henry followed, knowing they clung to a thin hope. Their daughter would not knock at the door of her own home.

In the open doorway stood a boy, perhaps fourteen years old. The urchin wore a short coat of brown wool and trousers, both with worn cuffs. He looked cold and thin. The policeman who had been stationed by the door gripped him by the shoulder.

"He says he's got a message for Mr. Weber," the officer said.

The boy thrust out his hand, shoving a crisp white envelope toward the gathered group. Edmund reached to take it, but the detective got there first and slipped it from the boy's grasp.

"Detective, I must protest." Edmund held out his hand. "That is addressed to me. It could be nothing more than regrets for our party this evening. Which we have already canceled." He closed his eyes and bowed his head, resigned.

The detective carefully opened the envelope and pulled out a sheet of paper. He skimmed it and then handed it to Mr. Weber. Henry could not read it from where he stood, but Mr. Weber's reaction was enough to let him know it wasn't good news.

"Who gave you this message?" The detective waved the empty envelope at the boy.

The boy stumbled over his own tongue. "A-a-a man, sir. Older gent, well dressed, don't know his name. Gave me ten cents to deliver it to this address. Even put it on the envelope so I wouldn't forget."

"And where were you when he gave it to you?"

"On Coulter Street," the boy offered, as if those words would release him. "The gentleman seemed very nice." His face brightened as if he had just had an epiphany. "He had a little bit of an accent."

"Thank you for your help." The detective motioned to the policeman, and he released the boy. The messenger paused for a moment, then darted down the walk and away up the street.

"Why did you let him go?" Henry snapped at the detective. "He might know where Sophie is!" He didn't even bother to correct himself for using her given name.

The detective shook his head. "He told us everything he knew." He indicated the letter, still in Edmund's hand.

"Is this the man you were referring to earlier?"

Edmund nodded. It could have been a trick of the light, but Henry swore Herr Weber's eyes turned moist. "Yes. He has made good on his threat of so many years past. Alexei Faber has taken my daughter."

CHAPTER III

THE FRONT DOOR OF THE UNASSUMING, SLIGHTLY RUNDOWN HOUSE on Coulter Street flew open with a crack and a splintering of wood. Police officers poured inside, followed closely by Detective Thornton, Herr Weber, and, of course, Henry.

They had raced through the falling snow, following the light of the streetlamps and the instructions contained within the note. The correspondent stated that Sophie would be found safe at this address. Henry still didn't understand who had taken her, or for what reason, and Herr Weber had not been forthcoming with details. It really didn't matter to Henry what the man's reasons were if he was true to his word.

The policemen scattered throughout the house, nightsticks drawn. Upstairs, boots pounded across the floor, rattling the ceiling fixtures below and sending plaster powder down onto Henry's head. Against the detective's advice to wait until they had cleared the house, Henry ran from room to room, calling Sophie's name. The kitchen, the parlor, the dining room. He returned to the entrance as empty-handed as the rest.

"She's not here!" Herr Weber smacked the wall beside him, sending down another flurry of plaster-snow. "Faber lied."

"Why would he do that?" Detective Thornton pulled a cigarette case from his jacket. "Why lead us here and leave no further clue?" He removed a cigarette and tamped it on the outside of the case before putting it in his mouth and lighting it. "Perhaps you should come to the station with us, Herr Weber, and tell us everything you know of this man, so we can move forward in this case."

"This case?" Herr Weber's face turned red. "This *case* is my daughter! And she has disappeared! You will find her, Detective, and you will find her immediately. There must be some clue here that will lead us to her."

Henry listened to the argument, his heart crumbling. He walked slowly through the house again, searching for any sign that he or the police might have overlooked. He ended up in the tiny parlor, where he fell into one of the dusty, frayed overstuffed chairs and watched the snow pile up on the edges of the frost-bitten window.

The misery of helplessness overcame him. He stood and paced the length of the small room. He could not get the image of Sophie out of his head. Sophie, alone and probably afraid, with a man whose intentions were unclear.

He leaned against the wall beside a dusty bookshelf and tried not to let his imagination get away from him. But unwanted and disturbing scenarios crept in around the edges of his thoughts, serving no purpose except to make him more anxious and angry.

Damn! He pounded a fist against the wall in frustration and pulled his hand back in pain. Something stuck out from the side of the cabinet, something hard. He looked for the offending bit, but it was dark. Carefully, he ran his finger along the place where the cabinet met the wall.

"Detective, could you come here for a moment?"

The tromping of a dozen feet heralded the arrival of Thornton, Herr Weber, and four of his men. Henry waved them over.

"Look at this."

The detective called for a light. One of the men handed him a small oil lantern. He held it up to the place Henry had indicated, peering closely.

"Is that...?"

"A hinge? Yes, it is." Henry knelt beside the bookshelf. "There is another one here. This cabinet swings like a door."

Detective Thornton barked a few orders, and immediately the police sprang into action. They scurried about, looking for tools, crowbars, and hammers that could be used to remove the obstacle. Henry, meanwhile, chose a less violent course of action, examining the bookshelf and the wall around it. He looked for the mechanism that opened the door. The room was shabby, the furniture worn, and everything covered in dust. The chandelier and sconces were black with tarnish.

"Except this one." The brass of one of the fixtures attached to the wall adjacent to the bookshelf shone, as if it had been touched many times. The sconce's globe was dust-free. Henry tried to turn the fixture on. It did not light. Instead, one edge of the bookshelf separated from the wall, swinging outward slightly.

"Here." Henry pushed it open a little further.

"Very clever," the detective remarked. "How did you figure it out?"

"I'm an engineer. I can see how things are supposed to work in my head." Henry had no other explanation. It was something he had been able to do since he was young, when he was very good at taking apart pocket watches, but not yet good at putting them back together. Everything inside the secret chamber was darkness, but there was the sense of space. He leaned inside.

"Sophie? Sop—Miss Weber, are you here?"

Someone grabbed him by this coat and dragged him back. He spun around, twisting from the assailant's grip, and came face to face with Detective Thornton.

"I will go first, if you don't mind."

Henry squared his shoulders, making himself as tall as possible. "With all due respect, detective, I found the door. If Miss Weber is in there—"

The policeman pulled him further from the door, keeping his voice low. "Faber may have left some kind of trap. She may not be in there at all. Or he may be in there himself, waiting with a pistol to shoot the first man to enter."

Henry felt the blood drain from his face. "Excellent points." He stepped back and gave the detective room.

"Wait here until I give the all clear."

With his pistol leading the way, he pushed the door open further and stepped inside. Henry held his breath. There was no sound of a gunshot, or a struggle. But also, nothing to indicate Sophie was inside, which did nothing to assuage the fear that gripped Henry. He grasped his watch, worrying the gold case with his thumb. The faint scent of lavender mixed with a heavy smell of dust emanated from the room.

There was a sound, like something, perhaps a foot, hitting a metal object, followed by a muttered curse. "What is this? Can we get some more light in here?"

Edmund Weber stood beside Henry in the parlor. He studied the wall beside the doorway. Edmund reached out and turned a brass key Henry had thought was decorative. The key clicked and then a soft glow emanated from inside the secret room. The light shone from fixtures on the ceiling, revealing a startled Detective Thornton.

"I recognized this switch," Herr Weber offered with a shrug. "It controls the new incandescent bulbs." He pointed to the glowing globes on the ceiling.. "We're installing them in the factory. No gas jets to cause a fire."

Henry entered the room. Based on the wallpaper, it seemed to have originally been part of the parlor. The windows had been covered with black paint, blocking the outdoor light and hiding the room's contents from prying eyes.

"Herr Weber, if would you please join me over here." Detective Thornton called.

The room appeared to serve as a workshop. One wall was taken up by a long wooden table, covered in tools and strange-looking instruments. Brass casings and glass fronts reflected the overhead lights. The workbench was littered with things familiar to Henry; gears, springs, and bits of machinery like those in his father's clock shop. This man was obviously interested in mechanical things. What did he build?

The answer might lie in the stack of pages piled at one end of the bench. They looked like blueprints. He lifted the top sheet and pulled it close to his eyes to study in the strange light. The design was so odd-looking, he could not begin to guess what the purpose of such a machine would be. He picked up the second page when a sudden gasp made Henry's blood run cold.

"Oh, my Sophie. What has he done to you?"

Henry turned, the blueprints in his hand, his stomach a lump of lead. Edmund stood near the back of the room where a large but ordinary-looking wardrobe stood in the corner. Herr Weber stood nearby, a sheet in his hand, his attention arrested by the object that it had covered.

On the floor sat a large rectangular case. The bottom half was constructed of brass, while the top was glass. Knobs, dials, and several gauges decorated the front. A pair of polished brass cylinders were attached to one end of the case; copper tubes ran from the cylinders to one end of the glass portion. Something lay inside the case. Henry approached slowly. He knew what he would find, but loathed to confirm his fears.

Sophie.

She looked as if she were sleeping, her eyes closed and her hands at her sides. Her clothing was different than what Henry had last seen her wearing. In place of her trousers and peacoat she wore a delicate gown of snowy white. Sophie's hair was unbound, spread across the satin pillow beneath her head. A perfect angel, sleeping in a case of glass. A coffin.

"Oh no. No." Henry put his hands on the glass, and hissed as he snatched them back again.

"Is it hot? Are you burned?" Detective Thornton asked.

Henry rubbed his palms together. "No, it's cold. Freezing cold." He leaned in close, watching for the rise and fall of Sophie's chest. But it did not move. Tears splashed onto the glass, turning to jeweled snowflakes, and it took Henry a moment to realize they were his own. He wiped them from the case with his coat sleeve, and that was when he noticed it... His gift.

The locket he had bought Sophie for Christmas, an oval-shaped pendant of gold, lay on her chest, the delicate chain around her neck. Inside was a picture of himself. Such a personal gift was an indication of his declared intention to court Sophie. He hoped she had been able to see it and realize what she meant to him before... this... had been done to her.

"She looks perfect." He inspected her more closely, wishing he could reach through the glass and touch her pale cheek. There was no sign of violence on her skin. A hand gripped his shoulder, and he looked back at Edmund. Henry had never known him to be demonstrative, not even with his own wife. But the look in his eyes as he gazed at his daughter reflected the heartbreak that lodged in Henry's own chest like a knife.

"We found this."

Detective Thornton held out a second envelope. It was inscribed with Edmund's name, in the same script as the note that had been delivered to the house. Herr Weber snatched it and ripped it open. He pulled out the page within and scanned it, lips moving slightly. As he read, his face turned to a mask of horror. Henry could not stand it any longer.

"What does it say?" There were no words that could relieve his grief, but Henry had to know.

Edmund looked at Henry, confusion and pain so clear in his expression. He closed his eyes and handed the letter to Henry, who took it with a shaking hand.

Edmund,

The hour of my retribution has arrived. years ago, I swore to you, that I would have my revenge. You see before you your own child, the shadow of death upon her brow. Now you know the pain you brought upon me. Losing your child is like having your own heart ripped from your chest.

But she is not dead, Edmund. The machine in which she lies — do you recognize the design? It has placed your Sophia into a deep sleep, one from which she will not wake until the designated time has passed.

One hundred years. Then the machine will revive her, perfect and healthy. Do not attempt to open the machine or otherwise tamper with it. To do so would seal Sophie's fate — she would indeed die.

You, Edmund, will grow old and watch your daughter sleep, ageless and beautiful. She will always be in your sight, but forever out of your reach. You will never hear her laugh again, or watch her marry, or see your grandchildren.

My curse has been fulfilled.

Alexei

Henry sucked in a ragged breath. So many questions begging to be answered, but one leapt to his lips.

"What does he mean, Sophie is asleep?" Her face was pale as death, and no breath fogged the glass above her. What kind of sorcery could put a person in a sleep so deep they appeared dead? And then keep her there for — Henry looked at the letter again — a hundred years?

Edmund covered his eyes. "How arrogant I was, to think that I could keep her safe from him forever." He stared into the case, his gaze unfocused. "Oh, my darling Sophie. I am so sorry. So sorry you have paid for my ignorance. My arrogance."

"She's not dead." Henry latched on to that bright spot, clutching it for dear life. "There has to be a way to get her out of there." His fingers scrabbled along seam of glass and brass, looking for a latch, but found nothing. He scanned the room, looking for something to break the lid. Finding a hammer on the workbench, he raised it over his head, ready to strike.

"Henry, stop!" Edmund caught his hand. "You'll kill her."

Henry pulled away from Herr Weber and lowered his arm, the hammer falling to the floor. "I only wanted to... listen, do you hear that?" He held up a hand, tipping his head toward the device.

Tick, tick, tick.

The unmistakable but faint sound of a clock. Henry knelt in front of the strange prison, looking for the source. It wasn't hard to find. A small glass door set into the brass looked inside the machine, where sat the innermost workings of an average clock. Gears large and small, springs, all put together with precision and skill. He didn't see a winding mechanism, but beneath the door was a small, three-numbered dial, showing the number 100. A keyhole, surrounded by an ornate brass plate, had been inserted next to the dial. Finally, a series of brass buttons had been inset into the panel in a circle, numbered zero through nine.

"This looks like some kind of countdown mechanism. When it reaches zero, the case will open." Henry ran his hands through his hair. "But how can this madman expect us to believe he could keep Sophie asleep for a hundred years? It's impossible. Isn't it?" He skimmed the note again, standing to face Edmund. "He asks if you recognize the design. Do you? Who is Alexei Faber?"

Herr Weber's face turned a nauseous shade of green, guilt filling his eyes. It was gone as quickly as it had appeared, and the stoic man Henry knew returned. He grabbed the edges of his jacket and pulled them as straight as his visage.

"Detective, I want this contraption moved to my home immediately. Sophia needs to be with her family."

The detective's jaw fell open, and Henry thought the man was about to make the mistake of objecting. But he closed his mouth, inhaled slowly, and heaved a sigh. "Yes, Mr. Weber. As soon as we dust it for fingerprints, we'll move it. I suppose we can collect evidence from it at your house just as well as anywhere else. I'll make all the arrangements."

Sophie gasped, struggling to breathe. Her mind strained to make sense of her surroundings while she fought against something that held her legs. Finally she realized she was in her own bed, the bedclothes tangled around her. She pushed the blankets off and swung her legs onto the floor, the rug soft beneath her feet. A deep sigh of relief pushed its way from her lungs.

It was just a nightmare. Her jumbled thoughts began to sort themselves out. It had started as a pleasant dream, with Henry chasing her through the snow, but had turned strange and dark.

Sophie shivered and realized she was freezing. She crossed the dark but familiar room, feeling her way to the wall, searching for the knob that turned on the lamps. They hissed into life, casting an oily yellow glow around her bedroom. Everything looked exactly as it should, but something did not feel right.

That's silly. It's that horrible dream, making me jumpy. She brushed back the errant strands of hair that had escaped her nighttime braid. She couldn't even think about going back to sleep. *I'll go to the kitchen and make a cup of tea. Maybe that will settle my nerves.*

Wrapping her dressing gown around her, she stepped into the chilly hall. The sconces were lit, but the house was eerily quiet, with all of the doors in the hallway closed. That wasn't unusual — keeping the doors closed kept the heat from the evening fires inside. Still, Sophie could not escape the feeling that something was out of place. Icy fingers of foreboding ran up her back, making her shiver again.

She crept down the stairs and toward the kitchen. The lamps blazed here as well, which *was* unusual. The wood was cold, and Sophie wished she had remembered to put on her slippers. The doors to the parlor and the dining room were closed. Also odd. Normally they were left open at night, since the fires were out and the rooms empty. She reached to open the double doors that led to the dining room.

Her face collided with the wood, her nose bearing the brunt of the force. She stepped back, her hand to her face. She tried again, with no better result. There was a keyhole, but she could not ever remember the doors being locked. Strange. She tried the parlor door. Also locked. She tried every door on the lower floor, but they were all locked tight. That feeling of wrongness crept up her spine again.

Sophie raced up the stairs, her bare feet thundering on the treads. She pounded on the door to her parent's bedroom. No one answered. Her hand shook as she reached for the knob but it opened easily, and Sophie ran inside.

The bed stood empty.

She searched the room, panic blossoming in her midsection, climbing into her throat like a vine. She looked in the closet, wondering if her mother and father weren't playing some terrible kind of joke. No one was there.

Every other room on the floor was just as empty. She called out for everyone, anyone, even up the stairs to the third-floor servants' quarters. She received no reply.

Where could they have gone? Sophie could not fathom any reason that everyone would leave the house in the middle of the night, let alone without her. It was as if they had vanished. She ran back to the safety of her room, slamming the door shut and leaning against it. The cold air stabbed her lungs like knives. Never in her life had she ever been utterly alone. The prospect she had always longed for now filled her with terror.

Putting her hand to her chest as she tried to catch her breath, she touched something small and cold. A pendant, unfamiliar to her fingers. Sophie followed the chain around and undid the clasp. A round, gold locket on a fine chain slid off into her hand. The face was engraved with loops and swirls, an elegant letter S in the center. Where had it come from? She slipped a fingernail into the locket's seam and tried to open it, but it was as if the locket were glued shut.

Clasping it back around her neck with an irritated sigh, she stared out into pitch dark outside the window. It must be night, but what the hour? The dark didn't frighten her as much as the uncertainty of what had happened to her family. She would go and find help.

Having something to do besides panic like a ninny made her fear ebb a little more.

The Rittenhouse's lived close. She would go there.

It was incredibly inappropriate to call at a gentleman's house unchaperoned at any time of day, never mind whatever ungodly hour it must be. Not that she cared about what was appropriate. Which was something that had been a constant source of contention between her and her caregivers—first her governess, and then the headmistress of her boarding school. But if she was going to Henry's, she could not go in her nightclothes. That was just impractical. She grabbed a simple skirt and blouse from her closet, and a pair of stockings from the drawer and pulled them all on as quick as she could. The clothing felt different without a corset, but that would take too long to put on by herself. Unencumbered was fabulously comfortable.

Was this how men felt every day?

With her boots buttoned, she prepared to leave her room again. She had made enough noise on her first trek downstairs that any intruder would have heard. Just in case, she needed to protect herself. There wasn't much in her room she could use. The pitcher by the dry sink was heavy but unwieldy. A hat pin was long and sharp but wouldn't do much damage should she need to incapacitate someone. Sophie lifted the fireplace poker, its cast iron weight hefty in her hand. Heavy, but easy to maneuver. *This will do.* With the poker in front of her, she crept back downstairs.

Her long wool coat hung on the brass rack beside the front door. Like a church mouse, she slipped it on. According to her mother's prized grandfather clock it was midnight. The clock had been damaged around the time she was born, or so she had been told. But Mr. Rittenhouse was the best watchmaker in the city, and he had repaired it to like new. It told time as well as Big Ben.

Midnight? Not so late after all. During the Season, midnight was when the best parties turned interesting, if she were to believe the stories of older girls. Sophie faced the front door, realizing at that moment that she had no idea if it would open.

She reached for the knob. Sophie hissed and snatched her hand back. The metal was cold as ice.

"How odd." Not the oddest thing she had encountered in the last half-hour, but it was strange. She patted the pockets of her coat, found her gloves, and put them on before attempting the knob again.

It turned. With a relieved sigh, she pulled it open and ran onto the veranda.

And let out a bone-shaking scream.

A forest of thick, black-thorned plants grew across the front of the house. The stalks grew taller than Sophie, winding past the edge of the veranda's roof. Some of the plants were thicker than a man. The thorns were easily a half a foot long, tapering to a wicked point. She ran from one end of the veranda to the other, but the deadly-looking plants twisted around each other like snakes, forming a chrysalis of vegetation woven so tightly Sophie could not see anything between them.

Dropping the poker, she walked backward into the house, her eyes never leaving the vines. The heel of her boot caught the threshold, and she tripped and fell inside. She didn't bother to get up. Reaching out, she shut the door.

Henry stood outside Alexei Faber's kitchen door. Two hours ago, the police had taken the machine containing Sophie back to the Weber's, which had required a considerable bit of manpower and the unfortunate use of a funeral carriage. Detective Thornton had ordered the house sealed to anyone but police and stated that he would be back to collect the evidence in the lab once daylight had come. Henry's parents, the Weber's best friends, had been waiting when they returned. Henry had retold his story, while his mother consoled the heartbroken

Marta. It was well past midnight when he slipped away, under the pretense of going home to sleep. Instead, he returned to Coulter Street.

Thornton had left two men to guard the house, but they maintained their position at the front door, only circling around once every fifteen minutes. Henry waited in the shadows for them to make their rounds. As soon as they were out of sight, he sneaked to the kitchen door.

It was locked, of course. But Henry had come prepared.

He slipped a small case from his coat and opened it. Jeweler's tools, appropriated from his father's workshop when he was twelve and carried with him ever since. He selected the tools he needed and slid them into the keyhole. With the careful amount of pressure applied, the door was open. There was a moment he considered that he was breaking the law, but it was at the very bottom of his list of concerns.

Henry pushed open the kitchen door and winced at the creak of the neglected hinges. With steps feather-light, he stepped inside and shut the door. Despite his best efforts, the dusty, bare wooden floor protested his intrusion with squeaks that made Henry skittish. Sneaking about wasn't his usual *modus operandi*, but extreme situations sometimes called for appropriate measures. Sophie was the risk taker—sneaking about in boy's clothing, climbing too high in trees, riding horses people said were too wild while her parents called after her, never far away. Leading young men on chases through the snow. *And look where all of that got her*. His heart squeezed painfully at the thought of her lying encased in cold glass, like a specimen in a jar.

Using his hands out in front of him to avoid any surprises and noisy collisions, it seemed to take hours to get from the kitchen to the parlor. Even longer to cross the parlor to the secret workshop's door. Thornton had left it wide open. Henry turned the light switch and scooted inside, pulling the door closed.

In the tomb-like quiet, the room looked even more ominous than it had when he first set foot in it. Faber's tools glowed dully in the light, once-innocent looking instruments taking on a more sinister cast. The entire room was draped in gloom, despite the illumination. What had been going through Sophie's mind when she was here, alone and afraid? He blocked out the thought. He needed to do what he came to do and get out before he was discovered.

What sounded like shuffling footsteps outside the room made him jump with alarm. He listened, hoping the policemen hadn't decided to check inside the house. He had closed the kitchen door. Hadn't he? He ticked off ten seconds in his mind. Nothing. His breath escaped in a *whoosh* and he resumed his inspection.

What was he doing here, sneaking about like a thief? He needed to find something that could help Sophie, before the good detective carted it all away. The tools told him nothing, likewise the odds and ends of machinery on the workbench. Henry scooped up a gear and rolled the teeth across the pads of his fingers. He spotted what he had come for — the stack of blueprints. Thank God the detective had not yet taken them. Slipping the gear into his pocket, he scanned each drawing, flipping to the next, searching for the one he needed.

The plans for the machine that kept Sophie prisoner.

Edmund Weber had never revealed why Faber had written that he would recognize the machine. But when Henry had looked into Herr Weber's eyes he knew it was the truth. The machine seemed to require a key to open it before the timer ran out, but Henry obviously didn't have it. He might be able to pick the lock, except there could be a mechanism that would kill Sophie if he did. If Henry had the blueprint, he could probably figure out how to deactivate the contraption. The police would look for Faber, of course. Thornton had declared a man-hunt would begin immediately. But Henry wouldn't put his faith solely in the police; he would do anything he could to save Sophie himself.

Faber had a great collection of designs, most of which were ridiculous. One was for some kind of automated carriage that didn't use horses to move, another for a clockwork man. Henry snorted in derision. While Faber was brilliant, he was obviously also mentally unstable. As if a man made of brass with clockwork innards could actually do the work of a man made of flesh.

None of the drawings looked like the machine that held Sophie prisoner.

"Damn, it's not here!" Henry, frustrated, threw down the pages so forcefully they slid from the top of the bench and onto the floor. One landed on his shoe, and he bent to pick it up. The design was of an upright rectangular box, about the size of a wardrobe, but with all manner of machinery attached. He had passed it over before, but now that he had a second look, the blueprint's title caught his eye. He had to read it three times before he was sure it said what he thought.

"Oh, he couldn't possibly believe..." All of the other designs at least made some kind of sense, useful things that Faber had merely modified. But this? This was absolutely impossible.

The man put Sophie in a chamber where he believes she will sleep, unchanged, for one hundred years. Clearly this man's definition of impossible and mine are vastly different.

As ridiculous as the idea of the machine was, Henry could not seem to put the page down. He was enthralled by the way the machinery fit together, captivated by the explanations for how things worked that Faber had written in painstakingly small, neat hand. Which is why it was so shocking when he felt something cold and, if he had to guess, shaped exactly like the barrel of a pistol, pressed against the side of his head.

"Hello, chum. I think you need to give that to me."

Henry sucked in his breath, hoping the prowler would not mistake it for resistance. "I'm sorry, I don't think this will be worth anything to you. If you're looking for valuables, they're more likely to be upstairs."

"I'm not after valuables. Just what you've got there."

Henry let his hand come down slowly, the diagram still in his fingers. He couldn't turn his head to see his assailant, but there was a polished piece of metal above the workbench, in which he saw his own surprised reflection. The pistol appeared beside him, of course. Though it didn't look like any weapon he had ever seen. The barrel was a strange tubular shape, made of brass, and there seemed to be a dial of some kind on the side.

It also floated in mid-air.

No fingers gripped the pistol's handle, nor was there anyone in evidence behind him to hold it in position. It wasn't *exactly* floating. It was pressed into his head with a great deal of force, held steady by something unseen. Something with a low, gruff voice.

"Are you listening? I said give it to me."

Henry was shocked into a response. "What could you possibly want with this? It's not worth anything." How odd it was that anyone would want to steal a diagram of such a flight-of-fancy contraption.

"Never mind why I want it. It's not your business. Just give it here. Don't make me hurt you."

Henry held out his hand, the paper limp in his fingertips. As he watched in the makeshift mirror, the paper slipped from his grasp and flew away, seemingly under its own volition.

"Thank you. You've done your country a great service." The gun pulled away from his scalp. "Time to go, chum."

He was just going to let Henry go? The man was not much of a criminal. On the other hand, it was not as if Henry could go blathering to the police. He wasn't supposed to be here either. Nor could he identify his attacker, and he could only imagine what would happen if he said he had been threatened by an invisible man wielding a strange-looking weapon. On the whole, Henry figured he should capitalize on his good fortune before the man decided to rethink his position. He backed toward the door, grateful to be in one piece. When he reached the parlor, he turned and ran through the house and out into the snow without looking back.

Sophie sat in the foyer, her back to the front door. Time had come to a halt, crushing her, pulling everything into one point inside her chest. She was not typically a girl who cried. Not since she was six years old and her favorite china doll had slipped from her hands and shattered into a million pieces. But tears spilled down her cheeks now, splashing onto the front of her coat and turning to bits of ice in the frigid air.

First there was the lovely dream about Henry, which turned into the horrible nightmare about the man who had kidnapped her and put her in the glass coffin. Then she had woken up to find that everyone in the house seemed to have been spirited away. Which seemed impossible, considering how carefully she had been watched her entire life. So often she had wished for such solitude, a day when she could walk into her own yard, or down the street to the sweets shop or the tearoom without the watchful gaze of her governess, teachers, or parents. And now she had exactly what she wished for, and all she wanted was to hear her mother's voice.

And yet, the thing that had reduced her to tears was the bizarre wall of thorns. Their size was disturbing enough, but the thought of pricking her skin on one of the foot-long spikes nauseated her. How had they grown so quickly and so completely around the house?

Suddenly, the grandfather clock sang its Westminster chime. Sophie didn't look up, only listened to the familiar, comforting sound, her breath slowing and her heart calming. When it finished, it rang the hour. Sophie expected a single chime since it had been midnight when she had last looked at it. But the bell continued, Sophie's confusion mounting with every one.

Twelve. Twelve?

Sophie must have miscounted. A knot of lead and acid formed in her stomach as she stood to look at the timepiece's face. Both hands were still on the twelve. What had happened to the time?

"Don't be such a goose, Sophie Weber. There is obviously something wrong with the clock." She turned away and startled at her reflection in the large mirror that hung in the hall. The streaked cheeks and wild eyes that gazed back at her inspired terror. With a shudder, she gazed back at the clock. Maybe it was twelve and she had only misread the time the first time. That must be it. The thick wall of thorns made it impossible to see if it was midnight or noon. She should find out just how far the ridiculous plants had gotten in taking over her home. Maybe there was still a chance to escape.

All of the doors downstairs were locked, so up the stairs she went. In her own room, the windows showed the inky black of night. Nervous, she pulled one of them open and let out a moan of disappointment. The thick, black, thick plants covered the window. The vile, thirsty thorns reached toward her fragile skin, looking for a place to draw blood. She slammed the window closed and jumped back. What kind of devil's root grew so thick and tall? It seemed to reach for her as if it was grasping for dinner.

Sophie made her way downstairs. Something bothered her, besides the shut doors and the missing people. It nagged at the edge of her mind, but she couldn't quite put her finger on it. The hall looked the same. The windows on either side of the door were frosted over, which was unsurprising. What was it she had expected to see?

What month was it? January? No, December. What day? The last she remembered, it had been Christmas Eve afternoon. She had wanted to go riding. She must have fallen asleep and dreamed she snuck out in her boy's clothing, and all the rest, before she woke up in her own bed to an empty house.

Decorations! That was it. Not a garland or red bow in sight. The doors to the parlor were still locked, but she would guess that the Christmas tree, topped by its brass angel with clockwork wings, was gone as well. The angel had sat atop their family tree for as long as she could remember. It had been a gift from Henry's family, made by Herr Rittenhouse himself. It was a working clockwork, with a mechanism that, when wound, made the wings flutter. She eyed the front door, but knew it was pointless. Her gaze moved again to the grandfather clock. The hands had not shifted from the stroke of midnight. *How could that be?* Sophie had been upstairs for at least ten minutes. She leaned in closer. The clock itself was silent, the pendulum still. Sophie opened the door in front and touched the brass pendulum with one shaking finger. It, like the doorknob, felt cold as ice, and even though it normally took only the slightest bit of pressure to set it swinging, it would not budge. Time, it seemed, had frozen.

Sophie snatched her hand back, her rapid breaths frosting in the air. How had the clock chimed? Where was the ticking sound coming from? Though soft, it permeated the hall. *Tick, tock.* There were no other clocks in the house that made such a sound.

Sophie forced her nerves to stillness, refusing to allow another inexplicable thing to upset her. There was something very wrong here, and since there was no one to help her, she must figure it out for herself. She scanned the foyer, searching for some kind of clue.

Her examination concluded at a small table. It looked as it always did, with the calling card receptacle against the wall, the rest of the surface waiting for any letters or parcels that were delivered to the house. In the center sat a long brass key, which she was certain she had never seen before. It sat innocently on the table, and yet Sophie got the distinct feeling that it was anything but innocent. She picked it up, pinching it between her fingers.

"Curiouser and curiouser." She scrutinized it closely, as if her steady stare could force it to reveal its secret—for she was very certain the key had a secret to tell. But the key remained a key and said nothing. She wrapped her fingers around it, the metal warming in her hand.

And that was when a light appeared beneath the parlor door.

CHAPTER IV

ENRY SKIDDED TO A STOP AT THE END OF THE STREET. THE SMOOTH soles of his shoes slid on the snow, and he grabbed a lamp post to keep from landing on his backside. He righted himself with the heat of embarrassment flooding his face and the cold air biting into his skin. He had run away, but what could he have done differently? Someone had threatened him with some type of weapon, and he would be no good to Sophie if he were dead. Away from danger, he felt pathetic. He had thought himself so brave and clever, sneaking into the house and avoiding the police, and yet at the first sign of trouble he had turned into pudding.

The man had appeared to be invisible, which had been as shocking as the surprise of his attack and the strangeness of his weapon. The whole affair struck Henry as odd actually. People could not become invisible. It had to have been some kind of illusion. And he had only glimpsed the reflection of the man's weapon. Perhaps his eyes and mind had played a trick on him. Which did nothing to make him feel better.

Henry's heartbeat slowed, and the logicality for which Sophie always teased him took over. The burglar, regardless of his skill at prestidigitation, had wanted Faber's diagrams. Henry had thought it ridiculous, as the machines were, at best, flights of fancy. *Especially the last one – the most ludicrous of all! And yet, that was the one the burglar had seemed most interested in.*

A strange and hopeful idea stole into Henry's thoughts. Faber seemed to have perfected the deep-sleeping machine, so maybe some of those other diagrams weren't quite as impossible as they seemed. If the burglar saw value in the designs, perhaps he knew how they worked. If he were a reasonable sort, perhaps Henry could convince him to assist him with the sleeping-machine.

And had the man had said something about Henry being of service to his country? There was *definitely* something besides ordinary burgling going on.

Henry was only slightly surprised to find that by the time his brain was finished following that train of thought, his feet had carried him back down the sidewalk to the front of Faber's house. The policemen were nowhere to be seen. Had they found the burglar? Since it was unguarded, Henry tried the front door, finding it unlocked. The door to the secret room hung slightly ajar and light spilled through the crack. Henry tiptoed to it and peeked inside.

Three people were in the workshop. A tall, muscular man with dark skin and a bowler hat inspected the workbench, rifling through the tools as if searching for something. A second man, shorter with curly, light-brown hair and a scowl, leaned over the table, his gaze pinned to the pile of blueprints that had so recently been in Henry's hands. The third burglar stood in the far corner, hidden by shadow, and Henry could not make out a face or decipher the person's activity.

Henry slid from the door and pressed his back to the wall beside it. He hadn't counted on the man having accomplices. One he might be able to overpower, or at least outrun should his request for assistance go unappreciated. Three presented a problem, especially taking into account that if one was armed, it was a fair bet that the others were as well. He needed to think.

Something small and dark scurried out of the door. Henry froze. At first, he thought it was an enormous rat. It stopped in the shaft of light from the workshop and sat upright. Jewel-bright eyes pinned him with an intelligent gaze. The thing bared a set of brilliant white teeth, like razor-sharp bits of ice in the blackness of its face. Before Henry's muscles could recall their proper function, the creature let out a screech similar to what Henry imagined a demon of hell sounded like.

The animal leapt at him, claw-like hands grabbing the lapels of his coat. Henry held up his arms in defense. The beast snatched Henry's scarf and scurried back into the workshop.

"Tesla, what have you got there?"

A soft voice, tinged with a British accent, floated out of the room. Henry debated between remaining where he was and once again running for his life. Before he could choose, a woman appeared in the doorway. An amused smile pulled at her lips.

"Hello, Henry. My, my. You are a persistent one, aren't you. Gabriel, Alphonse? We have company."

The light seeping beneath the parlor door was not the muted, flickering light of gas lamps or a fire in the fireplace grate. It was brighter, as if the sun has risen behind the double doors of this one room. The key in Sophie's hand grew warmer. She gripped it tightly and understood it would open this door and only this door. She pressed her free hand against the wood and put an ear to the surface. Only silence.

"Oh, just get on with it, you silly girl." Talking to herself was becoming a habit. She thrust the key into the lock and turned it. With a deep breath, she pushed the doors open.

Light flooded the hallway, forcing Sophie to hide her watering eyes behind her arm. After a few moments, she peeked. The parlor was gone. Instead, Market Square, the hub of activity in Germantown, spread out before her. People crowded into the square. Neighbors and friends.

"Oh, thank goodness!"

Her joy was short-lived. Not a single soul turned to look at her or showed the least bit of surprise that a parlor door had suddenly appeared in the middle of the market. In fact, nothing moved. It was as if the entire scene were a painting.

A slight breeze, warm and full of the promise of spring flowers, blew through the doorway, inviting her in. She looked back at the hallway, still covered in winter midnight, and back again.

Whatever kind of magic this was (and she had no doubt it was magic; after all, how else could the entire square fit into the parlor?) it had to be better than standing in the freezing cold. She would leave the door open, just in case she needed to step back into the hallway.

The moment her boot touched the grass, the square came to life. A cacophony of familiar sounds washed over her. People bustled about their business, but not a single soul turned to greet her. *Odd.* Perhaps they hadn't been able to see her when she had been on the other side of the door, but now she was right before them.

Mr. Adler, her neighbor and the owner of the general store, stood in front of his shop. He helped a customer load her packages into a carriage. Sophie walked toward him a greeting on her lips, but something drew her up short. She had seen Mr. Adler a day or two ago, when she had helped her mother with the shopping for the annual Christmas Eve party. The man before her had less gray in his hair, the lines on his face not as deep.

She took a step, meaning to approach him and solve the mystery, when she was cut off by a blue streak that turned into a golden-haired child in a blue dress.

"Sophie! Sophie Weber, come back here this minute!"

Sophie searched for the caller, tears of joy flooding her eyes. Her mother was easy to spot, just a few yards down the street. Sophie lifted her skirts and ran toward her, unheeding of how unladylike she looked.

"Mother! I'm so glad to finally have found..."

Sophie's words died in her throat. Her mother had not so much as turned her head at the sound of her daughter's voice. Sophie stood directly ahead of her, but she might as well have been made of glass.

"Sophia Alexandra Weber! I am speaking to you!"

Sophie slowly waved her hand before her mother's face, but the woman's gaze remained fixed at a point over her shoulder. She turned to follow her mother's irate stare and caught a flash of robin's egg blue disappearing into the crowd. Sophie immediately remembered the dress.

It was *her* dress. It had been her favorite when she was eight, the robin's egg blue with the ruffled skirt and the cream satin sash that came from France. Sophie studied her mother more closely. Like Mr. Adler, the lines around her eyes were not as deep as she remembered. And her clothing was nearly ten years out of date, the train of her walking dress sliding behind her as she rushed off after her mischievous daughter. *After me.*

Was this a memory? Had this day somehow been pulled from her mind and plunked down in the parlor? *This is definitely magic.* She turned around, and there was the door, standing open to the darkness of the hall. It seemed to be just as invisible as she was to those around her. Should she go back to where it was safe? Well, safe probably wasn't the best choice of words. It was cold and empty, with locked doors, surrounded by a wall of giant, bloodthirsty thorns.

If this was a memory, it felt incredibly real. She lifted her skirts again and followed her mother, but walking instead of running like a decapitated chicken.

Her mother called after her wayward daughter again, fear and panic apparent in her features and her voice. She always sounded like that whenever Sophie left her sight. Why was she always so worried? This was home, and the little girl was known to everyone in town. No one was there that would harm her.

Where am I? I mean, where did I go on this day? She had no idea of the date. It could be any Saturday. She scanned the crowd and spotted her younger self.

Little Sophie ran between people, laughing with delight as her frantic mother called after her. Sophie-the-elder dodged the crowd as she tried to keep the child in sight. She mused on how little had changed. Even in the present, Market Square was just an empty park during the week, perfect for taking a stroll or sitting on a bench to enjoy the fresh air. But on any given Saturday morning from early April until late October it was a carnival of sights, sounds, and the most delicious smells. When she had been sent to boarding school, it was the memory that made her the most homesick.

Little Sophie passed a row of cloth merchants and headed for the Market Building, a huge barn at the end of the square. The bleating of sheep poured from it, clearly heard above the murmurs of the people.

It must be April. If the weather and the scent of flowers hadn't told her, the noise of the sheep made it obvious. The farmers came to town to sell their wool to the textile mills that dominated the Kensington part of the city. The mill buyers came to Market Square and chose their wool to be sheared and dyed before it went back to the mill for spinning and weaving.

The child Sophie's golden curls bounced in the sunlight as she raced along. She was happy to be free of her mother's clutches for a few stolen minutes. Sophie followed her former self past the barn, the scent of hay and lanolin filling her nose. Little Sophie ran into the shade of a blossoming apple tree and leaned against the trunk, her cheeks pink with running, her smile wide as she enjoyed freedom and the warm, apple blossom-scented breeze. Big Sophie smiled at her joy as she stepped into the shade.

"Hello there."

Both versions of Sophie gasped in surprise. A man hid in the shadows behind the tree, barely visible near the slender trunk. The sunlight that peeked through the tree's canopy dappled his dark hair with spots of gold as he stepped toward the child. The older Sophie stepped back, dumbstruck, her heart thundering and her palms turning dry.

As the man came toward her younger self, Sophie grew dizzy. The colors of the apple blossoms brightened, the bleating of the sheep grew loud. She reached for the shoulder of her child-self, but her hand went through as if the little girl were made of air. She tried again, desperate to pull the little girl tight, to shout at her to run from the man who approached with such easy grace and a welcoming smile. His name still escaped her, but there was no doubt.

This was the man from her nightmare. She knew she had met him, but that had been years after this day, and years before her current age. She had no memory of meeting him on a Market Day.

Little Sophie eyed him curiously. Older Sophie moved behind her protectively, even though she knew it would do no good.

"I don't know you," Little Sophie said. "Mother said I shouldn't talk to strangers."

The man looked abashed. "I didn't mean to frighten you."

Little Sophie pulled her shoulders back and jutted out her chin, a look of defiance her older self knew well. "You didn't. I was only surprised because I didn't expect anyone to be there."

The man smiled at her in amusement. "Where is your mother? Or your nurse?"

Little Sophie put a hand on her hip. "My *governess* has the morning off. And my mother..." She scrunched up her face and older Sophie knew that the little girl had considered telling the man a lie, but then decided it didn't matter what he thought of her.

"...is off in the Market."

The older Sophie looked over her shoulder but did not see her mother. Where could she have gotten to? After years of wishing to be left alone, she wanted nothing more than for her mother to materialize beside them. *She must be losing her mind at this moment.*

Sophie took a breath. If this was a memory, then nothing bad could have happened, or she would have remembered immediately. But she was no longer sure it was a memory. Her nightmare came back to her, and her chest tightened in fear.

The man narrowed his eyes in obvious mock suspicion. "You don't know?"

Little Sophie shrugged. "I ran away from her."

"Why would you do that? Isn't she a kind woman?" The man took a step closer and leaned against the tree's trunk, his arms crossed over his chest. Older Sophie held her breath and took a half a step toward them. What would she do? What *could* she do?

Little Sophie blushed and looked at her dust-covered shoes.

"She is kind, sir. Except she never lets me have all the sweets I want and makes me wash behind my ears. Mother doesn't like it when she can't see me. But I'm not a baby. I want to run and play."

The man knit his brows and nodded sympathetically. "I see. Do you think she is worried about you at this very moment?"

Little Sophie glanced over her shoulder, but her mother was nowhere to be seen. "I won't stay away long. I just want to have a bit of fun."

The man smiled at the child, and older Sophie felt her trepidation slip away. "Of course. Children are meant to have fun."

Little Sophie put her hands behind her back and studied the man. "Do you have any children?" She spoke to him as if she had known him all her life.

I was positively precocious! Sophie had never been shy, despite her parents' constant reminders not to talk to strangers. But all the parents said the same thing to their children, especially after what had happened to little Charley Ross. Charley had been kidnapped when Sophie was six years old. The boy and his friend had been snatched from his own front yard and never found. The incident had been in all the papers and whispered about by all the adults in all the parlors of Germantown.

Strange, the things we remember. Ten years had faded it from the neighborhood's memory, but this conversation brought it back at once. Again, Sophie took a half a step forward, though she knew it was pointless.

"I had a daughter, once." The man's green eyes turned stormy. He reached into his jacket and pulled something from his waistcoat pocket. A watch swung from the end of a gold chain. He flipped the cover back and showed it to Sophie. On one side was the watch face, with gold filigree hands telling the time. Inside the watch's cover was a photograph of a little girl with dark hair in ringlets and a large bow on her head.

"She's very pretty." Little Sophie frowned. "What do you mean, you had her once? Where is she now?"

The man was quiet as he closed the watch and put it back into his pocket. "She is gone. She died eight years ago."

No wonder he looked so sad. Little Sophie looked as sad as older Sophie felt. "I'm sorry."

The smallest smile ghosted across the man's face. "Thank you, my dear, but please don't be sorry. It's..." he paused, and Sophie got the impression there was something important he wanted to say. "It was long ago."

The silence that followed was uncomfortable for everyone.

Little Sophie kicked at a pebble. "I should be getting back to my mother now. It was nice to meet you, Mr... oh! I didn't even ask your name."

Older Sophie held her breath and leaned forward to listen.

But he shook his head. "It doesn't matter. It was very nice to meet you as well." The man bowed to the child, and she dropped a graceful curtsy before turning and running off into the sunshine. Sophie, relieved, stayed a second longer to study the man's face, and then followed.

"There you are!"

She jumped, startled. Could someone actually see her? The voice had sounded familiar, but like everything else here, it was from the past.

"Hello, Henry," little Sophie called in greeting.

Older Sophie's breath came out in a *whoosh*. A boy ran toward her younger counterpart, and she laughed out loud when she realized who it was.

Eleven-year-old Henry Rittenhouse stopped beside young Sophie, his face red from running, his brown hair flopping into his eyes, as always.

"What are you doing here?" He sounded annoyed, which made older Sophie smile. He had always sounded annoyed when they were younger.

"I was talking to that man." Little Sophie turned and pointed to the apple tree, but there was no one there. "Oh. He's gone."

Sophie craned her neck, looking for the man. How she wished he had given his name! But he was nowhere in sight, swallowed by the burgeoning crowd in the square.

Henry didn't seem care. "I've been looking all over for you. Your mother has everyone searching, you know. She's been frantic."

Little Sophie lifted her chin, squinting in the sunlight. "And how is that different from any other day?"

Sophie laughed again, delighted. She had been so defiant, so cheeky. And he had been so practical, even at eleven years old.

"Come on, Sophie." Henry took little Sophie's hand and dragged her away. Sophie followed behind, listening to their discussion.

"I thought you were going to your father's shop today." Little Sophie deliberately walked slowly, forcing Henry to pull her along behind him. "You *always* go to the shop on Saturday."

"I was going to, but he's busy, and the shop's closed."

Little Sophie pulled up short. "What do you mean, closed? He never closes the shop, especially not on a Saturday."

Sophie furrowed her brow, just as surprised. Rittenhouse's Watch and Clock shop was one of the best in Philadelphia. People flocked to Chestnut Street to purchase his beautiful pocket watches and carriage clocks, and when they needed a repair, they trusted no other. She had only been there a handful of times, but when they were children, Henry had spent nearly every Saturday at the shop. He had always told her, with no small amount of pride, that he was a great help to his father. But Sophie had once overheard Fraulein Rittenhouse telling her mother that he spent at least half the day next door at Grimm's Book Shop, browsing and, as always, reading.

Little Henry let out a very-put-out sort of huff. "Normally he wouldn't, of course. But there's only a few weeks until the Exposition opens, and he's a member of the Franklin Institute's board, so he has to help oversee the final arrangements. He's spent every waking moment it seems in Fairmount Park, making sure everything goes as it should."

Henry leaned toward the little girl, and older Sophie also leaned in, so she could hear his conspiratorial whisper.

"Though, if you ask me, he just wants to get an early peek at all of the machines. He told me there are some of the most amazing things on display, things beyond your imagination."

Little Sophie *harrumph*ed and pulled her arm out of Henry's grip. "Who wants to see dirty old machines. I doubt I'd be surprised anyway. Unlike you, I can imagine quite a lot."

Henry's mouth fell open. "That's not true. I have plenty of imagination. I just don't believe in nonsense. I can imagine going across the sea to Europe, but I know I can't fly there, like a bird. I'll have to take a boat."

"And you never, ever like to have fun."

"What do you mean? I do so like to have fun."

"Not the kind of fun I mean. You only do what you're told, what you're *allowed* to do. You'll want to visit Europe and see a bunch of boring buildings and museums. I want to have an *adventure*."

The longing in her younger self's voice made Sophie wonder. Had she always felt the need to see what else was out there in the world? When her father sent her away, she had been devastated to be pulled from her family, but also excited to be away at last. But too soon, the polish had worn off the new country. There were more rules to follow, and different eyes to watch her. A new prison.

Henry took Sophie's elbow and pulled her along again. "Adventures are nothing but trouble. Look at you, running off, making your mother worry and sending everyone to look for you."

Little Sophie rolled her eyes. "I know I shouldn't have. But what could possibly happen to me here, Henry—"

"Watch out!" Henry yanked Little Sophie back, just as a man ran right across the place where she had been standing. A moment later, two other men also raced through, chasing the first man.

Sophie knew two of the three men. One was the man her younger self had been talking to beneath the apple tree mere moments ago. Except she could have sworn he had been wearing a brown coat, and now he was wearing a gray one. The second was a curly-haired young man she had never seen. The last was Henry. Not the child Henry, who still stood beside her, but the nearly-twenty-year-old she had dreamed of leading on a chase through the snow in exchange for a kiss. He might even have been wearing the same clothes as in her dream.

Impossible. How could he have been here, on this day? This was definitely not a mere memory, but some stranger magic. Had the men come through the same door she had used? If that was so why had the children moved out of the way? They had seen the men, but hadn't spotted her. It made no sense.

She should return to the house, then, to see if they had come through that way. Maybe Henry would be there and could explain everything.

The two children resumed their walk, Henry's hand still tethered to Sophie's arm. Little Sophie continued her tirade.

"She never lets me do anything. She keeps me prisoner."

Sophie cringed at the whine in the child's voice.

"Oh, stop being so dramatic." Henry dragged the little girl around a group of people gathered outside a potter's booth and back toward the Market's gate. And there, like a lighthouse beacon on a foggy night, stood the door. It remained open, the foyer's darkness a hole in the brightness of the day. Waiting for her.

Little Sophie shook her head and her curls bounced. "I'm not being dramatic. I am always either with my governess or Mother. She never leaves me alone, not for a minute. It was all I could do to get her to come to the market today, and we live just down the street. What kind of adventure could I possibly have three blocks from home?"

Henry shook his head. "I'll say it again—adventures are nothing but trouble."

Sophie paused at the door, taking one last look at her younger self. She never had listened, not to him, nor her mother, nor her father, nor her governess. Even if it were possible for her to speak to her younger self, she probably wouldn't have listened. If there was one thing Sophie knew, it was that she often preferred to do things the hard way.

Hoping to find some answers, she stepped through the parlor door.

CHAPTER V

ENRY SAT ON A CHAIR IN THE MIDDLE OF THE SECRET WORKSHOP with his hands in his lap. He tried to appear as if being held captive was a daily occurrence. Appearances, as it is often said, can be deceiving. While his posture was that of a man without care, the thumb of his right hand rubbed continual circles on the case of his pocket watch. The three people who had raided Faber's workshop stood before him, each with a different expression on their face.

They were much younger than they first appeared to Henry. The dark-skinned boy crossed his arms over his chest and sported a pensive look. He appeared no more than twenty. Henry got the impression he was the leader. The one with the curly hair, who might have been sixteen or so, must be the master of illusion Henry had seen — or rather, not seen — earlier. He had come to this conclusion when the boy had, once again, pointed the odd weapon at him and forced him into the chair. As strange as it looked, he had no doubt it was still deadly, and was grateful the leader had ordered the boy to stop threatening Henry with it. And so instead he tried to injure Henry with a razor-sharp scowl.

The third member of the party shocked and puzzled Henry. The girl who had discovered him stood beside the dark-skinned boy, the same amused look on her face as when Henry had first seen her. Her clothing was nigh on scandalous. What looked like a dark skirt covered her legs, but it was split up the middle, like voluminous trousers. If that wasn't enough to cause an uproar, she wore a leather corset like armor over a blood-red blouse. Her skin was smooth, except for a long, angry-looking scar that ran down the left side of her face. Despite that, or perhaps because of it, Henry thought she was rather pretty. Her dark hair was pulled to the nape of her neck into a sleek, smooth bun. If Henry had to guess her age it would be around seventeen. A gray silk top hat balanced on her head, tipped just so that her scar wasn't as noticeable. A pair of odd-looking brass goggles adorned the brim.

Henry couldn't imagine what father would allow his daughter to leave the house dressed so. Of course, she was here skulking in the secret workshop of a madman inventor, so perhaps the point was moot.

The supposed demon perched on her shoulder. Which turned out to be a small monkey. He was covered in black fur, except for a patch of white on its head. His tail draped around his mistress's neck, while one paw clutched her finger. He pinned Henry with an unnerving look.

"What do we do with him, Gabriel?" the curly-haired one asked his leader. "We can't send him home. He's seen us."

The tone of the man's voice made Henry uncomfortable. He reached up to loosen his collar but thought better of it when the pistol twitched in the man's hand.

"Easy, Alphonse." Gabriel pushed his bowler back onto his head and rubbed his hairless cheek. "I understand the predicament he's put us in, same as you."

Henry thought he cottoned on to the men's meaning. "Oh! You're afraid I'll tell the police? Well, then, gentlemen, and lady, please put your minds at ease. I won't say a word to Detective Thornton or the officers outside. I'll take it to my —" His face fell as he realized that his choice of words might not be prudent. "Well, let's just say no one will ever hear it from me."

Alphonse smiled, though the expression did nothing to ease Henry's mind. "Those two bumblers you call police officers? They won't be taking any statements from you."

Henry felt the blood run from his face. "Did you... kill them?"

Alphonse's expression shifted to indignant shock. "Oh, no, definitely not. They're just taking a nap. Point is, they can't help you."

"Alphonse, stop scaring the poor boy." The girl's accent was, as Henry had first thought, British. She stroked her pet's fur, never taking her eyes off Henry. "He's harmless."

"Harmless or not remains to be seen." Gabriel scrutinized Henry like a difficult puzzle. "He came back when he was told not to. And what, exactly, were you doing here in the first place? Who sent you?"

"No one!" It came out so quickly even Henry wasn't sure he believed his own words. "I mean... I was looking for the plans to a particular machine. This Faber person, whoever he is, has placed Miss Sophie Weber inside the contraption, and it's keeping her in some kind of deep sleep. His note said she won't wake for a hundred years." Even as the words left his mouth, Henry realized how insane they sounded.

His captors, however, did not laugh. They did not even blink in surprise.

Alphonse shot Gabriel a sideways glance. "We know."

Henry leapt from the chair, knocking it over backward. "What do you mean, you *know*?"

Gabriel held up his hands in a placating gesture. "Calm down. What Alphonse means is that we know about the machine. Our intelligence says Faber had been developing it for nearly two decades. We didn't actually know about Miss Weber. Or you, for that matter. What is your name again?"

Henry stood there with his mouth open, the air completely taken out of his sails. "Henry Rittenhouse. I'm Sophie's..." What was he, exactly? He was not officially her suitor, not yet having secured her father's permission. He decided upon the most accurate description. "I'm her friend."

The girl tilted her head. She pursed her lips and narrowed her eyes, her gaze boring into Henry. There was a strange sensation in his mind, like the tickling of a feather. It made a shiver run up his spine.

"No, I don't think so. You love her," she said as if talking about the weather. "You came back here because you wanted to ask us for help."

Henry pulled his coat tighter around himself, feeling somehow violated. He cleared his throat. "Well, I... how did you know that?"

Gabriel smirked. "Irene here has a number of talents, as do we all. She's very good at reading... people."

Alphonse chuckled. "That's one way of putting it."

The mood in the room shifted. The choking weight of their gazes turned less heavy, and Henry took the opportunity to ask his own questions.

"All right. Now I've seen you, and I know your names." He paused, wondering how prudent it was to show his hand, but there was nothing for it but to press on. "And I *did* wonder if you could help me. I mean, you don't seem to be average burglars, so—"

"So what are we doing here, looting the place?" Irene finished his sentence for him.

Henry once again had the notion that his thoughts had been invaded. He nodded, emboldened by civilized conversation. "I'm sure there are more valuable things in this room, things the average petty thief could pawn. Copper, brass, the tools would fetch a good price. But you're very keen to have those diagrams. Why?"

Gabriel shifted his weight again. "This Detective Thornton you mentioned. I imagine he is looking for Alexei Faber, to solve the case of Miss Sophie Weber, correct?"

Henry nodded. "Faber and Soph—Miss Weber's father have some kind of history."

Gabriel raised an eyebrow. "Thornton will be collecting evidence from this room tomorrow, correct? Probably right after his Christmas breakfast and presents with his children."

"I suppose so." Henry had no idea if the detective had a family, but it was a good enough guess.

"And that's why we're here. We can't let him take certain items from this room."

"Like the blueprints?" Henry replied.

"They would be useless to him, but we needed to get them before they became locked up in a police station. Other people are after them, people with far less noble intentions than ours." Gabriel clasped his hands behind his back. "The good detective will make a valiant effort, I'm sure, but he won't find Faber."

"And you can?"

Gabriel smiled, baring a mouth full of straight, white teeth. A Cheshire cat's grin. "That's our job."

Henry furrowed his brow, confused. "How do you even know about Faber?"

Some kind of silent communication passed between Gabriel and his companions. He returned his attention to Henry, then reached inside his waistcoat. Henry flinched.

"Relax, Henry. No one's going to hurt you." The girl, Irene, spoke in a calm, even voice.

Gabriel pulled something from his pocket. He showed Henry what looked like a small leather billfold and flipped it open. There was no money inside. Instead, it held a large gold, star-shaped badge, reflecting the overhead light.

"The United States Government, Mr. Rittenhouse."

Henry peered closer at the badge. The words *United States Secret Service* looked back at him in raised lettering. He leaned back and shook his head. "You can't work for the Secret Service. The two of you look barely old enough to shave, and she's—" he pointed to Irene. Henry didn't want to insult her but couldn't find any words that wouldn't.

"British. And not a boy." Irene shrugged, which caused the monkey to bristle indignantly. "Brilliant observation on both counts. *My* employer is Scotland Yard." She indicated her pet. "And this is Tesla."

Henry barely had time to wonder why a member of Scotland Yard would be in Germantown, Philadelphia, before Gabriel brought the conversation back on point.

"You're right, of course. We're not the usual type of people who work for government agencies. We were hired because we have certain... attributes... that tend to be useful in this kind of situation."

Henry didn't want to know what those attributes were. "What 'situation'? What does the government want with Faber? He's a criminal, surely, but why the Secret Service? Has he been printing his own money?"

Alphonse responded. "It may have gone better for him if he had. Alexei Faber has been of special interest, for many reasons. We have been monitoring his correspondence and movements for a while now."

"You've been *spying* on him? An American citizen, being spied upon by his own government?" Henry could not help his indignation, despite the fact the man whom he was defending had imprisoned Sophie in a most egregious fashion.

Gabriel raised an eyebrow at Henry's outburst. "Mr. Rittenhouse, I'm not here to debate policy with you. Take it up with President Arthur, or President-elect Cleveland if you prefer. Write your congressman. I'm pretty sure none of them will have any idea what you're talking about. That's not the point. Despite our surveillance, we missed Faber. And now we need to chase after him. Which we are about to get on with." He reached back to the workbench and held out Henry's hat. "This is where we part ways, sir. I trust you can show yourself to the door."

Henry took the hat but wasn't about to leave. "You can't just throw me out! I still need your help. A-and if you don't help, I'll tell Detective Thornton everything."

Irene giggled. "Oh, I like this one, he's got a little pepper in his shorts."

Henry blushed at her forwardness, expressing ideas about his shorts.

Gabriel smirked. "Detective Thornton couldn't do anything about us even if he believed your crazy story. We answer to a much higher authority."

Henry ran his hands around the brim of his hat. "Fine, I won't tell. But if you understand the diagrams, could one of you at least come and look at the machine? There has to be a mechanism for opening it sooner than one hundred years."

Alphonse rolled his eyes. "Of course there is."

Henry's mouth fell open for the second time. "If you know, why didn't you say so in the first place?"

Alphonse shifted on his feet. "I didn't say I knew what it was, only that it exists. Or most likely, anyway. It's something any good inventor would include. But that's not our job. Our job is to find Faber and bring him back."

Gabriel tried to soften the blow. "I am sorry, Mr. Rittenhouse. But Alphonse is right. We just don't have time to spare. Besides, you said yourself the diagram for the device isn't here. Without it, I'm afraid we're no help to you. Unless you want Alphonse to go tinkering around in there and accidentally kill your Miss Weber, which I don't think you do."

Henry felt the blood drain from his face. "Of course not."

"It seems to me, then, that the only way to save Miss Weber is to let us do our job. We'll find Faber, and when we bring him back here, we'll... ask... him how to open the machine. Does that sound fair?"

Henry didn't appreciate Gabriel's flippant attitude or tone. This was Sophie's life they were talking about. He stood toe-to-toe with Gabriel.

"No, it's doesn't. How do I know you'll keep your word? You have no problem sneaking around, breaking into homes, or spying on people. I'm coming with you." The last bit had run out of his mouth before he had a chance to consider it, but he didn't dare take it back. This bunch may be odd, but if they led him to Faber, he'd follow them to the gates of hell. Gabriel shook his head. "Sorry, can't. You're a civilian, untrained. I'm not a nanny. You'll only get yourself into trouble and put us all in danger."

"I can watch out for myself, thank you. I'm willing to take the risk." Henry again was surprised at his words. What was wrong with him?

"But I'm not. Now, we have a lot of work to be getting on with, so if you'll excuse us..." Gabriel grabbed him by the shoulder, spun him around, and pushed him in the direction of the door. Henry stumbled, trying to think of another argument, but could not come up with anything convincing.

Alphonse and Gabriel had already forgotten about him it seemed, their heads together over one of Faber's blueprints. Only Irene continued to acknowledge his presence, watching him with that strange gaze. Her eyes were a lovely shade of blue gray. They widened and she sucked in a surprised breath. His face flushed, thinking she had known what he was thinking. Which was preposterous.

"Wait, Henry. Gabriel, he should stay with us."

Gabriel looked over his shoulder. "You mean he's still here?" He turned around fully and heaved a deep sigh. "Irene, I don't have time for this right now."

"We have trouble coming our way. There are three very large men outside the house who will do him harm if he goes out."

Alphonse dropped the blueprint and spun around, an unprintable word falling from his lips. "When did they get here?"

"Not long ago. They're here for the blueprints as well."

"Most wanted pieces of paper in the world tonight, I think," Henry said with a touch of misery.

Irene closed her eyes, one hand stroking Tesla's fur. "They're waiting for us to come out so they can ambush us. They found the officers you... relieved of their duties, Alphonse." A frown pulled down the corners of her mouth. "Unfortunately, they've disabled them permanently." She drew her hand across her throat in a slicing action.

"Damn!" Gabriel shook his head. "This was supposed to be a simple operation. Get in, get the diagrams, get out. Why must everything be so complicated?"

"Enough with the talking." Alphonse rummaged through the tools on Faber's workbench. "We need to get out of here." He pulled the strange weapon from his holster. "I'll just slip outside in my special way and take care of the problem."

Irene shook her head. "Wait, Alphonse. There's something... ooh, they're well-prepared for us, aren't they? Your particular brand of stealth won't work. They seem to be wearing some kind of special goggles. Feeling awfully smug about it, too."

Alphonse paled. "Where would they get something like that?" He looked at the blueprints, scattered on the floor. "Faber?"

"I can't see that, I'm afraid." Irene opened her eyes and rubbed her temples. "It was difficult enough to get that much. Almost like they knew I was in there, poking about, and were able to shut me out."

Henry, despite being completely lost about parts of the conversation, got the general idea. "What do we do? Charge out and plow through? It's three against three, even odds." He caught Irene's gaze. "Sorry, miss. Didn't mean to offend."

"No offense taken, Mr. Rittenhouse. I have been highly trained in hand-to-hand combat, so I hope *you* won't be offended when I say that it's still three against three." The monkey let out a shriek. "Oh, I'm sorry, Tesla, I forgot. It is four."

Heat rushed to Henry's cheeks. "I am a champion fencer, just so you know." It sounded weak, even to him.

"Unfortunately, I don't think these are the kind of fellows who fence," Irene continued. "Just before I was shut out, I saw their orders — retrieve the blueprints and don't leave any witnesses."

"Then we need to escape without them seeing us." Henry scanned the room. "Isn't there another way out of here?"

Alphonse snorted a laugh. "I don't think so, chum. And looks like fighting our way out is in the category of last resort." He picked up one of the blueprints in his free hand and studied it again. "I think we'll just have to move up the plan. Time to go."

A strange look came over his face, an expression of concentration so intense Henry was afraid the paper might catch fire. Gabriel leaned close, looking over his shoulder.

"Can you do it?" The words were so low Henry almost didn't hear them, but filled with such urgency they might as well have been shouted. Alphonse turned his head to meet Gabriel's gaze, his eyes so bright they could shoot sparks. He holstered his weapon, then scooped up tools from the workbench with one hand, and a random selection of gears and springs with the other.

"Of course I can. Give me eight minutes, and make sure those buffoons don't come in." He walked to the large, elaborately carved wardrobe in the corner and dumped all of the tools except a screwdriver onto the floor. Gabriel pulled the topmost blueprint from the pile and rolled the rest. He dug a thumbtack out of a box on the bench and used it to attach the diagram to the wardrobe's door. Alphonse did not look up at it as he began to work, fitting gears together and attaching them to the outside and top of the wardrobe.

"What are you doing?" Henry asked. "We're trapped in here and you want to waste time tinkering with Faber's flights of fancy?" He recognized the diagram Gabriel had tacked up, and if they hadn't been in mortal danger, he would have laughed. "To what possible purpose?"

Gabriel clapped Henry on the shoulder. "Our mission, Mr. Rittenhouse. We were going to do this back at headquarters. But circumstances being what they are, we're moving things up. It's not a perfect solution, and we may have to do a bit of... creative engineering. But, I have complete faith in Alphonse here. He's got a knack for this sort of tinkering."

Henry still didn't understand. "What are you going to do with that, that thing?"

"Catch Faber, of course. We already told you that was the mission." Gabriel pointed to the floor. For the first time Henry noticed four scratches in the wooden floor that formed the corners of a large rectangle. "He took the first train, so to speak. We're going to follow his tracks."

Henry stepped back, suddenly thinking he might take his chances with the three brutes outside. If they even existed. "You're all insane. You come here with some story about being from the government, and now you expect me to believe that Faber is... and that you're actually building..."

Gabriel held up his hand. "Believe what you want, Mr. Rittenhouse. We have to get to work. And if you want to keep breathing, I'd suggest you stay with us and out of the way."

Sophie stumbled out of the parlor, tripping over the threshold as the door slammed behind her. The cold hit her like a slap, shocking her into a gasping breath. She put her hands out to catch herself, smacking her palms into the wall, her legs colliding with the little table, which rocked dangerously on its spindly legs. Sophie managed to grab the top and right it before it fell over. She plopped down on the floor, her mind spinning. The ticking sound taunted her, pervasive even though the clock remained still.

What she had experienced had not been a dream. The warmth of the sun, the smells of Market Square, were all too real. Not to mention she was wide awake. It seemed like a perfect reproduction of her own memory, but it also... wasn't.

If it wasn't magic, she was hallucinating. Perhaps that was the answer. Someone had given her something that was making her see and hear things. Perhaps it was the same person or persons who had taken her parents and the household staff. She had heard stories of people who took opium or drank absinthe seeing fantastic visions. But she certainly hadn't done either.

Maybe the magic had allowed her to step *back in time* to that day on Market Square. Sophie put her hand to her mouth to stifle her laugh. *What a preposterous thought! If I had physically gone back in time, wouldn't everyone have seen me?*

The strange key fell from the parlor door lock and hit the floor with a *clunk*. She picked it up to find the shank once again icy to her touch. She gripped it tightly, certain that it wouldn't unlock the parlor door again. She was anxious to try the key in another lock.

But which door? She faced down the hall toward the kitchen, then turned toward the dining room and library doors. There was no bright light, nothing that pulled her toward any of them. She tried the dining room. Alas, they key did not turn. The library was no better, and the kitchen door stuck fast. What now? Just to be sure, she tried the door to the linen closet. It opened easily, but behind it she only found linens, neatly stacked.

Sophie's shoulders slumped. Shivering, she climbed the stairs to her bedroom, where she could think in comfort.

Though the maid usually made the fire, Sophie had watched her do it hundreds of times. Perhaps she hadn't done it before herself, but she certainly knew the steps. It took several false starts, not to mention twice pinching her fingers and acquiring three splinters, but in the end a fire crackled in the grate. At last, Sophie sat in the chair before the fireplace, holding out her hands to warm them. It was cozy, and com- fortable. She was tempted to just settle in and fall asleep, waiting for someone to come and rescue her. She had no guarantee that would happen, however. If she were to be rescued, she would have to do it herself.

The downstairs rooms were locked, the front door offered no escape, the back door was inaccessible. Of course, doors weren't the only ways to exit a house. She had become quite masterful at escape through unconventional means. But that required a change of clothing. She lifted the lid on the chest at the end of her bed. Beneath a crocheted blanket and a quilt her grandmother had made lay a neatly folded bundle of clothing. Sophie lifted it out and set it on the bed, then began to undress. This time, she grabbed her corset and slipped it on. She had begun to feel strange without it. She couldn't tie it as tightly as usual, which was a blessing, but it provided her with another layer for warmth. Her new locket lay against her chest. It was still a curiosity, but she had more pressing matters to take care of, so she tucked it under her chemise.

When she was finished, she admired herself in the long mirror. *All girls should experience how light boys' clothing feels.* The trousers, jacket, and hat — pilfered from one of the gardeners at school — were a disguise she had worn more often than she cared to admit.

Maybe that was why she had dreamed she was doing the same thing, just before meeting her dear Henry on the walk. Why couldn't she have continued that lovely dream instead of being kidnapped in a carriage house?

The thorns were too close to make her bedroom window a viable escape. She checked the other bedrooms, but the windows were all as black as her own, the plants close enough to her parent's bedroom window that the thorns scratched the glass.

She opened the door at the end of the hall and climbed the stairs to the attic. It was even colder than in the rest of the house. Sophie reached into the pockets of her wool jacket and pulled out a pair of gloves.

The maids' quarters were neat as a pin, their few belongings put away, their narrow beds with the serviceable but plain quilts made up smooth and tight.

There were a few windowed dormers in the room, and the light that came through was muted. But at least there *was* light. Sophie unlocked a window that faced the front yard and pushed it open.

The wall of black thorns reached up from below, the tops nearly touching the attic windowsill. The thicket stretched across the entire front yard. She couldn't even see where it ended, because the house and bramble were surrounded by a fog as thick as a London Particular. She pulled herself up into the window, prepared to climb onto the roof for a better view. This wasn't the first place she'd escaped from; it had been her preferred route out of the dormitory at school. After shimmying down the drainpipe, they would run off to an abandoned bungalow at the far end of the grounds, where someone had inevitably stashed a bottle of wine stolen from the cellars.

What would Henry say if he knew I had done such unladylike things? She knew how he felt about her. They had exchanged letters for years, and she was certain he was going to ask her father if he could court her. That was probably why she had dreamed of him, of wanting him to kiss her, though she knew he wouldn't because he was a proper gentleman. Always proper, that was Henry. Then, right after her one and only visit home from boarding school, things had changed. His letters, still proper, changed.

He would be trying to rescue her, thorns or not.

Sophie leaned to the right, one hand still on the windowsill, the other reaching for the copper drainpipe attached to the side of the house. Just as her gloved fingers skimmed the metal, something tugged at her foot. Thinking she had gotten snagged on a nail or a splinter, she tried to yank herself free.

And something yanked her back.

A glance at her foot made her blood run as cold as the air. A tendril from the treacherous thorn plant had reached up and snaked itself around her ankle. In her precarious position, it was impossible for her to try and pull away with any kind of force. Slowly, cautiously, she found her balance and gripped the window frame tightly with both hands. She lifted her free foot and slipped it back inside the window, lowering herself to solid ground.

Sophie then tried to pry the vine from her ankle. It had a grip like iron, and even the tips bore tiny thorns that pricked her fingers through her woolen gloves. It seemed to like the taste of her blood. The vine tightened its grip and pulled harder. Her foot slid from the sill, taking her leg out the window. The fog ate her scream. Both of her hands returned to the window frame, her grip tight, the only thing keeping her from being pulled out of the window and into the grasping, greedy plant. Another vine slipped over the windowsill, coming to assist the first. It twined itself around her calf.

Sophie's fingers ached from clutching the wood. The leg outside the window began to go numb, and her other leg began to cramp. Soon her strength would run out, and the plant would drag her over the edge and to her death. She looked around for anything that could help her. Beside the window stood a sewing dummy. A pair of shears hung from its neck on a ribbon. With all the strength she could muster, she thrust her body sideways. Her hand clutched the shears and ripped them off of the dummy. With both hands, she plunged the tip of the shears into the plant.

Greenish-black fluid spurted from the wound, and a high-pitched scream rose from somewhere below. The plant released her, and she fell to the floor, grabbing her injured calf. For the second time in mere hours, tears streamed from her eyes, running down the sides of her face into her hair.

There was no escape.

Henry and Irene stood beside the laboratory door. He listened for any sign of the intruders Irene insisted were outside, waiting to ambush them. Henry had weighed his options and decided it prudent to stay the present course. It seemed rather stupid that they had been pressed into lookout duty; Gabriel had locked the door from the inside, and the entrance was hidden by the cabinet. Henry thought it was more likely they were trying to keep him out of their way. Which was fine by him, given he thought they were all off their rockers.

He leaned against the wall, arms crossed over his chest, trying to look like he was unimpressed and failing miserably because he couldn't pull his gaze away from the strange and amazing feat being performed in front of him. In the last five minutes, Alphonse had taken gears, springs, and other bits of machinery from the piles on Faber's workbench and turned them into... something. He had put them together as if they were pieces of a jigsaw puzzle, just waiting to be reunited. Once he was satisfied, he attached them to the top of the wardrobe. Gabriel assisted, piecing sheets of spare metal together before hammering them on the corners and the sides. Several wires hung from the contraption, snaking their way inside. The whole of it was strangely beautiful.

Watching Alphonse's nimble fingers reminded Henry of his father, who could assemble a carriage clock with his eyes closed and have it work perfectly. Alphonse barely glanced at the blueprint tacked to the wardrobe's door, working either from a frighteningly good memory or some kind of instinct. Henry's own skill for mechanical things was good, but even he couldn't put something together that he hadn't designed without looking at the plans. He still didn't believe by any stretch of his imagination that it would do what the diagram said it would, but Henry was impressed.

"What makes you think Faber's machine works?" he asked for what must have been the fourth time. Prior attempts had garnered him admonishments by Alphonse to be quiet, or stern looks from Gabriel that made the words shrivel in Henry's throat. This time, it was Gabriel who looked down his nose, his lips pursing in annoyance.

Irene intervened, with a look of sympathy and a gentle hand on his arm.

"Henry, it's not important *how* we know. Honestly, it's all very technical and boring, anyway. And to be completely truthful, it involves the use of equipment that is strictly top-secret. So you see, if I told you, I would then have to kill you, and that would be a terrible shame, because I rather like you."

She said it with such nonchalance, as if they were conversing over tea, that it took Henry a moment to realize what she had said. Before he could react, she gave him a wink and turned back to her companions. "How much longer? Our friends outside are growing impatient." She paused, a listening expression on her delicate features. "They've begun to break things. And they're thinking some rather less than complimentary words about us and our mothers. Oh, my."

Alphonse, a tool in his teeth and another in his hand, mumbled something incomprehensible. Gabriel reached down and took the tool from his mouth.

"Alphonse, once more please. Without the screwdriver."

Alphonse stood. "I said, I'm just about finished. I've had to make some modifications. Faber built his own chamber, likely reinforced with iron and brass to keep her together on re-entry. We have to make do with what we've got, but she should get the job done." He leaned forward, putting his nose close to the blueprint and squinting. "Just need one last thing."

A sudden crash sounded outside the room. It was followed by the thudding of heavy footsteps.

"I think our guests are tired of waiting." Henry backed away from the door. "Whatever plan you've got in mind, I believe that now would be an excellent time to put it into action."

Alphonse swore. "Where is it?" He patted his pockets.

"What are you looking for?" Gabriel reached inside his waistcoat and pulled out the brother to Alphonse's strange-looking weapon. He pointed it at the door.

"My watch. Damn." He looked around the room, scanning for the missing timepiece.

Irene pulled Henry back even further, putting herself between him and the door. "We only have a few moments before they find this room,

Alphonse. Now is not the time to worry about your accessories." She reached into her reticule and removed a smaller version of Gabriel's odd sidearm, which she also pointed at the door.

"That's not what I mean, Irene. We need a watch to set the temporal target. Or would you like to just go bouncing around in time, hope we find Faber and then pray we make it back?"

Irene loosened one of her hands from the weapon and pulled at something on her corset. "Will this do?" She held out a small ladies' watch, attached to an ornate gold pin.

"'Fraid not. Too small, it'll burn out." Alphonse whipped around and strode toward Henry. "But I think I know where we can get one that'll fit the bill nicely."

Henry stepped away, his hand going immediately to his pocket. "You can't have mine. It's... it was a gift." He looked to Gabriel. "Surely you have one he can use?"

Gabriel shook his head. "Sorry. Lost mine in a card game last week."

A sudden thump against the secret entrance to the lab made the wall shake, loosening a blizzard of plaster dust. Irene's grip on her weapon tightened. Tesla shrieked his displeasure, jumped from Irene's shoulder, and darted into the darkness of the wardrobe.

"They've found us."

Alphonse held out his hand. "We're out of time, chum. Is your watch worth your life?"

Henry rubbed his thumb along the outside of the watch case, feeling the cool, smooth brass. Another thump. The door cracked, splintering wood joining the plaster dust. With reluctance, he pulled it from his pocket and handed it to Alphonse.

"I don't know what good it's going to do you. This isn't going to work."

"No time for arguments." Gabriel grabbed Henry by the sleeve. "It's time to go."

Her weapon still trained on the door, Irene backed toward the wardrobe, and stepped inside.

"You next." Gabriel gave him a rough shove, and Henry stumbled toward the open wardrobe door.

"You are all mad." He debated the idea that he would be better off facing whoever was on the other side of the workshop door but decided it didn't matter much anyway. Any second the men would break in, and they would all be trapped like rats, crammed inside a wardrobe. His goal was to not to get caught in the crossfire. After all, this wasn't his argument. He slid to the back of the cabinet, behind Irene and Alphonse. Once the machine failed to work, and the inevitable fighting started, he would look for a chance to escape.

With his pocket watch.

Alphonse fitted Henry's watch into a brass plate attached to the inside of the wardrobe while Gabriel continued to cover the door from outside. The thumping continued, and then there was the sound of something being ripped from a wall.

"They're not too bright, are they?" Gabriel said.

"I told you, I didn't read them as Oxford's finest," Irene said. "Alphonse, what's taking so long?"

Alphonse flipped open the watch case and started to set it.

"It was set to the correct time, you know," Henry protested. "And I wind it every morning."

"Not worried about the winding, and the *correct* time is relative, chum. Now, unless you want to pay a visit to the sixteenth century and end up hung as a witch, shut up." Alphonse left the watch, then turned a crank several times. Finally, he spun a knob in the control panel, watching the needle on one of the dials as it rose. "Almost there." He grabbed the crank arm again, giving it another few turns.

The machinery suddenly whirred to life, gears spinning, a soft hum coming from somewhere above. It was at that moment the outer door finally gave way in an explosion of wood and plaster. Two hulking men in gray military uniforms with splashes of red on the shoulders strode into the room, each carrying a large weapon that looked like a cross between a hunting rifle and a crossbow. It emitted a strange, blue glow. Both were trained on Henry and the others, the men's fingers on the triggers.

"Alphonse..." Gabriel gripped his weapon tighter, aiming it level with one of the men's barrel chests. Henry had the sinking feeling they were outmatched, pitting peashooters against cannons. His escape from this mad situation seemed less likely, and he pulled at his collar, which suddenly felt like a noose.

"Give us the blueprints," one of the men said. His voice held a familiar guttural accent. "Or we'll kill you."

"And if we give them to you, you'll let us go, I suppose?" Irene lifted an eyebrow, her aim never wavering.

The man's smile sent a terrible shiver down Henry's spine. "No. But we'll make your deaths less... messy."

"As tempting as that sounds," Gabriel replied, "I think we'll pass." He slid his feet back slowly, putting himself closer to the wardrobe.

"What are you doing?" The other man tilted his head, gaze suspicious.

Henry pressed himself further into the back of the box. Maybe they would all shoot each other and he would be left alone. Didn't seem likely, however. He was going to die here in the workshop of a madman, cowering in a wardrobe. But there was nothing for it now. He wasn't stupid enough to run out unarmed and try something grand, like a hero in a penny dreadful. Hopefully when the detective arrived in the morning and saw the carnage, he wouldn't tell Henry's family where he had been discovered.

The machine's hum pitched higher, and the wardrobe vibrated. Alphonse, who hadn't moved since the men burst into the room but had continued to watch the dials on the panel, cleared his throat. "Sorry to be so rude, fellows, but we must be going." In one lightning-quick move, Gabriel jumped into the wardrobe and pulled the doors shut. It was cramped, but not unbearable. The men's shouts of surprise were muffled by the wood, but Henry knew once the shock wore off they would be pulling the trigger. He braced himself for the blast.

Alphonse must have pushed a button or flipped a switch, because a new sound, like the grating of metal, erupted from the machine. It was unlike anything Henry had ever heard, and quite terrifying.

"Hang on to your hats, lady and gentlemen." Alphonse's voice was barely audible over the sound of the machine. The dark interior of the wardrobe was suddenly disrupted by what looked like lightning. His hair stood on end and there was a strange odor in the air. A blue-white flash blinded Henry. He waited for a shock to rip through his body and stop his heart. But it kept on pounding as the sound of his blood rushed in his ears.

The wardrobe shook so violently that Henry was sure it was going to fall apart. There was precious little space inside already, but enough for the four of them to jostle about, ramming into one another. Henry took an elbow to the gut, and he was sure he kicked someone in the shin. Everyone shouted, adding to the general chaos.

After about thirty seconds, the wardrobe stopped its bone-jarring shaking with a sudden *thunk*, as if it had been dropped. The noise wound down, becoming less alarming until there was silence. Henry's heart, on the other hand, beat like a bass drum on parade day, while his lungs heaved in and out like he had just run across the city. His companions were quiet, as if all three held their breath. Henry dared not speak, not that it would have been easy for him in his current state. He waited for his doom to be visited upon him in the form of bullets and whatever else those thugs in the lab had in mind.

Finally, Alphonse broke the silence. "That wasn't too bad, was it? Shall we see when we are?"

"You mean you didn't know to what *when* we were going?" Gabriel's shout made Henry jump in surprise.

"Nope. I just locked on to the most recent temporal disturbance and calculated from there." Alphonse's voice betrayed how proud he was of himself. "I have absolutely no idea when we've gone."

"Well, can we please get out sooner rather than later?" Irene's accent barely covered her annoyance. "It's a bit cramped back here. And ungodly hot if you haven't noticed."

Henry finally got control of his breathing, but he was unable to hold back his own irritation. "This game has gone on long enough. We have gone absolutely nowhere. The light show was impressive, though. Those men are waiting out there to murder us."

"Then why haven't they fired?" Gabriel asked quietly.

"Well, I, uh..." Henry stammered, trying to come up with a rational argument. But his clever mind failed him.

"Let's just end the suspense, shall we?" Alphonse did not wait for an answer, merely rattling the door as if trying to open it. A rude word shot from his mouth.

"What is it?" Irene asked. "Open the door already."

"That is going to take a moment." Alphonse sounded irritated. "You see, in all the rush, I forgot one important thing about wardrobes."

"And what is that?" Henry asked.

"They only open from the outside."

There was a choral groan.

"Not to fear, this won't be difficult." A rustling sound, and then something metal scraped against metal, followed by a *click*. "There we are. Welcome to... whenever." Alphonse pushed the door open.

Henry sucked in his breath. The hinges of the door gave a high-pitched squeal, which was followed by a deep and strange silence.

"Anytime you're ready to join us, chum." There was a distinct note of amusement in Alphonse's voice.

Henry peered out. It was dark, shadows laying thick in the corners of the small, extremely familiar room. "Holy hell." The curse was from his lips before he could prevent it.

Alphonse smiled as he clapped Henry on the shoulder. "That about sums it up, chum. So, how do you feel? You've just traveled in time."

Are you having me on?" Henry considered his companions had escaped from an asylum and were living out some sort of delusion. If they were, they were doing a marvelous job.

"No, sir." Alphonse looked offended. "Why would you say that?"

"Because we're still in exactly the same place we were." The "time machine" had given a terrific show, full of light and sound, and the feeling the world had dropped out from beneath them. He wasn't sure what he had expected to see when he stepped out of the wardrobe. He knew time travel was impossible, but he felt a sense of disappointment that they were still in Faber's workshop.

"I can see how you would think that." Alphonse leaned against the workbench. Gabriel and Irene stood by the door, the former looking annoyed and the latter amused. "I only said we'd travel in *time*. I never said anything about space. We've moved in time but stayed in one place. You'll notice the distinct lack of large German men pointing weapons at us. And look, no debris on the floor. If we didn't travel in time, where did all of that go?"

Henry opened and closed his mouth but had no words. He could only shake his head.

Gabriel made an impatient sound. "The pertinent question becomes *when* are we?"

"Not too far from where we came, if I had to guess." Irene grazed a glove across the top of a nearby table. "It looks almost identical."

Gabriel turned the switch on the wall, and gas lamps jumped to life. "And before he installed the electric lights."

"Cripes, let's just go out and see." Alphonse strode to the door and pulled it open. He stuck his head outside for a moment and then pulled it back.

"The house seems empty."

"Neither Faber?" Gabriel quipped.

Henry shook his head, confused. "What do you mean?"

"If we're back along Faber's timeline, but not where we left, then our Faber is a future Faber. There will be a present and a future version here somewhere. We'll need to keep out of the way of the present one."

Henry laughed out loud. "How can anyone be in two places at once? There can't simply be two of him." He had had enough of this joke, but it was amusing to see the extent to which they took the charade.

Gabriel ignored Henry's ranting.

"We'll figure out when we are, and that will probably help us find Faber." Gabriel pushed Henry out of the way and marched into the next room. Irene, with Tesla on her shoulder, followed, as did Alphonse, giving Henry a wicked grin.

A small key stuck out of the wardrobe's lock. Henry turned it, still unconvinced he had gone anywhere. He noticed, as he did so, that there was a second cabinet, not unlike the one he had recently exited. *Exactly* like it if he were being precise. He shook his head again. *It must have been there before and I just didn't notice. Because there was no other possibility. As for their pursuers, he had no answer for where they had gone. Maybe they were outside waiting for them. Which wasn't much comfort, but he followed the others anyway.*

"Really not a clue as to when this is, is there." Irene wandered to the window and picked up a dusty silver picture frame. Inside was a photograph of three people, but Henry was too far away to see them clearly.

"Whatever year it is, he must have a reason for choosing it." Gabriel lifted a lace curtain and peered outside.

"Faber's family." Irene held up the picture. A stoic-looking man stood beside a pretty blonde woman. A child, about eight years old, stood in front. She wore a frilly white dress, her dark hair in thick sausage curls.

Henry looked at the picture. Alexei Faber, whom he had never seen, looked every bit an ordinary man. "He has a family?"

Irene glanced at Gabriel, and a look passed between them that Henry could not interpret.

"His dossier says he had a family at one time." Irene set the frame back on the table.

"I don't remember that photograph being on the table when we left." Gabriel gave his associates a sharp look and moved toward the door. "We're not going to find him standing around here."

The four of them stepped out onto the house's small front porch. It was day — had they been inside so long? The air was warm, and Henry pulled off his coat.

He looked at the street before him and felt suddenly off-balance.

The snow was gone. The breeze was scented by flowers, instead of the biting winter wind that had been blowing when he stepped inside the house.

"Oh, my God." He didn't like using such rude language yet found himself doing it with increasing frequency. The proof was right before him. It was no longer Christmas Eve, it was... he didn't have any idea. He felt sick.

"Problem, chum?" The words *I told you so* danced across Alphonse's lips but remained unspoken. "Irene?"

Irene narrowed her eyes and focused on Henry for a few moments. "It's not pretty, what's going on in that head of his. All noise and confusion." She shook her head as if to clear it. "Is that what's it's like to be you? How do you stand it?"

"Fine. I suppose I have no choice but to believe you," Henry mumbled. His stomach churned as if he were on a boat in rough seas. He had actually traveled in time. It was almost too much to bear, despite the evidence in front of him. Alphonse patted him on the shoulder.

"It's alright, you'll adjust."

Henry looked at him, his upper lip beginning to sweat. "And have you traveled in time a great deal?"

"Well, no. This is a first for all of us. But I've seen enough to say that this isn't really all that strange." Alphonse smiled wide and walked away, just as Henry leaned over the porch rail and heaved his stomach contents onto the flower bed below.

"Better?" Alphonse called back. Henry wiped his chin and nodded.

"If we're through playing around?" Gabriel chided. "We have to find our Faber and get him back to the proper time. The faster the better."

"I say we split up." Irene set Tesla on top of the porch rail. "We'll cover more ground that way. We know what he looks like, we just have to find the *right* one."

"Excellent plan. Except *he* stays here." Gabriel pointed at Henry. "The rest of us will look."

"What?" Henry was no Secret Service agent. He had no real desire to chase down a criminal, but he also didn't want to be left alone when the bottom of the world may might fall away at any moment. "Why?"

"Because you're a liability. I want this extraction to go as smoothly as possible and be over quickly. You have no training."

Henry didn't deny the accusation, but it still stung, being treated like a nuisance. "Fine. Where do you want me to wait?"

"You can't be out in the open, someone might recognize you. And you can't stay in the house, present Faber could come home." Gabriel scratched the back of his neck. "You can't go to your home, for obvious reasons."

Henry had almost forgotten they were still in Germantown. It looked the same as every other day. Suddenly he was overcome with the desire to explore. What would his childhood home look to his nearly adult eyes?

"I guess I could wait in the carriage house," he offered.

"Fine." Gabriel pulled a small case from the inside pocket of his jacket. It looked like a cigarette or cigar case. "Irene, Alphonse, let's do a communications check." Irene pulled a similar case from her reticule, and Alphonse from his back pocket.

All three opened their cases. Inside were wires, knobs, one dial, and a small switch. Above them was a small, round, convex piece of glass. Gabriel fiddled with the knobs and flipped the switch. There was a buzzing sound, like an angry insect had been trapped inside. Light filled the glass. Henry leaned in to get a better look, his curiosity and surprise fitting together like two perfectly balanced gears.

"Can you hear me, Irene?" Gabriel's voice reverberated strangely, coming from both his mouth, and from the box in Irene's hand.

"Loud and clear." She held up her device to show Henry. Gabriel's face appeared in the glass. It was distorted, as if he were looking at them through the bottom of a bowl.

"Over and out." Gabriel fiddled with one of the dials and his face disappeared from Irene's device. He repeated the procedure with Alphonse's.

"Photophones," Gabriel explained, likely noticing the amazed expression on Henry's face. "Wireless communication."

"Where did you get them?" Henry had never seen such amazing devices. "How do they work?"

"No time for questions." Gabriel took Henry by the elbow and guided him down the steps to the sidewalk. "We'll walk you to the carriage house, and then we're on the hunt."

CHAPTER VI

SOPHIE LAY ON THE ATTIC FLOOR, GASPING FOR BREATH. HER LEG throbbed in time with her heartbeat. What *was* that thing? The plant acted as if it had a mind of its own. Who had planted it and how had it grown so quickly? She could only have been asleep for a few hours.

Sophie swallowed, and her throat made a dry *click*. She needed both water and a new plan. Neither would be accomplished from the floor. She stood, ignoring the protest of her sore calf. After double-checking that the window was locked and expressing her thoughts about the wall of thorns with a rude gesture, she tromped down the attic stairs, locking the door behind her for good measure. Luckily, the second-floor bathroom had running water. It had been installed with the flushing commode a few years ago. After filling a glass and drinking her fill, she stoked the fire in her room and contemplated her remaining options.

There were none. Every option was closed. The plants were a better guard than her governess and could even teach the headmistress at Montgomery House a thing or two. Sophie slammed the glass down on the small side table. It broke, spilling water and glass over her hand. Carefully, she shook the glass off and inspected the damage. Just a few nicks that barely bled. She leaned toward the fire's light to get a better look. The gold locket, which must have slid from beneath her shirt during the struggle, swung forward on its chain and caught the firelight. Sophie grabbed it with her uninjured hand and held it up.

She hadn't had much chance to think about where it had come from. There was something vaguely familiar about it, just touching the edges of her memory. It had been part of her dream. She was in the carriage house, hiding from Henry, waiting for him to find her. He had chased her because she had stolen a small, silver-wrapped package from him. Inside the carriage house, she had torn the wrapping, just a little. Before she could stop herself, she'd had the paper in her hand, and the box was uncovered. A jewelry box, dark blue. The stamp on the top was of from a jeweler on Samson Street.

The dream must have been her own wishful thinking. She was in love with Henry, and she was almost but not quite positive he felt the same. His letters had been so sweet, and he had alluded to wanting to court her. But they hadn't had time to speak in person since she had returned from school.

If he *had* given her a locket like this, it would mean he was making her a promise. In her dream, she had taken the lid off the box and peered inside. She had glimpsed what looked like a locket before the dream changed into a nightmare. Before the man from her long-ago memory arrived and kidnapped her.

Her fingers rubbed the locket face, feeling the small etched grooves in the gold. How could something from a dream show up here, around her neck? It was no less puzzling than the house being empty, surrounded by homicidal thorns, or the clock coming to a complete stop while continuing to tick.

Thinking about Henry brought her back to the scene in Market Square. The boy with the sensible notions had always been a part of her life, a grounding force to her whirling dervish. When she had gone to boarding school, she thought she was off on an adventure. But she had missed home. She had missed Henry. When they first started exchanging letters, they were full of pleasantries and news from home. She was sure he was just being nice to a homesick friend. Likely his mother had made him write.

Then last summer she had come home for a visit, and it all changed. Henry was so different. Tall and handsome, smart and kind. She had imagined he was more than her friend. And her mother and father were still, even after all their time apart, so vigilant about watching over her.

Actually, Sophie was rather surprised he wasn't already betrothed. He was older than she, able to go to parties and dance and meet girls, whereas she was still too young.

At the end of the summer, she had returned to school to finish her last few courses before returning home for good. Henry had *asked* to continue to write to her. She had agreed, and the tone of his letters changed. He sent poems, and hints of romance. She had replied to every letter, hopefully making her interest as plain as she could without being untoward. Since coming home, she had barely had time to see him. He was obviously invited to the Christmas Eve party, but half the town would be there, with no time to talk together except during a dance, perhaps. Her cheeks grew warmer than the fire at the idea.

She had dreamed he gave her this locket, engraved with her initials, as a gift. A dream that had somehow appeared here in her hand. She tried again to pry the locket open with her fingernails. But it stuck fast.

She sat back and watched the fire dance in the hearth, her eyes growing heavy.

A rustling sound from somewhere in the house jolted her completely awake. She listened, straining to hear above the crackle of the fire. There it was again—someone or something moving. She crept into the hall with light steps, certain the pounding of her heart would betray her. A creak of the floorboards at the top of the stairs. Someone running, quick as a flash. A flutter of something going down the steps caught her eye. Sophie tiptoed behind, listening as footsteps fell on each step of the staircase.

It could be Henry, come to find me. But Henry wouldn't creep around like a thief. Sophie followed the mystery person, trying to avoid the same creaky stair treads that the intruder didn't.

The person, dressed in trousers and a tailed coat, turned at the bottom of the stairs, toward the back of the house.

Downstairs, the parlor door stood open. Sophie was a little disappointed to see the actual parlor behind it, with its wood-and-velvet furniture sitting atop a Persian carpet and the portrait of her grandmother hanging over the fireplace. She paused just long enough to see the room was empty before she followed her visitor down the dimly lit hall.

No one was in evidence. The soft click of a door closing drew Sophie down the hall, any attempt at stealth gone. She grabbed and turned the knob of each door in turn, but the dining room and library remained locked.

"Hello? Where did you go? Can you help me?" Her only reply was the incessant *tick-tick-tick* that seemed continued to permeate the house. She kicked the library door in frustration, which was more of an insult to her foot than to the door. Favoring her foot, she approached the last door at the end of the hall, which led to the kitchen. The door, under normal circumstances, was a swinging pass-through.

Now there was a shiny brass lock that shut her out of the room. She peered through the keyhole. As she touched the cold metal, two things happened at once: the grandfather clock struck midnight again, and a warm sensation blossomed in her pocket. At the clock's chime, she jumped, and a surprised scream leapt from her throat. Sophie leaned her head against the door and took a few breaths, eyes locked on the light spilling from under the kitchen door. She reached in her pocket and pulled out the warm brass key.

Sophie slipped the key into the lock and turned it. The well-oiled mechanism clicked open. Butterflies waltzed in her middle, a dance of uncertainty. Would she find the past again, or the kitchen, with its well-stocked pantry? When had she last eaten? Her stomach gave her an estimate of *far too long*. There was something else to consider: would her mysterious visitor be behind the door, waiting? The butterflies' waltz turned into a polka.

She pushed the door inward. A wave of heat nearly knocked her off her feet.

Her own garden, decked out in summer green, greeted her.

Gabriel shut the door to the carriage house, leaving Henry in near darkness. If he hadn't known he had traveled in time, this place wouldn't have given him any clues. It looked the same as it always did. It smelled of leather, horses, and spring oil. It was much warmer than the last time he had been there, the day Sophie disappeared. The still air was stifling, which didn't matter, because he wasn't staying long.

He waited another minute by the back door for Gabriel to be gone. Or what he thought was a minute since he had left his watch with their time machine. It was odd, not feeling its comforting weight in his pocket.

The door creaked slightly as he opened it. Henry peered out but saw no one. He stepped onto the path. He could draw a map of this town from memory but was at a loss where to begin. A look along Germantown Avenue was a good place to start. He rounded the corner of the carriage house and slipped into the space between it and the next building, his presence shrouded in deep shadows. Technically he wasn't disobeying Gabriel's edict, since he was out of sight.

It had to be nearing mid-day, but there was not a single soul on the street. Not a carriage, either. Henry heard something in the direction of the square, though. A crowd?

It was Market Day.

Henry crept from his hiding place. He still didn't know what year it was, but Market Day was one thing about Germantown that never changed. It appeared to be spring, the blossoms on the dogwood and crabapple trees that lined the streets suggesting early April.

He strode down the street, feeling much more in control of this situation. After all, he was more qualified to go about town than Gabriel or the others. He knew every building, every bump in the sidewalk.

Every person.

Henry stopped short. Gabriel was right, someone might recognize him. Any other day that wouldn't concern him, but what if he were only a few years from where he left? Could he run into himself?

"Figured it out, chum?"

Henry spun, looking for Alphonse. No one was there. *Wonderful. Now I'm hearing voices.* He walked another ten paces.

"Where do you think you're going?"

This time Henry whipped around, expecting Alphonse to be directly behind him. Again, nothing. "Where are you, Alphonse. If you're there, just come out and stop playing games."

"But why? Games are so much more fun." Alphonse heaved a deep sigh from somewhere nearby. "Fine, if you insist."

The air two feet in front of Henry shimmered, like a summer heat haze. And then, Alphonse was there, an amused smirk on his face.

"Boo."

Henry leapt backward and screamed. He tripped and fell to the pavement with an *ooomph*. "Where did you come from?"

Alphonse chuckled. "I'm following you. I figured you'd try and poke around, so I kept close by."

"No, I mean..." Henry couldn't make himself say the words.

"Oh, you mean my party trick?" Alphonse looked surprised. "I thought you realized I was the invisible man when I was holding my little toy to your head."

"I wasn't sure what I saw. I was preoccupied... since you were try-ing to kill me."

Alphonse waved the words away. "Naw, I was just trying to scare you. Besides—" He pulled the same weapon from his jacket pocket. " — It doesn't have to kill if I don't want it to. It's a clever thing." He studied Henry a moment. "Sorry I scared you. Again. Just my way of having some fun."

"So, uh, what are you?" It came out sounding much ruder than he Henry intended. "If you'll pardon my asking."

Alphonse's expression turned serious. "I'll try not to be insulted by that. I'm human, just like you. Short version? I had an accident. You don't think the Secret Service hired me for my mechanical skill and rugged good looks, do you?"

Henry sat with Alphonse's words a moment. "Well, you are very good. And I speak as an engineer. Very fast, as well."

"That is all me. Machines and I have an understanding. I can look at a blueprint once and build whatever it is. This?" He held up the odd-looking weapon. "Made it myself. And the photophone."

"How did you come up with them?" Henry's fingers itched to grab it and take it apart. *Machinery* fascinated him. He just never wanted to be a watchmaker. Which he knew disappointed his father, even though Henry had never confessed so aloud. Watchmaking had been the family business for generations.

"Well, I... we... sort of browsed through the patent office. Never mind that, though." Alphonse's cheeks reddened; he quickly changed the subject. "Where were *you* off to, chum?"

It was Henry's turn to blush. "I just wanted to see."

"Being nosy?" Alphonse's tone said he didn't really believe Henry.

"In general, yes. No ulterior motive." Henry had no desire to take on Alexei Faber alone. Once Gabriel and his associates captured him, Henry would be able to find out how to save Sophie.

Alphonse crossed his arms over his chest, the weapon hanging from his fingers. "Fine. I guess you won't go back and wait patiently. If you're going to walk about, I should accompany you so that you don't muck things up."

Henry tried not to be insulted. "I can manage a walk to Market Square. I believe it's Market Day, which means I can blend into the crowd."

Alphonse let out a long whistle. "Thinking like a spy, now, aren't you? Good. Come on, let's go." He walked around Henry and led the way as they started down Germantown Avenue.

"Don't worry about what Gabriel said," Alphonse called over his shoulder. "About being recognized. If this is far enough back into your childhood, they won't know it's you, since they haven't yet met this version of you, if that makes sense."

Henry tried to understand but couldn't quite wrap his mind around it. "Not really."

"One question, though — whom do you favor, your mother, or your father?"

"My father, I suppose." Henry had often been told he looked like his father. "Except for my ears. And my eyes."

"Then don't be surprised if someone mistakes you for your father." Alphonse chuckled at Henry's horrified expression. "Just keep your head down and your eyes open. Avoid talking if possible."

They arrived at the square's entrance. The half-acre of open space in the center of town was jammed with people, milling around, and looking at the wares displayed in makeshift booths.

"This is sometime before 1883," Henry murmured.

"What's that?" Alphonse replied.

"The Civil War memorial. It was built in the center of the square two years ago." Henry paused. "I mean, two years from when we came from." More proof that they had truly time traveled. "It's not there."

"I had no idea. Maybe it's a good thing you came along, chum." Alphonse clapped him on the shoulder. "What else do you see?"

The rest of the market looked as it always did.

"That's the Fellowship Fire Engine Company, there." He pointed to a small brick structure that stood along the edge of the square. "And the German Reformed Church. That's the Deschler-Morris house. George Washington stayed there during the Yellow Fever epidemic." He felt as if he were reciting lessons or giving a tour. "But none of that helps us figure out the year, I guess. Most of these were built during the Revolution."

Alphonse seemed impressed. "Very good. But you're right, it doesn't help."

"Maybe Gabriel and Irene are having better luck."

A barn, open at both ends, took up the far side of the square. "That's the main market. And if it's Wool Day, that's where they'll have all the sheep."

"I don't think Faber is here to buy wool," Alphonse said. "He's probably not here at all."

"Sophie! Sophie Weber, where are you?"

The voice made Henry's voice catch in his throat. He found the caller easily, a little boy walking through the crowd. He wore short pants and a jacket, like the other boys his age. His brown hair was combed. He hated having his hair combed, though he couldn't remember why. Henry stepped into the square, his heart beating strangely and his stomach feeling like preserves.

"Where are you going?" Alphonse grabbed Henry's sleeve.

"Sorry. I was following my... that boy. He's looking for Sophie." *He's always looking for Sophie.*

"Why? We need to find Faber."

"He's me. I wanted to see where he was going."

Alphonse's gaze followed the path of the boy Henry. "You were a skinny little thing, weren't you?"

Henry pulled his arm from Alphonse's grip. "I'd like to see you at that age."

"Sorry." Alphonse wiped his hand on his jacket. "Can you tell the year yet?"

Henry returned to watching his younger self. The boy continued calling for Sophie as he walked through the crowd. It was strange to see himself at this age, a serious-looking boy even then. Feet always on the ground. *If that boy only knew.*

"I'm around ten or so. 1875, maybe 76."

Henry scanned the market. It was an unlikely place for a time-traveling kidnapper to be, given the crowds. And given that he might run into himself. *What a mad idea. Then again, today has been full of them.*

Movement at the far edge of the market caught his eye. By the apple tree, branches heavy with blossoms, with deep shade beneath the boughs. A man stepped into the sun and walked away. The same man from the photograph.

"There he is." Henry indicated Faber with his chin.

"We'll watch a minute and see which way he goes." Alphonse slipped his hand into his pocket and pulled out his weapon, keeping it hidden between them. Faber walked toward and then down Germantown Avenue. If he had seen Henry and Alphonse, he made no indication.

"That's not him." Alphonse said quietly. "I mean, it is, but it's the younger one, from this time."

Henry turned and followed Faber's progress. All he could see was the back of the man's head. "How can you tell?"

"He's not old enough."

Henry barely heard him, his attention drawn back to the apple tree. From the shade stepped a young girl. Sophie, already beginning to look like the woman she would become. He smiled, and then frowned.

What were they doing under that tree? Henry's mind whirled with terrible ideas. He studied her a moment, looking for some sign of distress. She looked happy as she skipped away. Her smile changed to a frown when his own younger self caught up with her. Their conversation was animated, younger Henry most likely berating Sophie for disappearing. She had probably run away from her mother, as usual.

"Why didn't he just snatch Sophie on this day?" Henry asked quietly. He had her, right there. So why?

Alphonse shrugged. "My guess? He hadn't finished the machine at this point. We didn't see it in the workshop, remember?"

Of course. It seemed so obvious, except that time travel forced one to think in odd, circular ways. An idea occurred to him, one that made him want to go back to Faber's house right away. Unfortunately, that was likely where the Faber they had just seen was headed.

Which presented another problem.

"Uh... what's going to happen if *that* Faber finds our time machine?"

Alphonse paused his eyebrows lifted. "That's a good point."

"Well, I did lock the door," Henry offered.

"It's a wooden cabinet, not a safe. A ten-year-old could pick that lock with a hairpin." Alphonse looked over his shoulder in the direction the younger Faber had left. "We probably should go after him and do something about that."

Which was when another Faber walked by, moving among the crowd as if he belonged. No one seemed to notice that his doppelganger had gone off in another direction not a moment ago. He didn't appear to see either Henry or Alphonse.

Alphonse beckoned Henry forward. They crept through the crowd, trying to keep out of Faber's line of sight. Now that Henry had a proper view, he noticed what Alphonse had been talking about. This man appeared much older than the one who had passed them not long ago, as if he had aged twenty years instead of eight or nine.

Faber might have sensed he was being followed. Or perhaps he just turned his head at an inopportune moment. Either way, he spied Henry. Faber's eyes widened slightly, and then he raced away through the square.

"Great." Alphonse pushed his hat tighter on his head. "I hate this part."

He forged a path between the people, darting around bustles and finding clear space between prams. Henry followed right behind, reaping the benefit of the other's path-clearing. He focused on the back of Alphonse's coat. Finally, people jumped out of the way, making it easier to follow, but Faber fled the square.

"He must be headed back toward his own time machine." Alphonse didn't even sound winded. Henry wasn't exactly gulping air, but he didn't have the ability to form complete sentences.

Faber headed north, the opposite direction of his own house.

"He's heading... to Upper... Germantown," Henry announced.

"There's an upper and lower Germantown?" Alphonse asked. Henry nodded.

Faber raced past the Mennonite Meeting House, the Maxwell Mansion, and the elegant homes that lined the street. Henry hardly noticed they had reached the Weber's house until they were almost past it.

Faber turned suddenly and disappeared through a gate set into a high stone wall.

The Upper Burial Ground.

Alphonse stopped beside the gate. With his free hand, he pulled the photophone from his pocket and handed it to Henry.

"I'm going in. He could be anywhere, and he could be armed. You stay right here. Call Gabriel and Irene."

Henry opened the photophone's case and looked at the dials and knobs. "How does this work?"

"You'll figure it out. It's not like you're going to accidentally get the wrong person. There are only two others in the entire world."

Before Henry could argue, Alphonse literally disappeared. His clothing, his hat, all of it. Henry had only seen the reverse. This was just as disconcerting. The gate opened, seemingly of its own accord.

"The problem is, I don't know if he's left or not." Henry muttered. There was no answer, and he got the feeling that he was, indeed, alone.

CHAPTER VII

SOPHIE STOOD IN THE OPEN KITCHEN DOOR. HEAT AND LIGHT RADIATED through it, along with the smell of damp, stale air that made her cringe. And as cold as the house was, she preferred it to being blanched like a piece of asparagus, as only a summer day in Philadelphia could do. The scene on the other side of the open doorway paused, frozen in time, like Market Square had been in the parlor. There was no sign of anyone in a long-tailed coat.

This was clearly a different day than the one in the parlor. Everything seemed to sag in the hot, humid air. The only flowers that thrived in these conditions were the black-eyed Susans, the day lilies, and the daisies.

And of course, the roses. Sophie could practically smell their heady scent as she slipped off her heavy jacket and dropped it on the hall floor as she crossed the threshold. The sun warmed her chilled bones and felt wonderful on her skin for the moment. She ran to the roses, her nose filling with their perfume, memory washing over her.

"Please? I'll just be outside in the garden."

"Fine, if it'll get you to stop whining, go. But just for an hour."

"Oh, thank you, Miss Abernathy. Thank you!"

The voice came from behind Sophie. The door she had come through remained, same as last time. It opened into the cold and dim hall. Like before, it stood in the middle of nowhere. But the rear facade of her house was *also* there, like some kind of optical illusion. The back door flew open, and for a second Sophie had a glimpse of the inside of the kitchen at the same time as the inside of the hall. *Strange.*

But no stranger, perhaps, than watching herself walk out the door. Not the eight-year-old version she had seen last time, but one that more closely resembled her current self. This girl was a few inches shorter, her face a little rounder, her bosom and hips less so. If she had to guess, she would say the girl before her was about twelve. Her dress was pale pink with eyelet trim, and her arms were full of books as she trounced across the garden toward the large oak in the corner.

The woman's voice belonged to Miss Abernathy, who had been her governess until she had been sent to England. A part of Sophie wanted to run through the back door and see her again. She had been strict, like every other adult in her life, but kind. *Considering how obstinate her charge was,* Sophie thought, *she had been an absolute saint.* As much as she wanted to visit with Miss Abernathy, she knew it wouldn't be possible. Better to stay here and see what kind of trouble her younger self got up to.

Young Sophie flopped in the shade of the tree, her books falling to one side. She glanced back, to make sure no one was watching, and then pulled her skirts up to her thighs. With a sigh of relief, she leaned back against the tree's trunk, her eyes closed.

Sophie giggled. This was one of dozens of days where she would beg Miss Abernathy to go outside, pleading for fresh air and promising to study while she enjoyed the slight breeze that made all the difference in the stifling weather. The woman would finally relent, and Sophie would bolt from the house and sit as her younger self was now, skirts hiked up as high as she could get them, letting the air dry her sweaty skin. It was the only place she could do so without being scolded for indecency.

The girl didn't make a move toward her books, and Sophie couldn't blame her. How could anyone be expected to concentrate on irregular French verbs on a day like this, when the very air endeavored to suffocate her? Her own skin had begun to develop a sticky, disgusting film as the hot air turned from welcoming to irritating. Her dress was much too warm for this time of year, and she lifted her skirts, waving it them in an attempt to cool herself. She moved into the cooling shade of the tree, just to the other side of the trunk from her younger self, to avoid being broiled and steamed all at once.

"Hello there."

Sophie swiveled her head toward the voice just as the girl's head popped up. Her eyes snapped open and then squinted against the sun. A man stood on the other side of the garden wall, his arms leaning against the stone. The same man that had approached her child-self beneath the apple tree in Market Square when she was eight. The nightmare man. He looked a little older than before, but not as old as he had appeared in her nightmare. The object of his steady green gaze pulled her feet close and yanked her skirts down, and Sophie's own cheeks burned in embarrassment.

This scene tickled something in the back of her mind. She tried to think, but her mind refused to cooperate, thoughts slipping into a fog when she tried to grasp them. Maybe it just seemed familiar because she was in a familiar place. She shook her head, trying to clear the confusion blooming in her brain.

Young Sophie pulled herself together remarkably well. "Good afternoon, sir," the girl said politely. "Are you lost?"

The way the girl said it bordered on cheek, but it was a valid question. Delivery men or servants used the back gate, and occasionally family. This man was dressed in a fine linen suit, a straw boater on his head. A gentleman. And *not* family.

The man shook his head, amusement in every line of his face. "No, I'm not lost."

Young Sophie stood and straightened her skirt, serious, as if she were the lady of the house.

"Well, sir, if you are calling on my father, you should go around to the front door and ring the bell." A look crossed her face, as if she wanted to say something else and thought better of it.

The man leaned one elbow on the top of the wall and propped his head on his fist, his eyes dancing.

"You don't remember, do you?"

"Remember what, sir?" Young Sophie stood, and subtly dusted off her backside.

The man sighed. "I don't suppose you would, though. Our conversation was brief, hardly enough to make an impression."

"I'm sorry, sir, do you mean to imply we have met before?" The girl tilted her head and studied the man's face, trying to place him. Sophie couldn't believe her younger self had forgotten him so quickly. It had only been four years.

"If so, I'm sorry but I don't remember."

The man lifted his head, hesitating. He shook his head and smiled. "No matter. It's not important."

There was an awkward pause. Young Sophie opened her mouth, either to make her exit as politely as possible or offer the man a glass of lemonade. The man's hand moved toward the gate beside him, as if he were going to open it. Sophie moved, instinctively, to protect her younger self, like she had beneath the apple tree on Market Day. Young

Sophie stood there, debating with herself about what to say, or if to say anything at all.

Footsteps crunched on the gravel, making made the decision unnecessary. The man pulled his hand back as if the gate's latch had burned him. He glanced toward the footsteps, and then pulled out his pocket watch. The case was a bit more scratched, the gold a little less bright. When he flipped up the cover, Sophie caught a glimpse of the photograph inside, the little girl with sausage curls and a large bow on her head. The man glanced at it, a shadow of sadness passing over his features.

"I must be going." He tipped his hat. "My dear Miss Weber, until next time." He turned sharply and walked away, in the opposite direction from the sounds of the footsteps.

Young Sophie finally found her tongue. She ran to the garden wall and peered over.

"Sir! Whom should I say called?"

The man paused. He glanced over his shoulder, an odd look on his face that made older Sophie shiver despite the sweltering heat.

"Tell him... tell him Alexei Faber came to call. And please be sure to tell him that I will call again." Alexei straightened up and continued on his way, his steps long and quick. Both Sophies watched him until he disappeared around the corner at the end of the block.

"What are you doing out here, Miss Weber?"

Both Sophies moved in tandem, jumping in surprise, their heads turning.

"Oh, Henry!" Young Sophie's cheeks flushed, and she clapped a hand to her mouth. "I mean, Master Rittenhouse."

Sophie smiled at Henry sauntering up the alley. Fifteen or so, all arms and legs, and still the most serious boy she had ever met. To her sixteen-year-old eyes, he was adorable. She could already see the man he was going to be starting to take shape in his cheekbones and the angle of his jawline. Dark curls peeked from beneath his hat. It hadn't felt right, the first time she called him by his surname instead of his given name, like he was some stranger instead of someone she had known her entire life. But her parents had insisted, saying that it was improper at their ages to be so familiar.

"I would think that on a day like today you would prefer to be indoors." Henry closed the book in his hand, a perpetual accessory, and tucked it beneath his arm.

"I... oh..." Suddenly, the girl's cheeks turned red, and her tongue seemed to tie itself in knots. Sophie furrowed her brow in confusion. She certainly hadn't been such a ninny, and definitely not around Henry.

"Did you forget why you came outside?" Henry's laugh was a happy one, but it stung her younger self. He was speaking to her as if she were a child. Which she supposed she was on that day, but Henry didn't need to act so uppity, did he? The girl went back to the base of the tree, where her French book lay on the grass.

"No, I did not. I came outside to study." She showed the book to Henry. "Miss Finch says that I am nearly fluent. I should think I will be perfect when I arrive in Paris." Miss Finch had been her French tutor. Sophie also remembered her fondly, mostly because she brought Sophie lovely pastries, but also because she always talked about the places in the world she had visited and all the adventures she had had. It seemed like a fantastic life to Sophie.

Henry lifted an eyebrow, still seeming amused rather than impressed.

"Paris? And just when, *mademoiselle*, are you expected in Paris?"

Sophie could practically see anger seething beneath her counterpart's skin. The girl pulled her shoulders back and squared them. "When I go for the Season, of course. When I am seventeen, I will go to Paris and make my debut." She looked Henry square in the eye. "And I will find a handsome French man to dance with me." She jutted out her chin. "A dozen handsome French men, and I shall be the toast of France."

Sophie's jaw fell open, shocked by the sudden realization that she had been in love with Henry, even then.

The girl's attempt to make him jealous did not have the desired effect. Henry managed to contain his laugh this time, but Sophie could see it just behind his lips, trying to break free.

"So you won't be making your debut at the Assembly Ball, like all of the other girls in Philadelphia?"

"Oh, no. That's much too... domestic. A Season in Paris, that will be an adventure."

Henry leaned on the wall, his smile still dancing in his eyes. Sophie wished she could slap him.

"Adventures are fine for storybooks and children. But as for me, I will stick to the practical things." He held up his book. "Science.

Engineering. Engineers aren't prone to flights of fancy. They are men of reason, building things that make society better, like bridges. I'm going to attend the University of Pennsylvania and become a civil engineer. I'll design tall buildings. Aquifers. Streets. It'll be wonderful."

Young Sophie made a face that did nothing to prove she was not the child Henry considered her.

"Sounds perfectly boring." She pulled her French book close to her chest and crossed her arms over it. "I want to see the world."

"Not likely. Girls don't have adventures." Henry's tone was matter of fact.

Both Sophies' faces flushed with anger. "Why does everyone say that? What's wrong with a girl traveling the world?"

"Because men are better suited. Women faint at the first sight of anything dangerous," Henry responded. "You wouldn't last a single day."

That was enough to break the girl's tenuous composure. She stamped the ground, sending up a cloud of dust. "You are wrong, Henry Rittenhouse. And one day, I'll prove it to you."

Before he could respond, and without an apology for using his given name, she turned her back and stormed across the garden and into the house, being certain to slam the door behind her. Sophie followed her going with a turn of her head, and something by the corner of the house caught her eye. It was gone in flash, but she was sure it had been a person, perhaps a woman, but she seemed to be wearing a top hat. Sophie marched across the yard toward them and looked down the alley between the houses, but whoever they were, they were nowhere to be seen. She ran down the alley to the front of the house. They had vanished as if by magic. As Sophie returned to the yard, she considered if it would have done any good even if she did catch them.

The yard was empty. Henry was gone, who knew where, but likely his nose was back in his book. Sophie still burned a little at his treatment of her younger self. She had thought she knew the moment she had fallen in love with Henry, but if this were indeed a memory, then it seemed she had been keeping a great secret from herself for many years.

That was just one of several things about this little scene that gnawed at her, and she needed to think on it in quiet. She turned toward the door that led back to her present-day home, the one steeped in dark and cold. The hall gaped at her like a hungry mouth. She hovered in the doorway and considered staying here in the garden for a bit longer. Perhaps she would sit by the tree and do her thinking, despite the heat.

At the far end of the hall, something moved. A person in a tailed coat dashed across the foyer, from the study to the parlor. Sophie's heart pounded as she raced through the door after them.

Henry peered through the cemetery gate, but there was no sign of Faber or Alphonse. Not that he expected to *see* Alphonse. Henry shuddered. A man shouldn't be able to disappear so completely in that manner. It was unnatural. Who was to know if he did something or went somewhere inappropriate? But an ideal ability for a spy to have, he supposed.

He looked at the photophone in his hands. It wasn't as complicated as it had looked at first, but nothing was labeled. He flipped the only switch, and the device emitted a buzzing sound. That was promising. Maybe one of the dials would bring up Gabriel's or Irene's face. That did no good. There was a button, so he pushed it.

"Alphonse? What's happening?"

Gabriel's face appeared in the glass a half-second after his voice came from somewhere inside the device. In his surprise, Henry nearly dropped it.

"Um, it's not Alphonse." He wasn't sure where he should direct his voice. "It's Henry."

"Yes, I can see that." Gabriel's tone held no amusement. "Where are you? Why aren't you in the carriage house? Where is Alphonse?"

"Well, I... it's a long story. Listen, we found Faber. Both of them, actually. But the right one ran off into the Upper Burial Ground. Alphonse is following him."

"He went alone?" Gabriel muttered something that sounded very much like a curse.

"He left me here to contact you. And he's... you know. Hidden." He couldn't bring himself to say the word *invisible*. It was quite enough that he had been forced to admit that time travel was possible.

"That doesn't make him invincible, no matter what he thinks. Don't move. I'll be right there." There was a *pop*, and Gabriel disappeared before Henry had a chance to say anything more. He thought about trying to contact Irene, but Gabriel hadn't said anything about notifying her. And he wasn't even sure how to use the photophone to make that happen.

Henry leaned against the cemetery's wall to wait. He peered through the gate. The Concord schoolhouse stood at the far end. The one-room school hadn't been used in almost a century, and Henry had always been puzzled as to why there was a cemetery in the same place as a school. It had an odd air about it that made Henry shiver.

Someone shouted. Henry put his hand on the gate and listened. No other sound, but he began to worry. Shouldn't Alphonse have returned by now? Henry should wait for Gabriel. But as he was already opening the gate and stepping inside, it was likely too late for that.

Henry scanned the cemetery. The grave markers stood silent in their lines, like granite soldiers. The oldest, from before the Revolutionary War, were barely legible. He looked toward the schoolhouse. It too stood silent, its mullioned glass like dark, empty eyes. He saw no one.

Henry left the gate open for Gabriel and stepped further along the path. His stomach churned, and his hands shook. He had no weapon to defend himself—what was he thinking? He moved deeper into the cemetery but no one revealed themselves. Which, unfortunately, left only one place to look.

Henry crept around the side of the schoolhouse and peeked through a window. Only the rows of old student desks and the blackboard along the front wall. With his back to the wall, he slid along it until he reached the corner. Leaning out just far enough so that he could see behind the building he turned his head.

Still no one. And yet, something both more interesting and frightening. Faber's time machine. This one looked far better constructed than the one Alphonse had cobbled together. The wood was thick and polished, trimmed in gleaming brass. There was no mere key lock on the door, but an intricate metal box with both a keyhole and a series of raised, numbered buttons. Henry would not be picking that lock with his tools anytime soon. It was doubtful that even Alphonse could crack it. Henry walked around the machine, both admiring the craftsmanship and looking for some weakness. He returned to the front no closer to a solution for how to get inside but completely enamored by the beauty and complexity of the machine. The familiar feeling of wanting to take it apart gnawed at him. He shook his head, focusing on his task.

"Where is Faber?" he murmured to himself, as he often did when picking at a problem. "The machine is here, so he's not gone."

"Right here, my boy." The voice came from behind him. Henry flinched and started to turn when a blinding pain raced through his body. Stars burst across his vision, and then darkness.

Wait!"

Sophie ran through the kitchen door, chasing the intruder. She only took a few steps over the threshold before the icy fingers of the frigid air grasped her throat. She gasped as needles of cold stabbed her lungs. The freezing air seeped through her blouse, turning her sweat-drenched skin to ice. She snatched her jacket from the floor, shoved her arms into it and pulled it tight around her body.

It was quiet in the house, except for the Ticking of Unknown Origin. She didn't even bother closing the kitchen door as she raced down the hall in hope of catching the man in the tailed coat.

"What? Where did he go?"

The parlor door remained open, the room exactly as she had glimpsed it before and still quite empty. Sophie stumbled into the parlor in disbelief, her heavy breath fogging the air in front of her. She looked behind furniture, under the piano in the corner, even in the cupboards, but there was no one there.

Thoughts flew about in her head like tiny birds, each chirping their need for attention. She turned on the gaslights and flopped onto the love seat, with its uncomfortable flowered-satin upholstery. It was for guests and not lounging, unlike the sitting room upstairs, with its worn and plush cushions. For the first time, Sophie realized that without holiday decorations, the parlor was actually a rather dreary room.

The last memory-scene had given her a speck of clarity. Finally, she had a name to go with the face that had somehow lodged in her unconscious. Why had he been in her nightmare? There was something else there, having to do with the man himself. He seemed a pleasant enough gentleman, but there was just... something. Maybe he was responsible for all of this, the memories, her missing family, and her prison of thorns. If that was so, then it only stood to reason that he was the man in tails sneaking about the house.

She jumped from the sofa, ready to search him out, but found herself suddenly overcome with fatigue. Her limbs were heavy as iron. The parlor became fuzzy, the furniture doubling. The ticking, which had become so pervasive she barely noticed it anymore, seemed to skip a *tick*. Or was it a *tock?* It hurt her head to think about it.

Sophie fell back, landing hard on the sofa. Leaning over, she put her head close to her knees, closed her eyes, and concentrated on her breathing. Focusing on anything was difficult. Henry's face floated across her thoughts. The boy, scolding her for running away; the studious fifteen-year-old who wanted nothing more than to change the world one building at a time. And finally, the young man on the edge of adulthood, his bright blue eyes piercing her right through her heart. She reached for the locket, the solid feel of it grounding her. Once she was free, she would find out once and for all what Henry Rittenhouse felt for her. She let herself imagine the kiss she had wanted from him. Were his lips as soft as they looked? Low in her belly, a not-unpleasant flutter made her gasp. The dizzy, breathless feeling faded. She opened her eyes. One parlor. And the freezing cold, which was probably the reason for her sudden infirmity. Before she went looking for whoever was playing hide-and-seek, she needed to warm herself.

Sophie made a fire in the parlor's fireplace (this time avoiding splinters) and sat cross-legged on the hearth, letting warmth wash over her. After a few minutes, she stood and shook out her limbs. Much better. The ticking seemed to have righted itself, but there was no sign of the intruder. He was here somewhere, and now she could properly search the house.

Before she took a step the clock chimed midnight. Again. She ran to the hall, the key in her hand, but spied no light beneath the dining room door, no warmth in the metal of the key. And no coattails disappearing around the corner.

The sound of voices made her turn so fast she nearly fell. She held her breath, listening, hoping it hadn't been her imagination. There was nothing but the ticking. *Am I going mad?* She supposed it was to be expected in such a situation, but she found no comfort in that.

Again—the distinct murmur of someone speaking in low tones. It came from the library.

"Marta, you must see reason."

Sophie's breath caught in her throat at the sound of her father's voice.

"Wake up, Henry. Henry, are you alright?"

Henry tried to pry his eyes open, but there was so much pain in his head he couldn't manage it. "I think so. Could you not yell quite so loudly?"

"I'm not yelling."

Henry heard the smile in Alphonse's voice. He did not find his current state half as funny. "What happened?"

"I was hoping you could tell me, chum. I was poking around the cemetery, looking for Faber. I found him." Alphonse paused, a strange look on his face. "Or rather, he found me. He could see me."

"He *saw* you?" Gabriel said. Henry hadn't realized he was there.

Alphonse nodded. "He was wearing a pair of strange-looking goggles. Must be the same kind Irene said those men who came to kill us were wearing. He snuck up on me."

"I thought that shout was you." Henry put a hand on his forehead, hoping to push the pain out of his aching skull. "That's why I came inside."

"That's why you disobeyed my orders, you mean?" Gabriel took no care to keep his voice low, which Henry thought might have been on purpose. "You're lucky Faber didn't kill you."

"Are you sure he didn't? This feels very much like death." Henry managed to get his left eyelid open a fraction of an inch. "Which would make you two angels, I suppose. Oh, lord, no. I guess I survived."

Alphonse laughed. "You made a joke. And here I thought you had no sense of humor."

"Come on, get up." Gabriel's tone brooked no argument. Someone clasped Henry's hands, his arms pulled upward so forcefully that his body had no recourse but to follow. He opened his eyes fully, which did nothing to ease the ache in his head.

"What happened?" the blurry shape that vaguely resembled Alphonse asked. "Faber clobbered me and I was out for a few seconds. When I came to, I found you, but he was gone."

"He—" Henry swayed as the world spun, and then regained his balance. "He snuck up on me, too, while I was busy looking at his time machine. I have no idea what he hit me with, but it feels as if I've been run over by a hack."

"You're sure it was him?" Gabriel's question struck Henry as odd, but to be fair, he hadn't actually *seen* Faber.

Henry rubbed the back of his neck. "Who else could it have been?"

The pause that followed made Henry uncomfortable.

"We aren't positive that Faber is alone." Gabriel finally replied. "But we've no proof he isn't, either."

Henry slowly, painfully, turned his head toward Gabriel. He was a little less blurry than Alphonse had been. "I didn't see anyone, just his time machine. It appeared rather better done than ours." Something occurred to him. "How did he get it all the way down here to the cemetery? When we traveled, we stayed in one place."

Alphonse, who was nearly in focus, rubbed his chin. "There are two possibilities. First, the most likely, is that he moved his machine to the cemetery back in our time, and then left from there, so that he will always travel in the cemetery. The advantage is, of course, that the cemetery is a fairly solitary place that has been and will likely remain the same over many years. He won't be landing inside someone's house, or in the middle of a road. Of course, it's quite a bit of work to wheel a giant cabinet down the road without anyone noticing."

"And the other?" Gabriel sounded impatient.

"That's a bit more frightening." Alphonse pulled on the rim of his cap. "That he's somehow figured out how to not only travel in time, but in space. So he can leave his workshop in 1885 and reappear in 1876 in the cemetery."

Gabriel furrowed his brow. "That does complicate things. He could hide anywhere in the world, anytime."

"And if *that's* true," Alphonse said, "why did he come back here? What's so special about this time and place?"

"Why did he travel in time at all?" Henry blinked rapidly; his vision finally cleared. "Why not just run away to Europe, or South America? If he's only trying to hide from what he's done to Sophie, why bother?"

Gabriel avoided Henry's gaze and question. "I have no idea why he came to this time. He's gone now, and that worries me more." He glanced over his shoulder. "We need to get back to our own machine and follow him."

Gabriel started back toward the cemetery's gate.

"But... isn't it a time machine?" Henry asked, jogging to catch up. "Can't we just follow him to whenever he goes and be there right away?"

"Theoretically. I mean, if you just want to travel in time, then yes." Alphonse walked beside Henry, his leisurely stride in opposition to

Gabriel's hurried gait. "I've never done this before, so it's all theoretical until it isn't. We're not just traveling in time. We're following his temporal disturbance. It's like a trail. And, again theoretically, if we wait too long, the trail will dissipate, and we won't be able to find him."

"Theoretically." Henry paused. "Who's theories are we talking about?"

"That's need to know." Gabriel opened the gate and stepped onto the sidewalk. He spun to face Henry. "And you don't."

The words felt like a slap.

"The only reason you're here is because I couldn't leave you behind. I would have, but I didn't feel like drowning in the paperwork that I would have to fill out if those men we left behind murdered you. Just because you're here, don't think you're part of our team. I told you to stay in the carriage house. You didn't. Alphonse told you to stay outside the cemetery. You didn't. Instead, you got hurt. You could have been killed, or gotten my operative killed."

He stepped closer, so that he was nearly nose-to-nose with Henry. "And now, instead of a no-muss, no-fuss extraction, we have a huge mess on our hands. Mr. Rittenhouse, don't make me sorry I didn't leave you behind."

As Gabriel stalked off, Alphonse gave Henry a sympathetic look and followed. He should be angry, being spoken to in such a way, but he wasn't. Nothing that Gabriel had said was untrue, although he didn't have firsthand knowledge of the paperwork part. He wasn't part of the team, and he wasn't sure how he felt about that.

"I have my own mission, remember?" He yelled at their backs. "To save Sophie."

Neither Gabriel nor Alphonse acknowledged a single word.

"And nothing you say will stop me." Henry hadn't meant to add that. It sounded at once both heroic and pathetic. His companions walked out of the cemetery and disappeared behind the wall. Henry sighed, his bravado deflating and his ego just a bit bruised. He stuffed his hands in his pockets and trudged in their wake.

Alphonse reappeared at the gate, a smile on his face. "Come on, Henry. You don't want to be marooned in 1876, do you?"

CHAPTER VIII

S OPHIE STOOD BEFORE THE LIBRARY DOOR, UNABLE TO BREATHE. HER
father's voice, even raised as it was in some argument with her
mother, sounded like an angel's song. She fumbled with the key
and stuck it in the lock, but it did not turn. She beat on the wood, tears
burning in her eyes.

"Papa! Papa, Mama, it's me. It's Sophie. Please, let me in."

There was no answer, only more murmuring. Why would they
ignore her? She pressed her ear against the wood and listened.

"But Edmund, she's our only child. Don't ask me to send her away."

"Marta, there can be no discussion. That man came to our home,
spoke to our daughter. Miss Abernathy should never have let Sophie
out of her sight. Imagine what could have happened." There was a
sharpness in her father's voice that Sophie recognized, but it was
touched with a fear she had never heard.

"Nothing happened, though. We can keep a closer eye. Miss
Abernathy will be dealt with."

"She is dismissed, I have already done so."

Sophie stood back, ready to begin her assault on the door anew,
when a sound took her attention to the hall.

She came face-to-face with herself once again. It was the Sophie from
the garden. Younger Sophie hovered by the stairs, her eyes wide and
fearful as she hugged the bottom spindle of the banister. She watched
the library door for a few moments before tiptoeing across and pressing her ear to the door, completely ignoring the older Sophie. Another
memory, perhaps?

"She is going to England, Marta, and that is that." Her father's voice
was clear now. "The arrangements have already been made."

"How could you do such a thing so quickly?" Sophie's mother's
voice was an angry whisper. "Unless this was always your intention."

"No, it was not, Marta. Of course I don't *want* to send Sophie away, but neither do I want Faber to make good on his threats." Her father heaved a sigh so heavy with weariness Sophie thought it might fall through the floor. "I have had this plan in place for a long time now, as a precaution."

A familiar squeak from behind the door. Her father had leaned back in his chair. "It has been so many years since we last heard from Faber I had thought he had decided to leave us alone. But now... this is what must be done. I have already written to my cousins in New York. She will stay there for a week or two until I can secure her passage to England. Montgomery House has held a place ready for her, and I have written the headmistress as well, explaining everything."

"I cannot believe we can't protect her, Edmund."

"This *is* protecting her, Marta. Now, you must help her to understand, and get her things together. She will leave for New York tomorrow."

Sophie and her younger self both straightened, with tears in their eyes. The girl turned and looked up at Sophie, their eyes meeting.

"We didn't do anything wrong. It's that man. He's the reason we were sent away."

The girl ran upstairs, the thundering of her footsteps echoing in Sophie's heartbeat. Shock, surprise, and confusion swirled in her mind like a storm at sea as she stumbled back to the parlor.

The memory-girl had spoken to her, actually *saw* her. She should follow her upstairs, see if she was alright, ask her what she knew. But she was drowning in the storm of her own thoughts. Sobs burst from her throat. Her chest tightened as if being squeezed, and she pressed held her hand to her heart as she cried. Resentment toward her father, who had never been an easy man to love, flowed away in the flood of tears. She had thought him angry with her and that's why she had been sent to boarding school. Bundled into a carriage one day, with no explanation given, sent to New York, and then put on a boat to England. She had vowed to never forgive him, but now her heart ached to hug him tightly and beg his forgiveness.

She breathed deeply. Father wasn't here, he was somewhere outside, trying to get to her. If he would send her across the ocean to keep her safe, he would certainly be trying to free her now. She owed it to him to help herself.

Why had her father feared Alexei Faber? He had made no threat to her. Her father mentioned a vendetta. What did he mean?

Why hadn't she remembered this overheard argument until now? So many of these memories had been locked away in her mind and only whatever magic she was tangled in had released them.

The voices had fallen quiet, and Sophie was left only with the ticking, the cold, and her loneliness. She returned to the parlor and stoked the fire. The more she thought about it, the angrier she grew.

She tried to think back to the time before she had woken up. What had she done yesterday? Gone shopping for the party with her mother, of course. Then decorated the house and tasted all the treats. Her mother had told her to take a nap before the party. Then the dream, the nightmare… and then she woke up to find everyone gone, and the house dark, cold, and empty, with no sign that it was a holiday. The memories, the key, the locket?

None of it made any sense. Sophie stood, determined. She would make it make sense.

The long walk from the Upper Burial Ground to Coulter Street was covered by awkward silence. Henry kept his head down; the words Gabriel had spewed at him fermented with every step. He hadn't volunteered for this. He had just been trying to find the blueprints for Sophie's machine. *Sophie's machine. When did I start thinking of it so?* It sounded ghoulish.

He supposed he was at least partly to blame. Henry wasn't a rule breaker. He did what he was told, ever since he had been a child. That seemed to go right out the window where Sophie was concerned. He had broken into a man's house, ignored the police, and disobeyed several of Gabriel's directions, all because he wanted to save Sophie.

He felt as if he had always loved her, though he knew that wasn't true. When they were younger, she had been annoying, always underfoot and getting him in trouble.

Then she had been sent off to finishing school. Which had always puzzled him. Her parents had never wanted her out of their sight and then suddenly she was halfway around the world. Henry and she had exchanged letters. Mother had said she would be homesick and need some comfort. He had done it, because he always did what his parents wanted, and then later because it seemed ungentlemanly to stop. She had written back. They were silly girl letters at first. Then, suddenly, they became more sophisticated, and instead of whining about missing home, she conveyed stories of her experiences. A shopping trip in London, a visit to the theater.

He found himself anticipating every missive.

She had returned for a visit, and that's when he knew that she was the girl he wanted to spend forever with. Still a spitfire, she had grown into a beautiful young woman full of surprises and not likely to follow the rules. His heart had spoken loud and clear.

"Whoa, Henry! Where do you think you're going?"

Henry stopped walking, but not of his own accord. Someone gripped his jacket, impeding his progress.

He turned and pulled his coat from Alphonse's fingers, with his hands forming fists, ready to defend himself. Alphonse raised his arms in a gesture of surrender.

"Easy, there! What are you going to do with those?" Alphonse pointed to Henry's fists. "Sorry, chum, but you were about to walk past the street." He pointed in the direction Gabriel was now heading. "Head in the clouds?"

"Just thinking." Henry lowered his hands. "And I am a pretty good boxer, by the way."

"Absolutely. A fencer *and* a boxer. Got it. Have you ever been in a street fight?" Alphonse clapped Henry on the shoulder and steered him up Coulter Street. Gabriel didn't bother waiting for them, just walked in the front door. Irene was already in the parlor, Tesla, as usual, gracing her shoulder.

"About time. Faber came back an hour ago."

Henry was only confused for a moment this time. Which was either an improvement, or unsettling. "And he's here? Now?"

"No, I locked him out of his own house and thought he'd just go away. Of course, he came in. I took care of it." Irene held up her weapon. Henry's stomach churned as he looked around the parlor. There was no sign of a body.

"No, Henry, I didn't kill him. What kind of person do you think I am? That would completely mess up the timeline." Irene put her weapon in her reticule and set Tesla on the floor. "I set it to knock him out. It's painful, but not lethal. Of course, now *our* Faber will probably have some kind of memory of this, but I was careful, and it couldn't be helped."

The idea that something that just happened could affect the memory of a person who wasn't even present made Henry's head spin again.

"Can we *please* move along?" Gabriel opened the secret door to the laboratory and held it for the others. Tesla ran in first, followed by Alphonse, then Henry, and finally Irene. Their time machine remained where they had left it. Alphonse tried to open the door.

"I forgot. Henry locked it." Alphonse smirked.

"I have the key right here." Henry held it out to him.

"What fun would that be? Now I'll show you." He stood before Irene. "If you don't mind?"

Irene rolled her eyes. "You are such a showoff." She reached behind her head, pulled out a hairpin and gave it to Alphonse.

"Yes, and you wouldn't like me half as much if I wasn't." Alphonse slid the hairpin into the lock and jiggled it around until the lock mechanism clicked open. "See? Simple." He hopped inside the wardrobe and began turning dials and flipping switches.

Henry crossed his arms over his chest. "To be fair, you aren't ten years old."

"Yes. But when I *was* ten years old. I could still pick that lock."

Gabriel gestured to Irene and Henry to get inside, and then he followed, shutting them into darkness.

"Here we go. Hold on to... well, just hold on."

A flash of light, like blue lightning, scored Henry's field of vision. It left behind a ghost-image that made him rub his eyes. As before, the time machine shuddered and shook, and the strange grinding noise assaulted his ears. His stomach lurched. The assault on his senses continued for what felt like hours but was likely seconds.

The change from cacophony to absolute silence was disconcerting. After a moment, there was a scraping sound.

"Remind me to put a handle inside, will you?" Alphonse continued to fiddle with the mechanism. "And that torch we have would be useful here, you know? Ah, never mind, here we are."

The door swung open, and light flooded inside. Tesla screeched.

"What the hell?" Gabriel said.

Henry turned his head away and tried to put his arm up to block the invading, blinding, light, but ended up hitting Irene instead.

"Ow! Watch out, if you please? Either close the door or go out!"

There was a release of pressure as either Gabriel or Alphonse stepped out of the cabinet. Henry stumbled behind them. He wiped his watering eyes, blinked a few times, and looked down.

Grass beneath his feet caused him to whip his head up. This time he was ready for the blinding sunlight.

"I thought we were supposed to stay in one place?" Henry's voice was layered with disbelief. Faber's workshop was gone. The house was gone. The entire *neighborhood* was gone.

Henry stepped away from the time machine and then looked back. The wardrobe stood in a large field, like an odd sort of outhouse. A few feet away ran a rutted dirt track. Off in the distance huddled a cluster of unfamiliar buildings.

He turned to the others. "Where are we?"

Irene looked as confused as he felt. Alphonse scratched his head. Only Gabriel appeared calm.

"We are still in the same place."

Three sets of eyes locked on to Gabriel. "Think about it."

Alphonse laughed. "Of course. We've gone back again. To a time before Faber's house was built." He clapped Henry on the shoulder. "Welcome to your hometown, in the Year-of-Our-Lord-We-Have-No-Idea."

"Oh, this is tedious! Just how to do we figure out what year it is?" Irene soothed Tesla, who sat curled in her arms, his head nestled at her neck.

"Well, it's hot." Alphonse took off his hat and jacket and wiped his forehead with his sleeve. "This has to be summer."

"Well, that certainly narrows it down. Some summer day in the long period of time before people lived on this spot."

Gabriel shaded his eyes with his hand. "We don't have time to argue over it. We're bound to be noticed sooner rather than later. And if we're as far back as all of that, we'll likely need a costume change."

"Unfortunately, our luggage has been misplaced," Irene quipped. "We'll have to... improvise." She gave Alphonse a pointed look, which he seemed to understand. He handed his hat and his jacket to Gabriel.

"Of course. I'll be right back. Don't miss me too much." With a grin, he sauntered back up the dirt road toward the village. Before he reached the buildings, he disappeared into thin air. It was no less disturbing watching it the second time, Henry thought.

"Where is he going?" he asked Gabriel.

"Reconnaissance," Gabriel replied, his gaze still pointed in the direction Alphonse had gone. "Next item of business is to figure out where Faber is and why he came here. He's definitely out of his own timeline, so there must be something or someone here he needs."

"You don't know?" Henry shouted. "I thought that was the whole point. I thought you knew everything about him."

"Stop shouting." Gabriel glanced over his shoulder, but they were still alone on the side of the road.

Henry was tired of being told what to do. "I thought this would be a simple matter of finding him and taking him back to our time."

"I never said that." Gabriel looked at Irene. "Tell me, did I ever say that?"

"Well, perhaps you did, but it's never that simple, is it?" Irene stroked Tesla, who now sat contently on her shoulder, seemingly unperturbed by recent events. Her expression softened. "I like you, Henry, and your heart's in the right place. But I know what you're thinking, quite literally. Please, don't do anything rash. We all really want the same thing here."

Damn, how did she do that? Henry *had* been thinking of going off on his own again. "I don't think that's true. I think our objectives are very different."

"No, our *reasons* are different." Irene kept her voice soft and soothing. "We can help you, but not if you make our job more difficult. By the way, you are probably the most open person I have ever met."

"I have no idea how it is even possible that you can read my mind, as you say." Henry's anger rose like a kettle of boiling water. "But if you are, and not pulling a charlatan's trick, please stop."

Irene seemed unperturbed by Henry's words. "I can't help it with you. Gabriel and Alphonse have learned to muffle their thoughts. You can try that. I'll try not to pay attention, but it's like you're shouting in my ear."

Henry had no idea how he could change his way of thinking, but he would try to be more mindful of *what* he thought when Irene was around.

"Good idea," Irene replied to the unspoken idea. "Oops, sorry."

Gabriel leaned against the time machine, his arms crossed over his chest. "Can we please get back to business? Think about where Faber might be."

Henry had an impressive thought. "What about the Upper Burial Ground? If Faber's machine is like ours, and can travel through time only in one place, shouldn't it be there now?"

Gabriel seemed surprised by the suggestion. "Good thinking. Does the Burial Ground exist in this time, I wonder?"

"The Burial Ground is as old as Germantown." Henry pointed to the buildings in the distance. "Unless we've gone back to before 1692, it's there. And if we are further back than that, the machine will be in the same place, no matter what is there."

"That will be our first stop, then, once Alphonse returns."

"Ask and you shall receive."

Alphonse reappeared with a full burlap sack over his shoulder. In his other hand he held a rolled-up piece of paper.

Gabriel tilted his head. "Record time. What do you have for us?"

Alphonse deposited the sack on the ground at their feet. "New garments. Enough to make sure we blend in." He held out the piece of paper. "This is much more important."

Gabriel took it and uncurled it. Scanning it for a moment he returned it to Alphonse with an incredulous look.

"You're sure this is correct? It's not old?"

"I lifted it from a corner boy on Market Square. It's current."

Gabriel's brow furrowed. "Then we have a big problem." He turned the paper around to show Henry and Irene. It was a newspaper, called *The Pennsylvania Gazette.*

"I've never heard of that paper." Henry pulled it from Gabriel's fingers so he could give it a closer inspection. It read like a history book. There were several articles espousing patriotism and reviling the Crown, as well as a list of military actions by John Hancock.

"It went out of business eighty-five years before we left," Gabriel replied, as if he kept that fact hidden in his pocket on the off chance it might come up. "That's not the important part. Check the date."

Henry skimmed the paper's masthead. On finding the date his jaw dropped.

"July 3, 1776."

CHAPTER IX

SOPHIE'S STOMACH CHURNED WITH BOTH HUNGER AND FEAR. HOURS and hours had passed and no word from the outside world.

Had it been hours? Or days? How can I know, when the clock refuses to tell proper time? She stood again in the parlor, closed her eyes, and listened. The ticking. Steady as her own heartbeat, pervasive as air. No other sounds. Where was her illusive intruder?

She slipped from the sofa and headed back into the entrance hall. Away from the fire, the cold crept into her bones again, and she shivered as she buttoned her jacket all the way to the top. The ticking seemed the same out here as in the parlor. She trudged upstairs, searching each room for the person in the tailcoat as she listened for any increase or decrease in the sound. Neither goal found satisfaction.

Back downstairs, the dining room and library doors remained locked. The kitchen door, however, swung open easily. It was back to its usual familiar self, just like the parlor had done. She stood in the middle of the room, alone, but the ticking wasn't louder or softer here either.

"It seems to be coming from the house itself." She had grown quite comfortable with talking to herself, it seemed. Her stomach growled in response.

Sophie grabbed a jar of canned peaches from the pantry and took them to the kitchen table. A quick rummage through the drawers elicited the church-key opener. A second later there was the satisfying *pop* of the jar opening. She tried to use a spoon to scoop out the delightfully sweet peaches, but her hunger soon overtook her, and she ended up with the jar in her hand, slurping the fruit from it, juice running down her chin.

Once her growling stomach was satisfied, she cleaned up herself and the mess. Her mind was clearer, but she was no closer to answers. The cold seeped through her clothes. She took herself back to the parlor and sat cross-legged in front of the hearth.

She tried again to recall what had happened before she woke up. Her mother telling her to go and rest before the party. Going to her room and closing the door. And then... she couldn't recall if she had actually lain down. She had thought about going riding. No, she only dreamt she had climbed down the drainpipe and met Henry at the bottom. She must have because she woke up in her bed. Why couldn't she remember lying down?

She touched the key in her pocket, willing it to grow warm.

A soft *click* caught her attention, barely audible above the ticking and the crackling of the fire. Slowly, carefully, she crept into the corridor. Empty. She tiptoed along the hall, stopping exactly where she had before.

The library door had opened, just an inch. There was no sign of the intruder, but he could already be inside. A few steps more brought her to the threshold. The scent of cherry tobacco wafted out into the hall. The smell of her father. She gave the door a slight push, and it swung open. Like every other room, it was stood empty.

This room doubled as her father's study. Sophie crossed the floor and sat behind his big, heavy desk, in his leather-covered swivel chair. She leaned back, the chair letting out the familiar creak. Her father sat here, she didn't know how many hours, keeping the books, managing the factory's inventory, writing the payroll checks for his employees. She had grown up watching him at his desk.

Leaning her elbows on the desk, she propped her chin in her hand. Everything looked as it always did — the green ink blotter, the bottle of ink, a canister full of fountain pens. A snow globe that had come from Germany, as a gift from his great-aunt. Sophie picked it up and shook it. Swirls of snow engulfed the tiny village inside, a beautiful winter wonderland that made her smile. She put it back and her eye wandered over a pile of letters stacked neatly, as usual, at one corner of the desk. The envelope on top bore familiar handwriting. She picked it up and discovered the penmanship was her own. The letter was addressed to her father.

"Of course, it is," she said. "This is his desk, who else would it be addressed to?" The letter was open, the top edge sliced cleanly by her father's slim brass letter opener. Sophie bit her lip. It was terribly rude to read another's personal correspondence. Then again, she had written it, so it wasn't as if she were reading something private.

She pulled out the paper, unfolded it, and began to read.

Henry stared at the date on the newspaper, the full weight of the situation falling on him like a brick building. "We're in 1776. *July* 1776?"

Alphonse's crooked smile did not mock him. "At least we know you can read. Maybe we know why Faber came here, then?"

"Forgive me, gentlemen, but explain it to me, if you please?" A crease had formed in the middle of Irene's forehead, matching the one on her pet. Tesla hadn't moved from his mistress's shoulder, only studied his surroundings with what seemed like distrust.

"Sorry, my darling Brit. I forget that you might not recognize the date." Alphonse bobbed his head in a small bow. "Though I'd think you know the date America told good ol' King George to stick it up his bum."

"Nice, Alphonse." Gabriel took the paper from Henry and rolled it up. "Two days ago, the Continental Congress officially declared its independence from Britain. Tomorrow, many of the Founding Fathers will meet at Independence Hall and sign the Declaration of Independence. The final wording will be approved at that meeting, and the day will live on forever in the hearts and minds of Americans everywhere."

At Gabriel's words, the color drained from Irene's face.

"He means to stop it from happening?"

Gabriel shook his head. "I have no idea what he means to do, whether to stop it or alter it or kill George Washington so the patriots lose the Revolution. Doesn't matter, none of it is good. The repercussions would ripple across history."

Alphonse rubbed his chin. "Why would he want to do that? It doesn't make any sense. I completely understand the revenge angle back home, after what happened with his—"

Gabriel shot him a look sharp enough to cut skin.

Alphonse closed his mouth with a snap, leaving Henry with the feeling he was missing an important piece of information.

"This must be his primary mission, the one he's being paid to do. His previous stop was for something else, maybe something personal. We know who is pulling his strings, thanks to Irene."

"I think we'd better move along, gentlemen." Her gaze was fixed on the distant buildings, but Henry saw nothing. It actually looked as if she were listening rather than looking. "Before we're noticed." Her gaze shifted to meet Gabriel's, communicating something Henry did not grasp.

Gabriel, however, seemed to get the message loud and clear. "Alphonse, you said you have our new attire?"

"If you'll step this way," Alphonse swept his arm toward their unconventional conveyance. "I will show you a lovely array of the finest garb the 18th century has to offer." He opened the sack and pulled out bundles of cloth.

"Where did you get these?" Henry asked.

Alphonse only winked and smiled a rakish grin.

"Why do I get the feeling that someone will be missing these from their washing line?" Henry said with an admonishing look.

Alphonse shrugged. Henry didn't argue. The three boys walked behind the wardrobe to change. Irene followed and began unhooking her corset.

"What are you doing?" Henry shouted. A fierce heat that wasn't from a Philadelphia summer rose in his cheeks. Apparently, Irene had left her modesty back in 1885.

Irene didn't even look up at him. "I'm changing my clothes, what does it look like?" Only one hook remained on the corset. "Are you embarrassed? Because I'm not. It would be a silly thing, you all changing out here while I suffocate in that box."

"I'm sorry, but I'm not comfortable with this." Henry wasn't sure which shocked him more—Irene's behavior or Gabriel and Alphonse's lack of propriety. "I must insist you change out of sight."

Irene finally did look up at him, her corset in her hand, her shirt untucked from her split-skirt trousers. "Have you ever worn a bustle? Or three petticoats? Of course you haven't. A lady needs room to move when she dresses. It's almost an acrobatic feat." She looked at Henry and sighed. "All right, fine. Not for my sake, but before your head explodes." She marched around the corner and into the wardrobe. "But I'm leaving the doors open so that I don't perish of heat prostration."

There wasn't any cover, so Henry tried not to think about who might be watching as he removed *his* wool trousers, shirt, shoes, and coat. As quick as possible, he pulled on thick white stockings, knee-length breeches, a linen blouse, an embroidered waistcoat, and a long-tailed jacket. It wasn't much cooler than what he had removed, but at least he looked the part. Alphonse handed him a black tri-cornered hat.

Irene stepped out of the wardrobe. "Well, what do you think? I don't have a petticoat, so this skirt is too long." Her simple dress was indigo blue cotton, with a square neckline and a white pinafore. A white mob cap covered her hair. She looked respectable, save for the mischievous look in her eye.

Tesla followed her from the wardrobe, hopping onto his mistress's shoulder.

"Irene, darling, you can't bring your pet. He's got to stay here." Alphonse's tone was gentle, and Henry realized the curly-haired boy fancied her. His gaze lingered on her scar for a moment. "We're trying to stay incognito."

Irene reached up protectively. "He can't stay here alone. If anyone asks, I'll say that I've just come from the Caribbean."

Alphonse opened his mouth to protest, then closed it again with a shake of his head.

He was dressed much the same as Henry, though the clothes were a bit looser on his slight frame. Some gentleman would be missing *two* sets of clothes from the wash.

Or three.

Gabriel stepped from behind the wardrobe. The clothes Alphonse had given him were still in his hand. He handed the clothes to Alphonse.

"I can't wear this."

Alphonse held up his hands. "What? Not a good fit? I did the best I could without a tape measure and chalk. I'm not a tailor."

Gabriel shifted his weight to one side, looking not amused. "It's not that, Alphonse. Look at that paper again. Not just the date, but the articles. There's a dozen advertisements, offering rewards for runaway slaves." He rubbed his hand across his short hair. "I'm not equal here. Not that I was exactly equal where we came from—"

"Gabriel," Alphonse interrupted. "You're in charge of this crew."

"You know what I mean. I can't even pretend I'm equal here. If I wear the clothes of a gentleman, or even a merchant, it will not go unnoticed. And we want to be unnoticed."

Henry had to admit, he hadn't even considered what people in this time would think of brown-skinned Gabriel, Secret Service Agent and Thorn in His Side.

"You can't know that," Irene interjected. "This is Philadelphia, after all, not South Carolina."

Gabriel shook his head again. "Take my word for it, this will not work. I'm going to need something less fancy."

Alphonse snapped to attention. "Your word is my command. Just wait right here." He disappeared into thin air once more, and Henry only knew where he was by the trail of crushed grass he left in his wake.

Alphonse returned in fifteen minutes.

Gabriel took a pair of trousers the color of mud and a plain white shirt from his hand. "Much better." He disappeared around the back of the cabinet.

"And this is for you." Alphonse handed a petticoat to Irene. "I hope it will do."

"Looks perfect, thanks." Irene pinched Alphonse's cheek and then proceeded to pull the garment on beneath her skirt. Henry turned his head away and changed the subject.

"So, can you all do that? Turn invisible?"

"No, of course not, that's ridiculous," Alphonse said. "Why would we need three people who can become invisible?"

"Right. So you do that, and Irene can... I can't believe I'm saying this... read minds."

"Yes, I can, dear." Irene pulled her skirt over the petticoat. "And don't think I didn't hear those thoughts about me while I was putting this on, Heinz."

Henry's face burned. "I never told you that was my name."

"I know. And I know you hate it. As I said, your thoughts are no effort to read."

Henry was almost afraid to ask. "How can you do that?"

"I have no idea. I've just been able to, as long as I can remember."

"I felt you in there, poking around," Henry whispered. He was a little afraid of Irene. Which he supposed she knew already. He hurried to change the subject. "So, Gabriel, you have some *other* kind of special... extra?"

Gabriel stepped from behind the time machine, buttoning his brown jacket. He put a round, wide wide-brimmed hat onto his head. "Yes. That's part of the reason we were recruited by the Secret Service and Scotland Yard."

"So that's how you can be so young and working for the government." At long last, something made sense to Henry.

Gabriel's gaze shifted quickly. "That's right."

"So, what can you do?"

Gabriel seemed not to hear the question. "We need to find Faber and bring him and his machine back to Washington." His business-like tone ended the conversation. Henry was sure Gabriel would reveal his ability eventually, like the other two had.

"Alphonse, you and Irene head to the Upper Burial Ground and see if Faber's time machine is there. Ask the locals if they've seen him, make up a story about being relatives or something. If you find anything useful, use the photophone. If you come up empty, meet us in Philadelphia." He dug in the pocket of his discarded jacket and pulled out a bit of paper and a pencil. He scribbled something down and handed the paper to Alphonse. "This address."

"I thought we were in Philadelphia," Irene said.

"Not at this time," Henry piped up, glad to be of some use. "This is Germantown, and in 1776, it's still separate from the city. Philadelphia is about eight miles from here."

"Which means we'd better get moving." Gabriel walked down the path, toward town. Henry remained for a moment, unsure whether to follow.

"Are you coming or not?" Gabriel tossed his words over his shoulder. Henry started to run after him, then ran back and locked the time machine again. His action earned him an eye roll and a shrug from Alphonse.

"It makes me feel better, all right?"

"All right, chum. Stay out of trouble." Alphonse tipped his hat, and Henry hurried to catch up to Gabriel.

"There won't be a train here for another fifty years at least," Henry mused, trying to make conversation. "We'll need to hire a hansom, or horses, or find out when the next coach leaves."

"*You* will go and find us a pair of horses." Gabriel reached into his pocket and pulled out some folded paper. He handed it to Henry, who unfolded it and goggled.

"You just happen to have a handful of Colonial currency in your pocket?" He flipped through the bills, an unsettled feeling in his chest. There were bills marked *United Colonies*, dated February 1776, and a few older bills from other colonies; Virginia, North Carolina, New Jersey.

Gabriel stopped and turned to meet Henry's astonished gaze. "In this line of work, it's best to be prepared. Let's just leave it at that."

"How could you possibly be prepared for this?" The question carried with it both disbelief and suspicion. "Even if you knew what

Faber was up to, you couldn't possibly know what he was going to do with the time machine, or when he would go." Realization hit Henry like a strike to the chest. He stopped in the middle of the dirt track.

"You *did* know. But how?"

Gabriel chuffed. "You can't possibly be this naive. It boggles the mind. Look, I told you, we've been monitoring Faber's movements for a while. Combined with intelligence from Scotland Yard. We were able to postulate a few scenarios if we didn't get to him before he used the time machine. We assumed it would work, and we prepared. Let's leave it at that and return to the task at hand."

Henry held the script out to Gabriel. "Why am I hiring the horses, then, if you think I'm so unqualified?"

"Because we don't have a choice. I can't leave you alone, obviously. Even in a time near your own you got into trouble. If I leave you alone here, who knows what would happen. Irene and Alphonse can use their skills to get information faster than we could. Which leaves you with me, and if I walk up to a stable and hand them a pile of money and ask to hire horses, there will be more questions than we need."

Henry had to think about what Gabriel was saying. "Black men have been free for nearly fifty years. Longer than that in the North. Black men fought in the Revolution. You work for the *U.S. government.*"

"Not today I don't. Things here aren't as bad as the South, but I can be hanged as a runaway or sold as property, even in Pennsylvania. Even if I was a soldier in the war. As much as it pains me to do it, I have to act like your servant." Gabriel grimaced. "Your slave."

"I won't treat you that way." Henry couldn't keep the quiver from his voice. "It's inhuman."

"You will or else everything will come undone." Gabriel's response was low, his tone dangerous. Then he sighed. "I appreciate the sentiment, but believe me, it will be nothing I haven't experienced before. Not everyone is as enlightened as you think you are, Mr. Rittenhouse."

Henry heaved a sigh. Of course, Gabriel was right. But it was one thing to have been told what happened in the past, and another to have to live history and pretend to be the kind of person that believes others are their property.

"Fine. But I'm going to be the kindest slave owner there ever was." He pressed his tri-cornered hat tighter onto his head. "If that's alright with you, Mr... you know, I don't even know your last name?"

"White." Gabriel's smile showed all of his teeth, the same color as his name.

Henry stared at him, open-mouthed. Could this get any more ridiculous?

"Of course it is."

Sophie read the letter twice before putting it back into its envelope. Her own words, written years ago, sounded as if they were written by a stranger. A *young* stranger. The missive was one of the first she had sent upon her arrival in England. She had begged to come home, begged to know what it was she had done wrong. Reading the words brought back some of the pain. There were more letters beneath the first, but she didn't need to read them. They all said the same embarrassing things.

Her parents had sent her away to protect her from Alexei Faber, for some reason she had yet to discover. Why did her father keep them here, on his desk? Was it so he could torture himself with her childish words?

She absentmindedly sorted through the pile of envelopes. At the bottom was one that bore very different handwriting. Bold strokes in black ink spelled out her own name and the address of her boarding school. A glance at the return address made her stomach fill with butterflies.

The letter was from Henry.

What was this letter doing here? Had her father *read* this letter? Sophie let out a little gasp. What if he had? They had written so many letters over the years. But it was Henry, so it wouldn't say anything scandalous.

She pulled it out and looked at the date. Not long after her visit home, summer before last. Usually most of the girls at school went home, to spend summer on their families' country estates or take trips to the Continent. But Sophie and one or two others had always stayed, until that particular summer. The school was closed for repairs after a spring of terrible storms, and no one could remain. Her father had wanted her to visit London, even suggested she take the time to get to know her cousins in New York. She had insisted on coming home to Philadelphia, though she had a feeling her mother had had something to do with his finally allowing it.

The summer had been too short. She had hoped to find her father less restrictive, since she was nearly fifteen. But, if anything, he had become even more so. Shopping trips had been carefully arranged; Sophie shuttled from carriage to shop door to carriage again. She was not allowed to visit any of her friends, or even her mother's friends. Guests came to the house, invited by her parents. She spent the entire summer sweltering inside, the only fresh air coming through the windows, and the only freedom she saw was what she could glimpse while getting in and out of a carriage.

The Rittenhouses were her parent's closest friends. They had come nearly every afternoon, gathered in the parlor over tea and cakes or occasionally a strawberry ice. Henry hadn't accompanied his parents on every visit, in fact, after the first time Sophie had been surprised to see him again at all. He had arrived looking glum, sitting on the love seat as if he had been condemned to death instead of an afternoon in the Weber's parlor. Sophie's father had engaged him in conversation, asking him about his studies. Henry had become animated, brightened at that, talking on and on about the most boring things Sophie had ever heard in her life. Bridges. Buildings. *Canals*. And oh, my, surveying! The conversation combined with the heat had made Sophie nearly fall asleep. Finally, his own mother had interrupted.

"Henry, dear, it's fascinating, and I'm so proud of you. Sophie, how are you getting along in England, my dear? Is it lovely there? Have you been to London?" There was a look in Mrs. Rittenhouse's eyes, a sparkle that spoke of a longing to see beyond Philadelphia.

"It is lovely, and I'm getting along well, thank you." There was no sense in burdening *Fraulein* Rittenhouse with the truth. She set her teacup and saucer down on the table, exactly as she had been taught. Her hands went back in her lap, and she was careful not to use them when she talked. "The courses are rigorous, of course, but I'm doing well in music and my French is fluent. I'm sure Miss Finch would be so proud."

Mrs. Rittenhouse nodded. Her smile was genuine, but the sparkle faded. "I'm sure, dear."

"However, I enjoy Latin the best."

"Latin? Whatever are they teaching that for?" Mrs. Rittenhouse nearly scandalized.

"A new, young teacher started it." Sophie tried not to convey the defensiveness she felt in her voice. "Only a few girls have taken it, but it's been enlightening." She had wanted to add that it was more interesting than sitting and embroidering all day, or learning to quill paper, but she held her tongue so as not to cause an uproar. She also decided not to mention the Maths course, to avoid unnecessary fainting.

"And yes, I've been to London. For shopping trips, and to see a play. It was wonderful, so much busier than Philadelphia, and even New York." Sophie lifted a cookie and took a bite, noticing the worried look she had received from her father at the mention of London. "But never without a bevy of chaperons, of course."

"You'll be returning to us again to us for your Season, I'm sure. To be presented at the Assembly Ball?" Mrs. Rittenhouse's voice pitched higher at the end. It was a question beyond casual conversation.

"I expect that I will." Sophie held back a sigh. Even though the Season was all the girls at school could talk about, she had no interest in attending any kind of ball. When she was finished school, what she wanted more than anything was her freedom. Obligation was nearly over, and adventures awaited.

Which was as likely to happen as her sprouting wings and flying away.

She stood, causing Henry and her father to jump to their feet. "Please excuse me, I'm tired. I think I shall lie down for a bit." Her parents and their guests bobbed their heads in dismissal.

She walked into the hall taking a long look at the front door. The temptation to walk out, just to take a stroll around the neighborhood, was great. She hadn't lied; she *was* tired. But more from inane, polite chatter than anything else. She was just about to go up when a voice stopped her.

"Miss Weber, could you wait a moment?"

Sophie had turned around to find Henry, standing just outside the parlor doors. He had pulled them nearly shut.

"Yes, Henry? I mean, Mr. Rittenhouse." She put her hand to her lips. "Sorry, am I being improper again?"

Henry had suppressed a smile. "No, of course not. I only wanted..." He had paused, as if waiting for something. "To ask you... if I could continue to write to you. At school."

Sophie tried to hide her surprise. "Of course. We are still friends, I hope."

Henry's smile faltered a little, and thinking back on it now, Sophie couldn't believe she had been so dense. Still, he had handled it well. He righted his smile and gave her a small, rather formal but oh-so-Henry bow.

"Thank you. I look forward to hearing all about your... adventures in England. Especially that Latin course." With that, he had gone back into the parlor.

Sophie's attention returned to the present. She considered the letter in her hand. Henry had thought a course in Latin was an adventure.

When she had mentioned the conversation to the girls at school, they had squealed with delight. At first, Sophie had pooh-poohed them.

"It's just Henry. We've written forever."

"Yes, but now he's *asked permission*," Alice, her best friend at school, gushed. "He's not doing it because his mother makes him anymore. It's completely different!" She had sighed deeply and fallen back onto the sofa, a hand to her breast. "It's almost as good as asking to court you!"

"Oh, stop it." Sophie had waved her silliness away. "It is not. It's *Henry*."

When this particular letter had arrived, the girls had swooned over his impeccable penmanship, the number of pages. She still brushed them off, but she found herself unwilling to read it aloud. Rereading it again, the letter *was* different than the previous ones he had sent. It was polite, of course, and appropriate. Just like always. Except the end:

> "I must admit that I was surprised at our meeting, Sophia. I hope you don't find me too forward for using your given name, but I feel it's appropriate in letter-writing where it's not in public. What surprised me was how much you have changed. When last we met, you were a child, with the ideas of a child. The young lady I met in your parent's parlor seems to have blossomed into something much more. You remind me of a rose. It begins as nothing more than a thorny plant, but it gives bloom to a flower of exceeding beauty."

The words took Sophie's breath away. How could she have missed it the first time? She was so afraid of saying something wrong, it had taken her weeks to reply.

She definitely hadn't shared this letter with her friends. Nor any of the others that had arrived in that year-and-a-half after. The letters became more affectionate, her replies easier to write. He had never asked to formally court her, though. Had he not intended to? She had never been courted, so she had no idea what was supposed to happen.

She looked at the pile left on her father's desk. *All* of Henry's letters were here. Sophie's face burned. How had they gotten to her father's desk? She had tied them all with a pink satin ribbon and placed them in her trunk when she left school for the final time.

Had her father read them? The idea mortified her.

She had no idea how or when they had gotten here, but she was going to take them back to her room. She just pulled the library doors closed when the clock in the foyer chimed the hour of midnight.

For the fourth time.

Henry and Gabriel rode side-by-side down a dusty, wheel-rutted road. Germantown faded into the heat haze three miles behind them. The man who ran the stable was only too happy to let him two fine steeds and some tack. Henry had the distinct feeling that he had been overcharged.

"What do you honestly think Faber is doing here?" Henry's question was mostly out of boredom. Eight miles wasn't that far to ride, but the road was deserted, everyone driven inside by the heat of early July.

Gabriel stood tall in his saddle. "I thought we had this discussion. I have no idea. And I really don't care, either. I have orders, that's all."

"Right." Henry swatted at a mosquito on the back of his neck. Something else ate at him, but he wasn't sure how to voice it without making Gabriel angry. Which, in his limited experience with the boy, was akin to juggling flaming torches while walking across a carpet of broken glass.

"You said you knew who was pulling Faber's strings. What does that mean? He's an inventor, not a... whatever you call someone who would muck up time." Henry looked sidelong at his dark-skinned companion. "And then there's our lady friend from Scotland Yard, and the two mountains masquerading as men who tried to turn us into jelly back in Faber's workshop. Their accents were definitely German."

Saying it all out loud was like snapping pieces of a puzzle together. He pulled his horse up short. "Faber's working for someone, and you know who it is."

Gabriel gave a resigned chuff and rolled his eyes. "Brilliant. University education certainly isn't wasted on you, is it. Yes, he is. Our intelligence says... look, it doesn't matter. Our mission is to bring him in and either turn him to our side, or at the very least get him to give us important information. Stopping him from whatever he's doing here in 1776 is a part of that mission."

"Who is he working for?"

Gabriel shook his head. "What does it matter? Would it change what you had to do, or what he's done?"

Sophie appeared Henry's mind, frozen in time beneath a thick sheet of glass, the years ticking away beneath her as the dial slowly counted out her hundred-year sentence.

"Because I need to know."

"You *want* to know why he's trapped Miss Weber." Something crossed Gabriel's face, a shadow of irritation and pensiveness.

"Of course. I've known Edmund Weber my entire life. He is an honorable, noble man, without an enemy in the world."

"Everyone has enemies." Gabriel steered his horse around a fly-covered pile of excrement.

Henry shook his head and slapped at another insect. "I heard what was in the letter he left. Obviously, there's some bad blood between them. I don't know why he chose an innocent girl as his weapon of revenge. And I don't know what any of that has to do with his coming to 1776."

"One has nothing to do with the other, really. But it does, too." Gabriel paused, then continued. "Tell you what. When we catch him, you can ask."

He kicked his horse, spurring him on ahead, leaving Henry scratching his head from more than mosquito bites.

Another half-hour brought them to the edge of Philadelphia. He pulled his horse beside Gabriel's and gawked. The town was so small, compared to the sprawling city he knew. Just a cluster of buildings on a carefully planned grid of streets. Philadelphia stretched from where he sat to the Delaware River, where giant masted ships floated across the glistening surface like something out of a pirate's tale. There was no palatial city hall, no elegant rowhomes on Delancy Place, no Academy of Music. No smoke-belching factories in Kensington. No Kensington.

Gabriel clapped him on the shoulder, making him jump. "Come on."

If the view from the city limits had been a shock, riding into town was enough to make Henry dizzy. He knew many of the buildings, but some were new to him, because they no longer existed in his time. Men and women walked the brick-paved sidewalks, their clothing outmoded.

Men in military uniforms marched around the corner. Their blue coats stood out against the dust and dirt of the street. They carried rifles across their chests, some affixed with bayonets.

"Don't stare, you'll draw attention," Gabriel muttered. Henry followed Gabriel's lead and kept his horse in place until the small regiment passed them by.

"That was... different." Henry pulled in a deep breath, just noticing he had been holding it the entire time the soldiers marched past. "I just didn't realize..." He didn't know how to verbalize what he was feeling.

Gabriel saved Henry from his anxiety. "This is a city at war. A country trying to be born. The Battle of Concord was a little more than a year ago, and just over a year from now will see both the British takeover of this very city and the Battle of Germantown. These are the hours of desperate men, taking a desperate act to secure their freedom." He didn't talk about it as if he were reciting lessons from a history book, but as if he had experienced it firsthand.

The Battle of Germantown. Henry knew of it, of course. Some of the houses in his beloved hometown still bore the scars. It was disconcerting to realize that if he went there right now, those black streaks and cannonball holes wouldn't be there.

It wasn't as if he didn't know a little about war, at least in the academic sense. He had two uncles he would never meet because of the Civil War. There were men in town missing limbs, or an eye, or a hand. Stories of battle were ones he had grown up with, romanticized through the lens of time and youth. But standing here on the brink of the American Revolution, the feeling of vulnerability was as thick as the humidity. Gabriel clucked softly to his horse and steered him in the direction the soldiers had gone. Henry followed.

"Where are we going?" Henry pitched his voice low, as if redcoats were hiding nearby and could hear him, waiting to brand him a traitor. A *patriot*, he corrected himself. These were the people who stood against a tyrant.

"Where do you go when you want to find out if anyone new has come to town?" They walked to the end of Market Street. Front Street and the river lay just ahead. Gabriel indicated they should turn left. Less than a block later, he pulled his steed to the curb in front of a row of shops. Henry steered his own mount to the hitching post beside Gabriel's and looked up at the sign above the door of a red-brick building.

City Tavern.

Gabriel swung himself from the saddle and landed on the dusty street. "The first Continental Congress met here, in 1774. Unofficially, of course."

Henry didn't ask how he knew that, only dismounted and met him beside the door. "Aren't we going in?"

Gabriel lifted an eyebrow and sighed. "Remember?"

It took Henry a moment to understand what he meant. "Oh, yes. Right. I'm still not used to this, sorry. Can you come in at all?" Henry hoped he wouldn't be on his own. He had no idea where to even begin asking about Faber.

"Not by myself, obviously. If I'm with you, it shouldn't be a problem."

An involuntary shiver ran up Henry's back. "I am no one's master, Gabriel, except my own."

"Oh, believe me, you sure as hell aren't mine. Just keep it together long enough for us to find out what we need to know, alright?"

Henry nodded and then pulled open the tavern door.

They entered a well-appointed hallway, with shining wooden floors and a staircase to the second floor. Henry hung his hat on the hook next to the door, beside a number of others. Gabriel also removed his hat, but made no movement to hang it.

"Last room on the left."

Henry followed his companion's direction. The room Gabriel directed them to had high ceilings with large, mullioned windows that looked out onto a walled garden filled with sunflowers. A wide fireplace took up most of the wall across from the door, the grate cold and dark. Gabriel subtly steered him toward a table in the corner. A serving woman, having delivered a pair of wooden tankards to another table, came to theirs.

"I'm sorry, sir, but this table is reserved for—"

"We know. We're meeting him." Gabriel's tone was low, but the words clear. The woman glanced at Henry, who nodded while trying to hide his confusion.

The server didn't argue. "Very well, then. Welcome to the City Tavern. Can I get you something while you wait?"

She directed her words at Henry alone. How did people ever live like this, as if other human beings didn't exist?

"Ah, well..." Henry's mind was blank. What did most people drink in a tavern in 1776? He decided to make the safest choice he could think of.

"An ale, please." He gave her a pointed look. "Make it two."

The woman glanced at Gabriel, her face unreadable, and nodded. "Certainly, sir."

When the server left, Henry leaned closer to his companion. "So, who are we waiting for?" he whispered. He didn't want to ask too many questions, though a hundred ran through his mind. When they had arrived in the city, Henry thought Gabriel was following a hunch. Now it seemed as if he had a specific plan. How could he be waiting for someone when everyone they knew, except Alphonse and Irene, were back in 1885? *Back, or forward?* Time travel was headache-inducing.

Gabriel sat back in his chair, pushing himself into the shadows. He waved Henry's question away, as his eyes scanned the room and returned to the door. Before Henry could press him any further, the serving girl returned with their drinks.

"Would you like something to eat, sir?" The barmaid said. "The cook's got a lovely pot pie for dinner today, smells delicious."

Henry didn't even think about it. "No, thank you." Even though he was starving—how long had it really been since he last ate? He didn't think it would do to be eating when whoever Gabriel was waiting for showed up.

"All right, then. Enjoy your ale." The serving woman left again.

Henry pulled his tankard closer to him and ran his finger around the rim. He was actually parched, though he didn't think the ale would quench his thirst. But now that he had asked for it, he had to at least appear to drink.

Gabriel took a sip from his own tankard. "Faber probably isn't using his real name here. He might have planned to, but now he knows we can follow him."

Henry bowed his head over his ale. He hadn't thought of that. Subterfuge and intrigue were not in his realm of expertise. Give him a river that needed a dam or a bridge, and he would be right at home. But spying? He couldn't say where to begin.

"Can you give me any indication as to why we are sitting in a tavern, drinking ale instead of out in the street looking for him?" Henry took a sip of the bitter drink, which made his mouth pucker. "I think I have a right to know."

Gabriel's expression did not change. "Enough questions. Just wait." He pulled a watch from his pocket and glanced at it. "Shouldn't be much longer now, anyway." He snapped the watch closed and tucked it into his pocket. "Hopefully he hasn't changed his habits."

Henry's eyes followed Gabriel's hand. "Didn't you tell Alphonse that you lost your watch?"

Gabriel shrugged and gave a small smile. Henry supposed it didn't matter now, but the lie irritated him. He had had to give up his own prized timepiece so they could escape their pursuers, while Gabriel kept his safe in his pocket. Gabriel's cryptic words only added to his headache.

A strange buzzing sound erupted from Gabriel's jacket, like an angry mechanical bee. Henry jumped, ale rushing up his nose, and he looked around nervously, waiting for someone else in the room to notice the noise. No one even looked their way.

Gabriel reached into his pocket. Despite his nonchalance, he slipped further into the corner. He pulled out his photophone and flipped open the lid.

"Hello, Gabriel." Alphonse's voice was tiny but no less energetic.

Gabriel lowered his voice so only Henry and Alphonse could hear. "Did you find Faber?"

"Nowhere to be found. But we *did* find his time machine. Right in the Upper Burial Ground, same place as last time."

Henry felt a little proud at having had the idea. Maybe he could be a spy, after all.

"Can you disable it?" Gabriel's nose was almost up against the glass. The screen glowed up at him, giving his face an odd cast.

Alphonse's tiny voice was loud and clear. "Not without destroying it. It's locked up tighter than a nun's knickers."

Henry nearly choked on his ale for the second time. His spluttering didn't raise an eyebrow from the bar's other patrons, but it did garner a smirk from Gabriel.

"I see what Henry was talking about, though. It's a real beauty."

"If you've finished admiring our fugitive's work? You two come into town, to the address I gave you. Now." Without another word, he snapped the case shut and slipped it back into his pocket.

Five more minutes passed in silence. Henry was just about to find the serving girl and tell her that he would indeed like some chicken pot pie when the front door slammed.

"Oh, it's hotter than Satan's fireplace out there, isn't it?" A deep, jocular voice asked someone in the front hall. "I'll be at my usual table, Abigail. Bring me an ale, would you? And whatever is good from the kitchen."

A moment later the speaker appeared in the doorway. He was short, with a large belly that preceded him. His bare head was balding, the hair line running around the top of his pate. A pair of small, round, wire-framed spectacles perched on his nose. He looked familiar to Henry, but how could that be? The gentleman headed straight for his and Gabriel's table. Although the man carried a cane, his steps were quick and sure. The concerned and slightly irritated expression he wore changed into a small smile on his thin lips.

"Why, hello there, Mr. White. I didn't think I'd see you again."

Henry finally recognized the man and wondered if someone had put something in his ale. Because he must be hallucinating.

Gabriel actually smiled as he stood to shake hands with the man. "Hello, Mr. Franklin. Neither did I."

CHAPTER X

THE CHIME RANG ON, AND SOPHIE DIDN'T EVEN BOTHER TO COUNT. She almost tipped the desk chair as she jumped up and raced into the hall. There was only one other door left to open—the dining room. The tell-tale tailcoat was nowhere to be seen. She pulled the brass key from her pocket, but it remained cold, so she waited by the dining room door.

The clock continued to ring—surely it had reached twelve by now, hadn't it? The chime sounded odd, a strange twang as if its spring had been wound too tightly. Something ground together, like two gears that had gotten stuck.

She yawned deeply, her mouth stretching wide. *So sleepy.* The feeling came over her suddenly, like it had before in the parlor. Her head felt as if it were stuffed with cotton. Her thoughts floated in a fog, and her hands had gone numb. The ticking still permeated the air but was it slower than before, or faster? She couldn't seem to focus.

What was I doing? She stared at the floor, trying to re-orient herself. The key in her hand still hadn't warmed, and she could use warmth right now.

She put her hand to the wood. Like everything else, it was like ice. She tried to knock, but her arm was too heavy to lift. Turning, she leaned against the door, cold gripping her lungs like winter's icy grip. *So, so cold.* The hall looked strange; everything shone too bright, little stars popped across her vision.

Perhaps Father and Mother have been hiding in there this whole time and were just waiting for me to find them! That was absurd. They would never be so cruel. She slid down the door and sat on the floor. Her limbs would not move the way she wanted them to. She tried to call out, hoping the man in the tailcoat would hear, but no sound came. A tear slipped down her cheek, leaving a frozen path. She yearned for her mother's embrace.

Without warning, a ribbon of warm air blew across the hall. It kissed her cheek, smelling like rose water. The same scent her mother always wore.

"Oh, my Sophie."

Her mother's voice came from far away, muffled as if she were behind a wall.

"Mother? Mother, where are you?" She tried to push herself to her feet, but her knees buckled, and she fell again to the floor. Somewhere, someone cried. Was it her mother? It seemed to come from everywhere, like the ticking. The *ticks* and *tocks* mixed with unnerving clanking sounds. Sophie managed to crawl to the bottom of the stairs, calling. "Mother, I'm here. Come and find me..."

"Sophie, come back to me." It was definitely her mother speaking. But she sounded so far away.

"I can't find you, Mother." The tears spilled down her cheeks. "Help me."

Another blast of air blew over her, numbing her further. The voice was gone, leaving only the ticking, which had turned steady again.

"Mother?" Sophie sat on the bottom step, her hands over her face, weeping. Had it all been a hallucination, or another trick?

Sophie's heart broke into a thousand pieces.

Warmth blossomed at the center of her chest. It spread slowly, seeping into her skin.   Sophie pressed her palm to the spot and felt the now familiar lump of the locket. She gripped it through her layers of clothing, letting the warmth seep into her hand.

She had dreamed that Henry had given this to her. Sweet Henry. She *would* see him again. And kiss him properly when she did, propriety be damned.

The clock chimed again. A perfect Westminster chime followed by twelve *dings*. With each chime it became easier to breathe, easier to think. She wiped her damp cheeks with her free hand before reaching into her pocket. The key was warm at last. *So nice of you to join the party.* She stood, her body on alert for the man in the jacket, determined to catch him this time. When she did, she would force him to tell her everything. She moved like a mouse in a house of cats as she scanned the entrance hall for signs of him, and, when she found none, crept through the lower level of the house.

The key in her hand grew warmer and when it became too hot to hold, she dropped it into her pocket, where she hoped it would not burn through the fabric. The dining room could wait.

In the parlor, the fire burned low. The idea of rekindling it tempted her, but she resisted. She was almost to the door when she turned around and grabbed the poker from the set of tools on the hearth. This one was made of brass, with an ornate handle, far fancier than the one she had left on the porch. She gripped it tightly and headed back out to the entrance hall.

"Come out, come out, wherever you are," Sophie called as she mounted the stairs. She was done playing hide-and-seek. It was time to catch the white rabbit.

Henry's mouth hung open, like a freshly caught fish. He stared at the man standing beside their table, knowing that he had heard the man's name correctly. Henry had seen his image hundreds of times, and he looked exactly like his picture. It was still hard to believe that this was...

"Benjamin Franklin. I don't believe we've met." The man who introduced himself as one of the most influential people in American history held out a hand to Henry. Henry knocked the chair over as he stood to grasp it.

"It's very nice to meet you, sir."

In his head, he cringed. He couldn't believe he'd just used the words *very nice* to describe meeting *Benjamin Franklin*. Incredible... amazing... fantastic... all were better adjectives. He was so busy staring at the man that he forgot to let go of his hand. Mr. Franklin gently pulled it from Henry's grasp with a small chuckle and a twinkle in his eye.

"Well met as well, Mr..."

Henry nearly forgot his name. "Ri—"

"Weber." Gabriel said the name louder than he needed to, which garnered him glances from the people sitting at nearby tables. "This is Henry Weber." Henry gave him a curious look, but Gabriel glared at him, his head shaking ever so slightly. Whatever reason there was for giving a false name, Henry wouldn't begin an argument here in the middle of the dining room. He sat and took a gulp of his ale.

Mr. Franklin pulled his brow low and looked at him over the top of his spectacles. "German, eh? Not a Hessian, are you?" His serious stare made Henry nervous.

"No, sir. Of course not." He pulled at his collar, which seemed to have tightened around his neck like a noose. Mr. Franklin's mouth curled into a smile. "Of course you aren't. You wouldn't be sitting here with my dear friend Gabriel if you were."

Henry's mind to snapped to attention as he realized that Mr. Franklin had indeed greeted his companion by name. "You *know* Gabriel, sir?"

"Yes, I do. For many years. Been in a few scrapes together, haven't we?"

Gabriel tried to hide his smile. "That we have, sir. But forgive my friend and I for completely forgetting our manners. Please, sit down."

Benjamin Franklin pulled out the seat across from Henry and lowered his considerable frame into it. The wood protested with a creak, but the sturdy chair held.

Henry remained speechless. There were a million more questions, to add to the million he already had. The idea that Gabriel, who was no more than a year or two older than himself, could personally know Benjamin Franklin, who had died almost a century before either of them was born, was impossible.

Unless Gabriel had traveled in time before. Which was a plausible explanation, despite his claims to the contrary. He had already proven himself capable of lying. *He's a spy, lying is practically his job.*

"To what do I owe the pleasure of this unexpected visit?" Mr. Franklin did not pull himself to face the table, but instead leaned to the side, so that his head was near to Gabriel's. "The last time we met, you said you were headed South, into the French territory."

Gabriel rubbed his chin. "Indeed, I was, sir. I got... sidetracked. At any rate, I'm here now, and was hoping you could help us."

"Of course, of course. Anything for a friend." Mr. Franklin tapped his cane on the floor.

"I'm looking for someone. A stranger to this area, newly arrived."

Mr. Franklin chuckled. "We're a port city. Newly arrived happens hourly."

"He won't have come by boat. And he may or may not be strangely dressed, though he's smart enough to try and blend in." Mr. Franklin looked confused by the remark, but Gabriel just held out his hands. "It's complicated. I'm afraid he's come for a nefarious purpose."

The older man leaned even closer to Gabriel, his brow furrowing. "These are troubled times, you know. Newly arrived is only second to nefarious purpose, it seems. Is he a British spy?"

Gabriel shook his head and put a hand on the other man's arm. "He may be a spy of sorts, but not for the British." He sat back and gazed across the room.

Gabriel continued. "I only know he's here. And with things being the way they are, I don't want to take any chances. Tomorrow is an important day, and I think he's going to try and disrupt it in some way."

Mr. Franklin's brows raised to his nonexistent hairline and his voice dropped low. "How can *you* know that, sir? It's not exactly common knowledge what is planned for tomorrow's meeting. We declared independence openly and officially two days ago."

"It doesn't matter how I know, just that I do. And so does our man. Alexei Faber is his name. We need to find him as soon as possible. He could be after the delegates, or Independence Hall itself. Or the Declaration."

"*What* hall?" Benjamin's question was loaded with surprise, and Gabriel looked as if he had been caught with his hand in the cookie jar.

"Uh, the State House," he said quickly. "He may be planning an attack on the building."

Benjamin, amazingly, broke out in a grin. "That means we must be doing something right."

Gabriel shook his head. "Don't joke about this, Ben. This is bigger than you know. I can't explain. Just know that we need to find this man before he..." He paused, perhaps deciding the best words to use. "Literally changes history."

Sophie didn't bother creeping around the house as she searched for the intruder. It was her house, and she was taking it back. The key remained hot, its heat radiating against her thigh through the layers of clothing, providing some respite from the cold. There was no sign of the tailcoat, so she looked under the beds, in the closets, anywhere that a human might fit, making quite the racket and using words she was certain would have drawn out anyone decent to scold her. Her parents' bedroom and the spare room were empty, as was the sitting room. The bathroom gave her no joy either. She rattled the attic doorknob, but it remained locked.

There was only one room left—her own bedroom.

The hall stretched out before her like something from a carnival. The closer she got to the door, the faster her heart beat. Her hands turned icy as the sweat from her palms hit the air. Her steps fell in time to the ticking, each one sounding like doom.

After what seemed like hours, she arrived. Her door was closed, though she couldn't remember if she had shut it. She gripped the poker tightly, and, with one hand, turned the knob. The door creaked a bit as it swung open, like a jaw opening the mouth of an unknown beast. The fire she had built earlier had died down to coals that burned with an eerie orange glow. Sophie turned on the lamps. Their dim yellow light did little to push away the darkness. The room was empty. She cautiously checked the wardrobe and beneath the bed, even behind the standing mirror in the corner. Nothing.

Before she could decide her next move, the clock downstairs chimed once more.

Sophie intended to ignore it, but an angry chirping erupted from her pocket.

She grabbed the key, which vibrated like a trapped bird. Hissing in pain, the key dropped from her hand. dropped it. The key, now scorching hot, fell to the floor with a heavy clunk, its furious noise muffled by the carpet. Obviously, she could not ignore it, or whatever lay behind the next door, any longer, though she was tempted to just leave it lying there. Would it continue to heat until it melted?

"Oh, alright, fine." Sophie grabbed a glove from her dresser. With her hand better protected, she picked up the key. "Besides, I don't want to ruin the carpet, now, do I?"

As soon as she entered the foyer, the key began to cool. She turned toward the dining room, the last door in the hall she hadn't opened. And there he was. The man in the tailcoat slipped through the sliding double doors, his polished shoes and tailored coat whisking through the just-wide-enough opening. Sophie ran after, but the doors slammed together, very nearly pinching her nose.

"Oh, you are not getting away that easily. Not this time." She ripped off the glove and jammed the key into the lock, probably harder than she needed to. Wrenching it around, she pushed the doors open.

A wall of darkness greeted her, thick as black-strap molasses. Sophie was almost afraid to turn on the gas lamps. Cautiously, she extended her arm through the doorway. It was swallowed by the dark. She bent her arm around the door frame, fingers reaching for the familiar roundness of the switch.

It wasn't there. Neither was the wall that held it. A warm breeze blew across the threshold, smelling of damp earth. That was her only clue as to what memory she faced.

She took a deep breath, as if she were getting ready to dive into a pond. Then she stepped through and plunged into the darkness.

Not complete darkness, she realized. Pinpricks of light grew visible as her eyes adjusted. Stars. Of course. How had she failed to notice the half-moon hanging in the sky? It was behind her, out of sight from the doorway, that's how. She stood in the middle of an English garden, which backed up to a huge manor house. The house stood half in shadow, but Sophie knew the familiar turrets and gables. The place she had called home for the better part of four years.

Montgomery's School for Fine Ladies.

The walls of the enormous house rose from the ground, the gray stone of the manor turned the color of pewter in the moonlight. Windows dotted the facade, twinkling like the stars above. The air was warmer than back in the hall, but not warm enough to leave behind her jacket.

What am I doing here? She had given up trying to see any kind of rhyme or reason to the places the magic showed her, other than the fact that both Alexei Faber and Henry had been in all of them, until now. There was no possibility of her meeting either of them in this place.

Giggling, followed by a sharp and distinct *shhhh,* disrupted her thoughts. Before she remembered she couldn't be seen, she ducked behind one of the shrubs that made up the extensive and well-kept landscaping. She tried to pinpoint where the voices had come from.

"C'mon, it's not that hard." The voice spoke in a harsh whisper, carried on the still night air. It seemed to come from above her.

"But I don't think I can, Sophie..." There was a slight whine to the second girl's voice, which barely covered her fear.

"If you're not going to try, then I'm afraid I'll have to leave you behind."

Sophie recognized the sound of her own voice, of course, and where the voices originated. The third-floor windows were all shut tight, the drapes drawn against the night's chill. Except for one. The last window's sash was pushed up as far as it would go, curtains fluttering out on the breeze. Two girls leaned out of the window, looking at the ground below.

There was Sophie. A Sophie that could be the same one that stood in the garden. The memory version of herself leaned dangerously far across the sill. A younger girl with a round, pale face like a small moon, huddled beside her. The girl's blonde curls hung down the sides of her face, while Sophie's tresses were tucked beneath a boy's cap.

She recognized the girl immediately, even from three floors below. Rose Wilmont, the girl who had been one of her roommates in her last year at Montgomery House. She was a timid thing, a proper English flower whose head was filled with finding a husband and living a life of blissful domesticity. Sophie had made it her personal mission to show Rose that life could be more exciting.

"Well, I'm going." Sophie-from-the-near-past sat on the sill and swung her body around so that her feet hung over three stories of open air. Present Sophie, never having seen it from this angle, gasped at how dangerous it was. She held her breath as she watched herself clamber down the drainpipe like a circus acrobat. She reached the bottom and dismounted the pipe with a flourish.

"C'mon, Rose. You can do it."

Rose's mouth, which had hung open for the entirety of Sophie's display, snapped shut. She shook her head so hard that her curls swung across her face. "You are insane, Sophie Weber." Her harsh whisper was softened by her accent. "What if we get caught?"

"We won't, but even if we do it'll be worth it." When Rose looked unconvinced, Sophie went on. "Come on. Let's have an adventure we can smile about when we're old ladies."

Rose paused, looking down at Sophie then back over her shoulder. "Oh, all right. But if I break my neck, I'm coming back to haunt you."

"Fair enough." Sophie talked the girl onto the ledge and then the pipe, which was more difficult since she wasn't wearing trousers like Sophie. Rose's skirt got caught on the stone of the facade more than once, pulling up the fabric and exposing her legs. By the time the girl reached the ground, she was red as a beet from exertion and blushing.

"Good girl." Sophie hugged Rose.

"I can't believe I did it." Rose's voice and her body trembled slightly. "I thought I was going to fall."

Sophie-the-slightly-older was thinking the same thing, given that Rose's arms were used to holding nothing heavier than an embroidery needle.

"But you didn't. Now let's go and meet the others." Sophie grabbed Rose by the hand and drew her across the moonlit lawn.

Rose glanced back at the house. "We'd better not get caught."

The real Sophie followed the girls through the gardens that surrounded the monstrous manor house. The two memory-girls hid in the shadows of trees and garden statuary, keeping out of the moon's bright gaze. While real Sophie traipsed directly across the garden, toward the woods on the far side.

There was a small, abandoned cottage in the woods that Sophie and a few of the older girls had discovered during her second year. They had cleaned it as best they could and secreted supplies into it, making it their own private clubhouse, where they could talk about anything they wanted, not only what was proper.

Sophie couldn't remember the aim of this particular night's outing. There had been so many. But this had been Rose's first time attending, it seemed. *Oh, no.*

She caught her balance with a hand on the trunk of a tree, putting the other to her chest. Absorbed with watching, she hadn't thought about *that* night. She had pushed it so far to the back of her mind she had almost forgotten.

Sophie could go back to the door. She didn't have to stay.

Despite herself, she ran into the woods.

Henry and Gabriel sat with Mr. Franklin for another quarter hour, finishing their ale and talking. Between the ale and the heat of the day, Henry's stomach churned. His thoughts whirled at the even *more* unbelievable turn events had taken. He barely listened to the conversation, only able to stare at the man before him. Inventor. Ambassador. Writer of History. Founding Father. Henry had no words; all his questions sounded ridiculous even in his own mind.

When Gabriel got up to leave, he shook Ben's hand. "Remember what I said. Be careful. I don't know what's going to happen."

Benjamin Franklin chuckled. "None of us do, my friend. You take a chance when you go out your front door."

Gabriel started toward the exit, beckoning Henry to follow. Henry, however, couldn't seem to get out of his chair.

"I think your friend is having some trouble," Benjamin said with a laugh. "Are you sure he is quite all right?"

Gabriel grabbed him by the shoulder and pulled him up. "His only problem is he thinks too much."

Henry found his tongue and held out his hand to Ben. "It was an honor to make your acquaintance, Mr. Franklin."

Ben took his hand and shook it. "As it was to make yours, Mr. Weber. Any friend of Gabriel's is a friend of mine. We'll be seeing each other again soon, I am sure." He winked at Henry and nodded to Gabriel, giving him a significant look.

"Yes, sir." Gabriel nodded in return as he dragged Henry toward the door. Outside, the sun seemed to blaze even hotter than before. Henry emerged from his star-struck fog. Before Gabriel could get to his horse, Henry grabbed him and dragged him beneath the shade of the building's eaves.

"You need to tell me exactly what is going on here," Henry demanded. He leaned close to his companion, pinning him to the wall with a hard glare.

"You already know. Faber came here to do something. He's also trapped your sweetheart, in case you've forgotten."

"Don't you dare use Sophie to change the subject." Henry's anger made him hotter than the sweltering temperature. "You don't care if she lives or dies, just that you catch Faber."

Gabriel pulled Henry's hands off his coat. "Alexei Faber is a bad man. He works for worse men."

Henry shook his head. "That's not what I mean, and you know it." He pointed at the tavern door. "How could you *possibly* know Benjamin Franklin? He acted as if you were old friends."

Gabriel ran his tongue over his teeth, beneath his lip. "We are. But it's a story for another time. We have to meet Alphonse and Irene." He walked to where the horses waited. Henry stayed behind for a moment, seething, before stalking after him.

"Mr. White, I demand you tell me. Now." He grabbed onto the reins of both horses, preventing Gabriel from untying them.

"Don't make me hurt you, Henry. You're a nice fellow, even if you are a pain in the arse." He pulled the reins from him and finished untying the horse. "Don't worry so much about the truth. It's rather overrated, much of the time." He swung himself into the saddle and looked down on Henry. "Now, you can come with me, and hopefully make it back to your sweetheart alive and able to help her, or you can stand there pouting like a spoiled child. Up to you."

Henry remained where he was, "Why should I trust you, if you won't give me simple answers?"

Gabriel adjusted his hat. "I could ask the same of you. Why should I trust you?"

"What reason have I given you not to?"

Gabriel smiled. "None, actually. Listen, the story isn't that interesting, and now is not the time to tell it. We have, as they say, bigger fish to fry." When Henry did not move, he shrugged. "I have an appointment with Irene and Alphonse, and a mission to finish. I don't have time to soothe your hurt feelings."

Henry, feeling beaten, untied his own horse and climbed into the saddle. "I'm not giving up, you know."

"I'd be disappointed if you did, Henry." Gabriel clucked to his horse and turned him up the street. "Very disappointed indeed."

Henry followed, still sulking.

CHAPTER XI

SOPHIE RACED THROUGH THE WOOD. THE TREES HADN'T YET LEAFED enough to block out the scant moonlight, but even if the night were black, she would have been just as sure-footed. She knew every tree and root. Soon she caught up to the two girls, who were chatting and giggling. Or Sophie was. Rose whined. About getting caught, about being in the woods and getting dirty. About her dress and her shoes and the walk. *Ugh, I had forgotten about that.*

She emerged in a clearing, like something from a fairy tale. The cottage stood in the center though perhaps *standing* was being generous. The roof sagged, and the glass in the windows was mostly broken out. Sophie and her friends imagined it had been the residence of a gamekeeper or gardener when the manor had been a private residence.

Pilfered candles illuminated the inside with flickering fairy light. Voices drifted on the air. Sophie crossed the clearing, anxiety tying her into knots.

A tendril of smoke wafted from the cottage's chimney. The girls had cleaned the flue themselves, getting covered in soot in the process. That had been difficult to explain to the headmistress, but they had devised a story about an accident involving a coal scuttle.

Sophie stopped in the doorway.

"You should have seen Rose's face, scrambling down the drainpipe!" Her other self squealed. "She was terrified."

Rose stammered something unintelligible while Sophie talked over her. "But I'm very proud of her. She finally plucked up the courage to escape from her cage, at least for tonight."

Herself and three other girls were toasting Rose's bravery. They drank out of mismatched glasses, lifted from the kitchens.

The amber liquid in their glasses was either rum or scotch. Her younger self took a swig and made a face. Scotch. Real Sophie shuddered. Scotch smelled and tasted like dirty socks. But sometimes it was all they could swipe from the headmistress's cabinet.

"Where are they, do you think?" one of the girls asked. Was that Jamie? Sophie couldn't see. She stepped all the way into the cottage.

"I dunno. Maybe they had trouble getting out?" Another girl replied, and her voice made Sophie gasp. Alice. Sophie's best friend sat on a bench covered in old, slightly mildewed cushions. She held her glass loosely, her posture leisurely. "You know how boys are."

Alice and Sophie had arrived at Montgomery House around the same time and been assigned as roommates. Sophie had cried from homesickness for weeks, and it had been Alice who had patted her hair and told it would be alright. She had shared a tin of cookies (biscuits, Alice had called them), and made Sophie tea.

Together, they learned the best ways to sneak about the school. Eventually they started sneaking *out* of the school. It was only a matter of time before they recruited other girls to their cause. Two others of their number — Jamie and Edith — sat about the cottage. They were one year older than Sophie and Alice.

"I'm still not sure about this." Rose hovered by the door, shifting on her feet like a nervous animal ready to bolt. "If anyone finds out we were here, drinking and carrying on like hooligans, our reputations will be ruined."

"Maybe I don't care," Sophie replied. "What's to be had by a reputation, anyway? Making a good marriage? Becoming someone's property?"

"It's obvious you don't care. Cavorting about in men's trousers. Just look at your legs." Rose flopped onto a dusty seat. "You'll care when the headmistress writes to your parents and sends you home in shame. At least you'll go back to America, where no one will know."

Both Sophies snorted a laugh.

"I'm not ashamed. That's the difference between you and me. I'm having fun."

"And what about when you go home?" Alice always had to play devil's advocate, though she had admitted to Sophie she would love to leave England and see the world. "You're not worried some suitor will find out about your wanton ways?"

"Oh, yes!" Jamie interjected. "What would your Henry say?"

Sophie laughed. "He's not *my* Henry. We talked over the summer. He sends me letters. That's all." She tossed a mildewed pillow at Alice. "He'll probably already be engaged by the time I'm home, anyway."

Memory Sophie sipped from her cup, hoping that put an end to the discussion.

We've told you before, boys of that age don't ask to keep writing out of obligation." Jamie said with a coy smile. "He's writing because he *wants* to."

Though it was impossible to see in the dim light, memory Sophie blushed. Real Sophie could tell by the look on her own face.

"I don't know about all of you, but I'm enjoying my freedom while I've still got it." Edith drained her cup and reached for the bottle. "In a few weeks, I'll be bundled off, and trussed up, and sent out to balls and parties. I'll have to be a *lady*." She made a face that conveyed just how she felt about that.

"There are worse things than being a lady." Rose's tone was defensive as well as admonishing. "You could be out on the streets or working in a factory. You could be a housemaid."

Edith opened her mouth, likely to tell Rose off, when a sound made everyone stop talking. Something approached, crashing and stomping through the woods like a large farm animal. Alice and memory-Sophie smiled. Jamie and Edith grinned. Only Rose looked nervous. The girls crammed themselves into the doorway.

Three boys in their late teens arrived in the clearing. They were inappropriately dressed for tromping through the woods, their trousers and waistcoats covered in foliage. The girls crammed themselves into the doorway.

"William!" Alice called. She waved. "What took you all so long?"

The tallest one returned the wave and jogged the rest of the way to the cottage. "Sorry. The headmaster was on a tirade. Something about a pig being let loose in the common room." He hugged Alice, swinging her in a circle. The girl screamed with delight while Rose made a tutting noise.

Real Sophie smiled. Alice and William had been so happy in their secret romance. Besides their clandestine meetings, they had sent secret notes to each other. Alice had swooned over his flowery words, though Sophie thought they might be copied from poetry books. Not that it mattered to Alice.

One of the other boys, shorter with neatly combed blond hair beneath his cap, stepped into the cottage and sat beside Memory Sophie. Real Sophie searched her mind for his name — Jonathan. "The old boy seemed very put out. Kept prowling the hallways."

"That's what you get for being so high-spirited," Alice scolded, but then smiled at William. "You should have climbed out the window, like we did."

"Obviously, we're not as brave or nimble as you." The third boy — *Charles* — leaned against the door frame. The boy was handsome, with dark hair and blue eyes. He looked positively rakish, but he was sweet and friendly. He never flirted, like the other two did, not in all the time they had met for these "tea parties," as Alice liked to call them.

This was exactly how Sophie wanted to remember her friends. Happy.

"Of course, you aren't. You're boys, after all." Alice's smile was coy, her head tilted a bit. She was getting very good at flirting. When her Season came, she would be a natural.

The party continued, with all the latest gossip tossed about. The scotch flowed, as did some rum the boys had brought along. Laughter poured from the windows. How they had never been caught, Sophie had no idea.

"I'm bored." Jonathan jumped from his seat. "We need some dancing." He held out his hand to Rose. "Would you do me the honor?"

Rose looked shocked and scandalized. "I certainly will not! There's not a chaperon."

Alice rolled her eyes. "You're sitting out here in the woods, with three boys, and you're worried about a chaperon? Sophie and I are your chaperons."

Rose studied Alice, then turned to Sophie. "There's no music."

"I'll sing, if you like." Edith piped up. "What would you prefer? A waltz?"

"A waltz sounds perfect," Alice said. "Come on, William, we'll dance. too." She held out her arms, and William swept her up once more. Jonathan remained with his hand extended, a smile on his lips. Rose, perhaps feeling the pressure from the other girls, reluctantly slipped her hand into his, and he pulled her close. She squealed and pushed him back.

"You will keep a respectable distance, sir."

Jonathan's eyebrows rose high, but his smile did not falter. "Yes, miss. Pardon me." He placed his one hand on her waist, and took her right in his left, leaving at least six inches between their bodies. Rose gently laid her left hand on his shoulder.

"That's better."

Alice could not stop her laughter. "Alright, then, now we're set. Edith, if you please?"

Edith began to sing, a waltz in three-quarter time. She had a lovely voice. The tune didn't sound like anything Sophie could identify, but she wasn't really paying attention to the music. A knot of anxiety sat in her chest like a sleeping snake.

The two couples twirled to Edith's music. Memory Sophie clapped in time, laughing and smiling. Charles remained aloof, lounging on a moth-eaten sofa.

It happened so fast, but also seemed as if time had slowed to a crawl. Jonathan, showing off, spun Rose, and her hip bumped a table full of candles. Two of the candles fell to the floor. Real Sophie yelled, a futile warning but no one heard. She reached for Rose, for the candles, but her hands went through them, as if they were made of mist. She wished the flames would snuff themselves out, or that Charles would see what had happened. But Rose and Jonathan blocked his view. There was Rose, her skirt just catching fire, a pillow alight. It took a few, precious moments for Rose to notice.

"What is that? Oh, help me!" The look of shock on her pretty face was horrifying. The flame raced up her back, licking her hair.

Sophie wanted to run back to the house, to where she could forget again. But she was rooted to the spot. The others scrambled to extinguish the flames, but the fire forced them away. Charles had a blanket in his hands, ready to toss it over Rose and smother the flames.

"Everyone, get out!" he shouted. William pulled Alice outside by the hand. Edith ran behind them. Jonathan stood, his mouth wide in terror, until Jamie shoved him out the door. Memory Sophie refused to leave.

"You have to leave." Charles pleaded. "I'll take care of her." His attempt to put out Rose had almost been successful, but then the fire on the floor caught the blanket. The tiny room was full of flame, leaping between Sophie and the other two. Rose's hair was ablaze, her screams piercing the night. Charles wrapped his arms around her and threw the two of them to the ground. He rolled her on the floor. Memory Sophie turned and ran. Real Sophie followed.

Both Sophies stood with the others, who had gathered across on the far side of the clearing. The cottage was engulfed, the dry roof providing ample fuel for the hungry flames. Edith had her hands over her mouth, while Jamie wept openly. Alice and William clutched each other's hands, their eyes wide. Jonathan stood like a stone beside Sophie. She called to them.

"Rose! Charles!"

There was no answer. Horror clawed at Real Sophie's insides, ripping open the wounds she thought had healed.

Her memory-self ran toward the house, determined to rescue her friends. William tried to grab her back but she slipped through his grasp. A shadow leapt from the woods and ran straight toward Memory Sophie. Real Sophie thought at first it was an animal, but it turned out to be a man. The man grabbed Sophie around the waist. She struggled, but she was no match for him. His face stood out in the light of the fire. Real Sophie gasped.

Henry followed Gabriel through the streets. He had been to the heart of the city hundreds of times, but today he saw it with fresh eyes and shook his head. His brain was still addled by the fact that he had just met Benjamin Franklin. The man who had *founded* Pennsylvania University. How could he have forgotten to mention that? It made him sick to think about the missed opportunity. But what could he have said that wouldn't have made the man suspicious? Gabriel had almost done that very thing, calling the State House by its future name, and he didn't want to know what would have happened if Mr. Franklin had pursued the mistake.

Gabriel led them down Walnut Street, to where it intersected with Sixth Street. Although just a moment ago Henry had been thinking about how different the city was, he also marveled at how it hadn't changed. The buildings here were as familiar to him as his own home, only less worn by time, technology, and conflict.

"Where are we going?" As always, Henry had the feeling that his companion was keeping something important from him.

"To meet Alphonse and the lovely Irene, of course." Gabriel pulled to the side of the street, so as to let the horse walk in the sparse shade from the trees that lined Sixth. "And Tesla, of course."

"Yes, but where?"

"Just a little further along, you'll see." Gabriel turned in the saddle. "Oh, and you'll need to keep the name Weber for a while longer, dear fellow."

Henry clucked to his horse, prodding him to catch up. "About that. Why did I have to change my name?"

"Stop asking questions."

Henry cheerfully ignored the directive. "Where are we meeting them again?"

Gabriel turned them onto Chestnut. Henry's heart leapt a little as he passed the buildings. They had different names, sold different wares, but they were essentially the same as he remembered. There was a milliner's, which in his time was a bakery. And Grimm's bookshop was once an apothecary. *Fancy that.*

He glanced in the front windows, thinking about Mr. and Mrs. Grimm, and the scent of paper and binding glue. It was the aroma of his youth, hours spent on a Saturday poring over the pages of books. The young Grimm brothers, Benjamin and Harry, had been his playmates. Benjamin had loved building things, the same as he, but he longed for a life in the spotlight. Harry, closer to his own age, had liked science. There had been some kind of incident a few years ago, and Benjamin had disappeared. Harry never talked about it much, and Henry had lost touch with him once he had started at the university. Funny, how something as simple as a shop window could bring back such memories.

His gaze skimmed across the storefront to rest on its neighbor.

And his heart, which had felt so light, nearly stopped.

"Something wrong?" Gabriel looked as if he were trying to both remain serious and not laugh. He pulled his horse to a stop and dismounted.

"We're meeting Irene and Alphonse *here*?" Henry could hardly get the words out; they seemed to lodge themselves in his throat.

Gabriel's smile turned wide. "Yes, we are."

"But... I..." Henry put his fingertips to his forehead. "I don't understand."

"For all your schooling, you don't know much, do you?" Gabriel pulled open the door to the shop and walked inside, leaving Henry to gape at the words painted on the sign above the door.

Rittenhouse's Clock Shop.

Gabriel held the door open for Henry.

Henry slid from the saddle of his horse and stood there, dumbstruck.

"You look like you've seen a ghost. Alphonse and Irene are meeting us here."

Henry took a nervous, shaking breath. This shop was in the same place it was a century from now. The same place it had always been. How had he not remembered? He had heard stories of the man who had founded this establishment, the great man who had begun a legacy of Rittenhouse watchmakers. That man was woven into the fabric of this city. Gabriel had to know of Henry's connection to this place. He knew Ben Franklin personally. Did Ben Franklin know David Rittenhouse? Gabriel had given this address to Alphonse and Irene, so he had planned to come here. Was that why he had introduced Henry to Mr. Franklin under a false name, so he wouldn't make the connection? Henry felt lightheaded.

"Why did you bring me here?"

Gabriel tilted his head. "Because we might be able to get information about Faber. Why else?"

"But... I... you know... why else?" Henry stuttered.

Gabriel waved away Henry's indignation. "Do you think I have time to play games? I don't know about you, but I'd like to return to my own time as quickly as possible."

Henry swallowed deeply. "You might have warned me."

"And spoil the surprise?" Gabriel's smirk was small but unmistakable. "What fun would that have been? We *do* have to go inside, that part is true. The look on your face is just an added bonus." He swept his free hand in toward the shop. "After you."

The smell of oil and metal wafted out and cleared Henry's head, as familiar to him as the scent of his mother's kitchen. Memory pulled him across the threshold and into the shop. The fragrance of the watch shop had been ground into the wide floor boards, into the wood of the door and window frames. The smell was accompanied by an incessant ticking.

He automatically turned his head to the right, as he did every time he entered the shop. Behind the display counter was a workbench. In front of the bench was a man, seated on a stool. He turned to face them, and it felt to Henry like all the air had left the room. The salt-and-pepper hair, the wrinkles around the gray eyes behind thick magnifying spectacles.

"Hello, there. Give me a minute and I'll be right with you." The man's gruff voice brought tears to Henry's eyes, although he didn't know why it should. David turned back to the workbench, slouching over a pocket watch, his posture exactly the same as Henry's father's.

"Thank you, Mr. Rittenhouse. No rush." Gabriel looked around the shop. "The rest of our party hasn't yet arrived."

Henry pulled his gaze from the watchmaker. The shop was essentially the same as in his present. Shelves held dozens of carriage clocks. Cuckoo clocks decorated one wall—all set to the proper time. He had always hated when the hour came around, because every one chimed at once, making such a racket he had to hold his ears. The display case was full of pocket watches, sitting on plush velvet.

Atop the counter sat a scale model of a mill. Henry looked closer. He knew the mill, of course. His own home was only a few miles from the full-sized counterpart. It had stopped making paper before he was born, but the building remained. A tiny sign hung from the model, meticulously lettered *Rittenhouse Paper*.

The bell above the door chimed. Henry turned just as Irene and Alphonse stepped inside.

"Hallo, chum." Alphonse gave him a little wave and a smile as he crossed the small shop. "Keeping out of trouble?"

Henry didn't know how to reply. Alphonse clapped him on the arm and smiled, an expression matched by Irene. Tesla, perched on his mistress's shoulder, held his hand up in some form of greeting

Irene tucked a stray strand of hair beneath her cap. "Sorry we're late. A bit of a slog out in this heat, and no way to hire a carriage." She looked at Gabriel. "You might have left us some money."

"Sorry." Gabriel looked genuinely cowed. "Next time, remind me."

"Yes, I'm sure there will be a next time," was Irene's sharp reply.

David Rittenhouse faced his customers, his spectacles pushed onto his forehead. "Well, this is quite a party, isn't it? What can I help you with on this fine day? A new pocket watch for the gentleman? I have some lovely pendant watches, quite suitable for the lady."

Irene's smile was genuine. "Thank you, sir but not today."

"A clock for your mantle, perhaps?" He walked to the shelves. "I'm afraid I do not have anything suitable for such a... fine companion as yours." David held out his hand toward Tesla. The monkey cocked his head quizzically, and then reached out and grasped one finger and shook it.

Gabriel cleared his throat to get the man's attention. "Mr. Rittenhouse we're not here for a clock. I've been told you're the man to see for information." He leaned close. "Mr. Franklin says that birds fly in the East."

Mr. Rittenhouse looked him square in the eye, his eyebrows lifting. "I see." He calmly walked to the door of the shop, glanced out the window as if looking to see if anyone were watching, and then locked it.

"Come with me." He led them through a doorway behind the counter and into the back of the shop. When all four of his visitors had come through, he pulled a curtain across the opening. The room, the same in which a younger Henry would spend almost every Saturday of his childhood — was tidy. Another workbench ran along one wall, delicate clockmaker's tools laid out on an oilcloth. A variety of watch parts and other bits of machinery were neatly arranged along the back of the workspace.

A table in the center held some very odd-looking machines, covered in gears and springs and glass lenses. Henry stared, but Alphonse gravitated toward them, his eyes sparkling and his fingers twitching as if he wished to reach out and touch. "These are amazing. Did you make them all?"

Mr. Rittenhouse beamed. "Yes, sir, I certainly did." He indicated a small mechanical device. It had gears in the bottom, attached to metal arms that were topped with spheres of several sizes.

"This orrery is a model of a larger one." He grasped a crank, connected to the gears, and turned it slowly. The clockworks set the arms in motion, twirling in their assigned orbits around the sun.

As Henry watched the little display a lump formed in his throat. He had often been told of the orrery his great-great-great grandfather had constructed for the College of New Jersey, but had never seen it. He didn't have the heart to tell David it was nearly destroyed in the Battle of Princeton. Which hadn't happened yet, of course.

"Now, how can I help you?"

Gabriel glanced at his companions. "We're looking for a man. We think he means some kind of harm, perhaps to the Congress."

David leaned against his workbench. "He'll have to get in line. King George isn't very happy with us of late. He's sent plenty of spies, soldiers, hired Hessians. Even Royalists, hiding among us, trying to stop us."

Gabriel nodded politely and continued. "This man, he's more dangerous than any of them. He has certain... knowledge that the others don't."

"A smart one, then?" David leaned against the workbench. "That's a change. But I'm sure he won't get past us."

"Please, Mr. Rittenhouse, he's our responsibility. I'm afraid that if your people approach him, they'll be injured."

David seemed to sense Gabriel's sincerity. "I see. What does this man look like? His name?" He crossed to a writing desk tucked in the corner. Stacks of parchment were perched atop it, along with assorted quills and ink pots. He sifted through the hodge-podge, and plucked out a small piece of blank parchment and a slightly bent quill. He dipped the point of the quill into one of the ink pots and poised it over the paper.

"His name is Alexei Faber." Gabriel crossed his arms over his chest. "He's about five-feet-ten inches tall." He held up a hand to show the estimated height. "Forty-five years old, wears spectacles. Lean build. He may or may not be wearing a wig, but if he's not, then he's got dark hair with gray at the temples. He may have a companion with him, but I don't have the slightest inkling what he might look like."

David scribbled everything down. "That's not much to go on. I could tell you five men this description would fit right now."

"Oh, yes, one last thing. He has an accent. German."

David nodded and added the detail. "That will make him slightly easier to find, but only slightly."

Gabriel nodded. "I understand. Any help you could give us would be beneficial."

David finished his scribbling, then folded the paper in half. He strode to the back door, which led to the small alley behind the shops, and stepped out for a moment. When he returned his hands were empty.

"There. Once the word spreads, we'll find your man. In the meantime, how else can I help you?"

Henry's confusion showed on his face. "How will you spread the word?"

David's smile was enigmatic. "This is a war, my dear lad. They have their spies, and we have ours." He waved a hand, dismissing the tension that had crept into the room like a low-lying fog. "Back to business. Once my people find this man you're looking for, how will I get in contact with you?"

Gabriel's gaze glided over the various gadgets that cluttered the workspace. After a few moments of weighted silence, he reached inside his jacket and pulled out his photophone. He handed it to David, ignoring the gasp from Alphonse and the muttered "Are you mad?" from Irene.

"With this device you will be able to contact us immediately." Gabriel reached over and opened the lid. David's eyes grew wide when he saw the miraculous machine inside. "Just flip this switch and turn this knob and start to talk. We'll answer."

Rather than push it away, claiming it was the work of the devil — as Henry half-expected — David pulled it closer, peering at it over the top of his spectacles.

"Such a marvelous invention! Did you build this?"

Gabriel laughed. "No. Young Alphonse is the master of mechanical things." He pulled the boy forward, who grinned from ear-to-ear.

"It's nothing, really. Bits and pieces put together." Alphonse held his hat in his hand, like a nervous schoolboy.

"I beg to disagree. It is amazing." David turned one of the knobs, his face lighting up in delight at the high-pitched squeal that came from the small speaking box below the glass. He turned the knob back the other way and closed the photophone's lid. "I shall keep this close. Wouldn't want the British or Hessians finding out about it."

"I'd appreciate that." Gabriel paused. "If you don't mind, would you please not show it to anyone? Not even Ben... Mr. Franklin?"

David looked a bit disappointed, but he nodded. "Of course." He slipped the photophone into the pocket of his vest. "I will contact you as soon as I get any information."

Gabriel gave a short, sharp nod. "Thank you. If you'll excuse us, we need to be going. It's probably best if we weren't seen leaving."

"Of course." David pulled the back door open for his guests. "God speed, my friends."

Irene and Tesla, then Alphonse, slipped into the alley. Gabriel put on his hat and tipped it to their host, then crossed the threshold, leaving Henry alone with David. Henry still didn't know what to say. He knew what he *wanted* to say, but also knew that the nature of time travel forced him to hold his tongue. All he could do was stare, in what was most certainly a rude manner, and commit to memory every detail of David's face. The way he lifted his eyebrows, just like Henry's grandfather, or how his eyes were the exact color as Uncle Florian's. How his half-smile mirrored Henry's father's. It was like looking at all the people he loved in one.

"Thank you, Mr. Rittenhouse." Henry bobbed his head. "For... everything."

David's smile turned into a quizzical look. "You are most welcome, Mr... I'm afraid we weren't properly introduced."

Henry's heart shoved his real name into his throat, but his brain got the upper hand and made the sensible choice. "Weber. Heinz Weber."

"Mr. Weber, then. Good day."

The others waited for Henry in the alley. Alphonse leaned up against the brick facade of the building while Gabriel paced a few steps away. He gave Henry an aggravated look.

"Everything all right?" Irene stood in the shade of the lone tree with Tesla still perched on her shoulder.

"Fine, thank you." Henry imagined shutting a door in his mind, keeping his emotions about David to himself.

"Very good, Henry." Irene smiled. "Keep practicing."

Henry focused on something else. "Why did you give that device to David? What about all of that nonsense you spewed to me about messing up time?"

Gabriel stopped his pacing and faced Henry. "Call it a calculated risk. I did what I thought was needed to catch Faber. If there's any damage, we'll try and fix it. It won't be as great as the problems Faber may cause."

"And what now, O great leader?" Alphonse pushed himself off of the wall and joined Henry. "Do we just sit around in a pub and wait for Faber to turn up?"

"As much fun as that sounds, we can't." Gabriel crossed his arms over his chest. "David's network might find Faber, but in the meantime, we need to keep looking. C'mon." He called over his shoulder as he headed down the alley. At the corner, he stopped and turned toward the little group, which hadn't moved.

"Let's go, troops. Move out."

CHAPTER XII

"L" ET GO OF ME! I HAVE TO HELP THEM!" MEMORY SOPHIE SCREAMED into the night. She struggled against Henry's grasp, but he held her tightly until she stopped struggling.

"Are you all right?" Henry put her feet on the ground but didn't let go of her just yet. Real Sophie, watching herself, felt the pain she saw on Henry's face as he held the struggling, stubborn girl.

Sophie's face shone with tears. She slumped against him. "Rose and Charles are still in there. We have to help them."

"I'll see what I can do." Another man appeared in the clearing. In the shifting light of the fire, Alexei Faber's face looked ghoulish. "You will wait right here. Do *not* follow me." He pulled up the hood on his long cloak and raced toward the cottage, his form a mere silhouette against the brightness of the flames.

"He's going to burn alive," Jonathan shouted. "Who is that man?"

Memory Sophie did not answer.

Real Sophie thought every second of that night had been seared into her memory by the heat of the flames. But she had no recollection of these two men being in the clearing. How had Henry suddenly appeared thousands of miles from Germantown? Her head spun, her middle squeezing and expanding like an accordion. Henry and Faber couldn't have been here.

She watched, overwhelmed and helpless, as the cottage was consumed. There was no sound except the crackling of burning wood, and the occasional pop of glass, until Alice called out.

"Look!"

She pointed to a dark shape among the flames. Faber emerged from the burning cottage. He seemed completely unscathed as he crossed the clearing, cradling a smoldering bundle. Across his back lay what appeared to be a human form, holding on around his neck. Jonathan and William raced across the clearing to help him. One of the boys pried the figure from Faber's back, while the other took the bundle from his arms and brought them to where the girls and Henry waited. Edith and Jamie clung to each other, tears drying on their cheeks in the fire's heat. Alice wrung her hands, fear etched onto her features. Henry still held Memory Sophie, his face unreadable as he rocked her gently.

"Are they... are they all right?" Lilly's voice was hard to hear above the crackling flames.

Real Sophie didn't want to look. She should turn and run as fast as her feet would carry her, through the woods and back to the door.

Her traitorous head turned, her reckless eyes refusing to shut out the horrific scene.

Charles lay on his side, coughing up smoke and moaning in pain. His blond hair was burned on one side, right to the scalp, along with the side of face. The back of one hand was red and covered in blisters. The rest of him looked untouched, except for the charred edges of his clothing.

The bundle must have been Rose, but there was nothing recognizable about her. Her hair was gone. Her clothes smoked, mere rags remaining of her dress. Her skin was black as the inside of a chimney, and split like an overripe melon. She did not move, did not cry out. Real Sophie was only able to look for a second. The terrible stench, like burnt meat. Memory overwhelmed her, and she stepped back. The others recoiled in horror.

"Rose? Rose!" Memory Sophie screamed the girl's name as she broke free of Henry's grasp and fell to her knees beside the body. Tears rolled anew down her cheeks.

Faber put a hand on her shoulder. "It's too late, child." A strangled cry erupted from Memory Sophie's throat. She stayed beside Rose, while Jonathan tended to Charles, whose screams had tempered to whimpers. Henry stood behind Sophie, looking helpless and dismayed as Alexei pulled on his jacket, as if to get his attention.

Henry slowly glanced over his shoulder at the other man.

"We have to go now."

An incensed expression on his face, Henry snapped, "Are you mad? She needs our help. We can't leave."

Faber rubbed his forehead with his fingertips, leaving soot on his skin. "We cannot stay, and you know exactly why. We've done enough, and now we must go." He pulled Henry close and spoke adamantly into the other man's ear. When he finished, he looked Henry in the eye. "You understand?"

Henry gazed at Sophie, his brow furrowed and his hands clenching and unclenching. Finally, he nodded and walked toward the heart of the woods.

"What are we going to do?" Alice stood away from the rest, unable or unwilling to come any closer. "We'll be in so much trouble if they find us. Oh, poor Rose! We can't stay here." William put his arm around her and pulled her close, her sobs muffled by his shoulder.

Faber knelt beside Sophie and whispered something into her ear. After a moment, he pulled her gently to standing.

"You understand?" His gaze was soft but commanding. "You must do as I say."

The girl made of memory turned her head slowly toward him, her gaze unfocused and her face emotionless.

"Sophia, please."

Real Sophie sobbed openly, her heart breaking all over again. She should have stayed; she should have told the truth of that night.

But she hadn't. She had done exactly as Alexei Faber had instructed.

He turned to Jonathan.

"Take your friend home. When you get there, tell them a story, anything that does not put you at this cottage tonight."

Jonathan nodded but did not reply. William gently pulled himself away from Alice and the two boys helped a still-whimpering Charles to his feet, lifting the boy's arms around their shoulders to bear his weight. They shuffled away, the deep shadows of the woods swallowing them as they left the clearing.

Faber turned to Sophie. "Go now, and take your friends."

Edith and Jamie had their arms around each other like frightened children. "But how can we go without Rose?" Edith sobbed, sucking in a hiccupping breath. "We can't leave her here."

"Don't worry about Rose." Faber insisted. "It's only a matter of time before someone sees the smoke, or before the forest catches fire and you are all lost. As I told the boy, none of you were here. Go."

Sophie watched her shadow-self grab Alice's hand and take a few steps toward the wood. Alice turned her head, her eyes wide with disbelief.

"We can't leave Rose here."

I'm sorry. We must." Sophie's gaze was clear, her expression determined. "It will be okay." She pulled Alice's hand again, and this time the girl didn't resist. Edith and Jamie followed, holding hands as well.

Sophie, the real one, watched them go. She knew what happened after. Faber moved Rose's body closer to the cottage. Then he, too, disappeared into the forest. Sophie followed, to see where he and Henry had gone.

The door that led back to the house blocked her path. She tried to go around it, but the door moved with her, preventing her progress. She turned her back on it, and it appeared before her, like a nagging nanny. Sophie uttered a frustrated grunt.

"Fine. I don't want to stay anyway." Weighed down with grief, she stepped back into her ticking, freezing prison.

In all the history books, no one ever seemed to mention how ungodly hot it was in Philadelphia in July 1776. Henry expected such ridiculous temperatures, having lived here his entire life, but attire in the late 18th century made it that much more unbearable. The wool stockings, in particular, itched terribly.

Gabriel led his strange little crew around to the front of the shop. Their horses waited patiently, flicking flies off of their rump with their tails.

"Poor things, out in this heat." Irene held out her hand and one of the horses nuzzled his nose in it.

Alphonse patted the neck of one of the flesh-and-blood creatures. "I've got an idea to build a horse from metal and clockwork. It wouldn't need food or water, just oil and a winding."

"You won't need to do that if those horseless carriages catch on," Irene replied. Tesla abandoned his mistress's shoulder, jumping onto the saddle of the chestnut mare.

The young man made a sour face. "Maybe. Perhaps I'll have to build one of those instead."

"Now don't be upset about it," Irene replied in a placating tone. "You can build anything you want. Literally, you've already built a time machine, so a horse should be no trouble at all." She unhitched her mount and gave it a pat.

"Are we going back to Germantown?" The thought of traipsing the eight miles back in the heat made Henry feel unwell.

"No reason to." Gabriel untied his horse. "I trust that Alphonse and Irene have done a thorough job searching it." He pulled the horse away from the hitching post. "First, let's get the horses to a stable."

By the time their errand was complete, the sun dipped toward the Schuylkill River.

"I'd say we should split up, but we may need to move quickly if David contacts us." Gabriel leaned against the stable.

Irene stretched. "If we don't find him soon, we're going to need to think about accommodations for the evening."

"There won't be any sleeping until we find him," Gabriel growled. "You can sleep when we get home."

They all groaned, and Tesla covered his face with his tiny hands.

"Fine, then where should we begin?" Henry's limbs weighed a thousand pounds. It was as if Gabriel's edict about no rest had made his entire body want nothing but.

"We can't sleep, but we do need to eat." Gabriel pushed his hat back on his head and rubbed his short hair. "I think I know just the place. Will that make you happy?"

Irene smiled. "Immeasurably."

"Fine." Gabriel led them down the street, toward the Delaware. Alphonse talked to Gabriel, saying something about how Faber's machine was an amazing piece of work, and how he couldn't wait to see inside. His tone was nearly reverential.

"You should see the craftsmanship! Amazing! And..."

Alphonse continued his praise, with Gabriel trying to steer him to more useful information. Henry walked behind, his body unable to continue at a faster pace. Irene kept pace beside him.

"These skirts make it so difficult to move." She pulled at the offending piece of clothing. "And they're rubbish for fighting. I can't wait to get my regular clothing back."

Henry nodded, happy for simple, friendly conversation. He wondered if Sophie was safe. He had to believe she was, because he didn't know what he would do if she weren't.

Irene laid her hand briefly on his forearm though she kept her gaze ahead. "You'll go on with your life."

"Pardon?" Henry snapped his attention back to her.

"I'm sorry, I didn't mean to intrude. It's a bad habit, peeking into people's minds." She reached up and scratched Tesla's head. "As I said, with you it's like you're shouting. When you're not making an effort to shut me out, that is."

"It's all right," Henry said. "I don't always mind."

Irene nodded. "I don't mean that you'll just forget Sophie and move along. It will hurt. You'll feel as if it's you that's died. But eventually, you'll remember that you have a life to live. You'll say you'll live it for her, that she wouldn't want you to spend the rest of your life mourning her. And that's true, of course, but you'll need to do it for yourself and no one else."

Henry was taken aback at her blunt words. He wondered who *she* had lost, but quickly squashed the thought before she caught onto it.

"I suppose I would."

Irene flashed a small smile. "Hold tight to your hope."

Henry nodded and rubbed his forehead. "I will. Thank you."

Irene turned her head and narrowed her eyes. "And I think you absolutely inherited your love of building things from your great-great-grandfather. Things like that... passions, gifts, talents, run in the blood."

"But my father is a clockmaker. A great one, to be sure, but not an engineer. He's spent his life huddled over springs and gears. He's never had ideas like David. Tracking the path of a planet? Even I can't imagine doing anything like that."

Irene dismissed the thought with a wave of her hand. "Your father has his own gift, but the same dexterity and understanding of mechanical things that David has."

Henry sighed. "I suppose."

"It takes a meticulous mind and a steady hand." Irene nudged him. "But sometimes things skip a generation. Look at me. My mother could barely form a thought independent of what the church spoon-fed her, let alone read the thoughts of others." Her words were bitter, but her tone rational. "But my grandmother... she had the Sight."

"The Sight?"

"She could see the future and the past. Like her own brand of time-travel, though she never left Nottingham. She had a real gift." Irene's voice caught in her throat. "Sorry, dust. It's really terrible out here, isn't it?"

Henry said nothing. It wasn't Irene's gift that frightened him about her. He wasn't sure exactly what did, except that maybe it had something to do with the idea she could quite possibly pound the piss out of him and not break a nail.

Irene continued, but Henry wasn't sure she was still talking to him. "Yes, indeed. Passions, gifts, talents. In the blood. Now, fear, *that's* learned. That's taught by people and institutions so many rely on to lead them on the path to righteousness. Even if it means they end up fearing the ones they are supposed to love."

Whatever she was referring to, Henry had a feeling it had to do with her scar. He decided not to ask. They traveled on in companionable silence for another block. Alphonse continued to talk Gabriel's ear off, listing his hypotheses of all the things Faber must have inside his time machine. Henry slowed, hoping Irene would match his stride. She turned her head, puzzled.

Henry took a short breath and watched the two boys ahead for another moment, then he slowed a bit more. "I want to ask you something, but I don't want Gabriel to hear."

Irene looked intrigued—perhaps waiting for him to say what was on his mind instead of searching his thoughts. Or maybe his thoughts on this subject were so jumbled she couldn't make sense of them.

"How well do you know Gabriel?"

Irene considered the question. "Not well. The first time I ever saw him was when I stepped off the boat from England a few weeks ago. Scotland Yard sent me to help them track down Faber. Why do you ask?"

"I just wondered..." Henry concentrated on his question, knowing she would hear it. *I just wondered if he'd ever told you that he'd traveled in time before. Specifically, to this time and to Philadelphia. More specifically, did he ever happen to mention that he was friends with Benjamin Franklin?*

Irene stopped short, her eyebrows rising in surprise. Tesla hadn't been prepared for the sudden loss of motion; inertia threw him forward. He landed on the ground and chattered his displeasure, giving Irene a very put-out look.

"Clearly, he did not." Henry scooped up Tesla and placed him back on her shoulder.

Irene settled her pet, stroking his head and cooing gently. "I don't expect Gabriel to tell me his life's story. We're colleagues, that's all."

"But don't you think he should have mentioned that when we got here? And what is his gift?" Henry felt it wasn't too probing a question.

Irene looked pensive. "You know, I'm not sure. It's never really come up." Her gaze flitted toward Gabriel, then back again. "I've never been able to read him. Not one bit. It's like a brick wall." Her brow furrowed, and Henry wasn't sure if she was trying to read Gabriel now, or if she was considering more deeply that she couldn't.

She smiled and gave a small shrug. "I'm sure he's got a good reason for not telling us everything. I *do* trust him."

"I didn't mean to imply we shouldn't." Henry carefully guarded the rest of his thought. *We don't have much of a choice.*

"Very good, Henry. I only caught half of that." Irene patted his arm. "It's probably best if we put this aside for now. Concentrate on the task at hand." She sped up and left Henry behind.

They were back on Front Street. Gabriel turned right, onto a small avenue.

"Where are we going?" Henry hadn't been to this part of the city very much, but it didn't look respectable. A pungent odor forced itself into his nose. Buildings crammed the street, which was split in two by a small creek. The water seemed to be the source of the offending smell.

"Right here." Gabriel stopped in front of a building with *Blue Anchor* Tavern scrawled across the sign above the door. The Blue Anchor, infamous for hosting Captain Kidd and Blackbeard. Every window in the establishment was lit, while the rest of the street was dark. It made Henry uneasy.

"So we *are* going to sit around a pub and wait, then?" Alphonse asked.

"What is that obnoxious smell?" Irene put her hand to her nose.

"Dock Street. The tanneries and breweries dump into the creek. That's Dock Creek." Gabriel pointed at the water. He looked at Henry. "They covered it over not long after the Revolution, so you've probably never heard of it."

"No, but I've heard of the Blue Anchor." Henry took a step back. "A legendary place of thieves and pirates."

"That is absolutely true. I said before, taverns are places to find information. *This* place will have a different sort of information than City Tavern." Gabriel held open the door, and raucous noise spilled onto the street.

Henry took a hesitant step. He caught the smell of something besides brewery waste. Something delicious.

"It can't hurt to get something to eat. And get more information, of course." He walked across the threshold, and his senses were assaulted. In one corner, a group of men sung a song with lyrics Henry was sure no lady should ever hear. Another group gathered around a table playing cards. Henry took two more steps inside when he was held back by something.

Gabriel grabbed both Alphonse's and Henry's collars and yanked them both away from the door. "Sorry, we have another appointment."

Alphonse looked murderous. "If I don't get some food soon, I'm going to eat your hat."

"We have a call." He indicated Irene, who held up her photophone. The device chirped furiously. They hadn't heard it over the noise of the tavern. Though there were several people on the street, no one gave them a glance. In this part of town, it seemed people minded their own business.

Irene handed her photophone to Gabriel, who flipped it open. The light of the device's little glass window shone bright as a candle on the dark street. David Rittenhouse's face appeared. Or at least part of it did. All they saw was a giant nose.

"Am I doing this right?"

"Yes, sir." Gabriel held the device closer and spoke softly. "But pull it away from your face a bit."

"Oh." David's entire face came into view. "Oh, yes, I see. Very good. There you are! What an amazing piece of machinery."

"How can I help you, Mr. Rittenhouse?" Gabriel asked.

"It's how I can help you, good sir." David's smile filled the bottom of the window. "I've found your man."

"You're sure?"

"As sure as I can be." David looked grim. "I'll meet you soon."

Gabriel nodded then clicked the photophone off, closed it, and handed it back to Irene.

They left the Blue Anchor Tavern and its delicious smelling food behind. The aroma reminded Henry of his mother's cooking; his mouth watered and his stomach complained.

He followed Gabriel back across the city, hungry and miserable. The night provided a little relief from the heat, but the sticky air hung around them like a damp rag. The cobbles on the street were coated in a thin film of dankness, making them slick.

Gabriel began the conversation, as if answering questions no one had asked. "Some of the designs we found in Faber's workshop were for powerful weapons. We think he's been making those for his employer, who is likely part of the German military."

Henry couldn't help himself. "I saw those plans. None of them had any hope of working. There was something called an Aether gun. What *is* that? It sounds insane."

Alphonse glanced at Gabriel before answering. "But it isn't insane. At least two of those designs work."

Henry kept talking. "I know Faber and Mr. Weber have some kind of history, but what does that have to do with his working for anyone? If he's working for the Germans, why would they want him to come back in time and change *American* history?"

Gabriel skidded to a stop and stared at Henry. "Excellent questions. We can only speculate, but it must be to change something that affects *our* present."

Henry felt compelled to continue. "What does any of it have to do with the Weber family?" That was the question that burned within him — what had made Alexei Faber so angry with Mr. Weber that he had taken the man's only daughter and put her in a state of sleeping death? The men had nothing in common, as far as Henry could tell. Herr Weber loved new gadgets, though he wasn't an inventor himself. He donated generous sums to the Engineering College at the university.

Was that the connection?

Gabriel waved him off. "Sorry, we'll have to save that story for another time."

They had reached the clock shop. The streets were deserted. The city's residents had left the shopping district, bound for their suppers and bed, with no idea of what their newly formed country would have to endure, or how soon.

The businesses were obviously closed for the night. Only David's shop bore light. Two candles burned in the window to the right of the door.

"This way." Gabriel led the way around to the back door and climbed the steps. "Keep an eye out."

Alphonse and Irene nodded. They split the alley, Irene watching one end and Alphonse the other. Gabriel knocked — three short raps, as David had instructed.

Footsteps on the other side of the door heralded someone's approach. "It's very late. Come back tomorrow." The voice was low, and not friendly sounding.

"I'm sorry to disturb you. I was wondering if you could tell me what time it is?" Gabriel kept his voice low as well. If they hadn't done something similar earlier, Henry would have found the exchange strange.

The pause was as heavy as the summer air around them. "What time do you think it is?"

Gabriel put his face even closer to the door. "The hands on the clock tower point to midnight." That was the code David had given them.

The door swung open. "Enter, friends."

Gabriel nodded and waved the rest of them inside.

Sophie's stepped into the icy foyer, taking one last look at the clearing as she closed the doors. The cottage was frozen in time, flames reaching for the sky. Rose's charred corpse lay where Alexei had left it, though thankfully Sophie couldn't make it out well. A wave of nausea came over her again. She turned away, fighting the feeling down.

She slid the dining room doors shut. The image was gone, but the pain remained. Sophie barely felt the cold as she walked straight upstairs to her room and closed the door behind her. She sat on her bed, unable to cry. There were no tears left in her.

Her thoughts vacillated between sorrow and anger. She had tried so hard to forget, to pack it away in her mind, like an overlooked trunk at the back of a dusty attic. Who had done this to her, and why had that night been chosen?

All of these memories directly involved Alexei Faber.

And Henry, of course, but they had been a part of each other's lives since birth.

The biggest difference in the last memory being, of course, that she hadn't remembered Faber or Henry being there. Completely contrary to her fierce desire to put the entire event as far from herself as she could, she forced herself to concentrate on that night.

Rose on the drainpipe. The cottage. Charles asking Rose to dance. The candles tipping over and everyone screaming and running.

Suddenly, the memory that had been so clear ran like water through her fingers. The vision in her mind doubled, and she saw herself running into the cottage and also being held by Henry. It was as if she had been split in two. She tried to focus, but her head spun to match her thoughts.

Something in her memory shifted, and it all became one again. It was Alexei Faber running into the cottage, pulling his hood over his head, and coming out with Charles and Rose's body. Faber and Henry had been there, and then walked off and disappeared into the woods. And she and her friends had returned to the school and continued with their lives.

The girls had made it back to the manor, smelling of smoke and forest. They snuck back inside with no one the wiser. Each had slipped into their nightgowns and laid down in their beds, waiting for the inevitable.

It hadn't come until almost dawn. The fire engines raced down the drive, bells clanging. Someone had seen the smoke or the flames. The headmistress had knocked on each door, checking on the girls.

When she discovered Rose missing...

They had never told, not one of them. The headmistress had no idea why or how the girl had left her bed, or what she had been doing at the cottage. Rumors abounded. She had been meeting a secret beau. She had been out for a walk and gotten caught in a rainstorm (despite the fact it hadn't rained at all) and had sought shelter in the cottage, which had been struck by lightning and caught fire.

The incident had come between Sophie and her friends like a wall of glass. They had barely associated afterwards, let alone talked about the mysterious men who saved Charles and kept Sophie from running into a certain death.

Even Alice, who had been her best friend. In the time between the fire and when Alice left school for her first Season a chill dropped over their friendship. They hadn't laughed in the same carefree way, and the silences between conversations were filled with the terrible guilt they couldn't admit out loud. Sophie had told herself that Alice was just preoccupied with her new life. Had they even written to each other after Alice had gone? Had Alice ever spoken to William again?

Who *was* Alexei Faber?

If he was a friend of her father's she had never been introduced to him. The first meeting seemed to be chance, the second he appeared to be looking for her father. *But he should have used the front door. Then, he appears halfway around the world from Philadelphia. And with Henry Rittenhouse, of all people!*

Understanding struck her like a thunderbolt.

Alexei Faber had sought her out.

Over and over.

Throughout her life.

Why? He had never made a move to harm her, had even risked his life for her. And yet, apparently, his very presence had caused her father enough panic to send her across the ocean to boarding school. Which hadn't even worked. He seemed obsessed with her.

So obsessed that he would lock memories of himself and her in the rooms of her house?

The idea popped into her head, unconsidered. Once there, it grew, like the bloodthirsty plants outside, rooting in her consciousness. Thorns of anger buried themselves in her heart. Her hands clenched so tightly that her arms trembled and her knuckles turned white.

Peeling her fingers from the bedding, she stood. The face of the man she couldn't remember fixed itself in her mind. It was his fault. *He* was the reason she had lived her life a prisoner. The reason she had been shipped away to school. The longer she thought about it, the more she was sure he was the reason she was trapped here.

Her anger propelled her from the room and down the stairs. "The game is over," she called. "You might as well come out." Her measured and determined steps took her through the downstairs level, where she systematically searched the corners of every single room. With each failure to find him, her frustration grew, like the dark, insidious vines outside.

Her rampage led her down the hall to the kitchen. She struck the door so hard it flew open and swung back and forth in her wake. Her search of this room was just as thorough the rest, with results just as miserable. Only the basement remained, but the door was locked. Which was normal. The door only locked from the outside, so the man couldn't be down there. Out of frustration, Sophie pounded the door, her anger unsatisfied.

Spinning toward the back door, she spied an ax leaning against the wall. Her father had kept it there for as long as Sophie could remember. Even though they could easily buy wood, chopping something her father insisted on doing himself, professing it was good for his soul.

Sophie wrapped her fingers around the ax's handle. The wood was smooth, polished by the rubbing of her father's hands. She picked it up.

"Fine. If you won't come out, let's see how your little pet likes this."

Determination and fury drove her steps as she strode through the house and out the front door. Stopping, she inspected her jailer for any weakness. The plant seemed do the same with her until the hairs on the back of her neck stood up.

Choosing a smaller vine at the bottom of the stairs, only as thick as her arm, Sophie took a deep breath and lifted the ax. She swung it down hard, striking the vine right in the middle. The blade cut the plant's flesh with a satisfying squelch. Somewhere within the mass of foliage sounded a cry of pain. The cry turned into a whimper, like an injured dog. If the plant was trying garner Sophie's sympathy it failed. She reveled in the black sap seeping from the cut. Raising her ax, she brought it down twice more, hitting beside the first.

The whimpering turned into a low moan of pain, which echoed in Sophie's ears but did not touch her heart. She swung again, this time with more confidence and much better aim. The blade again sunk into the first cut she had made, slicing deep into the heart of the vine. The moaning turned into a scream.

Sophie didn't even pause. She brought the ax up again, ignoring the burning in her muscles and shoulder joints. Sweat poured down her brow.

There was no way she would be able to hack her way to freedom. Just this one small vine had taken nearly all of her effort, and she hadn't even cut through. She didn't care. There was nothing else for her to do. She was about to bring the blade down one more time when the chime of the grandfather clock drifted through the open door.

The midnight hour was upon her once again.

CHAPTER XIII

HENRY AND HIS TRAVELING COMPANIONS ENTERED THE WORKROOM of the watch shop. An unfamiliar man held the door open, while David stood to the side, a lantern in his hand to illuminate their way. The flickering light threw his face into sharp relief, giving it an otherworldly look.

"This way," he whispered, without offering any pleasantries. The light bobbed off, toward the corner of the small room. Henry knew the way just as well in the dark as in full daylight. David opened the small basement door and disappeared inside. The man who had let them in watched them warily, and took up the rear.

Henry's stomach twisted around itself despite the familiar surroundings. The others followed David as if they had no care in the world, but they were likely used to clandestine meetings in the dark.

Henry's fingers found the rail and his feet the stairs. There were eleven stairs; he had counted them hundreds of times. Even so, his foot hit the floor with an abrupt finality, his arms flying out to catch himself. He collided with the rough stone wall, his palms scraping painfully, his nose barely escaping a similar fate.

"Careful, there." Alphonse grabbed him by the elbow and turned him to the right. He sensed open space. "Lucky you didn't smash up your pretty face."

Henry was too shaken to protest over being called pretty. "Too bad I can't see in the dark."

"Neither can I. Maybe I'll acquire that skill after my next terrible accident." Alphonse chuckled.

Henry realized he could make out Alphonse's profile. Scant light barely showed the cramped basement. It smelled exactly the same as he remembered, but seemed to be much smaller. More lanterns were held by two men Henry didn't know. One looked to be about David's age, but the other seemed just out of his teens. Both regarded the newcomers with suspicion.

"You are the ones looking for the stranger?" The older man asked.

"Yes, sir," Gabriel answered.

"I'd introduce you, but I'm afraid it's better if we keep things anonymous." David leaned toward the older man. "Ben vouches for them."

The men scrutinized Gabriel's motley band. Henry wished for a minute he had Irene's gift.

The older man nodded. "Aye."

David lifted his lantern, beckoning them further into the basement. "This way."

Henry wondered where he could possibly lead them, since a wall blocked their path.

David slipped through an opening in the wall. Henry stood, mouth agape.

"I knew it looked smaller," he muttered as he passed through the gap to the other half of the basement. It had been clearly arranged as a secret meeting place for the Patriots, though at some point in the future the wall would be removed. Pride swelled in his chest. His family had been involved in helping the Revolution.

The secret meeting space held a small table covered in papers, two chairs, and a bedroll in the corner. A map of the city hung on one wall. The older man pulled a piece of parchment from under his jacket.

"When we read the description you gave to David, we knew." The man set the parchment on the table and weighed it down with bits of broken brick. "Exactly who you were looking for." He punctuated his words by stabbing at the paper with one stubby finger. Henry and his companions crowded around. The page bore a sketch of a man's face. A thin man with prominent cheekbones and short hair, styled much like Henry's.

"Where did you get this?" Gabriel pulled it free from its weights and held it close to the light for a better look.

The man who had opened the door to them spoke. "One of our operatives drew it."

Gabriel turned the drawing around to show Henry. It was Alexei Faber. Gabriel pointed to the drawing and looked at the four men. "What do you know about him?"

The older man inhaled through his nose, letting it out in a *whoosh*. "Not much. Foreign, from his accent, but he's not been keeping with the Hessians, nor is he connected to any British battalion."

The younger man finally spoke up. "I still don't understand who you are, or who this man is. Or what any of it that has to do with us."

Henry tried to imagine how they looked to the Patriots: A young black man, two other young men, and a woman with facial scar and a suspect accent who carried a monkey. He looked sidelong at Irene. She turned her head toward him and smiled, then winked and turned away again. *She's been listening to their thoughts since we walked in here.*

"I assure you, we are only here to help." Gabriel said. "As soon as we find him, we'll take him off your hands."

The older man nodded. "I'll thank you for that. We've got enough to attend to." He sighed and sat in one of the rough chairs around the table. "We wouldn't have noticed him at all, except for who he was seen talking to."

"What do you mean?" Alphonse asked.

"George Williamson, a Loyalist. Yesterday morning. Like I said, up until then he was disregarded. Consorting with Williamson, that's something we pay attention to. That's when we made up that drawing."

Gabriel lowered his head and gave Alphonse a reprimanding look. "He was here yesterday? How did that happen?"

Alphonse shrugged. "It's time travel. He could have come to "yesterday" weeks ago, for all we know. And we're not exactly driving a top-of-the-line piece of equipment like he is. I followed his temporal trail, but with our machine it's possible we were off a bit. I got us here soon enough, didn't I?"

"Any sooner and we'd have been too late," Gabriel muttered, but Alphonse apparently heard him loud and clear.

"Look, considering I threw together a *time machine* in under ten minutes, using spare parts, I would think I could get some appreciation."

His voice had risen to a shout. Gabriel opened his mouth to reply, but stopped, realizing the room had gone quiet. David and the two other men's mouths hung open, while Irene's was clamped shut. Henry clapped his hand over his own to hide his smile at the comical array of expressions.

Gabriel tugged his lapel and cleared his throat. "Quite right. I'm sorry." He turned to their hosts. "Please pardon us. What were Faber and Williamson talking about?"

The man kept his wary gaze on Alphonse as he shook his head. "We don't know, but after their talk they went off together. Down to a building by the docks."

"Who owns the building?"

The man spat the words as if they tasted like dirt. "The East India Company."

Alphonse stepped back from the table. He seemed anxious. "What's in the building?"

The younger man shrugged. "All of the usual things the Company trades — spices, cloth, tea. Everything the bloody crown wants to tax us to death for."

Alphonse, his demeanor composed again, leaned on the table. His expression was entirely too serious for Henry's liking. "There's one other thing I know the East India Company traded — *trades* — in." He turned his razor-edged gaze on Gabriel. "Saltpeter."

The seven men and one woman stood still and silent, until Henry wondered for a moment if time had actually stopped altogether. Chemistry had never been his strongest science but even he knew the implications of Alphonse's revelation. The East India Company traded almost as much saltpeter as they did tea and spices. If that's what Faber was after, then there was only one thing he could want it for.

"A bomb." Gabriel pounded the table with his fist. "That has to be it."

"Why would this man want to make a bomb?" David stabbed at the drawing of Faber with his finger. "Who is he? A mercenary, hired like the Hessians?"

"Yes, but not hired by the British." Irene spoke for the first time. "Someone else. It's... complicated. And we need to stop him."

"He's going after the Congress."

Henry dropped the statement into the room and was met with silence. Every face turned toward him, expressions grim and surprised alike. He finished the thought, despite the stone of fear lodged in his throat. "It's the only thing that makes sense. He's going to blow up the State House, either before or during the Continental Congress."

Irene reached up and stroked Tesla's fur. "That's... extreme. You know what that would mean."

Henry shrugged his shoulders, apologetic for his statements but not retracting them. "No, I don't. I know what it will mean immediately, but over time..."

Gabriel knitted his brow. "The ripple effect... We can't know how it would change things, only that it would. Faber can't know either."

"I don't think he cares. It's not up to him, is it?" Alphonse's voice was low, his arms crossed over his chest and his chin down. "This is his mission. His employers gave him funds so he could get his revenge on Weber, and this is his part of the bargain."

Gabriel pursed his lips. "Yes. And we still have to consider that he's not alone. Whoever hired him likely sent someone along to make sure he finishes the job." He pulled out his watch, ignoring the *tsk* from Alphonse. "If he's really going to blow up the building, it has to be in place before the Congress meets tomorrow."

If that was indeed Faber's plan, the world Henry lived in wouldn't exist after tomorrow.

"I believe Henry is right," Gabriel said, breaking the silence. "It makes the most sense." Henry got the feeling that what he wanted to say was *"it will cause the most damage."*

"What are we going to do to stop him?" The youngest man said quietly.

Gabriel carried a lantern to the map on the wall. He pulled a pair of gold, wire-rimmed spectacles from his pocket and set them on his face.

"He got the saltpeter here." He put his finger on a building near the river, marked 'Delaware' in dark script. "And he's got to take it..." He slid his finger along the page, stopping at a rectangle larger than the others, marked State House. "All the way to here."

David shook his head. "He's got to have somewhere to mix it into gunpowder. He can't use it the way it is."

Gabriel held his finger on the State House and put another on the docks, measuring the distance between. "He must have moved it already. He'd want to be close to the State House, to avoid an accident while transporting it."

"We have lookouts all over the city." The oldest man added his finger to the map, touching seven or eight different locations. "I can move some of them around to cover that route. We'll find him."

Gabriel shook his head. "I appreciate it, but if he has a hint that we're on to him, he'll disappear. And we'll have to start all over again."

David sat in one of the chairs. "We already have men in place around the State House."

"Faber will find a way to get past them." Gabriel pulled off his spectacles and slipped them back into his pocket. "Believe me."

The meeting ended. Gabriel extended his hand to David and the other men. Everyone shook hands and made their courtesies to Irene. The humans ignored Tesla, over which he seemed to take great offense, because he let out a sudden screech.

Irene froze, her eyes wide. "Something's wrong." She looked ready to faint.

"What do you mean?" Henry moved to her side, ready to help her if she swayed.

"I'm not sure. I don't have the Sight like my grandmother, but this... *feeling*... is so strong. Something is definitely wrong."

Gabriel opened his mouth to say something. But the words were drowned out by an explosion. It shook the building, sending mortar and dust into the air, like a sudden summer snowfall.

"Zeus's beard!" He darted to the gap in the wall and through it. The rest of them followed behind him, up the stairs and out the front door.

The street remained empty. At the end, something glowed brightly.

"This is bad." Gabriel and Alphonse raced to the spot, followed by Henry, David, and Irene. In their wake trailed the sound of shouts and noise as those nearby investigated.

Fire.

A blaze engulfed a large structure a few blocks away. The flames reached into the night sky as smoke billowed, embers floating away, then disappearing into nothingness.

The Patriot men ran up beside them. "That's Elizabeth's house." The younger stepped forward, as if to run, but the older man caught his elbow.

"You can't, Robert. It's not safe."

Robert pulled his arm free. "Father, I have to see if I can help. I have to see if she's alright." Without another word of discussion, he ran toward the inferno.

"We should go, too." David said to Robert's father. "The fire department won't be able to handle it alone. They'll need us for the brigade." He hurried back into the shop, emerging a moment later with two leather buckets in his hand. The men ran after Robert, without a word to Gabriel or his companions.

Henry started after them, but Gabriel grabbed his arm.

"We should help." There wasn't a question in Henry's voice.

Gabriel didn't let go. "We have work to do."

Henry gave him an indignant look. "It can wait. We can help here. Four extra sets of hands may make the difference between life and death."

Gabriel shook his head. "We have to go, and we have to go *now*."

Henry held his hands out and then dropped them. "Why?"

"Because this is a distraction." Gabriel pointed at the house. "Faber is making his move."

Sophie held the ax above her head as she listened to the clock chime the final bell of the only hour that seemed to exist. Finally, her arms gave way, the ax falling with a dull, heavy thud. Tears and sweat streaked her face. Blood ran down her fingers from the blisters that burst on her palms. She pushed locks of damp hair from her forehead with a shaking, bleeding hand. The thicket still stood, every leaf and thorn in place. Black fluid ran down the vine from the cuts, rivulets of whatever it was that flowed through her vile captor's veins. The plant's cries had subsided to a soft weeping, barely heard over the never-ending ticks.

She did not want to go back inside. Rose's screams echoed in her mind. Sophie still smelled the scent of burning flesh.

It was only a memory.

The thought was meant to be comforting, but it did nothing to help. She wanted to talk to Alice, to cry with her over what had happened to Rose. And Charles — she never knew what had become of him. After that night she had never snuck out of Montgomery House again.

She jumped, startled, when the clock began to chime again. It sounded sickly. The ticking skipped, like an irregular heartbeat, only to then speed up, racing like a wind-up toy. She ran into the house, her gaze drawn to the grandfather clock, though she knew it was not the source.

The broken-clock sound heralded a wave of deeper cold that dropped over her like a curtain. Her vision doubled and she fell to her knees. It was hard to breathe, every inhale like shards of glass. She fell to the carpet, gasping for air.

And then it was over. As the chiming stopped, the ticking righted itself. Sophie finally sucked in a painless breath and her vision cleared. Rolling onto her back, she focused on making her breathing regular, while her heart thumped in her chest so hard it almost hurt.

After a few minutes, Sophie cautiously stood. The world remained stable and in singular form. How strange! It was almost as if she had been overcome with exhaustion. Her muscles ached with it. She wasn't even certain how long she had been trapped here. It felt like days' worth of hours, though she couldn't tell. The clock was no help.

Did time work differently inside the magic of the memories?

The four companions raced away from the fire, while dozens of people ran in the opposite direction, buckets in hand. Gabriel stopped in the shadows of the homes along the street and the others gathering around.

"Faber must have known the Patriots were watching." Gabriel wiped the back of his hand across his forehead. "That—" He pointed toward the conflagration a few blocks away. "—was deliberate and heavy-handed. He wants people to look over there. He also wants to pull the guards away from the State House. Come on, there's not much time."

Chestnut Street was dark and quiet. Everyone in the area had been drawn to the fire. The future Independence Hall rose out of the shadows, its bell tower and steeple piercing the dark like a needle. The steeple no longer existed in Henry's time. The bell was there, though, waiting to be rung a solitary time before it cracked. He was tempted to climb up and see it whole.

Shadows lay thick around the building. Which made it easier to sneak up on it, but harder to see if anyone else was there. Gabriel stopped and turned toward the group.

"Wait." He crept ahead, disappearing into the dark.

Henry, Irene, and Alphonse huddled at the edge of State House Yard. Henry felt exposed, with only shadow to shield them, but didn't dare breathe a word of his discomfort to the others.

A hissing sound floated from the darkness. Gabriel's signal. The three of them crept to the building where he waited.

For an engineering student, the historic buildings of Philadelphia were a treasure trove. Henry had spent days inside this one, days more poring over the blueprints. He pictured the first-floor layout in his head. The Assembly Room, where tomorrow the Continental Congress would meet to sign the Declaration of Independence, was on the other side of this wall. The importance of the moment suddenly weighed on him.

The windows were too far from the ground to see inside properly, but inside light painted flickering shadows on the ceiling. Henry tried different positions, attempting to get a better view, when someone yanked on his ear.

"Ow!"

Tesla sat on his shoulder, Henry's ear in his tiny grip. He turned his head to relieve the pain and noticed that the others had disappeared.

"Shhh! Take out an advertisement that we're here, why don't you?"

Alphonse's voice had come from around the corner. Henry crept along, not wanting to run into anyone by mistake.

The original Pennsylvania State House consisted of three buildings. The main structure stood in the center, while two smaller brick buildings, called wings, stood one on each side. The wings were connected to the main building by arcaded walkways called hyphens. It took Henry's breath away to see them, since they had been demolished in 1812. The shadows there should have been solid black.

However, there was light.

It was brighter than candlelight, steadier, and had a bluish cast. Henry's companions huddled around whatever was providing the illumination.

"There he is." Alphonse waved him over. "Don't get lost in the dark, now. Never know what's out there."

"Can we please be serious?" Gabriel scolded.

Alphonse almost looked offended. "Who's not serious? Am I not always serious?"

Henry, with Tesla still on his shoulder, drew close enough to get a better look at the light source. A brass tube with knobs and dials along its length. Gabriel held the unusual tube on one end, and the light poured from the other. He cast the light around the hyphen and their immediate area.

"It's a portable torch," Gabriel said in a low tone, surely having seen Henry's confused and awestruck look.

"Where did you get it?" Henry asked with more than a little fascination.

"Built it myself." Alphonse seemed pleased by Henry's admiration of his work. "After another design I, uh, acquired."

Gabriel swept the light across the ground. The hyphen led to a short set of steps up to the door of the main building. They tiptoed to the top of them and turned the doorknob.

Locked.

"Faber must have gone in by another door. We could should find that one." Henry patted his pockets. "I would pick this, but I left my tools in my other coat."

Alphonse stepped up to the door. "Never fear, chum."

Henry almost expected him to ask for Irene's hairpin again, but instead, he pulled something small and shiny from his pocket. It looked like a key, but it couldn't possibly be. Alphonse turned a tiny knob on the side of the device, as if he were winding a watch. Then he stuck the long end into the lock and pressed a button. After a few seconds, he turned the device as he would a key.

"Abracadabra." Alphonse twisted the knob and pushed the door open.

"Amazing." Henry breathed the word.

Alphonse pulled the device from the door and put it away. "Not my original idea. A girl I met in London made it. A magician's assistant, if you can believe it. Quite a clever one."

Gabriel handed Henry the electric torch.

"What do I need this for?"

"Because you can't have one of these." Gabriel lifted his hand and showed Henry the strange, pistol-like weapon they all carried. "And I can't leave you completely undefended. It's heavy enough that if you hit someone with it, it will hurt."

Henry took the light. It was, indeed, heavy enough to inflict damage. He directed the beam through the open door, revealing a tiny mudroom, with coat hooks along one wall. At the other end was a second door, this one without a lock. Gabriel crossed the space and pressed his ear to the door.

"Nothing. Either Faber's gone, or he's planting the bomb somewhere else."

"Or he's really, really quiet," Alphonse offered.

"Or he knows we're here and he's waiting for us," Irene whispered.

"Hopefully not." Gabriel put his hand on the knob. "Henry, turn off the light."

Henry had no idea how he might accomplish that. He turned one of the dials along the barrel of the torch, but that only made the light brighter. He quickly turned it back the other way, until it dimmed to almost nothing.

"Give it here." Alphonse took the torch. He and pushed a button on the end of the tube and the light flickered out. He handed it back. "Some engineer you are."

"Next time, label the button," Henry muttered.

Gabriel opened the door carefully. Silently. Light spilled into the opening. He poked his head in and then withdrew.

"All clear. But keep an eye out."

He disappeared inside. Alphonse followed next, his own weapon ready. Henry took a step but was pulled back by Irene. She put her finger to her lips, stopping his objection. With a wink, she went through the door ahead of him. Henry, his dissatisfaction growing, stepped into the room.

The Assembly Room was not as dark as Henry expected, between the risen moon filtering through the windows, and the glow of several lit candles. The space was filled with tables and chairs. To his left, placed between two fireplaces, sat the famous chair, engraved across the back with a half sun. The chair where General Washington would sit, presiding over the forming of a new nation. The same tables and chairs would remain in this room for at least the next century.

Unless Henry and his friends failed, in which case they would all be splinters and firewood, and with it their future.

"Tesla? Where are you going?"

The monkey ran across the room and through the arched doorway of the vestibule. "Come back here, you silly creature." Irene followed, disappearing into the dark.

Alphonse searched the far side of the room. "I don't see anything. Maybe we've gotten here first? Maybe he got caught up in that first explosion and we're rid of him."

"That's not funny." Henry retorted. If Faber were dead, he'd have no hope of saving Sophie. Would they even be able to get back to their own time, with no temporal trail to follow? As much as the possibility of Faber accidentally blowing himself up simplified things, it also infinitely complicated them.

Gabriel examined the inside of a closet. "I can't believe we'd get that lucky."

"You didn't."

The voice came from the shadow-filled vestibule. Part of a shadow took a half-step forward.

"I expected you to follow, once I saw you in Market Square. I had hoped to be finished with my work, though I had to move up my plans a bit when you showed up at the Blue Anchor."

His voice was low but strong, his familiar accent muted by years of being away from his native country. Gabriel and Alphonse trained their weapons on him. Henry finally remembered the torch in his hand, clicked it on and pointed it at the doorway. The man held up his hand to block the brilliant light.

"Both of your hands in the air," Gabriel barked. "Now."

The man made no move to honor the request. "But where are my manners? Allow me to introduce myself. I am Alexei Faber."

CHAPTER XIV

AS IF IN RESPONSE TO HER QUESTION, THE CLOCK CHIMED AGAIN, A quick twelve count. She picked up the key from where it had fallen on the rug outside the dining room door. It warmed her cold fingers. What else did the house want to show her? She had opened all the doors on this floor and the second floor, and the attic.

Well… Not *all* the doors on the first floor.

Sophie walked into the kitchen and to the cellar door. But the key didn't work. She plopped into one of the kitchen chairs and contemplated the key. It gave no indication of where the next portal might be. What was she supposed to do now?

Some help you are. She tossed it across the room, angry. It bounced off the back door and landed on the floor with a loud *clunk*.

The back door. It looked innocent enough. The thick, wavy four-panes *should* have been black as night, like the windows were. But light poured through. Bright but muted, like the winter's watery sunlight.

Sophie had gone out the front door half a dozen times so far. While she had been in the garden, that had been in her memory, and she had used the *kitchen* door to get there.

Scooping key off the floor, she rubbed the metal between her trembling fingers. Her memories had been sequential. Which meant something recent hid behind the door, something she might actually remember. She looked around for the man in the tailcoat but saw no sight of him.

Sliding the key into the back door lock, she turned it, her other hand gripping the knob. As the door creaked open snow blew inside, tiny flakes racing across the floor.

As she stepped out, her blood turned as cold as the snow.

Henry's emotions swirled inside him like a nest of snakes. Here was the man he had chased across time itself. Just standing there. He *still* didn't look like a monster.

Henry finally settled on anger.

"I never expected to be followed, of course." Faber gave Gabriel's weapon a pointed look. "My method of travel being so unusual."

Gabriel opened his coat with his free hand and showed his badge. "Secret Service. Alexei Faber, I'm placing you under arrest."

Faber stepped further into the room. "How nice to meet you. My employer said I was being watched. Well done, by the way. I probably wouldn't have known you were the one following me if I hadn't seen the boy." He pointed at Henry. "He was always close to Miss Weber, whenever he could be."

Henry's anger exploded. "Don't talk about her. You don't get to talk about Sophie."

"The white knight, riding to the rescue." Faber chuckled. "She never really needed you, you know. She's always been quite capable of taking care of herself."

"How would you know what she's capable of?" Henry tried not to choke on the stone lodged in his throat. "You know nothing about her."

"Enough. I'll say it once more, Faber," Gabriel growled. "Put your hands up."

Alexei strolled into the room. He did not wear a jacket, and his shirt sleeves were rolled up to the elbows. He held something in his left hand the size of a revolver. "How *did* you get here, if I might ask?" His gaze floated over the three boys. "I can't imagine how you built another machine. Unless you already had one. That would be the way, wouldn't it? I've spent my life working on inventions that will change the world, only to have them stolen from under my nose." He let out a weary sigh and shook his head.

Gabriel's aim never wavered. "Tell me what you've done here, so that we can undo it. Then we'll take you home."

"Where I will be given a fair trial, I'm sure." Faber pulled out a chair and sat, heaving another sigh. "All of this. And for what—someone else's ambition to rule the world."

"So end it." Gabriel didn't bother asking for clarification on who Faber was talking about. "Come back with me and tell us what you know. Help me stop it. No one's been hurt yet; we can help you if you help us."

Faber tilted his head and studied Gabriel. "Do you think they'll stop, just because you foiled one of their plans?" He barked a laugh. "Do you think they'll let me live if I fail? No, my boy. I made my bed, now I must lie in it."

Henry had tried to let Gabriel lead the way, but he couldn't wait any longer. "How can I save Sophie?"

The words echoed through the chamber, hanging in the air like smoke. Faber shifted his gaze to focus on Henry.

"I know you love her. I was in love, too. Once. I loved someone more than the moon and stars in the sky. Love wasn't enough."

Henry's fury boiled. He wished he had the ability to hide his emotions, like Gabriel. "Yes, I do love her. And I want to see her safe and sound, living her life and not trapped in that casket for another hundred years."

Faber shrugged, but there was a touch of guilt in his eyes. "Her predicament has nothing to do with her, or with you, or even with any of this." He waved his hand, indicating the room. "It's the settling of a personal account."

"What account? What could make you do this?"

Faber slid his gaze to Gabriel. "You did not tell him? You must know, I'm sure it was included in my dossier, or whatever you call it."

Henry turned to Gabriel, unspoken questions again piling up in his mind.

"Enough chatter." Gabriel took another step toward Faber.

Henry wanted to shake the agent by his collar. He was hiding important information. *Again*. Henry had trusted the man with his life, but he wasn't sure he could also trust him with Sophie's.

"You're a scientist." Alphonse made the statement sound like a question, and as if Faber's actions were a personal insult. "So, why?"

Faber barked out a harsh laugh. "When you bargain with the devil, eventually he demands payment."

"Where's the bomb?"

Faber's gaze locked on Gabriel. "If I do not succeed, I am a dead man. You understand that, don't you, Mr. Government Agent?"

"We'll protect you."

"Until you have no more use for me. I need to finish what I started. I am a man of my word. Maybe a new world *is* what we need."

Gabriel gritted his teeth and adjusted his aim. "You don't know what kind of world you'll be making."

"That's not my concern. I have nothing left. I leave the details up to the people who paid me."

"They might not ever exist if you succeed." Gabriel shook his head. "I wonder if they've thought about that."

"They have made arrangements to protect themselves from the consequences. That was part of our deal." Faber did not elaborate, and Gabriel did not press him.

Faber and Gabriel stared each other down, the tension in the air as thick as the humidity. Faber chuckled and stood. "Now if you'll excuse me, my task is complete."

"I don't know which word you didn't understand, Faber," Gabriel hissed. "But you aren't going anywhere except with us."

"That would most likely be true, except for one very important detail." Faber made no move against them.

"And what would that be?"

A feeling of dread came over Henry the instant the words were in the air. He barely heard Irene's warning cry before the shot rang out.

Henry ducked, his arms over his head. The light of the electric torch bounced around the room like an insect, highlighting tables, chairs, and the ceiling. His heart tried to make a desperate escape through his mouth, and his head smacked on the edge of a nearby table, sending blinding lights across his vision before he landed on the floor.

When he could see again, he lifted himself up just enough to glance over the table. Faber hadn't moved. Henry turned to where he had last seen Alphonse. He was gone.

A short, sharp cry of pain made him turn. Irene appeared in the doorway behind Faber. She wasn't alone. A man held her tightly. He was dressed as they were, in 18th century waistcoat, jacket, and breeches. But, like them, he did not sport an 18th century hairstyle.

He held a gun to Irene's temple—a modern one, not an antique pistol.

"He snuck up on me." Irene sounded angry. "Stupid." I was looking for Tesla and I didn't feel him behind me. He's got a mind like a pile of bricks."

The man grunted and shoved her further into the room. She scurried a few quick steps, but didn't fall, turning to face her captor.

"Are you alright, Henry?" She still sounded angry, but also concerned.

Henry, on the other hand, was terrified. "Yes."

"Where's my darling Alphonse?"

"I don't know."

"Figures. Always wandering off just when he's needed. Gabriel?"

There was no response. Henry made to move in the direction he had last seen Gabriel, but the man with the gun barked something at him in loud, guttural German. Henry knew the language, but his mind wasn't working properly. It sounded like a threat. Henry froze and held up his hands. Gabriel still didn't answer.

Faber made his way to the place where Gabriel had stood. He looked down, silent.

"Well, that's unfortunate." He turned to the German man. "No one was supposed to be hurt. At least no one who was not scheduled to."

Henry wanted to rush over and see Gabriel with his own eyes but knew he would be shot for his trouble.

"He is not innocent." The German man pointed his gun at Irene. "Neither is this one." His accent made the words sound sharp edged.

"Stop it." Faber said something else, in German, but it was too soft for Henry to hear. While the two men argued, he saw his chance to check on Gabriel. He slunk to the floor and looked beneath the tables, through the legs of chairs. His blood went cold.

Gabriel lay on the ground, still. Too still.

The men continued deep in discussion. Something about what to do with them, bits of English and German mingling together. Henry duck-walked toward Gabriel, his heartbeat seeming to slow with each inch he moved.

A loud *click*, very close to his ear, stopped him. He turned his head slightly, only to find that, once again, a weapon was pointed at him.

"That's far enough, young man." Faber's hands were steady as a surgeon's.

Henry raised his hands and showed Faber that he only had the torch. "I'm not armed. I'm not even supposed to be here." The last part came out mumbled and sorry sounding. "Let me help him."

Faber considered the request. He motioned his agreement with the pistol.

Henry scrambled to Gabriel's side. He was immediately glad they hadn't eaten at the Blue Anchor, or else he would have heaved up every bite. A gaping hole had been punched into Gabriel's chest, right above his heart. The linen around the wound was stained, the blood dark and shining. Henry checked for a pulse at Gabriel's wrist and neck. Nothing.

Henry wasn't a doctor but knew there was nothing to be done. He wasn't sure how he was supposed to feel, and it didn't matter, because he was numb. He had never witnessed a murder. It was nothing like he thought it might be. Not that he had given it a great deal of consideration.

As he stood, he locked eyes with Faber's. He shook his head. Faber frowned again, an expression of regret flitting across his face. He glanced at his companion, giving him an equally flitting look of reprimand.

"Finish now, and then we leave." The German man spat the words. Irene turned her head to look at Henry. Her eyes were wide, her face drained of color.

Faber left Gabriel and Henry where they were. He climbed onto the platform at the front of the room, where the head table and General Washington's chair waited. Faber disappeared beneath the table for several moments.

"It's done. Ready to go off during the meeting tomorrow."

"They'll find it." Henry was thinking of David and his men. They had heard everything Henry and his friends had talked about.

"Even if they do they won't know how to disarm it. They don't have the technological skill in this century."

Henry thought David might be able to figure it out. But he wouldn't be here, in this room—would he? He wasn't a signer. Maybe as an observer? The idea both uplifted and terrified Henry. If David tried to disarm the bomb and made a mistake he might die. And then Henry might never exist. He didn't know if David had any children yet, or even if he was married.

"They'll evacuate the building, then." Irene looked away from Gabriel's body. "No one will die, the Congress will be even more determined. You won't stop anything."

Faber shook his head. "I'm much more clever than that. I thought you would have guessed. All the doors have been outfitted with a timed lock. Once the locks are set, they will be trapped."

The German man grunted. "Enough chatter, Herr Faber. Let us leave this hot, wretched, disgusting place."

"It won't be the home you left you know." Irene said to him. "You don't know how what you're doing will change things."

"I *expect* a brand brand-new world. One that I will enjoy very much." He laughed again, and then suddenly stopped. The man's eyes rolled up into his head, and the hand holding the gun fell limp. As he crumpled to the ground Faber backed away, confusion on his face. He glared at Irene.

Irene held up her empty hands. "Don't look at me, I didn't do it."

Faber spun toward Henry, who also held up his hands. "I've been right here the entire time."

Faber cursed. "The invisible one." He touched his head as if looking for something. "I left my goggles in the machine."

Henry debated whether to stay put, or make a dive for Faber. He was closer than Irene, who remained unarmed. All he had was the electric torch, but, as previously noted, it would make a good weapon to strike someone with. He concentrated on what he was thinking, hoping Irene would hear. *We need a distraction.* Alphonse was nowhere to be seen, and Gabriel was dead. They were the only two left.

Irene gave no indication she had heard him. It didn't matter anyway. Faber slowly backed toward the door. "I'm sorry to leave you like this." He glanced at Gabriel's body on the floor. "But I can't pass up this opportunity." It seemed a strange thing to say.

"You know we'll follow you," Irene said.

"That's a very good point." Faber put his free hand into his pocket and fumbled with something. "And you'll likely also alert the Congress to the bomb. Which means, unfortunately, I'll have to dispose of you.

That was certainly not what Henry had in mind. How had this all gone so wrong? "Don't you think they'll be suspicious when they find our bodies on the floor tomorrow morning?"

Faber pulled his hand from his pocket. In it he gripped a small silver device the size of a cigarette lighter. "I honestly don't care." He held up the device and pressed a button.

A moment later there was a strange sound, like metal grinding on metal. It sounded familiar to Henry, and by the time he had figured out where he had heard it before, Faber's time machine had materialized behind him.

"What the hell?" Alphonse's voice came from somewhere to Henry's left and ahead of him. Faber jumped and turned toward the voice. "It moves through space?"

Faber spoke to the air, his gaze roving the area. "It was not part of the original specifications. I added it later." He held up the little silver box. "A simple transducer. Activated by this remote switch. The machine dematerializes from where it is and rematerializes wherever the signal happens to be." He backed toward the machine, gun still waving at empty air.

Alphonse's voice sounded closer to the inventor when he spoke again. "That's brilliant. I mean, I still have to stop you, of course, but it's amazing."

The inventor gave a small nod. "Thank you. A man always likes to have his work appreciated. And you can either stop me, or save your friends. Your choice."

Faber tossed a small, round object into the middle of the room.

Henry, thinking it must be some kind of incendiary device, dove away and flattened himself to the floor. The device buzzed and crackled, and the room filled with acrid, foul-smelling smoke. Across the room a door slammed. More grinding of metal. Then quiet.

"Irene? Are you alright? Alphonse?" Henry covered his mouth with his sleeve to block the smoke.

Someone coughed. He slid across the floor in the direction of the sound, and found Irene ten feet away. She sat on the floor, holding her mob cap over her mouth and nose.

"Alphonse?" Irene called, her voice muffled by the fabric. "Where are you?" There was no answer.

"If he's hurt, we'll never find him." Henry hadn't even thought of it before that moment, but he supposed becoming invisible had to have a downside. "Alphonse!"

A small shape moved in the fog, scratching along the floor. Henry found the electric torch. He turned it on and shone the light in the direction of the shape. A pair of beady eyes appeared, sparkling in the light, along with a mouth of sharp, white teeth and a loud a screech.

"Tesla!" Irene called her pet. "There you are. Where have you been hiding?"

Out of the way, Henry thought. *Maybe he's the smartest of us all.* Tesla raced to his mistress and clambered onto her shoulder. In his hand he held her missing weapon, which Irene gratefully took.

"Come on, we have to clear out whatever this stuff is. It doesn't seem to be harmful." She led the way to the edge of the room. Which was not as simple as it seemed. Henry nearly beat an innocent chair with the torch, and Irene accidentally shot a table. Once they arrived at the wall and opened one of the giant windows, the smoke fled, the room appearing before their eyes.

Faber's time machine was gone. The German man sprawled unconscious, face-down on the floor. Alphonse was nowhere to be seen.

Irene went to where Gabriel's body lay. "We need to find Alphonse and... clean this up." Her voice trembled slightly. "It won't do for the Continental Congress to come in tomorrow and find a corpse."

Gabriel's corpse took a great sucking breath and sat up easily, with no sign of pain. He pressed a hand to his chest, over the bloody hole in his shirt, and inhaled deeply, wincing in pain as his lungs expanded.

"Where's Faber?"

Henry jumped, a scream of shock and surprise erupting from his lungs. "You're dead."

"Obviously that's not true." He pulled on his jacket and grabbed his hat.

"Yes, you *were*. There was no pulse. And so much blood. You couldn't survive it." Henry kept his distance. Gabriel's sudden recovery might be a miracle, or it might also be something else.

"You made a mistake. Heat of the moment, bound to happen."

Henry looked at Irene for some kind of confirmation that she had seen the same thing he had. Her expression was unreadable. Henry pressed on.

"You have a giant hole in your chest. Even if I was wrong about how serious it was, and your injuries only made it seem as if you were dead, you've lost a lot of blood. There is no logical reason—"

"—We really don't have time for this now." Gabriel stood, strong and steady. Henry was almost certain that if he were to look beneath the blood-stained linen of his shirt, he would find the skin unblemished. He stepped away, his mind spinning a dozen horrors.

"What kind of demon are you?"

Gabriel laughed. "Demon? Is that the best you can come up with?" He shook his head and turned toward Irene. "What happened?"

Irene gave a brief account of events, including Faber's escape under smoke screen. "He made it sound as if he was going to kill us, but he didn't. Strange."

"He probably figures he'll be able to hide, somewhere in time." Gabriel looked around the room, his gaze hovering over the prostrate form of Faber's companion. "Where is our dear Alphonse?"

Irene's expression turned into worry. "I don't know. He was invisible. He knocked out that man, and then he was talking to Faber, and I think he was over there."

"You think?" Gabriel's didn't yell, but the irritation behind it was so intense he might as well have. Tesla, still sitting on Irene's shoulder, screeched. Gabriel flicked an icy glance at the animal, and he curled closer to his mistress's neck.

"He was invisible. Then Faber threw that smoke bomb and I saw nothing at all. He's obviously not conscious or visible. I didn't see any blood on the floor, at least not any that didn't belong to..." Irene let the words drift. "Given the circumstances, I thought you were the priority."

Gabriel strode to where the time machine had been. He swung out a leg, carefully, but found only air. Henry, still trying to recover from the shock of a dead man suddenly coming back to life, took a moment to figure out what Gabriel was doing. He and Irene moved around the room, walking carefully, looking for a solid mass of invisible man.

"Nothing," Henry announced from a far corner of the room. "He's not over here."

"Nor here." Irene called from the other corner "I don't feel his mind, either. Not that I would if he were unconscious."

Gabriel returned to the center of the room, his own search finished. "He's not here."

"Then where?" There was a note of panicked worry in Irene's voice. "Where did he go?"

Henry's realization filled him with cold dread. "Into the time machine with Faber."

"He must have gotten out before the door closed." Irene waved her arms low to the ground.

"He's not here, Irene." Gabriel said quietly. "He's gone."

There was a moment when Henry thought Irene might cry. "We have to rescue him."

"We will, when we find Faber again."

"And how will we do that?" Henry waved the torch in an irritated manner. "He was the one who knew how to operate *our* time machine."

Gabriel leaned against one of the tables. "Well, Mr. Engineer, I guess that's up to you now."

Henry's knees nearly buckled. "Me? Why me?"

"Why not you? You have to serve some purpose on this trip. I can't do it; I don't understand all that mechanical gobbledy-gook. Do you, Irene?"

"I'm sure I wouldn't have the slightest idea where to begin," Irene replied. "You're terribly clever, Mr. Rittenhouse. I have faith in you." The look in her eyes was far more doubting than her words let on.

The German groaned from the back corner of the room. He sat up, a hand on his head. Gabriel, without hesitation, aimed his weapon at the man and fired. A blue light burst from the end and hit the German directly in the chest. His eyes rolled up, showing the whites, and the man slumped over again.

"What are we going to do with him?" Irene nudged him with the toe of her boot. He grunted, rolled over, and started to snore. "He deserves to be left here, blighter."

"He does, but we'll need him to answer some questions." Gabriel shifted his weight, but he still moved as if he had not had half his blood recently spilled onto the floor. Henry, unnerved, put it aside.

"Before any of that, we need to find Faber's bomb and disable it." Henry hopped up onto the platform and knelt beside George Washington's high-backed chair. "Faber was messing about over here." He leaned his head underneath. "Uh-oh."

"That doesn't sound positive," Irene remarked.

Henry carefully turned the chair over and shone the torch's light on the bottom. Tucked beneath the seat was an iron box. Gabriel tenderly pried off the lid, revealing a small device. It was constructed of clock-work attached to small wax-paper wrapped tubes. Three numbered dials had been placed in the center. The device ticked softly.

Henry pointed to the dials. "It's the same type of countdown he used on his sleeping machine." Only these dials didn't count years, but hours and minutes. Twelve hours from now, give or take, the counter would reach zero. And then...

"I guess he didn't use all of the saltpeter in that last explosion." Henry turned his head to get a better look at the device.

"This wouldn't hold enough to do much damage. It's probably TNT. Much more stable, and a much stronger explosion. Or it's something completely unknown." Gabriel, with a feather-light touch, ran a finger over one of the dials. "It looks like the same type of device that was used in the Winter Palace bomb."

Henry had heard of the attempt to assassinate the Russian Tsar. He and his family had survived, but many others had died.

Gabriel turned to Henry. "Ideas?"

"Let's see if we can remove the box." Henry ran his fingers around the edge. "There's two hooks here." Henry pulled the hooks out, one at a time, holding the box with his free hand. He lowered the mechanism, slowly, and turned it upright. Gabriel took it from him and put it on the table.

Henry stood and shone the light into the box. "It seems simple. When the timer gets to zero, something makes a spark." His gaze followed the fuses that stuck out of the paper-wrapped tubes behind the timer. "Something behind here lights the fuses. And then..."

"Boom." Irene stood just behind Henry, looking over his shoulder.

Gabriel pulled up a chair and sat down. "Can you disarm it?"

Henry asked himself the same question. He studied the device's construction, building a blueprint in his head. It was harder than just taking apart a watch. The watch wouldn't explode if he did something wrong. "It should be as simple as disconnecting the explosive. Hold this and shine it right here."

He didn't think even Tesla's slender fingers would fit. "Do you happen to have a pair of tweezers?" Henry asked as a joke.

Gabriel pushed a button in the middle of the torch. Something popped out from the bottom. With his fingernails, he removed it and handed it to Henry.

"Will these do?"

Henry took a tiny pair of brass scissors from Gabriel. "It will indeed. What else have you got hiding in there?"

"If you knew, I'd have to terminate you." Though Henry was sure it was likewise meant as a joke, there was no trace of a smile on Gabriel's face. Henry turned back to the explosive device, which seemed less dangerous. He held his breath as he snipped the fuses of all the explosives. "That should do it. The timer will wind down harmlessly."

Without warning, the clock's ticking sped up.

Henry jumped back and dropped the scissors onto the table. The *tick, tick, tick* was like an insect's chirp, calling to the crickets outside. The numbers on the dial sped by, minutes going in seconds.

"It's boobytrapped," Gabriel said. "Damn Faber."

Henry had plenty of other words to describe the situation, but not a single one was appropriate for a gentleman to say.

"I don't suppose you know how to stop it?" Henry snapped. "Because we now have about twelve *minutes* before we all explode.

Or less." The ticking seemed to be speeding up instead of remaining steady.

Gabriel shook his head. "I told you this is not my area of expertise. Alphonse would be the one to ask."

"Great." Henry pulled off his coat and tossed it on the floor. "Light, please." His overly polite tone hid both his annoyance at Gabriel and his fear. He scanned the device once more, searching for the secondary mechanism.

"Maybe it's just for show, you know?" Irene offered the suggestion, likely trying to boost their spirits. "The timer is just winding down, and nothing will happen when it gets to zero? Like the smoke bomb. He could have killed us, but it was just a distraction."

Henry appreciated the effort. "I'd rather not wait to find out. Perhaps you and Tesla should go outside?" He didn't want to sound like a chauvinist; he knew full well that Irene was capable of taking care of herself. "In case things should go... badly."

Henry couldn't see her reply but heard the smile in her voice. "If it's all the same to you, I'll just wait here a bit longer. If I'm going, you're going with me."

"All right, then, we're all for one and one for all and we'll all get blown up together if you don't stop talking." Gabriel picked up the scissors. "Let's get this done, alright?"

Henry inspected the device once more. The dials were secured with tiny screws. He grabbed the scissors from Gabriel's hand and used them to loosen the fasteners, then pulled the faceplate away gently. The mechanism was made of small gears and springs, like any clockwork. Cutting the fuses to the explosive had started a secondary clock spring, which was wound tightly to speed up the timer.

Wads of cotton had been stuffed into the middle of the device. Henry carefully pulled out a piece. Beneath was nestled a glass vial filled with clear liquid. "What fresh hell is this?"

Gabriel looked over his shoulder. "That's probably pure nitro-glycerin. We're lucky we didn't blow up moving the box."

Henry touched the cotton padding, tucked in tightly around the vial. "Can we take it outside, let it detonate?"

"Too risky."

Henry's hands shook. There was so little time. He focused on the vial.

"A small hammer attached to the lever will break the vial and set off the charge. The entire building will be flattened, along with everyone in it." Henry talked through the problem. "So we can't move it. We just have to just stop it from going off."

"Thank you for the summary. Solutions would be nice." Gabriel's voice was sharp enough to cut glass.

"Stopping the timer so the hammer doesn't strike the vial is the best option." Henry said.

"One minute, gentlemen." Irene made no move to leave, but her body language said she could run from the room in record time if it were required of her.

She was right; the *ticks* were almost on top of one another now. Funny, they were in time with Henry's pounding heart.

Gabriel turned to Irene. "Go, now. We'll be right behind you."

Henry's palms were damp with sweat. Their lives were literally in his hands. Usually he had time to consider a problem, analyze whatever was in front of him. Now there was no time at all.

Henry's mind whirled like the gears. *The gears.*

"Ten seconds. Come on, we have to go." Irene's voice sounded far away.

Gabriel pulled at Henry's arm. "Time's up."

Henry scooped up the scissors from the table, and in one motion, stuck the pointed end into one of the gears.

The ticking stopped. There was a small grinding sound followed by a strange whining as the gears tried to continue their motion. Then silence.

"What did you do?" Irene's question broke the silence like gunfire.

"I just stopped the clock." Henry wanted to laugh, but he was afraid he might set off the device if he shook. "Such a simple solution. My father would kill me if he saw me break a clock on purpose."

Irene laughed. "In this case I think he'd be fine with it."

Henry put his hands on the table and bent over, not sure if he wanted to throw up or fall over.

Gabriel inspected Henry's work. "Not the most elegant solution but it is certainly effective. Well done, Mr. Rittenhouse."

"We need to dispose of it. If we had some lye, that would neutralize the nitroglycerin. I think." Henry had no idea how he knew that, except that he had a classmate who liked chemistry. He must have mentioned it to Henry at some point.

"Good. Lye is pretty prevalent in this time, I'm sure we can find some easily. We'll take care of this, and then we need to get back to the time machine and follow Faber."

"Did you say *time machine?*"

Gabriel and Irene whipped around toward the foyer where the voice had come from. Their weapons were out in the blink of an eye. Henry had nothing to defend himself with, not even the torch. He slid behind the other two.

"There's no need for all that, my boy." A second voice spoke from behind them. Three heads turned, but only Irene moved her arm, her aim swinging around to cover the second intruder.

"We're here to help." From the darkness of the doorway stepped a short man of rotund stature. The glasses perched on his nose caught the dim light.

"Ben." Gabriel greeted his friend but did not drop his weapon. "What are you doing here?"

"We were with the fire department, and—"

"Who's with you?" Gabriel asked.

"He told me what you had discussed. We realized that the fire was likely a distraction." Benjamin Franklin looked down at the unconscious German. "And that those who were assigned to protect the State House probably had left their posts. We thought it might be prudent to come here. It looks like we were correct."

Gabriel finally tucked his weapon into his shoulder holster. "David?"

Ben raised his voice slightly. "Come out, it's all right."

David Rittenhouse's skin looked pale, even for a moonlit room. He wore a strange look as he stared at Henry.

He had overheard everything.

"Rittenhouse?" David paused, the look on his face the same one Henry's father wore when a watch repair was being difficult. "You said time machine. I thought I heard you say it before, in the cellar. But I didn't believe it. You have come from the future?"

"I..." Henry didn't know what to say. He could think of no convincing lie. "Yes. I know it sounds impossible, but—"

"Please don't sound so apologetic, my boy." David's gaze was fixed Henry's face, studying it. "I've often wondered if it were possible to travel in time. After all, time is my business. Space is my hobby. I study the stars, watch their movements. I've pondered the idea that we don't have to be just passengers on this planet, but that we could be captains, going wherever and whenever we want." He finally tore his focus from Henry and shifted it to Benjamin. "But some don't share my vision."

"Flights of fancy." Ben's reply was distracted. He seemed to be working out some problem of his own, gazing at Gabriel with a wary look in his eye. "Have *you* come from the future as well? How is that possible when I've known you for years? You look exactly the same."

Gabriel puckered his lips, his eyes closing, as if he were in pain. "I would love to explain, Ben, but there's no time."

Benjamin pondered a moment more, his expression wavering between distrust and amazement. "I have seen and heard remarkable things in my life. But this will require a long talk beside a fire, and plenty of ale."

A smile flitted over Gabriel's lips like a ghost. "Perhaps. But now we need action. First, there is an explosive device in this box." He ignored David's gasp of disbelief. "It's been disabled. But it contains an extremely volatile substance that needs to be neutralized. We can't move it, or else we risk the entire building."

David gasped. "Good Lord."

"We need some lye," Henry added.

Benjamin gave a short nod. "We'll take care of it." He made no other inquiries about the device of or the people who had placed it there.

"Wonderful. And there are some timed locks on the doors that will need to be dismantled as well. Once that's settled, we will be in desperate need of transportation to Germantown. Horses will do, unless you happen to have something faster." Gabriel kept the conversation moving, perhaps to avoid the topic of time travel. And his strange history. And the fact Henry was a Rittenhouse.

David and Ben exchanged a glance.

"We have been working on something," David said. "It's a project we tinker with, mind. Never actually used it, not for as long as journey as you want to take. But it should do the trick."

Gabriel hopped down from the platform. Where is it?"

"Just the next block over, in my personal stable." Ben waved David across the room. "We'll get the lye and be back in a jiffy."

The two men disappeared into the mudroom, pulling the door shut behind them.

"And what about him?" Irene pointed at Faber's still-unconscious companion with her weapon

Gabriel nudged the man with his leg. "I suppose we'll have to take him back with us. But we need to make sure he can't cause any more trouble before then."

Irene found some rope in a cabinet. The German man was bound and gagged, still sleeping. David and Ben returned with the lye. Once the bomb was neutralized, Gabriel put the lid on the box and instructed David to toss it in the river.

Gabriel heaved the German onto his shoulder, as if he had never been deceased at all. And they all stepped out of the State House and into the hot night.

CHAPTER XV

I T WAS THE MOST UNLIKELY CONTRAPTION HENRY HAD EVER SEEN, WHICH was amazing considering the number of unlikely machines he had seen recently. Their band of two government agents, an accidental time traveler, one soon-to-be Founding Father, one famous astronomer, and a very quiet German mercenary gathered in the middle of Benjamin Franklin's carriage house, only half of which contained an actual carriage. The other half had been turned into a workshop.

They gathered around the back of a simple farmer's wagon. "Leyden jars?" Gabriel asked Ben. "You've made an electric wagon?" The back of the wagon was filled crates. Each crate was crammed with jars connected to each other by copper bars.

"Yes." Ben beamed. "You remember my experiments with electricity. That night with the kite, in the thunderstorm, and the key?" He spoke easily, seeming to forget that just fifteen minutes ago he had been wary of his friend's strange ability to travel through time.

Gabriel nodded. "I don't think I will ever forget. That night changed my life." He said the last part quietly, and Henry wasn't sure anyone was supposed to hear it.

"The Leyden jar holds the charge until it is discharged. Put several together, naturally I can store more electricity," Ben explained. "Of course, to move something large like a wagon, you need quite a bit of energy. Two horses' worth."

"It's a battery." Henry finally realized what he was looking at. He still had the electric torch in his hand. Its source of power was a small, single dry-celled battery. This was a much-larger version of the same thing. He held the torch behind his back, not wanting Ben to see. He had meddled with time and his own family history quite enough.

"Battery? Yes, it does remind one of a battery of cannons, doesn't it, all just waiting to discharge their loads." Ben chuckled. "I like that. Battery."

Henry ignored the scathing look he got from Gabriel. It was well-known that Benjamin Franklin had named the portable energy source, and why. What difference did it make how he had gotten there? History would remain the same in the end.

"How does it charge?" Irene asked. "We don't have to wait for a thunderstorm, do we?"

Ben laughed. "No, my dear. Like this." He showed them a small crank wheel positioned near the front of the battery. The outside edge of the wheel was wrapped in wool fabric. Ben positioned the wheel, which was on a swing arm, so that the edge touched one of the battery's copper bars, and then cranked it.

Henry understood. "The wool rubs on the metal and creates a static charge, which is then stored in the jars." It was brilliant. Wonderfully simple, but brilliant.

"Exactly. Just don't touch the jars, or you'll get quite the shock. And you'll discharge the battery, meaning you won't be going anywhere."

"This is fascinating, Ben, but how will this get us to Germantown faster than a horse?" Gabriel sounded both impatient and skeptical.

Ben raised a finger. "Ah, yes. This is only half the story. I contributed the power source, and my friend David contributed the driving mechanism."

David moved to the rear of the wagon. "Yes, you see, we needed to find something that would keep the wheels spinning since there's no horse to pull it." He crooked a finger at them, indicating they should follow, and then ducked down beneath.

Henry gasped. The undercarriage had been outfitted with large gears, like those from a tower clock. He followed the path of brass and copper, from the wheels to a single shaft that would drive them, to the center and the biggest clock spring he had ever seen resided. Henry's first thought as he scanned the contraption was *how amazing*. His next was how much his father would have enjoyed it.

David turned the hand crank, tightening the spring as far as it could go. When he finished, he reached out with one hand and grasped the empty hook, latching the crank in place so that the spring wouldn't unwind when he let go.

"Now we're ready. The spring will get us going, and once we've overcome the inertia, we can use the battery to maintain momentum."

"We?" Gabriel shook his head. "Just tell me how to work it and I'll get it going. You don't need to tag along."

"I'm afraid we do," David replied. "Or at least one of us does. In the first place, it will take longer to explain how to drive it than to just do it ourselves. In the second place, it sounds as if you aren't coming back to the city. Someone will need to return this."

Gabriel leaned against the wagon. "You're right, of course. But I don't think there's room for all of us, plus both of you."

"I'll drive." Ben hopped up into the driver's seat. He directed Henry and Gabriel to open the double doors of the carriage house. There wasn't a single soul on the street to witness the odd conveyance's departure. Henry wondered if the neighbors had ever seen it, or if the two conspirators had only ever driven it in the middle of the night.

Henry and Gabriel lifted the sleeping German into the open area of the wagon. Despite being tossed about like a sack of produce, the man still did not wake.

"Ladies next." Gabriel held out his hand and helped Irene in beside the German. Tesla hopped up and settled into his mistress's lap.

"You, you're on your own," Gabriel said to Henry. He hopped up beside Ben, discussing something with the inventor that Henry couldn't hear. A hand on his shoulder made him jump. It was David, his expression both concerned and puzzled.

"I'm still not quite sure who you are." He scanned Henry's face for the hundredth time. "And I'm not sure I'm supposed to understand. But if you are from the future, and my guess is correct, then... no, don't tell me." This was in response to Henry's intake of breath and open mouth. "It is not good for any man to know too much about his future. Or the future of his progeny, I expect. But seeing you, bearing my name, gives me great hope."

"Thank you, sir." The lump in Henry's throat made it hard to speak, and the words came out mumbled.

David patted Henry's shoulder again. "If I don't send you on your way, the future might not happen the way it's supposed to, and then this conversation might never take place."

Henry could only nod. He would love to sit down with this man, and discuss their family history, tell him all about his grandchildren and great-grandchildren. He also was a little afraid to say anything. His time at the university had been spent learning about arches and bridge spans, columns and cupolas. Everyday things. The man in front of him had wondered if it was possible to see the stars and built a machine that would allow him to do so. He was a man of action and adventure. The idea of time travel only seemed to intrigue him.

"Oh, don't forget this." David pulled the photophone out of his pocket and handed it to Henry. "It won't do me any good once you're gone, unless it can transport sound and pictures across time." He chuckled. "Though I don't mind telling you that I was tempted to keep it and pull it apart, just to see how it works."

Henry took the photophone with a smile. "Thank you." He hoped the words conveyed everything he meant. Grasping the side of the wagon, he pulled himself up and inside.

"Everyone ready?" Ben looked over his shoulder at his passengers. "Right, then let's be off."

"You're sure this works?" Gabriel's question was tinged with doubt.

"Absolutely. David, if you would be so kind as to let us loose? Oh, and give the boy his instructions."

"Instructions?" Henry had no idea what that meant, but it sounded like something Gabriel wouldn't forgive him for if he messed up. "I don't know if I—"

"—Oh, don't be silly. It's simple." David made a dismissive gesture and walked to the back of the wagon. "Now, once you get going, don't let the wagon slow down, or you'll have to start over." He leaned down and put his hand on the hook that held the spring. "There's a lever there." He pointed to the mechanism in question, beside Henry. "It will engage the battery. Let the spring go for a bit, to overcome the inertia, then flip the lever. You wait so that you don't use stored energy when you don't need it."

Henry nodded, excited he understood. "The kinetic energy of the spring and clockworks provide the propulsion, but they're not perpetual."

David's smile beamed pride. "Exactly. So, once you've flipped the lever, you'll need to keep the battery charged."

Henry knew before he was told. "I spin the wheel to keep the static electricity flowing."

"Precisely. I'm not sure how often you'll have to charge it." He knitted his brow. "We've never taken it as far as eight miles."

Henry was almost afraid to ask. "How far did you get before you had to charge it?"

"About a mile and a half. But you'll get further if you turn the battery off while you're on a down slope. Take advantage of gravity to give you a chance to build more charge."

"Are we done talking?" Gabriel roared. "It's only the fate of the world, I'm sure it'll wait until after tea."

"We're ready." Henry sounded far more certain than he felt. "I'll keep us going. Just be sure to keep us on the road."

"Ah, yes, nearly forgot." Ben jumped down from his seat and ran to the front of the wagon. He pulled a tinderbox from his pocket and lit a match. With the flame he lit the lanterns that hung from the front of the carriage and lit the wick.

"I don't know if that will be enough light to see the road at the speed we'll be traveling, but we have to make do with what we have."

Gabriel reached his arm back. "Henry? Hand me the torch."

Henry handed it over, wondering what help it could possibly provide. Its light would be too meager to see much in the dark.

Gabriel twisted something on the torch, pushing one of the three buttons that Henry hadn't bothered to press before. Light burst from the bulb, emitting a beam bright enough to see into every corner of the barn. He directed the beam in front of the wagon, where it illuminated the street in front, far beyond the reach of the lanterns.

"Well," Ben said with a chuckle, "that solves that. Just let me remove the brakes..." He pulled a lever beside his seat, and the wagon shifted slightly. "David? Let us loose."

David gave Henry one final wink. "Good luck to you, lad." He leaned down, pulled the hook that held the spring, and leapt away. The wagon rolled out of the barn, picking up speed as they reached the street. David ran to the door, his hand raised in farewell.

"Into the breach!" Ben pulled the reins, and the wagon turned the corner. The barn was gone, and they were on their way to Germantown.

It was cold, but that no longer bothered Sophie. However, standing in the snow with the sun shining overhead, her spine felt as if spiders crawled along its length.

She stood on the front walk of her house, the three stories coated in snow like a gingerbread house covered in sugar. There was not a single thorny plant in sight.

That wasn't what was caused her crawling skin, or the terrible, tight ball of fear in her midsection. Nor was it the fact that she had nearly been bowled over by Henry, who was striding up her own walk. It wasn't any singular thing, but the entire scene. Wreaths and greens, held in place with red velvet bows and strung across the front porch. A Christmas tree, visible through the front window. Henry's coat, his hat. He was distracted by a slight figure, dressed in boy's clothes, climbing down the drainpipe.

Sophie's chest tightened as if it were wrapped in iron bands. This *wasn't* a memory. It was her dream. The perfectly lovely dream that had turned into a nightmare.

Henry walked across the yard, traipsing over the snow-covered ground. He was dressed smartly in his long Petersham and top hat. It was Christmas Eve. In her dream, her mother's party wasn't for hours. Why had Henry come so early?

Her other self's feet touched the earth, and Henry was right there, grabbing her by the arm, accusing her of burglary. She couldn't hear what was being said, because her feet seemed frozen to the ground. She didn't need to move closer to know the conversation. He was gently trying to get her to come back inside; she was pleading her case for stealing away for a bit of riding.

Henry pulled the package from his pocket, silver paper catching the sunlight. It was tied with a green ribbon.

Quick as a wink, Sophie-dressed-as-a-boy snatched the package. She dashed across the yard, darting down the alley between the houses, her giggle trailing behind her. Henry ran after her, and then the lawn was silent, even the winter wind going still as this part of the dream ended. Sophie knew where her other self was going, but she could not move.

She did not *want* to move. This should not be here. It was a *dream*.

The ground swayed beneath her feet, and she stumbled to catch her balance. Since she had opened the parlor door and stepped into her own past, she had been trying to figure out the meaning behind it all.

She forced herself to move. Whirling around, she dashed down the front walk and out the gate. The carriage house was only a few doors down, but running through six inches of snow made it seem as if it took an hour.

Her heart thudded and her hands shook as she stepped inside. It was quiet and dark, the smell of horses and leather strong. The back door banged open, and her other self stumbled inside. Her hair was falling from beneath the boy's cap, her cheeks bright pink. She gripped Henry's package in her hand. Both girls looked toward the door, to see if Henry would open it. A second later, dream-Sophie tore the silver paper to reveal the jeweler's box.

The dream-girl was so focused on her task that she didn't see Alexei Faber step from the shadows behind one of the carriages.

"Hello, Sophia."

Smiling Sophie jumped and spun around. She held her free hand to her chest and laughed. "Oh, you frightened me. I didn't know anyone was in here."

Faber chuckled, his face the same fatherly-friendly it had been in every other memory. "I am sorry. It wasn't my intention."

Dream-Sophie tipped her head, surprised. "Have we met before, sir?" She studied him a bit, her forehead scrunched and her lower lip between her teeth. "You do look familiar."

Faber only smiled. "I suppose I have one of those faces. And now, I must apologize again."

Sophie, in her boy's clothes, snow melting and dripping on the floor of the carriage house, shook her head, "I'm sorry? Why is that?"

Faber took a step closer. Real-Sophie saw the cloth in his hand, but dream-Sophie did not. Faber moved quickly, reaching for the back of her head, the other placing the cloth over her mouth. Sophie watched herself struggle, the other girl's eyes wide in panic. The package was caught between them, and the silver paper tore. A slip of it fell to the floor, unnoticed. Soon enough, the struggling stopped. Dream-Sophie's body went limp her eyes fluttered closed.

The world around her went completely dark.

Henry kept his mind off the idea of careening to his death in a wreck of wood and metal by focusing on keeping the wagon's battery charged. It was mostly uphill from Philadelphia to Germantown, which meant he had to constantly turn the wool-covered wheel to keep the battery powered. The wind, at least, blew the sweat from his brow and kept him cool.

The experimental trials of this machine conducted by Benjamin Franklin and David Rittenhouse had failed to take into account one very important element—controlling the speed. It was impossible. They could only go or stop, and as long as the battery was charged, the wheels would keep spinning. They were only about three miles out when Henry felt his arm was sure to fall off.

At least Gabriel's torch hadn't failed. They saw everything in front of them. Which included cows, fences, surprised foot travelers, and at least one startled horse and rider. Henry was astonished at how crowded the road was for the middle of the night. Finally, the lights of Germantown appeared before them. Henry stopped cranking the wheel, letting the batteries discharge so that they could slow down before Ben applied the brakes. They rolled into town and came to a smooth stop near Market Square. The three companions clambered out, none of them the worse for wear save some dust on their clothing. Even Tesla seemed unruffled by the trip.

"Thank you, Ben." Gabriel held out his hand. Ben paused before taking it but shook it vigorously.

"I don't know what your story is, my friend, but I know the kind of man you are." Ben chuckled. "After all, each of us has our secrets."

Gabriel tipped his hat. "That we do."

Henry held out his hand to Ben as well. "Thanks again, Mr. Franklin."

Ben shook it as well. "You did well, my boy."

"But there's more to do, and I'm not sure how to do it." Henry found the words falling out of his mouth, his fears springing into the air.

"I'm sure you will be fine. You have a sharp mind, and motivation." Ben leaned toward him, his voice pitched low. "Unless you'd rather stay in 1776 with us, that is."

Henry took a step back. "No, thank you. I mean, it's lovely, but I need to get home."

"That's what I thought. Now, if you wouldn't mind charging me up and winding the spring?"

Gabriel and Henry hauled the German from the wagon. He started to stir, his eyes fluttering open, but still groggy. Irene kept her weapon trained on him, with Tesla also standing guard, while the men turned Ben's wagon around. Henry wound the spring, his arms burning like fire from all the previous work, while Gabriel turned the crank to charge the battery.

"I'm afraid it'll be a slower go home," Gabriel said. "You'll have to stop and recharge it, and rewind the spring, at some point. And sorry about the lack of light, but I have to take mine with me."

"Yes, it's a two-man job." Ben sighed. "But I'll get there eventually." He waved goodbye. "Good luck, my friends."

Gabriel dragged them off before Ben was gone, hurrying them along the road to where they had left their time machine. The wardrobe remained in the same place they had left it, not that Henry expected anything else. Although now that he thought about it, he wondered that no one had bothered with a wardrobe standing in a field beside a footpath.

Irene took the key from Henry and unlocked the door. She reached inside. When she stood back, her hands were full of bundled clothing.

"I think we should change before we leave. Or else people will think a theater troupe is running the streets."

Gabriel shook his head. "We don't have time. Faber's well ahead of us. Last time we followed him we ended up coming in a day behind."

Irene shook her head. "A slight miscalculation." She pulled at the bodice strings of her dress. "Besides, I'm not going home until I'm properly dressed."

Henry and Gabriel turned their heads before Irene actually removed any of her clothing, and so the argument was ended. They grabbed their own clothing and changed as well.

"We don't have anything for him." Henry jabbed his chin in the direction of the German. The man had woken up with much bellowing and struggling against his bonds. He only calmed down under threat of either another jolt from Gabriel's weapon, or being left behind, whichever he preferred. He remained quiet after that.

The moment Henry had been dreading had finally arrived. He opened both doors to the wardrobe. Gabriel used the torch to light up the inside. The instrument panel was all gibberish to him, springs and gears and cogs and tubes. Something emitted a ringing sound, but he couldn't tell what. He felt Gabriel's glare, burning through his jacket.

"I..." Henry didn't dare say what was in his head. There wasn't a choice — he could not fail. His pocket watch seemed to be the heart of the contraption. Alphonse, for all his hurry in constructing the machine, hadn't even scratched the case.

"Can you do it or not, Rittenhouse?" Gabriel's voice was a growl.

"One moment, please." Henry touched the watch, his fingers gliding over the glass that covered the face. "It's not like there's an instruction manual."

"You managed to disarm a ticking bomb. Twice. I think this is fully within your capabilities." Gabriel handed Henry the torch and stood beside their prisoner.

The vote of confidence was unexpected, but not very helpful. "I can't quite figure out how to set the year." Henry was sure it had something to do with the rest of the jumble of machinery attached to the wardrobe's door. "The watch sets the day and time, but there's no way to set a year."

If he could figure out where to begin, he could see how it was supposed to work. The watch was attached to the panel, which was controlled by gears, turned by a spring attached to a hand crank, much like the one on Ben's carriage. He spun the hand crank, and the lights on the panel turned on. *That's something.* He still wasn't sure what it was that propelled them through time, but at least he had power.

Henry wanted to pound on the machine in frustration. Even if he *could* set the year, he had no idea what year he would set it to. It wasn't as if Faber had left a forwarding address. Alphonse said he had followed the other machine's temporal path. He studied the instrument panel again, willing it to give him the answer.

"Mr. Rittenhouse, are we ready to leave or not?" Gabriel's question wasn't polite by any stretch of the imagination. Henry felt the boy's glare on the back of his neck, and a flush crept up to his cheeks. It was impossible to think under such pressure.

"Uh… I'm working on it." Henry had no desire to tell Gabriel that he couldn't perform the task. He rubbed his head and started again, giving the hand crank a few more turns. The machine began to hum.

"If you could work faster, I would appreciate it greatly." Gabriel spoke through gritted teeth. "And can you bring that sound to an end?"

The ringing *was* irritating. "I'll see what I can do."

He shone the torch around, looking for the source of the sound. It seemed to be emanating from a button beside the dials.

"What's this now?" How had Alphonse managed to install a button in the ten or so minutes he had had to build this contraption? Henry had no idea what it did. But maybe if he pushed it the noise would stop.

The machine began to make its trademark grinding sound. The hands on his watch whirled.

"Uh… oh. Time to go!" He shouted the last bit. "Now!"

Irene grabbed Tesla and raced into the cabinet. Gabriel struggled with the bound German, who was shouting through his gag. The words were incomprehensible, but it was clear he didn't like the idea of getting into the cabinet.

"Leave him, if he won't come along," Irene called.

Gabriel dropped him and ran. The man's eyes widened; perhaps he realized what was happening, and he stumbled toward the door.

That was the last thing Henry saw in 1776.

CHAPTER XVI

THE TIME MACHINE GROUND AND GROANED ITS WAY THROUGH TIME, shaking as if in a high wind. It only took a few seconds, but felt like all of eternity. When it was over, the silence was heavy but short-lived.

"Damn." Gabriel punched the wall. "Damn, damn, damn."

Henry had no reply, and Gabriel didn't seem to be interested in one. He cursed as he struggled with the latch. Once he succeeded, he slammed the door open and left, with no concern about what was outside. Irene glanced at Henry, her expression unreadable, and then followed.

Henry wasn't sure why he felt miserable, but he was certain it was the appropriate response. He heaved a sigh and exited the time machine.

"We have no idea what this could mean to the timeline, don't you understand that?" Gabriel's hat was in his hand, his other tangled in his short hair. His eyes flashed at Irene, who wore a look of suffering patience.

"I'm sure it will be fine." Irene held Tesla, who seemed uninterested in the discussion, in her arms.

"Whatever I did, I'm sorry." Henry hovered by the machine's door. They were back in Faber's workshop. It appeared to be just as they left it, but what year it was, there was no clue.

Gabriel's frustration was etched on his face. "Henry, you... you did fine. I'm aggravated at the fact we left his accomplice behind. Not only could he have given us valuable information, but leaving him could have consequences." His voice rose to a near-shout at the end of his speech. He paused, took a breath, then shook his head. "Yes, he was an enemy combatant and our prisoner. But we cannot possibly know how it will change our own present, or the future."

"How can one man change so much?" Henry wasn't arguing, he was genuinely curious.

"Everything we do, every day, no matter how mundane it may seem at the time, affects something else." Gabriel spoke as if he was explaining something that should be obvious. "Drop a stone in a pond, it creates ripples. The same applies to time, in theory. This man may meet someone who is meant to die in the war, for example. But he doesn't, and so he goes on and has a family, and some great-great-grandchild grows up to be a cruel dictator."

"Or a wonderful artist, or a doctor." Irene's interjection was soft. "You can't know which."

"Or maybe the man we left ends up killing George Washington." Gabriel's pessimism would not be swayed. "We don't know what's changed out there." He pointed to the workshop door.

Irene squared her shoulders and huffed at Gabriel. "You may be right. The whole world might have gone pear-shaped. But what's done is done, and there's no use getting your knickers in a knot over it. We need to find Alphonse." She marched toward the laboratory door.

"Don't you mean find Alexei Faber?" Gabriel said in a soft, flat tone. He turned his head toward her slowly, his brown eyes steady.

Irene's jaw tightened, but she simply turned on her heel, opened the door, and stepped out.

Gabriel stared after her for a moment, then stalked out as well. Henry was alone. He took the opportunity to get a closer look at the laboratory. It was organized as before though there was less dust. No electric light either. They had arrived at a time before Sophie's kidnapping. There was nothing else that could give him a clue, so he followed the others into the parlor.

The furniture looked almost new; the carpet wasn't worn bare. Irene and Gabriel were nowhere to be found. It was so quiet Henry could almost believe he was the only person in the world. He went to the bay window and pulled back the curtain. After Gabriel's speech, he didn't know what he expected. A world on fire, perhaps, or maybe nothing at all. But Coulter Street appeared exactly the same.

"Maybe the whole world has changed somewhere else." He let the curtain drop. As he stepped back, he bumped a table. The same small silver frame that had been there before wobbled and fell to the floor. Henry picked it up. The tintype inside showed a family of three. Two adults standing behind a child. Alexei's family, Irene had said. He and his wife were perhaps in their late twenties. The child between them looked about seven or eight. She wore a dark dress with light trim, her dark hair dressed in thick curls, a stuffed rabbit wrapped in her arms.

"Her name was Angelica."

Henry nearly dropped the picture as he spun around. Irene watched from the doorway, rubbing Tesla's head. "The child, Angelica, died probably not long after that photo was taken. A strange, unknown illness. His wife died a year later, they say from a broken heart."

Her words hit Henry like a punch. Irene continued, her eyes never leaving the photo in Henry's hand.

"I guess that would make anyone go a little mad. Especially if you thought you had a way to save her but couldn't for lack of money."

Gabriel's irritated *cluck* announced his return to the parlor. "Why don't you just tell him everything?"

Irene made no apologies. "He deserves to know."

"No, he doesn't." Gabriel leaned on the door frame. "Emotion muddies the water, and you, Mr. Rittenhouse, are already emotionally involved. We have a mission, end of story." He pushed himself upright and crossed the room. "As long as he knows part, he might as well know the rest. Faber tried to save his daughter. He built a machine, hoping to slow the disease until a cure could be found."

Gabriel looked as if he were waiting for Henry to say or do something. "His theory was that this could be achieved by dropping the body's temperature, to slow down the body's systems functions or something."

Henry dropped the photo again, this time making no move to pick it up. "That's what he did to Sophie."

Gabriel nodded.

Anger and confusion gripped Henry's insides. "What does any of it have to do with her?"

"Edmund Weber was Faber's patron. He paid the man to invent things. But when he found out Faber was making that machine, Edmund cut him off. I don't know why. Maybe he thought Faber was trying to play God. Angelica died. Faber blamed Weber."

Henry fell into the overstuffed armchair, everything suddenly, horribly, very clear. "That's everything? The whole story?" He didn't think he could stand one more surprise revelation.

Gabriel glanced at Irene and nodded. "Now you know, as much good as it will do you."

Henry's hands shook with anger as he stood. Who he was angrier at, Alexei Faber or Edmund Weber, he wasn't sure. "Let's find him and finish this."

Gabriel lifted an eyebrow. "That's the smartest thing you've said since I've met you."

"I won't let it go to my head." Henry focused on the pattern of the carpet. "We need to know when we are."

"Another good idea." Gabriel's almost cheery tone didn't help Henry's mood one bit. "We'll go outside and poke around a bit."

Irene's lips pulled tight in irritation. "It's definitely hot. Must be bloody summer. Again."

Henry pulled off his jacket, and Gabriel did the same.

"All well for you two. Try wearing a corset." Irene pulled at the garment she wore over her blouse. "Why is America so hot in the middle of the year? In England it's a proper temperature where no one has to sweat if they don't want to." She pulled at the top of her blouse, lifting the fabric from her skin. "One of you run out and find a newspaper to see what day it is, unless you have an easier way to figure it out."

Henry shrugged. "There's less dust here. And it's after the picture was taken, but it doesn't look like a family lives here. So sometime after Angelica and maybe her mother died, but before the day on Market Square."

"That's not bad," Gabriel said. "Narrows it down to a few years."

Irene rolled her eyes. "Maybe we should just go out and see? Standing around here isn't doing us any good at all."

"I know you're worried about Alphonse, Irene." Gabriel's tone softened. "But he's well trained. He'll be all right."

Her face contorted and then smoothed, as if she had thought of a reply and then bitten it back. "I suppose you're right. What do we do now?"

"We search for Faber."

"He could be anywhere. His machine moves through space, remember?" Henry stated. "Oh, did I forget to mention? I suppose you missed that bit, seeing you were busy being—whatever it was you were—lying on the floor of the State House in a pool of your own blood."

Gabriel's look of shock was worth every syllable. "Well that's just fantastic. Just what we need." He ran his hands over his face. "Let's just go with what we have. The machine took us to whenever this is, so he must be in this year. Whatever he wants, it's not in here." He walked toward the front door.

"Brilliant deduction. Wish I would have thought of it," Irene grumbled. She and Tesla followed their leader.

Henry ran into the workshop and shut the door to the time machine. As he turned to leave, a large sheet of paper tacked above the workbench caught his eye. The sleeping machine. Henry ripped the paper from the wall and inspected it. There were slight differences between this one and the one he knew. This was an earlier design.

"Coming?"

Gabriel stood in the door, his weapon in hand. He looked ready for battle. "We haven't got all the time in the world, despite having a time machine. "

Henry nodded, then looked again at the paper in his hand. He wanted to tear it in two, destroy it.

"It won't do any good."

"Why not?"

"Faber knows what he built. Destroying the blueprint? It won't stop him from building the machine again. He'll still get the money to do it from the men who hired him." Gabriel stepped inside. "Or he won't be able to rebuild it and he'll take his revenge on Edmund Weber another way. One that could end even worse for Sophie." He plucked the paper from Henry's hands. "You can't know what kind of ripples you'll create."

Henry didn't care whether or not Gabriel was right. He didn't even care what happened to Faber, as long as the man told them how to free Sophie. One way seemed as good as another, if in the end she was safe.

"Come on, let's go find him. Maybe once you're outside you can figure out what's so important about this day." Gabriel must have sensed Henry's frustration, because his usual barking tone softened. He set the blueprint on the table. Henry grabbed his wrist.

"What do you think you're doing?" The softness in Gabriel's tone had disappeared, replaced by a more dangerous, warning edge.

"I'm sorry. There's writing on the back." Henry turned the blueprint over and smoothed the paper with both hands. The writing was in clear, neat hand near the upper corner.

Modulator needs work. Temperature fluctuations unpredictable. Unregulated warming and freezing without use of the modulator may cause subject to experience respiratory issues that could lead to death. Somehow connected to timing mechanism. Calibration?

The bottom dropped out of Henry's stomach. *Subject.* Sophie. Henry faced Gabriel, anguish in every muscle.

"He had to have fixed the problem, right? Before he... before he put Sophie inside?"

Gabriel seemed to measure his words before speaking. "Yes, I'm sure he did. He doesn't want to kill her, only keep her where Edmund can't reach her."

There was no possible way to know if that were true. If Gabriel was trying to make him feel better, he was unsuccessful.

"We need to find him. Now." Henry stalked out of the lab.

Irene was waiting; it didn't appear she had heard their conversation. "Oh, are we leaving now? It's about time."

Gabriel walked across the parlor, heading for the front hallway. "Irene, you'll need to —"

"If you say, 'stay here,' I am going to scream." Irene balled her hands into fists. Tesla, from his shoulder-perch, gave an indignant shout. "And then I'm going to knock you on your ass on my way out the door."

"I wouldn't dream of it." Gabriel opened the front door and peered outside. "I need you and Tesla to scout the area. See if you can find Faber's time machine. And anyone else you might come across that doesn't belong here."

Irene smiled in understanding. "If I find something, I'll call you on the photophone."

"I'll be waiting to hear from you," Gabriel said.

Irene nodded to the two gentlemen and strode off in the direction of Germantown Avenue.

"Should we head to Market Square again?" Henry asked.

"Faber knows we'd look for him there." Gabriel shaded his eyes with his hand. "Let's take a walk."

Gabriel and Henry turned onto Germantown Avenue. It was a fine day, despite the heat. They passed the carriage house, and the Weber's home. Everything looked perfectly ordinary. The streets were empty, but that might have had more to do with the temperature than anything. Based on the sun, it was probably close to noon. People were working or at luncheon, or just somewhere that wasn't directly beneath the blazing ball of fire above. Henry looked more closely at everything, trying to determine what year it might be. Everything looked the same as it had since he was a boy. Even the tree, just inside the gate of the church across the street from Market Square.

Not quite. He grabbed Gabriel's shoulder.

"What is it?" Gabriel sounded both annoyed and concerned.

"That tree." He pointed to the oak. It was tall and full, the trunk gnarled with age but vibrant. "It was struck by lightning when I was eight. The trunk split in two."

"So we're sometime between Faber's daughter's death and the tree being struck." Gabriel scratched his cheek. "Good work."

The church door opened. Gabriel pulled Henry out of sight as people spilled out. If it were a Sunday, that would explain the quiet streets. But it was a small group, not a whole congregation. The women's large hats obscured their faces, but Henry thought he recognized one of the men, though he was too far away to be certain. One of the women carried a small bundle wrapped in white, and another held the hand of a small boy, perhaps three years old. He wore short pants and pulled at the collar of his starched white shirt.

That collar itches horribly.

"Oh, my." Stronger words crossed Henry's mind, but he didn't speak them aloud. "I know what day this is."

Gabriel lifted an eyebrow, an unspoken question.

"It's Sophie's christening day."

Sophie held her breath. The darkness was complete. The scent of leather and horses still hung in the air, and when she stomped her foot, she heard the reassuring sound of her boot heel on wood.

Carefully she turned, away from where she had last seen herself and Alexei Faber. When she was almost sure she had turned far enough, she stepped forward, leading with her foot in case of unknown obstacles. The sound of her boots scraping along the wooden floor was almost as loud as her breathing. She counted her steps, cursing to herself that she had no idea how many steps she had taken when she entered. She figured it couldn't be more than ten.

When she got to eleven, the toe of her shoe hit something solid. She reached out, and her fingertips touched the rough wood of the carriage house wall. Sliding her hands around carefully until she found the doorknob, she pulled the door open.

The kitchen greeted her, dark and cold. Sophie leaned forward, so that her head was in the kitchen while her body remained in the carriage house. The ticking, her steadfast companion, waited for her. Behind her there was pitch blackness, ahead the cold and lonely house.

She dragged herself through the door and shut it behind her. The click of the latch seemed louder than it should.

Sophie leaned against it, feeling the door's panels with her back, not caring if it ever opened again. Her chest tightened, her breath frosted the air with every exhale. It was colder here than it had been in the memory.

No, it was a dream.

It *had* to have been a dream, because she woke up from it here, in the house.

No, I didn't. I mean, I did. But there was more before I woke up.

Everything had gone black in the carriage house, and then in the next part of the dream, she was somewhere else. A strange place, where she was dressed in an unfamiliar gown and encased in a casket of glass. *Then* she had woken up in her own bed.

She took a deep breath and tried to sort everything out. Her mother had told her to go upstairs and lie down before the party. She had gone to her room and... she thought she must have laid down and dreamed the scene she just saw. But had she? Or had she put on her boy's clothes, which she was wearing now, and gone out the window, where she met Henry?

Which would make what she just saw another memory.

If that was so, then how had she gotten here?

She had been drugged by Alexei Faber, of course. She had just seen it with her own eyes. And while she was asleep, he brought her here.

And surrounded the house with thorns.

And kidnapped her family.

And made time stop.

And pulled her memories from her head.

Well, it had started out reasonably, at any rate. Where had Alexei gone off to? Now she was even more convinced it was him in the tailcoat.

She sat at the kitchen table, her head in her hands, wishing that there was something stronger to drink than the milk in the cold box. Her father kept a collection of wines in the basement, but the last thing she wanted to do right now was open another door.

Sophie grasped the mysterious locket from beneath her shirt. She rubbed her thumb over the polished gold oval, feeling the engraving of the swirling monogram beneath her finger. She slipped the corner of her thumbnail into the small gap in the locket's lid and twisted. The locket resisted as it had before. She jammed her nail in a bit more, wincing as the nail lifted from the quick. It still would not budge.

Frustrated, she put her thumb in her mouth, sucking on it. The pain took her mind off her troubles. All she had left were her thoughts, and they seemed to be chasing themselves around like a dog after its tail.

The back door blew open, banging against the counter behind it. There was only thorny darkness outside. The wind that had forced the door was warm. It carried the scent of rose water and the soft sound of weeping.

"Mother?" Sophie jumped from her seat. The wind washed over her, warming the whole room as it blew across the threshold.

"Mother, where are you? I can't find you..." Sophie's call was barely a whisper.

There was no reply, but the sound of weeping echoed down the hall. Sophie ran toward it, searching for her mother. As suddenly as it had come, the warm breeze was gone, replaced by an icy wind that ran through Sophie like a knife.

With no warning, her limbs turned heavy, and her eyelids slipped downward. She forced her eyes open, and the hall doubled, two identical images beside each other. She shook her head to clear her vision. Taking a step, she fell, her hands and feet numb. The ticking had also gone strange again, first fast, then slow. The clock chimed a sick, twanging chime.

Sophie crawled into the parlor and grabbed the blanket from the love seat. She wrapped it around herself, but it did nothing to stave off the cold. Curled up on the floor, shivering, and weeping, she called for her mother with what little voice she had left. Her eyes were heavy, her limbs like lumps of ice. With no more energy to fight, she let her eyelids slide shut.

Henry and Gabriel stepped behind one of the tall bushes that edged the square and watched the little group of celebrants. Now that he knew who they were, Henry spotted his mother and father easily. His mother leaned over and spoke to young Henry, likely to scold him about touching his collar. Then she took his hand and followed the rest of the party out of the church yard and down the street toward the Weber house.

"There were spun sugar swans, and silver place settings. Something else happened..." Henry rubbed his head, the heat making it hard to concentrate. "I was in the kitchen, I think. There was shouting, and a crash. And..."

The air rushed from his lungs as an image flashed across his thoughts. What had looked like his father and a man standing outside the Weber's kitchen door. The feeling that he had missed a step going down. He grabbed Gabriel's sleeve and pulled him down the street in the direction the group from the church had gone.

"What are you doing?" Gabriel pulled back, his arm coming free.

"We're supposed go to Sophie's house." The conviction in Henry's voice must have surprised Gabriel, from the look on his face.

"What do you mean 'supposed to'?"

"You'll see. At least one Faber will be there. I know that's where we have to go, because I saw us."

Gabriel's expression darkened. "What do you mean?"

Henry didn't want to waste time with an explanation. Or was he supposed to explain, so that they would get there at the same moment he remembered? Meddling with time was, as Gabriel had said, complicated. He resumed walking, knowing Gabriel would follow.

Henry slipped along the side of the Weber's house. The garden was brown, withered in the late August heat.

Opening the back gate, he paused to wait for Gabriel in the shade of the tree at the corner of the garden. He had found Sophie leaning against the trunk of this tree many times, reading or playing cat's cradle. It was in this very spot Sophie had told him she was going to travel the world and meet a handsome prince. Henry had laughed, but deep down his younger self may have been jealous of the imaginary and future beau.

It didn't take Gabriel long to catch up, but long enough for something else to finally make sense. "I think this is the day Faber makes his threat against Sophie." He slapped his hand against his forehead. "That's why her parents were so strict."

Gabriel wiped his glistening forehead with his sleeve. "What are you blathering about?"

"Sophie always complained that her parents never let her out of their sight. I thought she was being dramatic, but now that I think about it, they did keep an extra-watchful eye on her. Whenever Sophie would run from her mother at the Market, she would panic."

Gabriel stepped into the shade, the mottled light painting his dark skin. "She had you there to take her to task."

"My mother told me it was my duty to keep an eye on her." Henry paused as something else fell into place. "This explains their sending her to England for finishing school. They wanted her as far from Faber as possible."

"It didn't work." Gabriel swallowed, his throat making a clicking sound.

A powerful sensation overtook Henry. "No, but we can stop it all, here and now." He marched toward the Weber's kitchen door and tapped on the glass, hoping that a maid or the cook would let him in.

Gabriel was on him in a second, his fingers vice-like around Henry's arm. "What are you doing?"

"I'm going in there. I'm going to stop Faber before he ever makes the threat. I'll tell Edmund what he does to Sophie, and then he'll be arrested and none of this will ever happen."

The agent squeezed tighter. "We can't change the timeline. It's against the rules."

"Rules? How can there be rules for something that just came into being?" Henry didn't wait for a reply before speeding on. "I couldn't give a whit about the rules. Since when do you?"

"I have no idea know what you mean. I'm strictly by-the-book, in case you haven't noticed."

"I don't care what you say, you died. You were shot and died. Then you... came back. You are on a first-name basis with *Benjamin Franklin*. You defy the very laws of nature and talk to me about *rules*?"

Gabriel's grip slackened slightly. "Yes, I died. Happy? And I came back to life. It happens more often than you think."

"Are you serious? How old are you?"

"We don't have time for this."

"You're right, we don't. I've got a disaster to avert." Henry reached for the kitchen door's knob.

"I told you, you can't. How will you explain yourself?"

"I'll make something up." Henry was a terrible liar, but he was desperate. "I'll say I'm the authorities, at least that's partially true."

"Not even in the slightest." Gabriel shook his head and gestured at the door. "If you stop Faber now, you create a paradox. Yes, he won't be able kidnap Sophie in the future. But then he'll never come back in time, and so we'll never follow him, so we'll never be able to stop him from coming here on this day in the first place." He let the confusing idea spin its way into Henry's mind before continuing. "We cannot change the timeline; we can only extract the older Faber from this time." He sighed. "I've spent a lot of time reading theories on time. I know you think I don't understand, but I do. We will fix this. But we have to be careful."

Henry shot him a look full of distrust. "You want to complete your mission."

"Yes, I do. But our aims aren't mutually exclusive."

He tried to find another argument but couldn't think of one that Gabriel wouldn't shoot down. Henry glanced through the window, and there he was. His three-and-a-half-year-old self stood just on the other side of the door, looking at the two men with an expression of surprise.

And dizziness, Henry thought. His own vision spun a little, probably a side effect of looking at himself.

Something made young Henry turn his head toward the dining room door.

"The grandfather clock," he mumbled.

"Excuse me?" Gabriel tipped his head.

"What I'm—the me there—looking at. I remember this terrific smashing sound. It was the grandfather clock. Someone knocked it over and it was smashed to bits. There was definitely an argument. And a shot."

"A gunshot?" Gabriel pulled Henry away from the door. Henry resisted. He still wanted to open the door, if only to find out what had happened. He managed to turn the knob (it had been unlocked the entire time) when Gabriel's pocket buzzed.

The agent pulled out his photophone and dragged Henry across the yard to the garden gate.

"Alphonse? Is that you? Are you alright?"

"Is that his name? Your invisible friend? He is fine." The voice was tinny and small, but definitely not the voice of their companion. "But, indisposed at the moment. An unfortunate run-in with a blunt object."

Henry peered over Gabriel's shoulder at the photophone's small window. Faber's thin, lined face was in full view.

"What do you want?" Gabriel, in usual style, did not waste time.

"Good, you didn't ask what I had done to them. A man of business. We need to meet, you and I. We have some important things to discuss. Come to my home in ten minutes and leave the boy somewhere where he won't cause a fuss." Faber's face and voice disappeared with a small pop, and the machine went silent.

Gabriel snapped it shut and slipped it into his jacket. Without a word, he left the garden, his long and rapid strides leaving Henry to catch up.

The boy glanced behind him. On the other side of the door was a small boy, wondering where the strange men had gone. By tomorrow he would forget all about the argument, and the gunshot, and the grandfather clock. None of that mattered to the child, and he wouldn't think of them again for many years.

He wished someone would have told him how this day would shape his future.

As they approached the carriage house, Tesla raced toward them. He jumped into Gabriel's arms chattering loudly, his eyes wide.

"Where did he come from?" Henry almost felt sorry for the little beast. He seemed so upset.

Gabriel stroked the monkey's fur, his mouth set in a grim line.

"Faber said 'them,' He's taken Irene, too."

CHAPTER XVII

SOPHIE SHIVERED. HER MIND STRUGGLED TO WAKE, BUT HER THOUGHTS were as thick and slushy as a half-frozen pond. She was so very cold, even with the layers of clothing and the blanket. And she was so tired! Bone-weary, as if she had been out in the snow all day, like when she was young.

Henry would come and collect her. They would meet some neighborhood children and go sledding down the hill behind the church, up and down until their cheeks were pink and their noses running. Then home for hot cocoa and fresh cookies.

That was a pleasant memory, Sophie thought. *Why couldn't the house have shown me that one?*

Oh, that wasn't a memory, silly. It was a daydream.

She had never been allowed out of the house to go sledding, not even with Henry to keep watch over her. She had watched him and the other children play in the snow from the parlor window, her nose pressed against the cold glass.

She pulled the blanket tighter around her. Why was it so cold? Somewhere very far away the clock had wound down. Or it was broken, because it clunked and clanked, chiming in an out-of-tune way that hurt her ears.

Sophie clutched the blanket. Alexei Faber's face in her cluttered thoughts. His face across time, from the man he had been when she was young, to as she had last seen him, with gray hair and lines around his eyes. His eyes, full of sadness Why was he was so sad? He had trapped her and somehow made her memories come alive. Thinking made her head hurt worse.

It would be easier to stop thinking and just sleep.

No, I have to wake up. I have to find Faber and make him tell me how to get rid of the thorns. Tell me where my parents and Henry are. He was with Henry in the woods... why was he with Henry...?

She struggled to pull her thoughts upward to clarity. They slipped back underwater.

Sleep.

Wake.

Sleep.

Sophie forced herself to toward consciousness, but her eyes shut. The cold pressed in on her. She concentrated on the only sound she could hear. The ticking of the clock. Someone must have fixed it, because it didn't sound broken anymore. Steady, like a heartbeat.

The clock chimed midnight.

Her eyes flew open.

Gabriel raced across town, Tesla holding on to his shoulder for dear life. He didn't stop until he reached the end of Coulter Street.

"Wait here." He lifted Tesla from his shoulder and placed him on Henry's. Tesla didn't exactly look pleased about it, but seemed to sense the urgency of the situation. "Do *not* follow me."

"But I—"

Gabriel stopped him with a hand. "I have two agents compromised. I don't need to look out for you, too."

Henry slammed his mouth shut, biting his tongue both literally and metaphorically. He tasted blood, and was surprised it wasn't boiling hot. What did he have to do to prove he wasn't a child who needed minding? Gabriel, satisfied his word would be obeyed, walked toward the house.

Henry waited until he had disappeared before running behind the houses.

"Tesla, I need you to be quiet. No one can know we're here. All right?" The monkey nodded. They crept along the row, Henry careful to keep his footsteps light and soft. The yards along the path were smaller than those on Sophie's street, the gardens more modest. Faber's yard and house looked well-maintained. Years from now, when Henry would sneak into this house in the dead of night on Christmas Eve, the paint on the clapboards would be chipped, the gutters hanging askew. Time was a terrible housekeeper.

He opened the gate and slipped to the kitchen door, glancing through the mullioned window. The kitchen looked empty. Tesla tugged on his hair in an inquisitive way.

"No, I don't have a plan. I'm making this up as I go along." He turned the doorknob, but it was locked.

"So much for that," Henry muttered, wishing he had Alphonse's tool that had been so helpful in unlocking Independence Hall. Picking the lock with his own tools would be too noisy. Tesla leapt from his shoulder and skittered along the back of the house. He jumped straight up, catching a windowsill. The windows were open; it was summer. The monkey disappeared inside. A few seconds later, there was a click from the other side of the door.

Henry turned the knob and it opened. Tesla stood on the other side, wearing, if Henry interpreted the monkey's expression correctly, a rather smug grin.

"Maybe you're not so bad after all," he whispered. He held out his hand, and Tesla scampered up his arm and onto his shoulder. Henry moved through the kitchen with as much stealth as he could, thanking the floor for not squeaking. He pushed into the dining room, the swinging door mercifully well-oiled. The house was dark and silent, his steps muffled by a thick carpet not yet worn through by another sixteen years' worth of walking. The door that led to the rest of the house was shut, but he heard the sound of voices close by. Henry pressed his ear against the door, but couldn't hear any better. He gently opened the door and peered out. The hall was empty. The voices floated across the space from behind the closed parlor door. Henry hesitated. There was nowhere to hide.

Tesla tugged on his hair again. This time it felt like encouragement.

"All right, fine. It's not as if Faber will shoot you."

He tiptoed across to the parlor door. The voices continued without pause, so apparently Henry was as yet undetected. He pressed his ear to the door.

"It's not my fault, you know. I didn't ask you to chase me. I was on other business when we met in Market Square, a few years from now." Faber sounded nonchalant, as if the two men were old friends and meeting for coffee. "I couldn't just let you keep chasing me, it would get boring. And I have other matters to attend to."

"Oh, we would eventually have caught you." Gabriel's tone lacked its normal undercurrent of annoyance. "But now you've saved me the trouble."

Faber laughed. "I led you here, remember? Do you think I'm going to let you arrest me?"

"That's what's going to happen. But why take us to this time?"

"Because this is where it all began, of course." A small clinking sound, like a teacup being set on a saucer, punctuated the break in Faber's speech. "I wanted you to see. And that boy, of course. That Rittenhouse boy. He doesn't understand what happened. What was at stake."

"He's in love. People tend to be protective of those they love. You should understand that more than anyone."

Faber's tone turned sharp. "And he should learn, then, as I have, that loving someone often isn't enough to keep them safe, or healthy. Not enough to keep them alive." Something was slammed onto a hard surface. "It's a lesson we all must learn, some a harder way than others."

"That boy has done nothing to you. Nor has Miss Weber." Gabriel remained remarkably calm. He either knew that Alphonse and Irene weren't in immediate danger, or he was a very good actor.

"Collateral damage." Faber's voice gave the impression he had shrugged as he spoke. "It's not personal to either of them."

"But it *is* personal."

"Edmund Weber took something precious to me. I am balancing the ledger."

"Fine, that's your business. You still haven't told me why you called this meeting." Gabriel's voice sounded closer than it had before.

"Because I want your help."

Henry almost jumped back from the door. Why would this maniac want Gabriel's help?

"I'm listening."

"I failed in my mission, obviously. My employers will be looking for me."

"We left your babysitter back in 1776. You know, when you tried to kill us?"

"He was a buffoon. And I didn't try to kill you, he did. Anyway, I made a stop before I came here."

"Where? Or rather, when?" Gabriel asked. Henry wondered why he was dragging out the conversation. "And why?"

"Because, as I was curious about you and your little band of misfits, I was also curious about what my employers were up to." There was a pause that grew heavier as the seconds passed. Was Faber waiting for a response, or was it dramatic effect?

"I went into the future. Not long, just a few decades. Early 20th century. I wanted to see what the world would become." Something rustled, like paper. "I brought this back. As you can see, my failure did not deter my employers. They are playing the long game. It seems my little assignment was one of many attempts to achieve their goal."

Another silence followed, stretched out so long that Henry wondered if Gabriel and Faber hadn't left the room.

"Your mission wasn't to start a war, or to end one. It was to eliminate an enemy in a war that hasn't happened yet." Gabriel's voice was like lead.

War? What war? Henry furrowed his brows at the thought.

Faber's tone was soft and unreadable. "Exactly. The Archduke's death will be the precursor to something much more... global. And America is a formidable force. Leader in industry, full of innovators. A powerful ally, but a dangerous enemy."

Henry's ear was practically part of the door's wood now.

"But if that force were no longer in existence..." Gabriel let the though hang.

"Exactly. If the Founding Fathers were murdered on the cusp of signing the Declaration of Independence, my employers must have thought that the colonists would give up the idea of independence. America would never have become, and this country would instead be a patchwork of British, French, Spanish, and Mexican colonies. Those countries would spend so long fighting over territory, spread their own government so thin in keeping their colonies in line, that no one would be so upset about the assassination of an Austrian Archduke and his wife."

Henry felt ill.

"But there was no way to know that it would work." Gabriel's tone remained practical. "Something else could have spurred the Revolution. Or the colonists could have fought back harder and won."

"I'm told my employers have someone who was impeccable with mathematics and statistics, and this was the course of action that would lead to their ideal situation. Their own existence would be unchanged — a machine or magic potion or something that would keep them safe from the shifting timeline. They never indulged me with the details, and it wasn't my concern. They gave me quite a lot of money so I could complete my work. In exchange, I built them an arsenal of unconventional machines, including a time machine. The last thing

I had to do was prove the time machine worked, by carrying out their task. I failed." Faber's reply was curt. "My debt to them remains unpaid. Now I need to escape."

"I'm not in the business of helping criminals escape. My job is to bring you back. You can help us or spend the rest of your life in prison. Your choice." That sounded like the Gabriel that Henry knew.

"Not even in exchange for the information you need?" Faber's offer dangled in the air, like a mouse in front of a hungry cat.

Gabriel didn't pounce. "When I want your information, I'll sit you in front of Irene for five minutes. And you'll do it back in Washington."

"Ah, yes, the telepath. She was tricky to catch, unlike your invisible man. At any rate, yes, I suppose I could do better. What about my time machine? I could let you have it."

"And why would I want that? I have one, and the blueprints as well."

Faber seemed confident. "Yes, your crude interpretation of my design." He chuckled. "It won't last much longer. I'd be surprised if it survives another trip. Especially if I decide to keep your mechanic. I assume it was he that built and flew it. You don't seem like the type, and the Rittenhouse boy doesn't have the imagination."

The insult stung, but he was more concerned over the rest. It was completely possible their machine might shake apart on the next trip and be scattered to... where? What did the inside of time look like?

"Fine. You have two of my team and a functioning time machine. That's your bargaining chip. What can I do?"

Henry couldn't believe his ears. He hoped Gabriel had some trick up his sleeve and was just having Faber on to get information.

"As I said, I need an escape. I will give you my time machine, and the information you want. I will tell you where your companions are and you can retrieve them, unharmed. You will take me to a time and place I designate and leave me there. I will disappear and you will forget ever having seen me."

Gabriel's silence seemed to say he was considering Faber's plan. "And what about Miss Weber? I can't let her remain on ice."

"That's not part of the deal."

"I don't care about your feud with Edmund Weber. Sophie won't last a hundred years, and you know it. The mechanism is faulty."

"That was an earlier design." Faber didn't sound surprised. "The machine I built for my sweet Angelica. After her death, I realized my mistake. If I had had the funding I needed, I could have done it properly. Believe me, I had plenty of money to build the second machine."

"Brilliance fueled by anger. Wonderful."

Henry's heart bounded in his chest. He wished they would quit dancing around and just say what they meant!

"It was the calibration, you see." Faber's voice became almost too soft to hear. "The regulator for the freezing mechanism was faulty. She got too warm, then too cold, her sleep was too deep. I couldn't bring her back... I believe I corrected the problem."

Henry ripped the door open and stepped inside before he had a chance to think about it. Tesla let out an indignant screech as he leapt to the floor and scrambled to the sofa.

"What do you mean, you *believe* you corrected the problem?" Henry's voice and hands shook with rage. The shock of his unexpected entrance showed on both men's faces.

"I told you to stay outside," Gabriel barked.

"Why? So you could bargain away Sophie's life?" Henry shouted. Gabriel didn't reply.

Alexei Faber did. "Mr. Rittenhouse, I'm sorry, but—"

Henry cut him off. "If you were sorry, you'd tell me how to set her free. I am almost certain it requires a key, which you must have. If you were sorry, you would make it right." Tears threatened, but burned up in his anger. "You are going to give me that key. Then we are going home, and I am getting Sophie out of that... prison."

Faber was quick to reply. "I do not have the key, Mr. Rittenhouse. That is the truth. It's safe, somewhere no one will find it. Miss Weber must remain where she is. Her father must pay his penance." The man's tone was not unkind, but factual. "She will be safe as houses for one hundred years; I can assure you."

A guttural growl grew deep in Henry's throat. As it escaped his mouth he leapt at Faber, tackling him to the floor. He put his knees on the man's arms, pinning him down.

"Edmund's penance? What about the rest of us? Sophie's done nothing wrong! Her mother has done nothing wrong, and I..." He held up a fist, ready to drive it through Faber's face. "I don't believe you. You have the key, and if you don't give it to me, today will be your last day."

"I can't let you do that, Henry."

Henry turned his head just enough to see Gabriel out of the corner of his eye. His weapon was aimed at Henry. "I need you to get off of him. Now."

"That won't kill me, Gabriel. We both know that."

"I don't want or need to kill you, Henry. He has Alphonse and Irene. If you kill *him*, we'll never know where."

"I'm sure I could find them. There aren't many places to hide in Germantown, they can't be far." Henry didn't want to feel the sting of Gabriel's weapon, but it would be worth it to feel Faber's windpipe crush beneath his hands.

"And what if they're not *in* this time, Henry? What will you do then?" Faber didn't look afraid in the least, despite being sat upon and bodily threatened. He looked smug. Which only made Henry want to punch him in the face even more.

Gabriel's tone softened. "You're not a killer, Henry. Think about Sophie. What would she want?"

"Don't talk about Sophie as if you know her!" Henry's anger bubbled over, despite Gabriel's threat.

"He might not, but I do, Mr. Rittenhouse." The pressure on Faber's chest was finally affecting him; his breathing became labored, his speech broken. "I have been watching her her whole life. I know her probably better than you do."

Henry, his anger fueled white-hot, put his hands around Faber's throat.

Faber's face turned red, choking sounds came from his mouth. Henry kept squeezing, his rage turning him deaf and blind to the man's struggle.

And to the sound of Gabriel's weapon.

When the bolt of electricity hit him, every nerve in his body tingled. There was a blinding blue light, pain, and then darkness.

Henry woke with another headache. The bright light was like knives to his eyes and he slammed them shut. When he went to lift his hand to rub his aching cranium, he found he could not move his arms. His eyes snapped open this time, his headache of lower priority. He was in an unfamiliar room, lying on the floor on his side, his arms tied behind him. He struggled against the bonds, but Gabriel had tied them expertly.

"Hello? Gabriel?" There must be a door, but he couldn't see it. No one answered him. He was able to lift his head, but that turned his throbbing headache into a brass band playing inside his skull.

A terrible idea occurred to him. Gabriel had taken Faber up on his offer, found Irene and Alphonse, and left him here. Wherever here was. The room looked like a library, or maybe a sitting room. The brightly colored Persian carpet beneath him was thick and soft. Bookcases stood against one wall. Between himself and the cases were a loveseat, an overstuffed armchair, and a coffee table with a full tea service. Tesla sat on the loveseat, munching on a cookie.

"Where are we, Tesla?" He didn't know what he expected from the monkey, but at least he knew Gabriel was planning on coming back. He would never abandon Irene's pet. A low hum came from somewhere, but he couldn't tell if it was real, his headache, or some side effect of being shot with an electric gun.

"Where did Gabriel go? Off with Faber?" Maybe Faber was tied up somewhere else. Either way, Gabriel probably had gone to find Irene and Alphonse. Henry gently set his head on the floor again. Here he was, trussed like a goose and of no use to anyone. Gabriel had been right to neutralize him. Losing his head and injuring Faber, as righteous as it felt in the moment, would not help anyone. Least of all Sophie.

If Faber wouldn't give him the key, then Henry would spend the rest of his life, if that was what it took, working to free her. If Faber was wrong about fixing the flaw, she might never wake.

Henry wiggled his hands. The rough rope bit into his skin, and the exertion had him sweating in no time. Finally, he let his body go limp. Gabriel was an expert at restraining people. Of course, he was. He was apparently at least a century old, and a spy, so he probably had lots of practice.

The sound of a key turning in a lock made him jump. Which caused his shoulders to scream in pain.

Henry tried to push himself around to see the door, but the carpet was not conducive to sliding. Tesla watched Henry's flailing with what looked like amusement.

"Ah, Henry, glad to see you're awake."

Gabriel stepped into Henry's view and knelt down. "I hope you've had a chance to cool down?"

Henry didn't appreciate the condescending tone. "Yes. Can you please untie me?"

"Absolutely." The ropes loosened.

Henry sat up and rubbed his burning wrists and worked out his stiff shoulders. "Next time you might leave a little room."

"Couldn't have you running off, now, could I?" Gabriel seemed to be in good spirits. It made Henry suspicious.

"You did it, didn't you? You gave Faber what he wanted. Where is he?"

Faber stepped through the door. "Welcome, Mr. Rittenhouse."

Henry's shock kept him from speaking for a few moments. "I'm sorry, where are you welcoming me to, exactly?"

Faber's smile was both wide and annoying. "To my time machine, of course. Now, get up if you want to save Miss Weber's life."

CHAPTER XVIII

THE PARLOR SPUN AS SOPHIE SAT UP TOO FAST. SHE SLAMMED HER eyes closed for a moment and took slow, deep breaths, moving her tingling limbs one by one. Her fingers felt frozen, and she blew on them, trying to restore warmth. The clock finished its twelfth chime, the last seeming to hang in the air. What was left to see? The last memory (*not a dream!*) had happened just before she woke up. She put her hand in her pocket, but the key wasn't there. She must have left it in the kitchen.

Climbing to her feet, Sophie trudged to the hall. The grandfather clock stood as before, both hands on midnight, the pendulum frozen.

"You've been no help at all, you know."

She found the key on the kitchen table, right where she had left it. The metal warmed her hand but gave her no comfort. It frightened her.

The clock would keep chiming if she ignored it. The key might get hot enough to burn her. Sophie set it on the table in the foyer. Maybe she would return to the parlor. Re-make the fire, that would keep her busy. And warm. She might even sleep.

A step before she reached the parlor threshold, the doors slammed in her face. She rattled the knobs, but it would not budge.

"Well, that's a fine how-do-you-do."

She grabbed the key from the table and tried to unlock the door, but the key would not fit in the lock. She crossed to the dining room, only to be met with another set of closed doors that would not take the key, which was now almost too hot to hold. Upstairs, every door was shut and none yielded to her attempt at entrance.

"Alright, fine, I'll play your game," she screamed to the air. "What door is left?"

She ran back downstairs and tried every door again, her uncertainty and fear growing. The front door opened, but there was only the porch and the thorns. The parlor, the dining room, the library, all unbreachable. The kitchen door opened at her touch. She went in slowly, looking for some clue. The back door again, perhaps?

It wasn't locked, but like the kitchen and front doors, showed her nothing more than the macabre, dark wall of thorns.

Sophie retreated, disheartened and confused. Obviously, she was meant to be in this room. "Where are you? If you want me to see something so badly, show yourself!"

There was a knock on the cellar door. Sophie turned toward it slowly, her grip on the key so tight her knuckles turned white. The door was tucked away in the corner, a plain, dark-wood innocent-looking door.

"It has to be you, I suppose? Fine. Let's get this over with."

She slipped the end of the key into the lock and turned it. The *click* was as loud as a gunshot, slicing through the quiet. She opened the door slowly, the hinges protesting, but only a little. A blast of frigid air and inky blackness greeted her. She gasped, but not because of the sudden chill.

The ticking grew louder.

Henry laughed in Faber's face. He really wanted to punch him, but had learned his lesson. "Your time machine?" He gestured to the room. "How can that be? I've seen your machine and it's not much larger than the wardrobe."

Faber didn't seem offended by Henry's disbelief. "I assure you, that is where we are."

In response, Henry marched to the door, opened it, and stepped out. He expected the rest of a house. He did not expect a dark and unfamiliar city street.

Henry spun. The box stood there, pretty as you please, looking exactly the same size he remembered it. Gabriel stood in the open doorway, apparently unconcerned that Henry would flee. He wore a patient look.

Henry stuck his head back inside. "It's definitely bigger inside. How is that possible?"

Faber seated himself on the overstuffed chair and fixed himself some tea. He took a sip, his expression unreadable. "It's complicated. A new branch of physics having to do with stuffing more space into a fixed space. Like how you fold clothes to put them into a suitcase. It's all mathematical and too long to explain. I figured it out after reading some papers by a man named Michael Faraday. Brilliant." Faber pointed to the wall to Henry's left. "It's not infinite, of course. I don't have an entire house here, just this room. I wanted to be comfortable."

Henry stepped past Gabriel and back into the machine. The wall beside the door was covered in dials and gauges, lights that blinked on and off, and switches. It was far more advanced than their own little machine made of bits-and-bobs, a spare wardrobe, and his pocket watch.

"Please, sit. Have some tea. And some strudel. You must be hungry."

Henry wasn't hungry. He was starving. It had been at least a day since he had eaten anything. Even though he really would rather poke himself in the eye with a sharp stick, he sunk onto the loveseat beside the monkey, fixed himself a cup of tea, and managed to eat a sandwich without cramming the entire thing into his mouth at once.

"Better? Yes, we shouldn't talk on an empty stomach." Faber sat back in the chair and crossed one leg over the other. "You remember our arrangement?"

Henry could only nod, though he tried to look as angry as possible while stuffing a cookie into his mouth after the sandwich.

"Good. I know you don't agree." Faber set his teacup on the table. "You are a fine, smart young man. In time, you'll be able to accept this."

Henry swallowed his outraged reply along with three more cookies that had wandered from the plate and into his mouth. He began to choke on them, searching for his cup of tea to wash them down. The food traveled to his stomach in a hard lump, where it lay like rock.

"I will never accept it." Henry clenched his hands into fists, preparing to launch himself at Faber again. "You said you needed me to help save Sophie? What was that about, if not giving me the key and telling me how to open the machine?"

Faber shrugged. "We'll get to that in a moment. We have a time machine. Nothing, not one thing, is pressing when you have a time machine. I've told you; I don't have the key any longer. And no, I'm not telling you where it is." He took a sandwich from the plate. "Incidentally, you leaving your time machine behind in my laboratory was what started me — the earlier version of me, that is — thinking about time travel in the first place."

Henry stared at Gabriel. "You didn't move it?"

Gabriel stood by the bookshelf, scanning a page of one of the books. He snapped it shut and tucked it under his arm. "How could I, alone? He wasn't exactly helpful, either." He lifted his chin in Faber's direction. "And you were... taking a break."

"So, what was all that about not changing the future?" Henry stood, his still-balled fists shaking. "Again, the rules seem to apply to everyone but you."

"Don't be too hard on him. I had always wondered where that machine had come from. And now I know. I imagine, though I have no way of knowing for certain, that I would have come up with the idea eventually. It was my work with time travel that seemed to catch my employer's eye in the first place. They were persistent I should help them. Which seems odd. I mean, of all the scientists to ask to help you conquer the world, why a penniless widower from Philadelphia?"

This time Henry choked on his tea. "Conquer the world?"

Faber waved the question away. "Mr. White will fill you in later."

Gabriel had closed the door to the machine and stood beside it. It was unlike him to remain quiet for so long, which made Henry nervous.

"For now, we have business to get on with." Faber placed his teacup on the table. "Come with me, please." He stood before the instrument panel. There his hands moved as if he were conducting an orchestra, flipping switches and turning dials. Henry could barely keep up.

Henry jumped from his seat. "What about Alphonse and Irene?"

Tesla had finished his cookie and was sitting quietly, his head cocked to one side as if he was listening. At the mention of his mistress's name, he clambered onto Henry's shoulder.

"All in due time, Mr. Rittenhouse." Faber spun a dial to his left. "Time is a... strange thing. Malleable, changeable to some degree. Oh, that reminds me..." He crossed the room to the bookshelves and scanned them. He stopped and reached between two books and pulled something out. "This belongs to you."

He handed Henry a pocket watch. *His* pocket watch.

"Where did you get this?" Henry patted the empty jacket pocket where he usually kept the watch.

"You left it in my lab inside your machine. I've had it in my possession for years, and yet you left it there only a few hours ago."

The watch's case was tarnished, as if it had sat untouched a very long time. When Henry wound it, the watch started to tick, just as if it were new. He slipped it into his pocket.

Faber returned to the instrument panel. "All will make sense very soon, or at least I hope it will. Now, we must save Miss Weber." He continued to fiddle with dials and knobs on the panel.

Henry watched him, trying to make sense of what he was doing. Some of the buttons and lights looked like the ones in their own machine, but there were many more he did not understand.

"There, all set." He Faber turned to Henry. "All you have to do is push this lever upward, and we will be on our way."

Henry hesitantly touched the end of the lever. "How will this save Sophie, if you're not going to give me the key to the sleeping machine?"

Faber smiled. "You're going to have to wait and see." He studied Henry's expression, seeming to read him as well as Irene. "This isn't some kind of trick. I have no interest in harming you or Mr. White over there. Once this last item is complete, I'm on my way. That's the deal I made with him, and with you."

Henry looked over at Gabriel, who sat on the loveseat, looking relaxed.

"I know you don't trust me, and you have no reason to, if we're being honest. If you want me to push the lever, I will," Faber continued. "But I think it should be you."

Henry swallowed hard and pushed the lever.

Sophie stared into the dark cellar for a few moments, waiting. There was no scene, no memory. Just the cellar stairs. Her father hadn't bothered installing gas lamps in the basement, or electric lights. The cellar was used so infrequently, he said it wasn't worth the expense.

Footsteps below got Sophie moving. She grabbed a hurricane lamp from beside the kitchen door and lit it. Holding it high, using its yellow light, she peered into the open space below. The stairs led to more darkness, with no sign of anyone. She tried to count how many times in her life she had actually been in the cellar. Three? Four? They kept nothing down there except vegetables, jars of preserved fruit, and her father's wine. The only person who really went down there was Cook, or sometimes a maid. Still, Sophie hesitated.

Spiders and dirt wouldn't hurt her, but butterflies still danced in her stomach.

She held the lamp high and slowly descended. The cold was painful, deeper than in the house. Her breath curled like smoke in the light of the lamp. The ticking grew even louder. Before it had merely been annoying, but suddenly it became ominous.

At the bottom of the stairs, the darkness pressed in on her. The low ceiling and emptiness of the space made her feel as if she in a cave. The musty, earthy smell did nothing to help her sense of foreboding.

She crept through the first room and its shelves filled with jars. In the shifting light, the contents looked as if she had walked into a witch's pantry. A jar of eyeballs made her jump, then laugh when she realized they were pickled eggs. On the far side stood the door that led to her father's wine cellar. It hung half open, and a familiar-but-unwelcome tailcoat was just disappearing through it.

Sophie raced to the door, which had closed behind him. Her hand shook on the knob, while the other tried desperately not to drop the lamp. Whatever was on the other side, she should just leave it alone, stop playing Faber's game. She lifted her hand and took a step back, then. another, scolding herself as she did. Who knew how long, how many ticks of that never-ceasing clock went by, as Sophie stood in the freezing, near-dark.

"He can't make me go inside." Her words were whispered to the deep shadows, and lost to the ticking. She should have run, should have turned on the spot and raced back upstairs. But her feet, to her horror, decided to walk her right up to the door.

And then through.

Sophie held her lamp high, trying to pierce the curtain of blackness that enveloped her. She crept along, looking for something unusual, listening for the source of the ticking. The air here was the coldest she had ever felt. The room seemed larger than it should be.

The light from the lamp fell on the wall. She had expected to find rows of wine racks, but instead she was in a room that might have been a workshop. A bench stood against one wall, covered in tools and machinery parts. But everything looked fuzzy, as if she were seeing it through a window that had been fogged over. The room's smell, however, was sharp and clear. A musty, stale smell with a slight hint of lavender.

She gasped and halted, reeling. The ticking grew so loud it nearly drowned out her thoughts. If this was that same room, then...

As if it had only been waiting for her to think about it, an electric light bulb began to emit a soft glow from above. The room was still indistinct and blurry, and there seemed to be whole gaps in the space.

Likely because this was as much as Sophie had seen of it. Her heart pounded in her chest, drumming a counterpoint to the ticking. Something lurked at the end of the room, covered in shadow. Sophie moved forward, her whole body shaking as her feet dragged across the wooden floor. A long, rectangular shape, waist-high, six feet long.

She drew closer, and the shape emerged from shadow a bit at a time. Brass glinted in the lantern light, while glass threw it back at her in reflection.

Sophie's heart, pounding just a moment ago, seemed to stop.

The sound of metal-on-metal wasn't as loud from inside the machine. Henry braced himself for the whir of a hurricane and bone-rattling shudder, but it they never happened. Just the strange grinding sound for a few moments, then nothing.

Alexei smiled. "Ah, we've arrived." He opened a cabinet, which Henry hadn't noticed previously, and pulled out a long woolen cloak.

"You will wait here, Mr. White." Alexei's tone wasn't commanding or suggestive, simply stating a fact. "Mr. Rittenhouse, come with me, and do exactly as I say. Do you understand?"

Henry stood there, open-mouthed. "You can't be serious? How in the world do you think I could possibly trust you?"

"You don't have much of a choice, do you?" Faber's voice remained even and soft. "I've already discussed everything with Gabriel over there, and we have an agreement. You have my word no harm will come to you."

Henry looked over at Gabriel. The agent remained lounging on the loveseat, a cookie in one hand and tea in the other. He lifted his chin toward Henry, an affirmation of everything Faber had said. Henry inhaled, a slow, shaking breath.

"Fine. I'm not saying I trust you. I'll go with you, only for Sophie's sake."

"Fair enough, then." Faber opened the door of the time machine and gestured to it. "After you, Mr. Rittenhouse."

Henry stepped out into a dark, cold wood. He shivered, both from the air and his surroundings. "Where are we?"

"You'll see soon enough." Faber pulled on the cloak. "If you'd be kind enough to use that fabulous torch of yours, we won't break our necks tripping over tree roots or rocks."

Henry turned on the torch, training the beam on the ground. It revealed dark soil traced with thick roots and a layer of detritus through which jutted sharp-looking rocks. Faber picked his way through the wood. Henry followed cautiously, wishing he had Gabriel's weapon to defend himself. The agent may trust Faber, but Henry still had reservations.

Faber held his hand up and stopped. "We're almost there. Mr. Rittenhouse. What you might see... remember your promise."

Henry let out an irritated sigh. "I wish you would just be direct and tell me what is happening."

Faber faced Henry. "If I told you everything, you'd rush off like a fool. We are here because it is of vital importance to both of us."

A sound nearby startled Henry. He clicked off the torch and listened, holding his breath.

"Come on, gents, this way." It was a male voice. Footsteps crashed through the underbrush. A small light bobbed between the trees. Henry stepped back, nearly falling over a lichen-covered stone.

"William, slow down, will you? We know you want to see your darling Alice, but we would also like to arrive in one piece." A second male voice floated through the woods. "Do you think that lovely Miss Weber will be there tonight?"

Henry moved toward the voices, but Faber caught him and held him, a finger to his lips.

"Ahhh, Jonathan. Seen something you like, mate? Well, sorry to say, old chap, but Alice tells me she has a gent back in America that fancies her."

Henry sucked in a shallow breath. *Back in America?*

"Really?" the second voice replied, and Henry realized both boys had British accents. "How does she feel about him, if you know so much?"

There was a pause, and then a crash and a curse. "It's alright, I'm alright. I'm not exactly sure, sorry. Alice says she thinks the feeling is mutual, but Miss Weber has not been especially forthcoming. Charles, are you coming or not? You don't want to get lost out here."

A third voice, smaller than the others, came from a distance away. "Yes, of course, William, but you've run off with the light and these woods are trying to murder me."

Laughter echoed through the darkness, and the light bobbed back the way it had come. "There you are, we can't have you arriving damaged. All the girls will take pity on you and Jonathan and I will have no chance at all."

The light changed direction again, and the three boys stomped off, laughing and chatting.

Faber pulled on Henry's coat sleeve. "Come on."

Henry clicked on the torch, keeping the beam dim and low to the ground. Faber paralleled the boys' path rather than following directly behind. He stepped lightly and carefully, avoiding branches that could crack beneath his feet and give away their position. Henry followed, mimicking his movements. Not that it seemed to matter—the boys' chatted with exuberance, punctuated by laughter that carried across the forest, drowning out any other sounds.

"Here we are, then." One of the boys said. Their lamp bobbed a few yards more, then disappeared.

"William!" called a happy-sounding female voice. Her accent matched that of the boys. "What took you so long?"

The young man's answer was indecipherable. There was a scream, which set Henry's heart pounding, until he realized it was one of delight.

Henry and Faber continued a little further and emerged into a clearing. The moonlight poured through, giving more than enough light to see the dilapidated cottage without the torch. Light flickered through the broken windows. Voices spoke from inside, those of the boys joined by at least two feminine ones. A party. They all seemed to be in high spirits, laughing and talking loudly, not suspecting that anyone could hear them in the middle of the forest in the dead of night.

"Where are we, exactly?" Henry's whisper was harsh.

Faber glanced sidelong at Henry before returning his focus to his cottage. "We're in the wood behind Miss Montgomery's Finishing School for Fine Ladies."

Henry paused, thinking. "I know that name. Wait... that's the name of the school Herr Weber sent Sophie to, isn't it?" He didn't wait for Faber to reply. "We're in *England*?"

Faber gave a one-shouldered shrug. "I told you we could travel in space as well as time. In this case it's a bit trickier. A lot of calculations. This is about eight months earlier than when you left home." He shifted his weight, his face taking on a more serious look of concentration. "Now please, be quiet."

Henry opened his mouth to argue but was cut off by a frantic scream. The light inside the cottage increased rapidly. A fire licked the edges of the dry, rotted old cottage. Those inside poured out of the door and into the clearing; two of the three boys they had followed through the woods, and four girls. All were coughing, trying to clear their lungs of smoke. They stopped midway across the clearing and turned to watch as the flames consumed the building.

"Rose! Charles!" Sophie's scream turned Henry's blood cold. He ran toward her before he thought about moving. She was steps away from plunging headlong into the flames when he caught her about the waist.

"Let me go! I have to help them!" Sophie thrashed about, making it difficult to drag her back to safety, but Henry managed to hold on to her.

"Are you alright?" Henry held her firmly but set her feet on the ground. Her back was still toward him, so she hadn't seen his face.

"Yes, but Rose and Charles are still in there. We have to help them."

"I'll see what I can do." Faber finally appeared in the clearing. "You will wait right here. Do *not* follow me." He pulled up the hood on his cloak, which nearly covered his face. And then he raced headlong into the fire.

"What's he doing?" One of the boys asked. "He's going to burn alive. Who is that man?"

Henry said nothing. He held Sophie as she went limp, tears streaking her face. He longed to stroke her hair, to give her comfort, but before he could, Faber reappeared. He carried two figures with him. One was a boy, not much younger than Henry. His face was badly burned, but he was alive. The other... Henry's stomach heaved when he saw the burden Faber carried from the conflagration. It was a charred remnant of what must have once been a girl. One of the boys took the remains and laid them on the grass.

Sophie tore herself from Henry's grasp, calling out the girl's name, her voice choked with horror and grief. She threw herself beside the charred bundle, calling "Rose!" Faber knelt beside her and muttered something into her ear, before standing and facing Henry.

"It's time to go."

Henry stood, dumbfounded. "Are you mad? She needs our help. We can't leave."

Alexei, his hands black with soot, rubbed his forehead with his fingertips. "We cannot stay, and you know exactly why." He leaned close to Henry and spoke directly in his ear. "We cannot save that poor child, and they must not know who we are or how we got here. Sophia is in shock, she doesn't yet realize who you are, which is in our favor. We have to go now or risk doing more damage than we can fix." He pulled his head back. "You understand?"

Henry's conflict paralyzed him. Sophie was in so much pain. But Alexei, as much as he hated to admit it, was right. His heart heavy, Henry nodded and walked off into to the forest. Shielded by the trees, he looked back at the clearing. Alexei was talking to the group. Then the two boys picked up their injured friend and headed toward the trees. The girls stood for a few moments longer, discussing something, at least one still sobbing. Sophie grabbed the hand of one of the girls and dragged them in the opposite direction the boys had gone. Faber took the body of the girl and laid it closer to the cottage. The fire had all but consumed the building, smoke billowing skyward like a beacon while embers swirled dangerously close to the nearby trees.

Alexei ran to where Henry waited and then past him, heading back toward the time machine.

"Why did we come here?" Henry called. He turned on the torch and pointed the light at Faber's back. "How did you know?'

Alexei stopped. He turned his head and squinted against the light. "It doesn't matter. Sophia was a hair's breadth away from dying tonight. In another…" he seemed to struggle for the word. "Universe, timeline, reality, whatever you want to call it, she *did* die."

Henry froze. "What do you mean?"

Faber sighed and rubbed his face with his soot-stained hand. "We have to get back. Your friends are still in danger, remember?" He turned and walked further into the forest.

Henry remained for a moment. Then he raced after the man, the light from the torch bouncing off the trees and rocks as he tried not to break an ankle on anything hiding in the underbrush.

The time machine was nestled between two ancient trees, just managing to fit in the space. Faber pulled the door open and slipped inside. Henry reached it just before the door swung shut and heaved himself through.

"Explain yourself, sir!" Henry's words were emphasized by the slamming of the time machine's door.

Faber ignored Henry's demand, choosing instead to fiddle with the machine's knobs and dials in preparation for departure. Henry grabbed

Faber's arm. "I am speaking to you. I demand you answer me, and now."

Faber's arm hung in the air, the two of them locked in a battle of iron wills. "Release me."

Henry's gaze bored into the other man's. "I will not, until you explain. Everything."

"Let him go." Gabriel drew behind him, and Henry was certain that if he turned around, the other boy's weapon would be pointed at him once more. Henry, for the briefest moment, considered ignoring the command. But the memory of the last time Gabriel had used his weapon on his person remained fresh.

"Fine." He let Faber's arm go and stepped back. "I want to know what you meant when you said Sophie died."

Faber paused, his hand on one of the dials. "It's difficult to understand. In the simplest terms, the night of the fire, Sophia ran into the cottage and tried to save her friend. She was overcome by the smoke, and she died. She never returned home to you. She never ran away from you in the snow on Christmas Eve morning."

Henry felt a blush creep up his neck. "That can't possibly be true. Obviously, she didn't die in the fire. I stopped her. She's at home, trapped in a freezing coffin."

"Yes. We traveled back to before she died, and we stopped her from running into fire. And because we did, she *didn't* die, and everything you know to be true happened after." His looked right at Henry. "You have no memory of it because for you, it never happened at all, you only remember that she came home, and she never said anything about it. We *rewrote* time. Just like I tried to do when you found me in Independence Hall, only this time, fortunately, we were successful."

Henry fell back, flabbergasted. He stumbled to the sofa and sat down hard. Faber pulled the lever that set the machine in motion. The grinding sound roared in Henry's ears, and the world seeming to turn upside down as the box spun through time and space.

Faber returned to the panel and spun the dials once more. Henry pushed through the utter chaos that had taken over his brain, and stood. "I saved her life. I saved her, just so you could take her away?"

"She is alive and will continue to be so. Be happy with that, my friend." Faber took his coat from the hook and put it on. "As for me, this is my stop."

Faber pulled open the machine's door and stood on the threshold, framed by the dark night of some unknown when and where.

"Goodbye, Henry. Go home and have a good life. Forget about me, forget about time travel. Mr. Government Man will try and stop some bad people from taking over the world. And I won't know anything about it. I've fulfilled my end of this bargain." He lifted his hands, seeming to indicate the entire room. "This is now all now property of the U.S. Government, I suppose. For all the good it will do them." He reached to his left, grasped the lever that started the machine, and pushed it before stepping out.

In the time it took Henry to cross the distance to the door, it slammed shut.

"No!" He tried to pull it open.

"It's too late. He's gone."

Gabriel was right. The time machine was already in motion, grinding and shaking its way through the ether to wherever Faber had sent them.

"I... I can't help her." Misery poured out with each syllable. "Sophie. I... failed." Henry fell back to the sofa, his hand to his chest as his heart shattered. Tesla, perhaps sensing how awful Henry felt, put a tiny hand on his leg.

Gabriel stood over him. "I'm sorry. I really am, Henry, but we don't have time for this right now. Irene and Alphonse need us."

The words slowly pierced through Henry's veil of sorrow. "What do you mean?"

"Faber's kidnapped them, remember? Another reason I was negotiating with him, I wanted to find out what he did with them. I don't know where they are or how much time they have. He only said he'd take me to them."

Henry jumped up, glad for the distraction. "What are we going to do?"

Gabriel held up a finger in pause. "Listen."

"I don't hear anything."

"Exactly. We've stopped."

Gabriel was out the door before Henry had a chance to take a step. Henry turned to Tesla, who still lounged on the love seat. "Well, come on, let's go."

They were back in Germantown. The cold air nipped at Henry's skin, and snow crunched beneath his boots. The Christmas tree in

Market Square was decorated and lit. Was it Christmas Eve? That seemed little help — this could be any Christmas Eve from his childhood, or one in the future. The scene gave no clues.

"Henry, come on!" Gabriel called to him from across the square. He stood on the steps of the church. The same church where Sophie had been christened. Tesla scampered across the snow, and Gabriel scooped him up, putting the monkey on his shoulder before disappearing inside. Henry paused for a moment. As Gabriel was so fond of reminding him, he wasn't part of their team. He was extra baggage. A burden.

"Henry! Get in here!"

Henry ran to the church door. The arched entryway swallowed him in shadow. Beyond, soft light filled the chapel. Gabriel stood at the front of the sanctuary, his back to Henry. He glanced over his shoulder. "There you are. I could use a bit of help, if you don't mind."

Henry jogged up the nave. Alphonse and Irene were laid on the altar, side-by-side, unconscious. A strange mask had been placed over each of their faces. The masks were connected to a box by a tube. Faber had attached a timer to the top of the box. The ticking reverberated through the cavernous room.

"Not again." Henry scanned the box for a vial of nitroglycerin and a small hammer.

"It's not a bomb. Faber said it was poison." Gabriel clicked on the electric torch and shone it at the box. "They're breathing in sleeping gas. He said if we didn't get here in time, it would change to cyanide."

There was one minute left, according to the timer. They could just pull the masks off, but then the sleeping gas and/or poison would spew into the air. Henry knelt beside the box and scanned the outside. A wire connected the timer to the box. "We left the scissors in 1776. You don't have a knife, do you?"

"You would think I would, in my line of work, but no."

Forty seconds left. Henry ran his hands over the outside of the box. On the far side, he found a button. It seemed strange to find a button. He had been fooled by Faber before, though. This button could do anything, including kill Alphonse and Irene. He looked at it more closely, squinting to see in the dim light.

Finally, something is labeled!

"Gabriel? Did Faber tell you what to do once you *found* Alphonse and Irene?"

"He said I would be able to stop the gas from dispensing." The words rushed from Gabriel's mouth. "He didn't say how."

Henry almost laughed. "Maybe like this?" He pushed the button.

The timer stopped, followed by the *hisss* of escaping air. Gabriel pulled the mask off Irene, then Alphonse. They coughed and spluttered, then sat up.

"Thanks, I needed that." Alphonse stretched his arms overhead. "Best sleep I've had in ages, though."

Irene swung her legs over the side of the altar. "I could have done without it. Tesla!" The monkey made several affectionate-sounding chirps and dove into Irene's lap.

"Now that we're back in action, what's next?" Alphonse hopped to his feet. "Where is that arse Faber? I'd like a chance to repay him for this."

Henry and Gabriel exchanged a look. Henry couldn't read Gabriel's expression, but his own anger resurfaced

"He's gone." Gabriel clicked off the torch.

Irene stopped petting Tesla. "Gone where?"

"Just gone. Into time. We can't follow him because we don't know when we left him." Gabriel said the words with no emotion.

"What does that mean?" Alphonse asked. "When are we?"

"We're home. I think," Gabriel answered. "I haven't had a chance to really see. We're in Germantown, that much is certain."

Henry said nothing. He was still angry with Gabriel, but almost as angry with himself. Faber had slipped away, leaving him with no way to save Sophie.

Sophie!

He ran from the church, across Market Square, and down the street to Sophie's house.

CHAPTER XIX

SOMETHING WAS WRONG. HENRY COULDN'T PLACE IT, BUT THERE was something wrong here. The Weber house looked exactly like it always did. There was only one light on, in the parlor. Sophie's mother, likely, sitting watch. If that was so, that was a good sign. It meant the machine hadn't malfunctioned.

It might not break, whispered the voice in Henry's mind. *He said he fixed it.*

"Hey, chum. Whatcha' doin' out here?" Alphonse sauntered up beside Henry. "I thought you'd be in there by now, saving your lovely lass. I know it's late, but I honestly don't think anyone will mind your bursting in."

"Yes, Henry, why are you standing around?" Irene and Tesla arrived right behind Alphonse. Gabriel was nowhere to be seen. He hadn't told them.

"I don't have the key. Faber said he didn't have it and wouldn't give it to me if he did. Sophie's release wasn't part of the deal." The words made the hole in Henry's heart larger.

"What? What deal?" Alphonse's shocked question carried in the quiet night. He looked around, to see if anyone had heard.

"The deal I made to save your lives and complete our mission." Gabriel had finally arrived. "We got Alexei Faber's machine, and information about his employer. You remember, the bad guys? Enough intel and tech to keep us working for another five years."

"But not Sophie." Irene did not pose it as a question.

Gabriel's face became a study in sharp edges. "No. Faber would not be moved on that point. I made the call that needed to be made." His tone said the discussion was over.

Henry finally realized what was wrong. "There are no Christmas decorations on the Weber house." Saying it aloud, Henry realized how significant it was. "There's a tree in Market Square. Look, wreaths on the neighbor's doors, candles in the windows. Marta Weber loves

Christmas above all other holidays. When we left, this house was decorated to the nines."

Alphonse's mouth dropped open. "Where is Faber's time machine?"

"Back in Market Square, why?" Gabriel asked, but the question was spoken to Alphonse's back as he ran toward the Square. The rest of them followed.

Alphonse waited outside the time machine. "It's locked. I hope you can open it?"

Gabriel pulled the key from his pocket and turned it, then punched a series of numbers into the keypad beside the lock. Alphonse pushed the door open and ran inside.

"Son of a bitch!"

Henry stepped toward the open door, but Alphonse reappeared, blocking his path. "A year."

"What are you babbling about?" Irene pushed Henry aside.

"Faber left us here, one *year* after we first left."

Henry stumbled back. "What?" Sophie had been in the machine for a year. A year of her parents watching her, with no hope. Not even the will to put up holiday decorations. And not a word from Henry. What must they think? That he abandoned her? His own parents, what must *they* think happened to him? The more he thought about it, the more horror-struck he grew.

"Let's just go back, then." Irene said. "Just all pile in and go back one year. Simple."

Alphonse shook his head. "I'm pretty sure I could do it, but not positive. This machine works differently than ours did. I need to figure out how to set the time and destination. It'll take me some time to do it properly."

"Even if we can, I don't know if that's wise." Gabriel stared at the sky. "We may make things worse, going back along our own timeline."

"All right, fine. So we've been gone an entire year with no word to anyone we know. We've disappeared." Alphonse shut the door to the time machine. "I can't say that's the oddest thing that's ever happened to me."

"We'll make a full report when we get back to Washington." Gabriel locked the door. The four of them stood in silence, looking at each other.

Henry's mind reeled. "I have to go and see Sophie." He had no idea what time of night it was, but he would pound on the door and make his apologies later.

"Where are you going, chum?"

He had only walked a few feet before Alphonse's question stopped him. "What do you mean? I told you where I'm going."

Alphonse shrugged. "All right. I thought you wanted to save her, but if you'd rather not, that's up to you."

Sophie stumbled and almost lost her grip on the lamp as she approached the thing that had been hiding in the basement. She knew what it was but had no name for it. The lower half was made of gleaming brass. The lid was glass. The ticking sound that had plagued her since she had woken here emanated from it, like a strange, sick heartbeat. Sophie wasn't close enough to look inside. Slowly, she shuffled forward. As she had no choice about entering this room, there was no choice *but* to look.

She touched the glass, then pulled her hand back with a hiss. It was so cold it burned her skin. What *was* the thing before her? It looked like a coffin, but sounded like a machine. Coffins weren't built of brass and glass or made to look into.

Or out of.

Sophie fell back with a cry of revulsion. She had run from Henry in the snow, and been taken hostage by Faber. Those were real events. This... this had to be a nightmare, the one she had between falling asleep in the carriage house and waking up in her bed. This could not have happened.

"Sleep well, Sophia."

She pulled her sleeve down over her hand and wiped at the glass in an attempt to clear it. But it was no use. The ice crystals that frosted the glass surface grew on the *inside*. Sophie looked for the latch that would open the lid, but there was nothing. She put her ear to the glass. *Tick, tick, tick.* The mechanism that made the sound was out of sight, beneath the pretty exterior. Sophie wanted to rip it open with her bare hands and crush it into silence. She lay with her skin on the freezing surface.

"When you wake, the world will be a very different place."

Sophie gasped. This was certainly a wholly different world. A world where she was utterly alone. And this beastly machine was at the heart of it all. She pushed her fear down deep and examined the contraption, but the buttons and gauges made no sense.

"Maybe if Miss Montgomery's Finishing School for Young Ladies had taught me something practical, I'd be able to get out of this mess. Conjugating French verbs won't help me here, will it?" Henry was good at this sort of thing, not her. She pounded on the machine with both fists, frustrated.

What would happen if she destroyed the machine? Would the wall of thorns disappear, and her prison open? There was nothing nearby she could use to break it.

She tore through the cold cellar and up the stairs. In the kitchen, she searched through the cooking utensils.

In the far corner, she found her salvation. A sledgehammer. Why there was a sledgehammer in the kitchen, she could not fathom. It was far heavier than the axe, but Sophie would find the strength to swing it if it killed her.

She dragged it into the basement, thudding its head on each step as she went down the stairs. The casket stayed exactly as it was, ticking away moments of her life. It gave no indication that it knew what Sophie planned to do.

Of course, it doesn't. It's only a machine. The thought gave her no comfort. Sophie had overheard horrible stories her father had told her mother, when they thought she wasn't listening. Accidents at the factory. A bit of loose clothing that was caught, and into the jaws of the machine the worker went. Machines could be dangerous, and Sophie likened this one to a sleeping beast.

Sophie wiped her hands on her trousers to warm them, and then wrapped them around the hammer's long handle. She bent her knees deeply and hoisted the hammer onto her shoulder. Halfway there. All she had to do was give it one big push over her head and let it fall.

"On the count of three." Talking helped to build her courage. "One... two... three!"

A yell erupted from her throat, anger and fear filling her lungs, pouring into her arms. The hammer sailed over her head and slammed into the glass.

It cracked but didn't break. Which was satisfying, but not nearly good enough. Sophie dragged the hammer back, heaving it for another blow. Before she could lift it, the ticking shifted. It slowed, then sped up, then slowed again. A chime rang, the music warped and distorted.

Sophie dropped the hammer, and it hit the dirt floor of the room with a dull *thud*.

What have I done?

I can't save her. I told you that already." Henry tried not to sound as annoyed as he felt in the face of Alphonse's glib comment. "Did that sleeping gas affect your memory, or your hearing?"

"Oh ho, the boy's got bite." Alphonse crossed his arms over his chest. "About time. Don't you mean, you can't save her *yet*? Because I know you're not giving up. Not if it took you the next ninety-nine years, you wouldn't just give up. Would you?"

Henry dropped his annoyance. "Of course not. I just don't know how."

"With the key, of course," Alphonse said, as if it should be obvious.

"He doesn't have it, Alphonse, he's already told you." Irene made a *tutting* sound. "Honestly."

"We don't have it *yet*." Alphonse wore a smug smile. "But maybe we can find it."

"What are you blathering about?" Henry wanted to throttle Alphonse, but he was just too tired. "Just spit out whatever you're thinking already."

Alphonse uncrossed his arms, snapping his shirt cuffs one at a time. "Faber said he didn't have the key, right?"

"Yes." Henry wasn't sure where Alphonse's thoughts were going. "Do you believe him?"

"I didn't, but I don't know. He had every reason to lie."

"Let's say he's telling the truth. Where would he have put it? We saw him, on a random Market Day." Alphonse spoke to them like something should be obvious.

"Yes, I remember. I was there. We were all there." Gabriel finally interjected into the conversation. "Your point?"

"My point is, what was *his* point? He didn't know we were following him, and it had nothing to do with blowing up the Continental Congress. What if he came here to hide that key?" Alphonse walked in a circle, gesturing with his hands for emphasis. "Think about it. He told you he would never give it up. How could he ensure that? By not actually having it on his person."

Gabriel held up a finger. "Let's say you're right. He would need to hide it in a place that was guaranteed not to change over the years, to keep the key from being found by accident."

"Correct." Alphonse pointed at Gabriel. "And where is the one place that is like that? Very unlikely to change, even over a century or two? What's a place no one would touch? And where in Germantown, specifically?"

Henry realized they had had this conversation before, but Irene must have read his thoughts.

"A cemetery!" she exclaimed.

Alphonse beamed. "I knew you'd figure it out, my sweet."

"There are three main cemeteries in Germantown." Henry said. "Plus crypts in the churches. It will take days to search them all."

"We don't need to search them all." Alphonse's eyes were so bright, they might have thrown sparks "We only need to find one."

The answer struck Henry like lightning. "We need to find Angelica Faber's grave."

Falling snow muffled the footsteps of the four figures that stepped through the iron-and-carved marble entrance to the Lower Burial Ground. The cemetery was at the opposite end of Germantown Avenue from the Upper Burial Ground where Henry had first encountered Faber and his time machine.

"She is most likely buried here," Henry said, more to break up the quiet, eerie dark than anything else. "This is the cemetery closest to Faber's house."

The wreaths and grave blankets placed on many headstones were the only sign of recent visitors. Gabriel swung the beam of the torch in wide arcs, yellow light skimming over the hundreds of markers that filled the grounds.

"Do we have any idea *where* in the cemetery Angelica might be buried?" Alphonse asked. "Maybe we should split up. "

"It's a good idea. But we only have one torch." Gabriel scanned another section of the grounds.

Alphonse jammed his hands onto his hips. "Well, now, that's not exactly true." He reached into his jacket and pulled out a second brass tube, smaller than the one Gabriel held. "I kind of built this one too, just in case." He pressed the bottom of the tube, and yellow light poured from the end.

"Why are you just telling me this now?" Gabriel didn't seem angry, just confused.

Alphonse shrugged. "We didn't need it before now, did we? I almost forgot I had it." He held out his hand to Irene. "Come on, love, let's go and find us a headstone."

Gabriel and Henry stared at each other, tension pulling like a violin string between them.

"It was Franklin." Gabriel's words fell like the flakes around them. "That experiment with the kite and the key?"

It took Henry a moment to process what Gabriel was talking about. "You mean, how you can—"

"Come back to life. Yes." Gabriel's words flowed, as if a dam had burst inside him. "I had been working with Franklin since I was eleven years old. I'd helped him on countless experiments, and that night, which was the second time he'd tried, I was the one holding the kite string." He took a breath. "The bolt hit me, and the next thing I knew I woke up in a hospital bed."

Henry didn't know how to reply, so he said nothing.

"That was 1767, I guess? Then the war happened. I joined the Patriot cause. 1777. When the British took over Philadelphia? I was there. I was shot, right there in the middle of town. I was dying. And then I wasn't. And that's how it's been, ever since."

Henry had nothing to say. He felt nothing for the man. Not hate, not fear. And Gabriel was a man, not a boy, no matter how he appeared. An impossible man, who had, by his own admission, lived over a hundred years already.

"Is that what living forever does? Make your heart shrivel and your soul die? No care for anyone, just the next mission?" Henry had wanted to scream the words, but they came out on a breath of quiet fury and despair.

"Because that sounds like Hell." He turned away.

Gabriel continued his sweep of the cemetery, the two of them moving from stone to stone as quiet as the graves. The wind picked up, the snow falling thicker and faster. Henry stuffed his hands in his pockets. When Gabriel's photophone buzzed, it was almost drowned out by the storm.

"We found it." Irene's voice was like a squeak, barely audible. "Follow our torchlight."

It took Henry and Gabriel ten minutes to reach them, slogging through the deepening snow, their light bouncing off the snowflakes.

Alphonse held his torch so the beam shone on the headstone, highlighting the words chiseled into the marble.

Angelica Faber
Beloved Daughter
Aged 8 years
1860-1868

Henry knelt on the cold ground, the knees of his pants instantly soaked. He flung the snow aside with both hands until he uncovered the earth below.

"It's frozen solid." Henry scraped at the ground, attempting to dig his nails into it, but there was no way to budge even a pebble.

Alphonse knelt beside him. "Let me see." He scrabbled against the ground. "I could get through this, but the tool I need isn't here."

Henry pounded on the ground with his fists. Frustration and grief filled him like a kettle.

"Hold on, Henry. Let's think." Alphonse's calm voice broke through the haze that had descended. "Faber didn't have time to dig a hole and bury anything. We followed him up from the Market."

"He had a time machine, Alphonse. He could do whatever he wanted. Who knew how long he was here before we caught up with him? Maybe we're wrong and he didn't leave it here at all." Henry couldn't allow any hope, no matter how small, to let him drop his guard. He couldn't bear it if it came to nothing. Again.

Alphonse sat back on his haunches. "I was so sure." Snow covered his tri-cornered hat, and lay in his hair. The storm deepened. If they didn't find anything soon, they'd have to abandon the cause before they froze to death.

"I don't think the man would have dug up the grave, do you? Maybe it's under the stone?" Irene offered. Alphonse stood and pushed the stone. His feet slid on the wet and snowy ground, and the stone did not budge.

"Guess not. Sorry." Irene's voice was small, soft.

"Come on, Henry. We'll figure it out. You and me." Alphonse might have meant his tone to be soothing. But Henry's grief was a wall, impenetrable.

A sleeping cherub's head had been engraved across the top of the marker, wings spread on either side. Henry touched it, feeling the engraving beneath his fingers. They were out of options.

He leaned into the engraving, meaning to push himself to standing. The cherub's head moved beneath his fingers and sank into the stone.

"What?" He jumped back, thinking he had broken the monument.

"Look at that," Alphonse whispered. "It's some kind of secret latch."

Pressing the head caused one of the cherub's wings to pop outward. Henry grabbed it with his fingertips and pulled. It came free, revealing a dark hollow behind it.

Alphonse directed the torchlight over Henry's shoulder as he reached inside the hidden space.

"There's something... got it." Henry pulled his hand from the opening. Clasped in his numb fingers was a leather pouch. He turned toward the light. He pulled the drawstring with shaking fingers. and upended the pouch. A large, ornate brass key fell into his hand.

Alphonse let out a long, low whistle. "You did it, Henry."

Henry let it sit in his hand for a moment, not sure it was real. "Not yet, I haven't." He wrapped his fingers around it so tightly his knuckles turned white.

Then he ran.

The streetlights glowed like stars among the thick, falling snow as Henry raced down the middle of the street, the key in his hand.

Finally, he reached the Weber's gate.

He ran up the walk, leapt onto the porch with thunderous steps, and burst into the entrance hall without knocking. In the parlor, Marta Weber jumped to her feet, her eyes wide with fear.

"Henry? *Henry*, where have you been? A year, gone. Your mother is sick with worry. And Sophie! My poor Sophie!"

Henry approached the machine. "What's wrong?"

Marta's voice maintained the same high, frantic pitch. "The machine, it sounds... sick." She moved her hands over her the glass, as if she were trying to soothe it. "It's happened a few times over the year but stopped. Then just an hour ago, it started again." She grabbed Henry's sleeve. "I think it's killing her."

Henry's eyes moved over the machine. The needles in all the gauges bounced back and forth. Except for one, labeled *temperature*. That one was pinned all the way to the left. Cold flowed from the machine, reaching for him with icy fingers. The counter dial read 001, mocking him with the time that had passed. Henry leaned closer. The clockwork inside *did* sound sick, skipping and grinding like the spring had slipped, or a gear was out of plumb.

A gasp from the door made him turn. Irene, Gabriel, and Alphonse stood in the parlor door. Irene's eyes were wide and filled with tears. "I can hear her thoughts."

Henry's breath caught in his throat. "You said you couldn't hear the thoughts of sleeping people."

"I usually can't. Hers are faint, almost a whisper. She's calling for you." She lowered herself into the overstuffed armchair by the fire, her face white as the snow outside.

"Faber didn't fix the calibration problem," Henry said. "Not enough for it to run for a hundred years. The machine is breaking down. It's making her too cold."

"What are you waiting for?" Alphonse replied. "You have the key."

Henry had nearly forgotten. He thrust it into the lock. The key turned easily, and the tumblers clicked.

Nothing happened. He pulled at the lid's latch, but it remained locked tight. The cold wound around his hands like death. Horror bubbled inside Henry, a poison that flowed through him. Sophie was freezing to death.

He looked for something to either smash the glass or pry off the lid. A poker by the fireplace caught his eye, and he grabbed it viciously. With strength he had no idea he possessed he jammed the tip beneath the lid's clasp.

"Henry. Henry, stop!" Irene's shout was followed by Alphonse grabbing his arm.

"She can't die in there! I won't let her." Henry struggled against Alphonse's grip, but it was surprisingly strong.

"Think, Henry. What do we know about Faber? He always uses redundancies, so if one system fails another takes over. There's nothing we can do to break in. It might even be booby trapped, and then we'll all die."

Henry stopped struggling. Alphonse was right. Faber was deranged and misguided, but he was also a genius. "What do we do?"

"We need the combination." Gabriel's voice cut through the chaos in Henry's mind like a knife. "Look." He pointed to the keypad beside the lock. "It's just like the one on his time machine. You need both a key *and* the combination."

"I thought that was to set the number of years," Alphonse said. He released Henry and examined the numbered device. "But you might be right. I think this disables the cooling mechanism. The lid can't open until the cooling is turned off."

As if it knew its secret was told, the machine gave a mighty heaving sound, the *tick, tick, tick* turning into a *clunk, clink, clank*. The dials on the front of the machine that were supposed to count off the years, began to rapidly turn. Year Two was gone.

"What happens if it reaches a hundred in the next few minutes?" Irene asked. "Will it release her?"

Henry wasn't about to wait. "Maybe, but by then she could be dead."

Alphonse shook his head. "We don't know the combination. Or even how many digits."

"Four." Gabriel seemed very sure of this fact. "If it's like the time machine, it's four."

"Do you think it's the same numbers?" Henry placed his hands on either side of the numbered panel, ready to punch in the combination.

"Not likely. He gave me the time machine combination without complaint. If they were the same, he knows I would tell you." Gabriel made no move to enter the room, as if he was unsure of his welcome.

Irene's voice was edged with panic. "It must be a number that means something to Faber."

Inspiration struck Henry.

"There's only one four-digit number I can think of that would be that important to him. One that he'd want Edmund Weber to remember." The same year as Sophie's birth. The year Angelica died. It was almost too simple, but then again, Faber was also arrogant. He never expected anyone to find the key, and without it, the combination was useless.

Despite the cold pouring off of the machine, Henry wiped sweat from his brow. "One, eight, six, eight." As he said each number, he punched the corresponding button.

The ticking did not slow. It came to a complete stop. The dial that marked the years held steady at twelve, and the gauges ceased their dance.

"Did we do it?" Alphonse whispered, apparently afraid that if he spoke too loudly something bad might happen.

Henry shook his head. "Don't know. Maybe you'd better step back, just in case."

Something made a sound beneath the case that held Sophie. Then there was a *whoosh* and a freezing blast of air shot from under it, frost turning to beads of water in the heat from the fire in the grate. Then silence.

Henry leaned over the machine's mechanism and scanned the gauges. All lay still, fallen to the right like they were sleeping. Except the temperature gauge. It rose, slowly, steadily. Henry held his breath, as he waited for what seemed like a hundred years. When it reached seventy degrees, there was a *click* from the area of the lid's latch.

Henry reached for the lip of the casket. With a prayer muttered under his breath, he lifted it.

Sophie felt as if she were falling down a hole. The clock's ticking was like her heart, racing and then slowing. Her hands went numb again, her breath feeling like shards of glass in her chest. The room turned into mirror images of itself. Gears ground together, though she couldn't tell where the sound came from. It was a horrific sound that blended with the clock's distorted chime like some kind of unearthly harmony.

Sophie dragged herself toward the door. She gulped for each breath, the expansion of her ribs a torture. At last, her fingers found the knob. The air was fresher on the other side, but the musty odor of the cold cellar hit Sophie's nose hard. She crossed the cellar in the dark and staggered up the stairs. In the kitchen she fell to her knees, unable to take another step.

"Sophie, my poor Sophie!"

Her mother's voice sounded miles away. But Sophie had no strength to search for her. Barely a voice to call out.

"Mother... help me..."

Sophie fought to keep her eyes open. She crawled to the kitchen door and lay across the threshold. The ticking continued in its strange way, fast and slow, high and low. The clock was broken. It would never strike midnight again.

Her hand found the locket. She gripped it like a lifeline. Henry.

I tried. I tried to get back to you.

"She can't die in there. I won't let her!"

Henry's voice. Was it her mind playing tricks? She struggled to hear, to keep her eyes open, to make her voice work. But it was as if she was being dragged under the ice of a frozen lake. Her mind held on to images of Henry. Every memory, every dream.

She pictured the kiss she had intended to give him, that Christmas Eve in the stable house. It was soft and warm, passionate and full of promise.

Silence fell. The ticking had stopped.

Am I dying? Am I dead?

"Did we do it?" The whispering voice was male, but didn't belong to Henry.

"Don't know. Maybe you'd better stand back, just in case." Henry sounded close now, his voice clear.

"Henry?" He must have found a way through the thorns, made it to the front porch. Why didn't he just come in?

There was a loud *click* from... everywhere. She touched her locket again, and found that it had popped open. Sophie gently opened it further. In one side was her own picture, one her mother had had taken when she had been home over the summer.

In the other side was a picture of Henry. Sweet Henry. Henry, wearing a dark, pinstriped tailcoat. Tears dripped from Sophie's eyes and over the image. It warmed her heart and her frozen limbs. She snapped the locket closed and rose. Henry's voice led her to the front door. When she touched the knob, it didn't burn her fingers with cold. She turned it but it was still locked. She banged on the door, calling Henry's name.

"I'm here! Open the door!"

Murmured voices continued to speak on the other side. Sophie raced back to the kitchen. The key had dropped from the basement door and sat on the floor, waiting. She scooped it up and ran back to the front entrance, her heart in her throat. The key slipped into the lock as if it had been waiting just for this moment, and Sophie held her breath.

She turned the key. It *clicked* open. Sophie released the air from her lungs as she turned the knob and pulled the door open.

"Henry..." Light and warmth flooded the hall, so bright she couldn't see. She took a step...

And woke, looking up into Henry's face.

Henry's beautiful face, lined with concern. "Sophie, are you all right?"

Sophie reached up and pulled his face toward hers. The kiss was as soft and warm as she had dreamed it would be. For a moment, Henry stiffened in shock, and then he was kissing her back, and her whole body warmed with the heat of it. She could have stayed there forever, in this moment, frozen in time.

No. She had had enough of frozen time. She broke the kiss and looked into Henry's gorgeous brown eyes. Eyes she never thought she would see again.

"I love you, Henry Rittenhouse." She had never said it aloud but couldn't possibly wait one more second to say what was in her heart.

Henry lifted her from the machine, cradling her in his arms. "I love you, Sophie Weber. Until the end of time."

CHAPTER XX

ENRY CLOSED THE FRONT DOOR TO THE WEBER'S HOUSE. HE NEVER wanted to leave Sophie's side again, but the Weber family needed privacy for their reunion. The whole house had awoken during the last half-hour: maids, cook, and Edmund all racing down the stairs just in time to see Sophie kissing Henry. Edmund hadn't shouted, probably because of the shock at seeing his daughter awake. But how much longer that generosity would last, Henry didn't know and wasn't about to test the boundary of his good fortune.

Irene, Alphonse, and Gabriel waited for him on the lawn.

"I'm so happy for you, Henry." Irene beamed at him. "She's lovely. She really loves you."

Henry didn't even bother to scold her for peering into Sophie's thoughts. "Thank you. I love her as well."

"You were pretty cool back there, chum," Alphonse said. He gave Henry's shoulder a lighthearted jab. "I was waiting for you to tear that machine apart with your bare hands."

"I almost did." Henry chuckled, but he wasn't lying.

"You should have seen him with that explosive device of Faber's." Irene's gushing made Henry blush. "He really came through for us. For history, too, I suppose. You saved history, Henry."

"And he wasn't exactly miserable at making our time machine work, either." Gabriel's grudging praise was appreciated, but Henry wasn't about to let him know it. He hadn't exactly forgiven the agent yet, despite everything working out in the end.

An awkward silence fell. No one seemed to want to be the one to speak the inevitable. Henry decided to take the plunge.

"I suppose you'll be off, then?"

Irene and Alphonse looked to Gabriel for the answer. "Yes. We have to take Faber's time machine back to headquarters. And there's likely to be a ton of paperwork."

"And I'd like to get out of this Colonial ensemble at some point," Alphonse said. "Or maybe I'll just start a new-old fashion."

"If anyone could do it, Alphonse, it would be you. Well, then I'll say goodbye, and good luck. It was... not boring." Henry turned toward the house.

"Of course, we should debrief you." Alphonse's words made Henry stop, one foot on the bottom step. "Right, Gabriel? We can't in good conscience just leave him here without a proper debriefing. Especially as he's a civilian."

Henry turned around slowly. "How long would that take?"

"Oh, I should say a good long while. Of course, we'll absolutely need to debrief Miss Weber as well."

As if she had only been waiting to be called, Sophie opened the front door. "Henry, there you are! Mother and Father want to thank you and your friends again." Her eyes were bright and full of mischief, as usual. She walked stiffly, her muscles slowly getting used to working again. "Miss Weber, we were just talking about you." Gabriel beckoned her to them. "I was wondering how you feel?"

Sophie seemed taken aback at the question. "Fine, I suppose. A little out-of-sorts, but I'm sure I'll be right as rain."

"Perfectly understandable." Irene stepped forward, looping her arm through Sophie's, as if they were the best of friends. "Have you met Tesla?"

Tesla stood on Irene's shoulder and bowed to Sophie.

Sophie laughed. "What an adorable creature."

"He likes you." Irene turned them away from the house. "I'm Irene. Henry tells me that you spent some time in England?"

Irene walked Sophie away from the boys, chatting away.

"She's a unique girl," Gabriel said in a musing tone. "Possibly even more now."

"What do you mean?" Henry asked.

Gabriel tugged at his jacket. "She's been through an experience unlike any other. Many times, the body... changes when it goes through something so traumatic."

Henry gleaned on to Gabriel's meaning. "You mean she might be like you three?"

"It's possible. We'll need to test her to find out." He didn't look at Henry. "Which might take a while. You're welcome to come, of course. In fact, I think you should. Alphonse is right, you should be debriefed."

Henry's nerves danced at the idea. "I won't leave her again. Would it be allowed? I don't work for you..."

"That can be easily remedied." Gabriel turned to Henry at last. "You have got valuable skills. Think of what you could do if you're given the means and opportunity to expand them. What inventions you might create."

"And I can build anything," Alphonse said, sounding like a child who had been handed a toy at Christmas. "We'd make a helluva team, chum."

Henry wasn't sure he was hearing properly. "Just a few days ago you said I was only going to be trouble. A burden, I believe was the word?"

"Without proper training, yes. But you might have the makings of a good agent." Gabriel didn't seem to be in pain or have a gun to his head, so he must be telling the truth. "Besides, we have a lot of work to finish up. We have to find the men that hired Faber, for starters."

"And who knows what other trouble we might get up to along the way," Alphonse added. "I mean, we *do* have a time machine."

Henry searched for an excuse in case this was some kind of test or tease. "We can't just drag Sophie away from her family, not when just when she got them back."

Sophie and Irene had reached the end of the walk. She ran back to Henry, eyes sparkling. "Henry, is it true? Are we going on an adventure?"

The look Henry gave Irene was a mix of scathing and surprised. "We... could. But only if you want to."

Sophie looked as if someone has asked if she might like to breathe. "If *I* want to?" She stopped suddenly, a pained look on her face. "Adventures are nothing but trouble, aren't they, Henry?"

Henry could hardly believe his ears. "Absolutely." He reached out and took Sophie's hand. "Sometimes, though, trouble can be awfully exciting."

Sophie's smile lit up the night. "I never thought I'd hear you talk that way, Mr. Rittenhouse. I would love to go on adventures with you."

Henry laughed. "But what about your family? Sophie, it will break their hearts." He really wanted to make sure they were both certain.

Alphonse stepped up. "We can come back, any time. Right to this moment. They'll never know you were gone."

Henry shot a glance at Gabriel, to see if this was true. He nodded. "As long as we're very careful, yes."

"Come on, Henry. We could be Lords of Time!" Alphonse's exclamation echoed across the night.

"Lords of Time?" Irene scoffed. "Sounds utterly ridiculous."

Henry was out of excuses. He couldn't see himself going back to the dull existence of building bridges. David, his great-great-great grandfather was unafraid to try anything. Everything.

Sophie gazed at him and the choice was made.

"Let's go."

ABOUT THE AUTHOR

ONCE UPON A TIME, CHRISTINE NORRIS THOUGHT SHE WANTED TO BE an archaeologist but hates sand and bugs, so instead, she became a writer. She is the author of several speculative fiction works for children and adults, including *The Library of Athena* series, *A Curse of Ash and Iron*, and contributions to *Gaslight and Grimm, Grimm Machinations*, and *Other Aether*. She is kept busy on a daily basis by her day job as a school librarian in New Jersey. She may or may not have a secret library in her basement, and she absolutely believes in fairies.

A Curse of
Ash and Iron

by Christine Norris

A Steampunk
Cinderella Story!

All The World's A Stage, As They Say...

In 1876 Philadelphia, Benjamin Grimm knows real life is much like
the theater—people play their parts, hiding behind the illusion of
their lives and never revealing their secrets. When he reunites with
his childhood friend Eleanor Banneker, his delight turns to dismay.
On learning she has been under a spell for the past seven years,
forced to live as a servant in her own home, he realizes how sinister
some secrets can be.

Ellie has spent the long years since her mother's death under her
stepmother's watchful and unforgiving eye. Bewitched and hidden in
plain sight, it seemed no one could help Ellie escape. Not even her
own father, likewise bespelled. When she encounters Ben one
evening, he seems immune to the magic that binds her. Her hope
rekindles along with their friendship.

But time is running short. If they do not find a way to break the curse
before midnight on New Year's Eve, both Ellie and her father will be
bound forever.

https://especbooks.square.site

NOT-SO-SECRET AGENTS

Abigail Reilly
Alex Jay Berman
Andrew Kaplan
Andy Holman Hunter
Anthony R. Cardno
Aysha Rehm
Bailey A Buchanan
Barry Nove
Benjamin Adler
bill
Bill & Kelley & Kyle
Brendan Coffey
Brian D Lambert
Brian Klueter
Brooks Moses
Buddy Deal
Caitlin Rozakis
Candi O'Rourke
Carla Spence
Carol J. Guess
Carol Jones
Caroline Westra
Cheri Kannarr
Christine Lawrence
Christine Norris
Christopher Bennett
Christopher J. Burke
Coats Family
Colleen Feeney
Craig "Stevo" Stephenson
Crysella
Dale A Russell

Danielle Ackley-McPhail
Danny Chamberlin
Denise and Raphael Sutton
Doniki Boderick-Luckey
Donna Hogg
Duane Warnecke
E.M. Middel
Ef Deal
Ellen Montgomery
Emily Weed Baisch
Erin A.
"filkertom" Tom Smith
Frank Michaels
Gary Phillips
Gav I
GhostCat
GraceAnne Andreassi
    DeCandido
Greg Levick
Ian Harvey
J.E. Taylor
Jack Deal
Jakub Narębski
James Aquilone
Jamie René Peddicord
Jennifer Hindle
Jennifer L. Pierce
Jeremy Bottroff
Joe Gillis
John Keegan
John L. French
John Markley

Jonathan Haar
Judy McClain
Karen Palmer
KC Grifant
Kelly Pierce
Ken Seed
kirbsmilieu
krinsky
Lark Cunningham
LCW Allingham
Lee
Lee Thalblum
Lisa Kruse
Liz DeJesus and Amber Davis
Lorraine J Anderson
Louise Lowenspets
Lynn P.
Maria V Arnold
Marie Devey
Matthew Barr
Michael A. Burstein
Michael Barbour
Morgan Hazelwood
Mustela
Niki Curtis
Paul Ryan
pjk
Rachel A Brune
Raja Thiagarajan
Reckless Pantalones
Rich Gonzalez
Rich Walker

Richard Fine
Richard Novak
Richard O'Shea
Rigel Ailur
Robert Greenberger
Robert Ziegler
Ronald H. Miller
Ruth Ann Orlansky
Scott Schaper
Shawnee M
Shervyn
Sheryl R. Hayes
Sonia Koval
Sonya M.
Steph Parker
Stephen Ballentine
Stephen W. Buchanan
Steven Purcell
Subrata Sircar
Susan Simko
The Creative Fund by BackerKit
Thomas Bull
Thomas P. Tiernan
Tim Tucker
Tom B.
Tracy Popey
Tracy 'Rayhne' Fretwell
Will "scifantasy" Frank
'Will It Work' Dansicker
William C Tracy
wmaddie700

Printed in the USA
CPSIA information can be obtained
at www.ICGtesting.com
LVHW091149051024
792941LV00005B/36

appeared in the light. And bells rang from all
over the world. And I was drawn up with
all of them into the heatless fire.

A heavenly voice rang out saying, "I
am the Way, the Truth and the Light. None comes
to the Father but through me." I got it!

That's when the ringing alarm woke me up.

Canto XXI

epilogue

A nurse turned off the alarm on what turned
out to be an IV pump. "She seems to
be coming around now," she said. Then a

Chinese doctor with a white goatee shined
a bright light – brighter than the sun – in first
one eye and then the other. His white hair

was neatly trimmed – no pigtail. Using Sun
Wun Liu's voice he said, "You may as
well discontinue the IV. She is

"doing well without it. Let us transfer
her off the unit into the ward." Then
my poor old mother, who still goes to church,

cried out, "Thank God!" and she rushed to hug my
neck. This gave me that gnawing feeling in
my chest which I've always hated. I tried

to remember what happened, but all
I could remember was the afterlife.
The Chinese doctor said to me, "You were

"in car accident, Pilgrim. Do you

remember what happened?" I shook my head,
which made it hurt. "You were drinking and your

"car went off the road. You were fortunate.
You could have killed yourself and others. It
looks like you have been given a second

"chance. My name is David Sun and I have
been your doctor. How are you feeling?" I
groaned. My mother cried. I wished they would all

leave. Dr. Sun did a few more neuro
checks and then said, "The police said they want
to talk to you as soon as you regain

"consciousness. I strongly advise you to
sign yourself into rehab before you
talk to them." "Please, Sarah darling, do it."

Again, that painful gnawing sensation.
I signed the papers and the next four weeks
would be many therapy sessions and

lectures on substance abuse. Luckily,
they encouraged us to write in journals.
Poor Mom supplied me with a dozen of

those little bound books and, as I promised
Master Sun, I remembered and wrote. And
I kept silent, saying only those things

in group therapy that I knew they were
waiting to hear. I even cried sometimes
to make it convincing and to distract

them from my writing. It was a nice try.
There is no privacy in Treatment, yet

the staff don't share what they've said about *you*.

So, one-way rehab communication
notwithstanding, I tried to read a bit
from my journals. One meth addict laughed and

asked if I was sure my drug of choice was
alcohol and not hallucinogens.
My counselor had an extra session

with me where she tried to talk me into
taking a new medication. But I
kept writing, cautious. I wrote after lights

out and hid my journals. I knew that they
would be branded the ravings of a drunk
again, or a psychotic who needs meds

if I revealed their contents before they
were ready, so I decided to say
they were fiction if they were discovered.

They were discovered, of course. I asked that
my writing not be disturbed until I
was done. They said it wasn't possible.

On an impulse, I demanded to see
Dr. David Sun. They refused. I told
my counselors that I would check myself

out unless I could see him. He showed up
the next day. I explained my dilemma,
saying that I knew he would understand.

Then I cried and begged him to talk to
my counselors. I said I was almost
finished, but I *had* to write. He agreed.

The next couple of weeks I was allowed
to write as long as I contributed
in group therapy. I listened and shared.

I filled one journal after another,
mostly at night, listening carefully
for bed check after lights out. And I wrote.

I wrote about Dante, of course, and I
remembered as much as I could about
Hell's motorcyclists and the souls that dwelled

there. I remembered as much as I could
about the Mount of Purgatory. And
I remembered Anandiel with

such a peaceful longing in my heart. One
morning I awoke to find a tiny
white feather on my pillow. Maybe

it was from the pillow itself. Maybe
not. I hid it with my journals and I
wrote. I remembered the firewall in

Purgatory, and Sun Wun Liu, and the
other worlds, and the beginner angels
and Enoch. I remembered and I wrote.

Day after day I listened politely
to the other patients and I told
them whatever I needed to say while

I daydreamed about my journals. One
day as my twenty-eight day sojourn was
nearing completion and Discharge Planning

was working on their summaries, a large pile of journals — mine — appeared at a group therapy session. At first I was horrified at the invasion of my privacy, but then I recalled that my duty was to share. Our therapist said,

"You've been so busy journaling, and I applaud your hard work on recovery. I hope you share your writing with the group."

I smiled and replied, "Yeah, I'm ready."